The Searching Three

The Searching Three

Steve Rieman

Columbus, Ohio

This book is a work of fiction. The names, characters and events in this book are the products of the author's imagination or are used fictitiously. Any similarity to real persons living or dead is coincidental and not intended by the author.

The views and opinions expressed in this book are solely those of the author and do not reflect the views or opinions of Gatekeeper Press. Gatekeeper Press is not to be held responsible for and expressly disclaims responsibility of the content herein.

Published by
Gatekeeper Press
2167 Stringtown Rd, Suite 109
Grove City, OH 43123

Copyright © 2021 by Steve Rieman
All rights reserved. No part of this publication may be reproduced or transmitted in any form or by any means, electronic or mechanical, including photocopy, recording, or any information storage and retrieval system, without permission in writing from the copyright owner.

The cover design and editorial work for this book are the product of the author. Gatekeeper Press did not participate in and is not responsible for any aspect of these elements.

Library of Congress Control Number: 2021930058

ISBN (Paperback): 9781662909061
ISBN eBook: 9781662909078

Contents

Acknowledgments.. vii
Foreword.. x

Chapter 1 1
Chapter 2 4
Chapter 3 16
Chapter 4 23
Chapter 5 30
Chapter 6 33
Chapter 7 36
Chapter 8 38
Chapter 9 41
Chapter 10 58
Chapter 11 85
Chapter 12 89
Chapter 13 96
Chapter 14 100
Chapter 15 143
Chapter 16 148

Chapter 17 154
Chapter 18 171
Chapter 19 187
Chapter 20 203
Chapter 21 255
Chapter 22 286
Chapter 23 288

Acknowledgments

Being that this is my first book, I have quite a few people to thank and recognize so please bear with me. I would first like to thank Matthew Juillet, Nathan Preci, and Bradley Jarret, (Rest in Peace Brad) for their character inspirations. I also want to thank the following people for their love, support, and friendship throughout the years: Samantha Schwenck, Bret Philpot, Brian Wilson, Reggie Mcatee, Linnea Posthuma, Wade Crawford, Josh Shroyer, Tony Delcoma, Jeff Cooper, Jeanette Janssen, Scott and Lisa Wexton, Cain Motter, Don Henderson, Jay Martin, Ken Gilbert, Robyn and Linda from Pappy and Harriets, Kenny Walden and Jimmy Willard. Also my family: My cousins; Leslie and Perry Irving, Shealyn, Chelsea, Meggan and Zach, Yvonne Williams, Nancy, my Aunt Mildred and Uncle Nelson as well as Gayle Hill. My nephew Stuart, and his mother Valeri. My loving sister Laura, and all of her side of our family including: Vic, Krystal, Jillian, Timothy, all of my grand nieces, nephews, and all the rest.

I'd like to also thank these bands and musicians for their talent and inspiration: Gram Parsons (Rest in Peace Gram) Todd Rutherford Johnson and Jesika von Rabbit of Gram Rabbit, Nate Lawler and Death on Wednesday, Elvis Suissa and Three Bad Jacks, Trent Reznor of Nine Inch Nails, Josh Homme and Queens of the Stone Age, Jesse Hughes and Dave Catching of Eagles of Death

Metal, "The Roadside Prophet"-John Doe of X and the Knitters, Ryan Bingham, Jesse Dayton, Sean and Von of Star and Dagger, John Garcia and Brant Bjork of Vista Chino and Kyuss, Brett Anderson and The Donnas, Brian Setzer and Lee Rocker of the Stray Cats, Jim Heath and Jimbo of The Reverend Horton Heat, James Mercer and The Shins, Kim Nekroman and the Nekromantix, Sarah Blackwood of Walk Off The Earth, Kenda Legaspi and The Creepshow, Nick 13 and Tiger Army, Bryan, Eli and Andrew from Hard Fall Hearts, Greta Valenti and Robin Davey of Well Hung Heart, Shelby Legnon, Josh Liem and Gary Marsh of The Chop Tops, Brett Black, Anthony Red Horse and Chango of The Rocketz, Sean Wheeler of Throwrag and Sean and Zander, Josh Mancillas and Eli from the The Howlers, Zak Victor and The Koffin Kats, Karling Abbeygate, Robert Lee Bell and Jason Carmen of The Sandbox Bullies, Jaysin and Sideshow from The Grave Slaves, Robbie Waldman of WAXY, Jack Kohler and War Drum, Angel Lua and Jamie Hargate of The Hellions, Wendy Lee Gadzuk of The 440's and Andalusia Rose, and too many more to list.

I want to recognize the following authors for their creative insight and inspiration: Carlos Castaneda, Hunter S. Thompson, (Rest in Peace Dr. Thompson) R.A. Salvatore, Terry Brooks, Michael Crichton, Richard Adams, Anne Rice, Stephen King, Robert E. Howard, Edgar Rice Burroughs, Louis L'amour, James Herriot, Dean Koontz, J.R.R. Tolkien, Isaac Asimov, and John Steinbeck, among many, many others.

I'd also like to acknowledge the entire Y.V.H.S. graduating class of 1992, and the Milky Way Scientists Facebook page for allowing me to use their photo for the book cover. Additional thanks to Samantha Schwenck for the Authors photo.

Most of all, I would like to thank my daughters: Adrianna, Sydney, Megan and Irene for being my biggest inspiration for writing. I want again to acknowledge Carlos Castaneda and the profound

Acknowledgments

effect that his books have had on my awareness and beliefs in life. This book is dedicated to the memory of my Uncle Les but most of all, to the memory of my loving parents: Ron and Loraine Rieman. I hope I've made you proud.

Foreword

The first thing I'd like to do is thank You; the reader. I appreciate your willingness to take this walk with me, for in doing so you will get to know me greatly through my writing. I want you; dear reader, to know up front that there is mention of the use of psychedelic plants and drugs not once, but all throughout this story. If that is an immediate problem for you, then you may want to set this book right back on the shelf from where you found it. However, I'd like to say that nearly all of my references to these certain drugs are cast in a very positive light and are meant only for personal growth in regards to what is best concerning the individual. Furthermore, I'd like to adamantly recommend that no one try to replicate or relive the experiences in these stories- especially on their own. I do not condone nor advocate radical or irresponsible use of drugs, especially for recreation. Psychedelic drugs should never be taken lightly and their effects should be respected, as they are often symbolic to the individual. I'd like yet again to acknowledge that the writings of Carlos Castaneda were, and always will be, a huge influence in my interpretations concerning these experiences. I can't attest to Castaneda's writings as being true or accurate, but I can tell you this; while this book is a work of fiction, not all, but many of the stories in this book are true. Some are actual accounts that I, among others, have personally experienced out in different parts of the desert. Some names and characters, as well as certain scenarios, have been

Foreword

switched around a bit to allow for a smoother story line, but many of the occurrences and descriptions were real. I have seen, heard and felt fantastic things in the vast stretches of the mysterious desert that has been my home for most of my life. Some were fascinating and believable while others were terrifying and seemed to defy logic- which in fact they did. Much of it did not make any sense to me until I started reading the Castaneda series. To me personally, it's the message that holds true and important concerning these events. My hope is that at least a few of you out there will relate to, or even adopt some of the philosophies that I expound upon in this book. If that's the case then it will all have been worth it for me. So with all that having been said, if you still hold any interest in proceeding with this amazing compilation of recollection and adventure, then buckle up! You're in for one hell of a ride!

Steve Rieman

"To seek freedom is the only driving force I know. Freedom to fly off into that infinity out there. Freedom to dissolve; to lift off; to be like the flame of a candle, which, in spite of being up against the light of a billion stars, remains intact, because it never pretended to be more than what it is: a mere candle."

don Juan Matus

Chapter 1

He stood staring vacantly out of his tenth story office building window, his eyelids at half-mast from lack of sleep and overexertion; both due to his increased work schedule. While gazing absently yet locked into a stare without focus, a sudden familiar, frantic voice called out from behind him shattering his peaceful, catatonic state.

"Brad! The bosses are demanding the updated version of the file for the presentation you turned in yesterday. Please tell me it's ready!"

Brad's eyes shut tight at the first syllabic onslaught and he replied irritably, "Yeah. I worked on it all damn night and got about two hours sleep this morning!"

"Thank God! Well, hand it over my man. They are screaming for it!"

Gary was a good assistant. Better than good actually, but he always had a flare for the dramatic and in this case, he was right on his game.

"I was just about to print it out on my new laptop..." Brad replied, as he spun around in a quick semicircle, the back of his elbow catching his three quarters full cup of steaming hot coffee and spilling it in its entirety all over his new computer. The screen started flashing on and off as a sizzling sound began to emanate from the keyboard and then suddenly it shut down completely.

"Son of a bi-" Brad started to scream but stopped in mid-sentence as he looked up to see one of the head clients in which he personally represented, standing in the doorway looking at him with a mixture of curiosity and disdain.

"Uh hum," the suit said in what would normally be a person clearing their throat, only it came out sounding more like; "Hey asshole. Why am I still waiting for my damn file?" Out of the corner of his eye, Brad saw Gary silently mouthing the word "Shit" as the suit walked up to view the laptop sitting on Brad's desk. "That's a pity," he commented, contempt dripping from every syllable. "I hope this doesn't affect me getting my file right now."

"Uh...no," Gary piped up from the corner as he took a few tentative steps forward. "Brad always saves his work on a backup, right Brad?"

Judging by the way Brad stared at the dark screen of his brand new, newly fried, twelve hundred dollar computer, Gary as well as the suit were suddenly not convinced.

"Brad? Buddy?" Gary asked, "You do have a backup..?"

"Mr. Coldblood, I am so sorry. I finished this just a few hours ago and didn't have a chance to save it..." Brad responded, backpedaling.

"Please tell me that you are joking Mr. Reid. I needed that file and list of presentation materials yesterday, and I'm not speaking metaphorically here," Coldblood angrily replied. Again Gary silently mouthed an obscenity, only this one started with the letter "F". "So, exactly what does this mean, Mr. Reid?"

"Sir," Brad hastily replied, "I will spend all day and night if need be preparing this and I promise I will have it first thing tomorrow morning. Again, I am truly sorry."

"My flight for New Mexico leaves in forty five minutes out of L.A.X. and if you don't have it now, you can bring it to me there. I don't want it faxed and I don't want it E-mailed to me. I want it personally delivered to me, by you, tomorrow at nine a.m. sharp

Chapter 1

and that is non-negotiable. You know where my New Mexico office is located," Coldblood stated, as he stormed out of Brad's office, brushing past Gary and causing him to involuntarily shudder.

"Brrr!" Gary shivered. "Guy sure lives up to his name, huh?"

"Coldblood," Brad spat. "Can you believe that there is actually a guy out there named Coldblood and I get stuck dealing with him? I do all the work and he presents it as if he'd done it all himself!"

"That's what we get paid for right? So what happened?" Gary asked. "Why didn't you take the thirty seconds to email it to yourself or save it on your home or even work computer?"

"When I said that I was up all night working on it, that wasn't an exaggeration," Brad replied. "I only finished it a few hours ago. I'm so tired I guess I thought I already had."

"Well, you heard the man...or beast. Whatever he is! You better have that file ready to rock and roll by nine or it's the Apocalypse. I'll get on booking your flight for you."

"Right," Brad said, venom coating the word. "There goes lunch with the wife and kids today and tomorrow."

"Oh, and boss?" Gary chided. "Leave the coffee behind this time?" he snickered, ducking out of the office just before a well-aimed stapler hit the wall where his head would have been should he have waited a second longer. "Just saying..." Gary added as he stuck his head back in the door for one last jab.

"Get ou-" Brad started to say, but Gary was already far down the hall.

Chapter 2

Early the next morning, Brad was on a long stretch of desert highway in what seemed like a desolate, forgotten section of New Mexico. His plane had landed him at Albuquerque International Sunport and he had promptly attained the rental that Gary had arranged for him. It was a Hyundai Sonata; a decent luxury car that offered a very smooth and comfortable ride. Coldblood's office and company headquarters were located up near the northern tip of Albuquerque towards Santa Fe, so it looked like he had at least an hour or so drive to get there. He'd left around six forty five a.m. just to be absolutely sure that he would arrive there early and then he'd wait until the office opened at nine. If he was really early he would just find a place to have breakfast and then he could read some of the book he'd brought to help pass the time. Brad had packed a book by Carlos Castaneda called: "The teachings of Don Juan- A Yaqui way of knowledge." He looked down at the worn out paperback with a fond reminiscence. He had figured it would be fitting to bring it with him since he was going to be out in the desert.

God, it had been years since he had read his favorite books or been out to any desert for that matter! Being locked into city life forever now it seemed, it occurred to him just then how much of his spirituality he had forsaken. He used to read the entire series of Castaneda books at least once every couple of years and he realized

Chapter 2

now that it had been more than eight years since he'd even picked one up.

"Far too long," he mumbled to himself.

How abstract and strange they had seemed to him at first! Then the more he read and understood the more they had made perfect sense. He could relate on so many levels to the various intense and often hilarious stories told within. Especially the ones involving psychedelics! So many times he and his friends had taken mind altering and psychotropic substances and had gone on hikes and adventures off in the desert when they had been younger. Everything seemed so much simpler back then. But hell, it was! Living out there in the desert, working a dead end job, and having no real hopes or dreams. With no money saved and a car that constantly broke down on him and yet for what it sounded like, it was a very happy time for him. It's not that he hated his life now, that was far from it. He had just felt so much more balanced back then, at least spiritually. He was in better shape and his senses and reflexes were so much keener back then. Of course we all lose some of that edge when we grow older but this was different. It was almost like he hadn't lost it; he'd sold it.

As his contemplations reached their zenith, he looked out to the eastern horizon just in time to see the sun come up over the mountains and that's when it happened. An enormous wave of emotion and wonder welled up from deep within him and he stared in awe at the beautiful spectacle he saw taking place before his eyes. He immediately pulled the car over and as he stepped out he almost had to catch his breath as the wondrous, yellow orb rose above the mountain tops. It was as if it were a show being played out just for him. He truly couldn't remember when he'd felt so much peace and serenity and wished that he could share it with everyone that he loved and cared about. When was the last time he even saw a sunrise?

Eventually, he shuffled back to the car, got in, sat down and suddenly he felt terrible. He knew that by tonight he would be back in

L.A. with the noise, smog, stress and the anxiety. Very mechanically he put his seat belt on, started the car and drove away wishing he had never seen that damned sunrise. He felt as though a cruel joke had been played on him and now he just wanted to get over it.

When he arrived in town he checked the time; Seven fifty. He spotted a little diner on the right, and pulled in for some breakfast. It was a quaint little coffee shop and he chose a booth that was kind of secluded so that he might triple check Coldblood's presentation materials in peace. Coldblood! he thought sarcastically to himself. He still couldn't get over the fact that this guy's name was Coldblood! That's like a doctor with the last name Hertz or a Narcotics Officer named Fink. And he had the pleasure of handing over a file that took him weeks to complete and was sure to be unappreciated. Skimming through the file he heard someone slide into the booth behind him. Perfect. Try to find a tiny bit of isolation and someone always has to intrude.

"Hey man, was that not something or what?" he heard in a voice thick with stoner, surfer dialect.

"Dude! I'm like still soooo feelin' the flow bro!" a second voice answered.

"Ha! I can go...with the flow!" the first one responded back and then they both laughed uproariously.

Great, Brad thought to himself. There are two of them. The cafe is all but empty save for an older guy with a graying ponytail in a cheap looking blue suit at the counter, and these two stoner schmucks had to sit right by me! He tried tuning them out with little success and started to get up to move to a different booth when one of them said something that stopped him dead in his seat.

"Man, that place out in the desert was exactly as those guys described it. Just like out of a Carlos Castaneda book! Dude, do you think that really was a power place we were at?"

Chapter 2

"Bro! Can you even doubt it? You should see yourself right now! Your like...aura, is glowing! At least I can see it."

"Dude, I thought I felt that! It's incredible bro! Yeah! I think yours is too!"

"Oh yeah, I knooow mine is bra!"

Now Brad was unbelievably intrigued. He moved his files over and set his laptop down on the seat next to him having lost all interest in work, and tried desperately to eavesdrop some more. Unfortunately, they both began perusing through their menus trying to decide on what to eat and they started talking about eggs and bacon instead of deserts and power places.

Brad ordered next and shortly after his food arrived, he found himself immersed in deep contemplation. God, wouldn't it be nice to take one more psychedelic run of it again? Maybe he could realign his energy and explore the mysteries of the Universe one last time! Ahh, what are you doing? he thought to himself. Not gonna happen, chief. You can't just take off like in the old days and go tripping off into the desert! You've got a wife who would never approve, a hectic work schedule with a deadline, and besides you couldn't do it alone. Who would go with you? Irritated once again, he got up and stalked off to use the restroom.

On the way back however, curiosity got the better of him and he peeked over at the two intrepid stoners. They looked up as well and what he saw genuinely amazed him. They were both about his age, had short unkempt haircuts with at least two days worth of stubble on their faces, but that wasn't the amazing part. They had an energy about them that was clearly noticeable and seemed as if they were actually somehow glowing! They looked peaceful yet energized at the same time! They all three looked down simultaneously like they had been caught doing something wrong, and Brad just shook his head in disbelief as he sat back down in his booth.

There was no disputing that those two guys had just experienced something fantastic and intense and now he had officially convinced himself. He's going to do it! He wasn't sure how, but he was going to make it happen. It'd have to be at least a three day trip and he'd need the proper provisions; namely Peyote. Or at the very least some mushrooms. Oh yeah, and food and water too. It was time for him to contact a couple of old friends that he'd scarcely been in touch with for some time, and convince them that they had to go on this trip with him. It would take some smooth talking and serious coercing, but he felt confident that he could pull it off. He thought then of his friend Jason; of twenty years, and his friend Nick; who he'd known for about twelve.

Back in the day they would have only needed the slightest nudge to do a trip like this. Now it would probably take a miracle. He would need to invent some kind of extraordinary circumstance to get them to partake in this little endeavor. He snapped out of his scheming scenario as the waitress set his food down and asked him if he needed anything else. After assuring her that he was good, he devoured his food and exited the diner quickly, excited now by the prospect of achieving this new mission that'd been set forth before him and his two unaware comrades.

Having already sent the file early that morning, dropping off the presentation materials at Coldblood's office went exactly as he had predicted. He was the epitome of unappreciation and made it clear that if he was not happy with the file, then he would be contacted immediately. Brad had never even needed to truly be there in person, it was just Coldblood's way of punishing him for his little laptop accident.

Normally that would have bothered him but not this time. Visions of colorful deserts, melting rock cliffs and swaying Saguaro cacti danced through his head. He suddenly decided that he would drive the rental all the way back to L.A. in order to enjoy the desert scenery some more and have time to figure this whole thing out.

Chapter 2

After he called his wife and his assistant, he was on his way once again traveling that long lonesome stretch of road he had been on earlier. Only this time everything was different. He had an immediate purpose and one he believed to be of enlightenment.

Working up a pitch for his amigos would be tricky but the hardest part would be in finding the psychedelics. Who in the hell did he know that might be able to come up with such things? He'd been out of the loop for years now and couldn't think of even a single person who might be able to hook him up.

"This could be a real problem!" he murmured to himself.

It was definitely a necessity to have something to help them discover some new found spiritual insight. He knew that he personally needed something to kick start himself out of his conscious hibernation in order to retrieve some of those dormant spiritual realizations. He was pretty sure that it would be the same for his two, as of yet, unknowing cohorts.

Casually cruising down the highway, he remained lost in thought until he spotted two figures walking alongside the road up ahead about a hundred yards away.

"Who the hell would be walking way out here in the boonies?" he muttered aloud to himself as he steadily drove ahead.

There was no way to get a good view of them as he approached because of the backpacks lifted high upon their shoulders. He passed them by, shaking his head when a glance in the rear view mirror stole his breath away. They were the two guys from the diner! He recognized them immediately. Without the slightest hesitation he slowed down, put his car in reverse, and rolled right up to them. If this miraculously worked out the way he hoped it would, it could solve the worst of his problems.

"Hey, you guys need a lift?" he asked cheerfully.

"Ah dude! That would be awesome!" the taller of the two replied.

"How far are you goin'?" the other one asked.

"All the way to L.A." Brad responded.

"Right on!" the first one said happily.

They put their backpacks in the trunk and hopped into the back seat and Brad turned fully around to get a good look at them. The taller of the two had sandy, blonde hair and a thin muscular build, similar to his. It was the other one that really set him back. He looked just like his former friend Steve that he had known years ago, only slightly stockier with shorter, curly, dark brown hair. Steve had been one of the best friends he'd ever had, who unfortunately and tragically ended his life in suicide. For a second he was assaulted by a wave of nostalgia until the guy started speaking to him.

"Hey! I recognize you! You were at the diner earlier right? So hey man, whatcha doin' in Albuquerque? Do you live out here or something? Oh, by the way; my name's Troy and this here's Dan."

"How's it goin' man?" Dan asked politely.

"Uh…I'm actually working," Brad replied, as he pulled back out onto the highway. "I live in L.A. and am heading back right now. How 'bout you guys? You look like you were out camping or something. Where are you guys from?"

"San Diego," Troy answered. "The closer you could get us there, the better."

"Yeah man we were out camping," Dan chimed in. "We hiked for three days and camped for two nights."

"Out here?" Brad asked incredulously. "What would make you guys want to come out to this desolate desert?"

"Ah dude…" Dan started to explain, "we found this totally awesome power place that we heard about from these guys, so we decided to-" Dan stopped in mid-sentence upon feeling a strong jab to his side from Troy as a signal not to say too much.

"Decided to what?" Brad prompted eagerly, and looked up to the rear view mirror just in time to catch Troy eyeing Dan scornfully, shaking his head.

Chapter 2

"Well, uh...we just wanted to come and check out the desert, that's all."

"Oh...okay." Brad replied, sounding disappointed.

"So, man. We didn't catch your name," Troy said a little suspiciously.

"Oh. Sorry guys, I'm Brad, nice to meet ya," he said, as he turned around as much as he could to lean back and shake each of their hands while he maintained the wheel.

"So, what do you do for work Brad?" Troy asked.

"Well, I'm actually a representative with a major advertising firm. We consult wealthy business owners, sports teams and even the occasional celebrity every now and then. But honestly it's not that glamorous, just tedious and stressful most of the time. So Dan...what were you starting to say about your camping trip?"

"Hey, Troy! Check it out! He reads Castaneda!" Dan said excitedly as he held Brad's book up for Troy to see.

At that Troy brightened considerably, and looking up at Brad said, "Far out! So you're into the Castaneda as well huh?"

"Oh, yeah!" Brad replied enthusiastically. "I've been reading Castaneda's books for years! Are you guys into him too?" he asked, already knowing what the answer would be.

At that point, Dan and Troy both started talking at the same time, almost on top of each other, and soon Brad found it hard to even shut them up. He was grateful though because he had found a way to break the ice and hopefully segue into his sixty four thousand dollar question. After a good forty five minutes of stories and conversation, Brad finally felt confident enough to pose his tentative inquiry.

"Hey guys. I was seriously thinking about going on a little journey with some friends here soon and was wondering if you might know where I could pick up some psychedelics?"

"What were you looking for bro?" Troy asked.

"Well...I was really hoping to score some Peyote but I can't imagine how hard that would be to get these days."

"Not for us!" Troy said with a wide grin on his face. "In fact, if you can take us all the way home, we can hook you up with some from a friend of ours. He's three quarters Mescalero Indian and has access to mescaline."

"Wow! Seriously?" Brad gasped. "That would be the coolest thing imaginable! I need enough for three people though," he added, biting his lip.

"That, and a little extra just in case!" Dan chimed in laughingly.

"Don't worry bro. We'll make it happen," Troy assured him confidently.

More elated than ever, Brad drove on. His destination now for San Diego. The three shared several more stories along the way; some hilarious, others bizarre and disturbing, but all very intriguing for Brad to hear. Eventually they both fell asleep and napped for almost the remainder of the drive.

Once they reached their residence in San Diego, the boys made good on their promise and hooked Brad up for his trip and for free nonetheless. Brad made a small protest about trying to pay for it but they both insisted that it be a gift, especially since he drove them all the way home. Along with the Peyote they also drew him a makeshift map of the area that they had camped in, which had the power place close by. Then they exchanged phone numbers and bid their farewells and Brad left wondering if they'd ever see one another again.

As he left San Diego he realized that there was no turning back now and that all signs were pointing to the fact that this trip was meant to happen.

For the first time in years he had a fierce desire to accomplish something that he believed would be spiritual and enlightening, and felt as though he was actually glowing during his entire drive back home!

Chapter 2

It was ten thirty at night when he finally pulled into his driveway. He took all of his effects out of the rental and strode up the walk and through the front door. He stepped inside to a chorus of "Daddy!" as his son and daughter rushed up to greet him. Nearly tackling him they immediately started asking him about his trip. He began to tell them all about the drive and the desert when his wife came up and gave him a welcoming hug and kiss.

"It sure does feel great to be home!" he said, and sincerely meant it with all his heart.

"Here honey, let me put that stuff away for you. I know you had a hell of a long drive today," Melanie said. "Eric and Christa have been waiting all day for you to get here. I told them that they could wait up to see you and...Brad...where's your new laptop?"

"Isn't it with my stuff?" Brad asked, not seeming too concerned.

"Uh...no. It's not here. Did you leave it in the rental?"

"No. I took everything out before I came in. I'm sure of it."

"Well you better double check. I seriously doubt that your network provider will grant you the insurance again so soon after your last little debacle."

"No, I doubt that they would," Brad agreed. "I had to fight them tooth and nail just to get it this last time around. I'll go look again."

As Brad searched the Hyundai he experienced a sinking feeling in the pit of his stomach as he realized that he must have left it somewhere. But where? When was the last time he used it? The diner in New Mexico! He had been sorting through Coldblood's presentation materials and got distracted by Dan and Troy! He remembered now setting it down on the seat beside him. Quickly, he ran back up to the house and grabbed his cell phone. Looking up Troy's number, he dialed it as fast as his fingers could punch in the digits.

"Yello?"

"Troy? Hey man, its Brad."

"Braaaad! What's up dude? Did ya get lost or do ya just miss us already?" Troy chuckled.

"Both, and neither man. Hey, do you remember the name of that little cafe we ate at this morning? I think I left my laptop there by accident."

"Ummm...hold on. Hey Dan! What was the name of that diner that we ate at this morning?"

"Carol's Diner!" Dan shouted out in the background.

"There you go. Carol's Diner. Good luck bro."

"Thanks man. Talk to you later."

After hanging up the phone, Brad immediately called information and got the number to the diner.

"Carol's Diner..." said the voice on the other end.

"Hi. I ate there this morning and I think I might have left my laptop on the seat of the booth I ate in. Near the back by the windows?" Brad asked hopefully.

"Oh yeah. That little black computer doohickey. We've got it. Come on by and get it, we're open till midnight."

"Thank you so much!" Brad said, elated. "I actually live out of state so can you hold it for me till tomorrow?"

"Sure, hun. Just come get it as soon as you can before it gets lost again."

"I'll be there tomorrow morning. My name is Brad, and thank you!" He set his phone down and looked up to see that his wife had heard the entire conversation.

"You left it in New Mexico. Might as well claim it as lost and get a new one rather than travel all the way back there."

"I can't!" Brad replied desperately. "I have six months' worth of clients files and personal information stored in that damn thing. I've got to get it back immediately, it's not an option!"

"Well great! There goes another lunch with your wife and kids. I think you did that on purpose!"

Chapter 2

"Come on doll," Brad said persuasively. "It was an accident. I miss you and the kids. We'll spend some time together soon but I have to go back for it. I'll make it up to you guys, I promise."

"Yeah, well you better," she said as she pushed her body up against his and laid a big kiss square on his lips.

"I will," Brad promised. "In fact I'll start tonight," he said seductively, as he gently kissed her ear.

Chapter 3

Early the next morning Brad was again at L.A.X. awaiting his flight back to Albuquerque. The flight was only an hour and a half long but he figured it should still be enough time for him to formulate a plan.

He had the place and the Peyote but he still needed to concoct a story for his friends to convince them to go on this trip. He could tell them that he was having marital or work problems and that he needed their support right now, but that just didn't feel right to him. He wanted to be convincing but he didn't want to outright lie to them. There must be a way he could get them to go along with his plan and at least involve part of the truth in doing so. He started to wonder if either one of them had been feeling the same way he had lately. Maybe there was a way to play that angle and get them on board with this little psychedelic escapade that he'd come up with.

Brad racked his brain the entire flight, trying to devise a scheme that would ensure that his buddies go with him, but with no success. He'd landed and was already driving his latest rental to the diner and had still come up with nothing. He couldn't stop thinking of Castaneda's adventures with don Juan though, even as he walked through the door of the cafe and up to the register. He was approached by an older waitress who promptly asked if she could help him.

Chapter 3

"Hi, my name is Brad and I called last night about a laptop that I lost-"

"Oh, yeah sugar," the waitress said loudly, interrupting him in mid-sentence. "I've got it right here," she cooed, pulling it out from behind the counter. "There you go, sweetie."

"Thank you!" Brad sighed, exhaling a deep breath. "I would be in real trouble without this little sucker! Thank you so much for finding it and holding it for me."

"Well, I did hold it for you but I wasn't the one who found it. Jack over there….now he was the one who found it," the waitress said, as she gestured towards a man sitting down the bar about fifteen feet away. As he looked down to the end of the counter he saw a middle aged gentleman in jeans and a gray blazer sipping coffee. Something about the man struck him as familiar but he couldn't put his finger on it.

"Would you like to order something, doll?" the waitress asked sweetly.

"Yeah, I'll just have a look at the menu real quick. I think I'll go ahead and sit next to Jack over there…oh, and put his ticket on my bill please."

"Whatever you say, sugar."

Brad made his way over and sat down right next to Jack. He casually picked up the menu and said, "I think I owe you a debt of thanks, Jack."

"Pardon me?" Jack asked, looking up inquisitively from the pamphlets he had just been reading.

"I was told that you found my laptop yesterday."

He stared at Brad squarely for a few seconds before responding. "That's right. That's right I did. Did you get it back?"

"Just now, thanks to you. I'd like to repay you by buying you breakfast if that's alright?"

"Is that the going price for a lost laptop these days? A breakfast?"

Brad stared at Jack for a second, dumbfounded and speechless. Jack just stared right back with a look so serious and intense that it actually stole Brad's breath away.

"I didn't mean..." Brad started to backpedal. "What I meant was...if you wanted a reward, I..." but before Brad could finish his stammering, Jack erupted into a loud bellowing laughter.

"Take it easy friend, I'm just messing with ya!"

"Whew!" Brad exhaled. "Wow! You really had me going there!"

"What's your name, guy? Or should I just call you the laptop loser?" Jack asked, smiling warmly from ear to ear.

"I'm Brad, nice to meet you," he replied, leaning over to shake Jack's hand.

"And I'm Jack Martinez. Unless you want to refer to me by my Native American name, in which case I'm called; Jack Red Feather."

After a moment's consideration Brad said, "I really like Red Feather, it sounds so much more earthy and majestic, but I'll stick with just Jack if you don't mind?"

"Well, you really know how to play out a formal introduction sir! And unless I miss my guess, you are in sales or marketing of some kind."

"How'd you know that?" Brad asked, amazed.

"Because I sir, like yourself, am also in sales."

"Ah! What kind of sales are we talkin' exactly?"

"Well...not your most prestigious line of work exactly..." Jack said, sounding slightly embarrassed. "I sell vacuum cleaners."

"Wow," Brad responded. "Is there much of a market for that these days? Especially when you can buy them online or from most any appliance or department store?"

"There is for me actually," Jack explained. "You see, I'm contracted through the state to give people discounted vacuums in exchange for their old ones thanks to a new program that the government just put

Chapter 3

into place. They get new ones at a seriously discounted price and I take their old ones away to be either refurbished or scrapped. This isn't exactly a rich area out here, if you know what I mean, and people will take what they can get."

"Doesn't sound too bad at all," Brad said. "Any money in it?"

"Well...enough to pay the bills," Jack stated with confidence. "And not much else. But hey, it's a living. I also do some acting on the side for local T.V. and radio ads. I'm not too bad either, if I do say so myself."

"Fair enough," Brad said. "And now I think I'll order some breakfast."

"You do that," Jack agreed.

After ordering, Brad pulled out the map that the boys had made for him from his pocket and started to examine it while he waited for his food. He thought he might have a little bit of time to possibly scout out some of the area before he left Albuquerque. After all, if he didn't do it today, when was he ever going to have time before he came back on the trip with his friends? He started going over some of the marked localities on the map when Jack happened to look over and take notice.

"Whatcha got there, something for work?"

"No...it's a map. Of this area in fact. Some friends of mine and I are actually planning to go on a camping trip out here soon."

"Out here?" Jack asked incredulously. "And are these friends of yours aware of where you're planning on taking them?" Jack asked, smirking all the while.

"Of course," Brad stated defensively. Jack raised an eyebrow at that and just continued to stare at Brad as though he was not anywhere close to being convinced. "Okay, well maybe they don't know exactly where yet, but they'll be fine with it."

"Uhhh...huh!" Jack snickered knowingly. Brad looked up from the map to see Jack smiling warmly.

"Boy. You can see right through me can't you?"

"I deal with all different types of people every day and I am a salesman, remember? Here, let me take a look at that map."

"Do you know this area at all?" Brad asked hopefully.

"I grew up out here. Born on the local Reservation."

Now Brad was excited again. "Hey, do you think that there's any way you might be able to help me find some of the areas that are on the map? I would consider it a huge favor."

"And do you always ask huge favors of people that you hardly know and just met?" Jack asked with a serious expression on his face.

Once again Brad was taken back but managed to give him a reply with a deadpan look that almost matched his own.

"No. But in your case I'll make an exception."

At that, Jack's ice cold countenance melted and a wide warm smile replaced his frown.

"Nicely answered," he said. "This looks a lot like a place that my Grandfather used to take me to," he added, pointing to a spot on the map. "Could be the same one. And since it is very slow for me today I shall accompany you to this area and see if we can't make heads or tails of it."

"Awww, thanks!" Brad replied gratefully.

Right after they finished eating they left the diner, quickly on their way to locate the areas on the map. They ended up getting better acquainted on the drive out as they filled each other in as to where they both worked and lived. They chatted idly about small things and upon arriving, pulled off onto a long rippled dirt road and parked over to one side.

"You see those boulders and that canyon over there?" Jack motioned with his chin as he and Brad both got out of the car. "We're gonna have to hike through those to get to the area in question, if I'm not mistaken."

Chapter 3

They hiked for about five minutes in silence then once they approached a wide flat area surrounded by huge boulders, Jack picked up the conversation.

"So, what's this camping trip all about anyway? You seemed to have picked a desolate spot. Couldn't you just go up to the mountains or along some beach? Why here?"

"It's kind of complicated," Brad said nervously.

"Oh, come on!" Jack bellowed. "Trigonometry and French Literature are complicated! I'm bettin' that this is simple compared to those."

"Okay," Brad said tentatively. "Here it is; I want to bring my friends out here so that we can rediscover ourselves through the use of Peyote."

Jack stared at him hard for a long time. Brad could hardly stand his piercing gaze and had to avert his eyes thinking that his look was judgmental.

"Now why would you think that I couldn't understand that? I am Native American ya know."

Brad let out a sigh of relief. "So have you taken Peyote before?"

"When I was sixteen. I was sent on a spiritual quest and it was required that I take it. But that was a long time ago and I haven't had a reason to take drugs like those for several years."

"I can respect that," Brad said, nodding his head.

"You had better be awfully careful if you're going to do that stuff. Especially around here. The desert can be a very unforgiving place. There are large packs of coyotes around here and even the occasional mountain lion."

"We will definitely take that into consideration," Brad replied.

"Well, here we are. What do you think?"

Brad had been so busy talking that he had not been paying much attention to his surroundings. He looked up to see that they were in a wide circular area that was surrounded by giant sized boulders, and past that was a sandy clearing enclosed by great cliffs on all sides. The sheer beauty of the place instantly inspired awe within him.

"To the north," Jack informed Brad, "is a long stretch of flat desert that you probably saw as we drove in from town. To the west is a little spring that comes right out of the rocks about two miles away. Good drinking water too. To the south there is a long mountain range with high canyons and some large sand dunes. And lastly, to the east; more scrub desert and a few small washes scattered intermittently throughout the terrain."

Brad watched Jack curiously as Jack just stared off into the east as if he could see fifty miles away. For the first time, Brad stopped and took a real good look at Jack. He seemed as though he might be in his late thirties like himself, but then noticed the streaks of gray in his hair and the crow's feet around his eyes. In the sunlight he could see the wrinkles that he hadn't noticed earlier.

"How old are you Jack?" Brad asked boldly.

"I will be forty nine in four months," Jack admitted, watching Brad for his reaction.

"Wow," Brad breathed in disbelief.

"I know, I know," Jack laughed. "I'm older than I look right?" he said, as he turned towards Brad.

Brad nodded his head in agreement and looked upon him with a new found appreciation. As he continued to stare at him, Jack reached up and removed the band from his hair and it all flowed down onto his shoulders as he shook it free to cool himself. Brad was amazed as he noticed for the first time his pronounced Native American features; his high cheekbones and sun darkened skin. He had an undeniably stoic look when his head was turned just right. It was then that Brad was suddenly struck with what he hoped was a brilliant idea.

Chapter 4

"You've got to be kidding me right? What is it you want me to do exactly?"

"I want you to be our guide," Brad answered, without hesitation.

"I assume you mean on your camping trip?"

"Exactly!" he replied happily.

"What even makes you believe that I'm qualified?" Jack asked doubtfully.

"You know this area! You grew up here. Your Grandfather showed it to you, you said so yourself!"

"That was years ago!" Jack said emphatically and threw his arms up in the air. "And even then I got lost all the time!"

"Look Jack, you still know this desert ten times better than I do and plus I need it to be you."

"There has got to be someone better suited for this than me and... wait a minute. Why does it have to be me?" Jack asked suspiciously.

"Because I need someone who looks Native American, that's why."

"And why is that, Mr. Brad?"

"Because...I..." Brad started to stammer.

"You are planning to trick your friends aren't you? You want me to pretend that I am some wise, Native American Shaman that's going to guide you in and out of the Spirit World, right?"

Once again Brad just stared at him in disbelief, speechless.

"How did you figure...?"

Jack erupted into laughter upon seeing Brad's face lose all color.

"I just put two and two together and came up with what you wanted me to do for the three of you!" Jack continued chuckling, and even Brad started to laugh as a man who'd just been made the butt of a joke.

"Okay...okay. You got me. So what do you say? Will you do it?"

"I don't know, guy," Jack said, shaking his head. "Seems dishonest. If they're your friends then why do you feel as though you need to fool them like this?"

"Look Jack. I know it seems that way, but they need this. I need this. It's for their own good. For all our own good! Pleeease!"

Jack gave him another one of his long scrutinizing stares and said, "Well..."

"I'll pay you three hundred dollars," Brad blurted out.

Jack looked up, then smiled and asked, "When do we go camping?"

They both ended up going back to the diner and spent almost two hours working out some of the details. Brad was amazed to find that so many ideas and insights for the trip came flooding out of him like a tidal wave of inspiration.

"Sounds like you've got this whole thing figured out," Jack commented, during a certain point in their planning and he seemed genuinely impressed.

"You know, it's funny," Brad said, chuckling to himself. "I'm really just making this up as I go along! Well, that and I've had huge influences from reading Carlos Castaneda. Are you familiar with his writing?"

"Carlos who?" Jack asked, raising one eyebrow.

"You've never heard of..." Brad started to ask, as Jack just stared at him with a blank expression.

"I read plenty of Shakespeare when I was in Theatre."

Chapter 4

"Theatre? Never mind. Anyway, I'll have more ideas for you when they hit me. Just be ready to improvise."

"Hey guy. I am not a professional actor, just an aspiring one okay? But for three bills, I'll do the best I can."

"That's all I ask!" Brad said, smiling.

After Brad and Jack exchanged numbers, Brad was on his way back home but this time he had to fly. He'd spent too much time with Jack to drive back again.

Once back home he started clearing his schedule three weeks away so that he'd have time to take the weekend off, buy some camping gear, and convince his friends to take the trip.

One thing he hadn't considered, however, was how he was going to tell his wife. He believed that she'd understand because they had a great trust and respect for each other, but he also knew that she'd be worried for his safety. After all, he'd be virtually unreachable out there in that desert. He knew that there was no cell phone coverage because he had checked during the whole drive back from the diner to the airport, and while he'd been out hiking with Jack. He felt confident that he could convince her however, but he pondered on how to break the ice with this one. He didn't have to wonder long though, for one night right before bed he heard a distraught sound coming from the bedroom.

"Braaaad!" Melanie's voice soared down the hallway. "What is this?" she asked, holding up the large zip lock bag half full of Peyote. "I know what it looks like but I must be mistaken. Right, sweetheart?" she asked with a mixture of sarcasm and concern.

Melanie easily recognized the substance having done her time on the psychedelic scene as well. She grew up in Oregon, mostly by the coast, and had had her share of hippy friends and experimentation. That was one of the things they'd both had in common and talked about when they had first dated.

"Oh, hey. I thought I had stashed that better. Yeah, that's actually-"

"Peyote!" Melanie cried out. "I know what it is Bradley! What I want to know is; what the hell is it doing here? You want to tell me what's going on?"

She used his full first name and anybody who's anyone knows that that is an indication of trouble to come.

"Okay, okay! I was going to tell you, I swear! I was just waiting for the right time."

"Tell me what darling?" More sarcasm coating each word as it spewed forth. "Please don't tell me that you are selling this shit! Are we drug dealers now?"

Damn. Now she's cussing! Brad thought to himself. His wife had an excellent vocabulary due to a good education and very rarely took the opportunity to express herself with any less than the finest articulation. Perhaps he underestimated her reaction to this little plan of his.

"No, no, no..." he said, getting ready to explain. "Okay, sit down. Please."

Melanie had assumed the classic defiant pose of; chest out with one hand on her hip, while the other hand held up the evidence at eye level. He grabbed the bag from her and then gently took her by the hands as he led her over to the bed and sat her down.

"Something happened to me recently. Something very profound."

"When you were in New Mexico?" she interrupted, still clearly very upset.

"Yes, but please hear me out. I can't explain it properly if you keep interrupting me."

She gave him the "You've got a lot of nerve asking me to be quiet" look, but then relaxed visibly and upon seeing this, Brad continued.

"First, I just want to assure you that I love my life as it is. I love and adore you and the kids. But more and more lately something has been very off-kilter with me. Everything we have together is great. No one could ask for a more lovely, sexy and amazing wife than you."

Chapter 4

"Keep talking," Melanie interrupted quietly.

"I will," Brad said, before he continued, "Taking that trip out to the desert really did something to me. It made me feel more spiritual then I've felt in a long time and yet it also made me realize just how lacking in spirituality I am these days. I never get out into nature anymore. I just spend all my time in the city. Now I do love living here, it's fine, but a person like me needs to get out more often. I've put this off for far too long and now I owe it to myself to make this happen."

"But Brad...we just went camping up in the mountains last month. The kids and I had a great time. We all had a great time. And make what happen? What are you talking about?"

"Melanie! Please let me finish without interruption, I'm begging you!" She rolled her eyes, nodded, gave a huge sigh and then relaxed her posture, so Brad continued. "Thank you! Yes, we all had a great time camping and I hope to do it again soon but this is different. I need a huge introspection concerning my life right now and I hadn't realized it until just recently. I'm talking about self-exploration. And no, before you say it, I am not having a midlife crisis...at least I don't think so. But seriously, can you just have enough faith in me and trust me enough to understand that I know what I'm doing? I wouldn't even think about doing this unless I believed it was necessary for me."

"Okay Brad. I'm not interrupting, I just have a question. And by the way, you know that I trust you...implicitly. If you feel that strongly about something then I will back you one hundred percent. All I want to know at this point is; what exactly is it that you feel you need to do, and where are you planning on going?"

"I want to go back to New Mexico and camp out in the desert for the weekend," he stated, and judging by the horrified look on Melanie's face, he felt that he had better elaborate quickly. "I'm planning a camping trip with Nick and Jason for three days and two nights there. We'll bring plenty of supplies; food, water-"

"And Peyote!" Melanie interrupted, practically shouting as she jumped up off the bed. "You want to go off and trip in the desert with your buddies just like you did in the old days, isn't that it? Don't bullshit me Bradley!"

Again with the cussing and the first name. Perhaps more explanation was required, and right away!

"Honey, listen to me," he pleaded calmly as he sat her back down on the edge of the bed. "You know what my spiritual beliefs are and you've always respected that about me. I met a couple of guys that found a very unique and powerful place and they gave me directions on how to get there."

"Brad! You don't even know New Mexico! Last week was the first time you've ever even been there, you said so yourself! What if you can't find this place? What if you and your friends get lost?"

"We have a guide," Brad blurted out. "He's Native American and he knows the area. He grew up there on a Reservation."

Brad paused for a few seconds to let his wife digest this newest bit of information. What he got in return was a look of suspicion and disbelief.

"What's his name?"

"Jack Martinez. Or Jack Redfeather as he's known on the Res."

"And this Jack…knows the situation? The whole situation?"

She's starting to react rationally now, Brad thought to himself. That's a good sign.

"He does," Brad responded. "He knows the terrain and has had many positive experiences with Peyote." A little fudging of the truth but necessary at this point, Brad again thought to himself.

"When were you planning on going?" she asked with a tone of resignation in her voice.

"In three weeks," he said quietly. He scooted closer and took her hands in his. "When was the last time I ever asked to do something like this?" he begged sincerely.

Chapter 4

She looked at him long and hard. "I can't even remember," she stated honestly, shaking her head.

"So please think of who I am as a person, and try to understand, okay?"

"What else can I do?" she asked in a tone of defeat. "It doesn't sound like I even have a choice."

"Hey, if you really don't want me to go, then I won't go," Brad announced seriously.

"Sure, but then you'd hold it against me right? Right? Be honest."

"It's true I might," he admitted. "I guess I just never considered the idea of you refusing to let me go do this. Especially when you knew how much it meant to me."

"You know I won't stop you it's just that I'll be worried about you, that's all."

"I know, but don't be. We have a professional guide." Embellishment. "We'll take weapons, plenty of food and water..." As well as a powerful mind altering drug. "and I have a detailed map of the area." Which was drawn by two stoner hippies. But hey, what could go wrong? That's right Brad, lay that sugar coating down thick. "Look, don't think about this any more for right now. We have time. We can talk about it some more later, okay?"

"Now I'm starting to wish that you were just dealing drugs instead of this. Boy. I bet you already had this whole thing planned out, didn't you?"

Funny. Jack had said something very similar to that.

"I have been thinking about it since I came back from New Mexico, yes."

"Mmm...hmm," she said. "Alright, enough for now. But this is definitely a 'to be continued'. You got me mister?"

"Yes ma'am," Brad said as he reached over to turn out the light.

Snuggling up to his wife he thought; well that didn't go so badly. Maybe it'll be even easier with Nick and Jason.

Chapter 5

"Seriously?" Jason asked. The doubt and skepticism more than evident in the sound of his voice as it came through the phone line.

"Dead serious," Brad replied without hesitancy.

"Yeah...no. I won't be doing that any time soon."

"Okay...so what's a long enough time, consist of? Three weeks?"

"Very funny, guy. No, what are you insane? I haven't even seen you in...what's it been? Five years?"

"Three years Jay and I've told you a million times not to exaggerate."

"Okay, so three years. And now you want to go traipsing off into the deserts of New Mexico on a camping trip and what's more, you want to drag me along with you?"

Interesting, Brad thought. Now Jason is sounding like his wife. Not good!

"Not just you. Nick's going with us."

"Really?" he stated more than asked. "And just how in the hell did you manage to wrangle him into this fiasco?"

"Uh...well, I haven't exactly asked him yet."

"Dude! You are a real piece of work these days aren't you my friend? Look man. I'm happy with my life. Family's great, job's great. Got no complaints. Not sure what you're going through right now and wish I could help but I'm gonna have to sit this one out."

Chapter 5

"Alright. I'm really happy for you. Sounds like everything is wonderful with you, but as my friend you're supposed to be there for me regardless of how you're doing. Don't you remember the pact we made years ago? The three of us said we'd stick together through thick and thin no matter what. And right now things are getting thin for me."

There was a silence on the other end of the line for a moment.

"Okay, talk to me Brad. Has the marriage gone sour? Your job stressing you out? Kids okay? What's up?"

"Everything's fine with job and family Jay, it's just that lately I've been feeling as though my soul is stretched too thin. I'm starting to get that old feeling, you know? Like; what is it all for? Can't you relate even a little?"

"Sure man. It's called a midlife crisis. All of us men have to go through it."

Brad's voice groaned over the other end of the phone.

"Jay, listen to me. Remember all the times we took those intense trips and hiked to all those radical places in the desert? Remember the closeness and comradery we shared together? Remember how we got to a certain point and it felt like time itself stopped and we were completely at peace within ourselves and with everything around us? For just a few moments we understood the secrets of the Universe and just for a second...we knew what it was all for."

All went silent on the other end of the line. That wasn't even a sales pitch, Brad thought. I just poured my heart and soul out there and if this doesn't work then I don't know what will.

"Yeah, how could I forget?" Jason fired back. "But we were also on some heavy hallucinogens at the time if you recall? So why do I get the feeling that there's something you're not telling me?" More phone silence then a long winded sigh from Jason's end of the line. "Alright man. You had me at; 'Remember all the times we took all those intense trips...'"

"Yes!" Brad said enthusiastically. "This will be one of the best things that ever happened to us, you'll see. You won't regret it!"

"Yeah, well if I do, so will you my man. Big time. Oh Christ. How the hell am I going to break this to the wife?"

"Good luck with that friend. Oh and Jay? Promise you won't mention any of what was just said to Nick. I want to explain it to him myself. Gimme your word."

"Okay, okay, fine. I promise."

Twenty minutes later, after he'd filled Jason in on the plan, Brad called Nick's cell phone.

Chapter 6

"Yello?"

"Hey old friend. How's it goin'?"

"Heeeyy! Pretty good man. Long time no hear! How you been?"

"Not bad, not bad. Could be better, could be worse."

"Yeah I hear ya. So, what's up? If I know you, there's a reason for this 'out of the blue' phone call."

"Well you got me dead to rights. I need a big favor."

Nick began chuckling on the other end of the line.

"Ah, sorry man. I can't help ya. I'm broke."

More chuckling.

"Aww come on man. I don't need that much. Just about seven hundred oughta do it."

This was a game Brad used to love to play with Nick. He would hit Nick with the hard stuff making him think that he needed a gigantic favor. Then when he had him hooked, anything else would seem small in comparison. It almost always worked like a charm.

"Seven hundred bucks?" Nick echoed emphatically. "What happened? Why so much? Did your car break down or something?"

This was Brad's favorite part.

"Look man. I wouldn't ask if it wasn't extremely important. Whaddya say? Can you help me out? Please? You're the only one I can turn to."

"Geez, guy! Alright. When can you pay me back though?"
"Just kiddin' bro. I don't need your money."
"Whaaat?" Nick exhaled, taken back.
Now Brad was chuckling.
"No man. What I need from you doesn't cost money."
"Whooaa guy! What are we talkin' about here?"
"Calm down friend. I'll explain it to you."

Brad got serious then and just for a second he considered giving Nick the same speech that he'd just given Jason but decided against it. It worked once but he didn't want to push his luck. It might be time to fabricate the circumstances of the situation just a little bit. Sure, he'll feel bad about it later but it seemed necessary at this point.

"Well...here's the thing. I just got off the phone with our old buddy Jason and it seems as though he's got a bit of a situation going on in his life right now and needs us."

"Aww, man, what happened? Is he okay?"

There was genuine concern reflecting in Nick's tone. Brad was starting to feel bad now so he felt he'd better get this over with and quick.

"Well I can't really speak on it too much. I'm just going to have to let Jay fill you in when we meet up."

"Meet up? When? Where?"

"Well, guess what? Pack your camping gear cause we're going to New Mexico in three weeks," Brad stated in a tone not unlike that of a game show host.

"Whaaat? New Mexico? For how long?"

"Just for the weekend."

"Why do you want to go to New Mexico?"

"Well it's not me so much as it is Jason. Apparently he feels as though he really needs to complete some kind of spiritual quest or journey, or something. Anyway I think we'd better humor him for the time being. Sounds like he's got something pretty major going on. Oh, and it's probably best that you don't ask him about it right away. Maybe just let him speak on it when he's ready. In fact, you should probably just pretend that you don't even know that anything is wrong. Know what I mean? He'll probably act like there's nothing the matter until he's ready to come clean anyway."

"Uhh...alright man. If you say so. You've known him longer than me so you probably know what's best."

"That's right and don't you forget it! Hell, bro! If it was you with the problem, there isn't anything Jay and I wouldn't do for you!"

"Ahh...it's cool man. Yeah, I'll be there. You better bring plenty of beer though. This trip is gonna cost you!"

"Oh, don't you worry my friend. I'll definitely bring plenty of something!"

"Something? Hey what are we talking about here, guy?"

"Wups, gotta go. Got another call comin' in. I'll call you back in a day or two."

Brad hung up the phone before Nick could get another word in edgewise. Well, that wasn't so bad, Brad thought. Another idea occurred to him just then.

"Time to call Jack," he stated to himself aloud as he dialed Jack's number.

Chapter 7

"Hey Jack, it's Brad."

"Yes, High Commander!" Jack's crisp tone coming through the phone line. "What new task have you prepared for me this time?"

"Well, first of all, you'll need to work on your character development. If you call me High Commander in front of the guys, then they'll probably think you're some kind of lunatic cult member."

"Got it chief. I mean...you gottem paleface!" Brad groaned over the other end of the line. "Hey, hey! Reeelaaax! When the time comes, I might just amaze you. I did take some Theatre back at Community College."

"Yeah, so you keep telling me! Anyway, have you scouted out any more of the area that you're gonna take us to?"

"Yes, I did as a matter of fact. I even checked with the local Ranger's Station to see if anyone was scheduled to camp out anywhere near there on that weekend, and they said no."

"Excellent. That was good thinking Jack."

"Thank you...thank you."

"Now did you find something to wear? Something authentic perhaps?"

"Yes siree. I found some things that belonged to my grandfather. Real Native American garb. Fits like a glove. Hey, ya know, I could

Chapter 7

call some of my old Theatre buddies and see if they want to get into the act if you want? I could have them meet us out in the desert!"

"No, no, no! Definitely not! No thank you. I don't need some prima donna upstaging someone or stealing someone else's line and blowing this whole thing for me. My friends aren't stupid. They'd figure it out in no time and then my head would be on the chopping block. Or worse yet, it could get weird and disastrous. Don't forget, we're gonna be on a serious psychedelic drug. Remember Jack, I want this to be a real spiritual experience for all of us. As real as possible anyway."

"Well then why all the deceit? Why not just tell them what is really going on? Get it out in the open so that you guys can have fun."

"Because if they knew what I was up to then I'd never get them out there! They'd never take me seriously. They'd think it was just a waste of time. Just some mind altered camping excursion."

"But that's what it is!"

"No! It'll be much more than that, you'll see. Or maybe you won't see, I don't know. We three will see, and that's all that matters. I'm doing this for all of us. I need it. So do they, they just don't know it yet."

"Boy, I sure hope you know what you're getting yourself into. Hope you don't end up losing two good friends."

"Are you kidding? I know these guys! They'll end up thanking me in their prayers!"

"I'll be saying some prayers for you, that's for sure," Jack mumbled under his breath.

"What's that Jack?"

"Uh, nothing. Call me back when you have something new for me."

"Will do."

Chapter 8

As Brad planned the trip in the upcoming days, the excitement for adventure was constantly flowing through his veins making him almost giddy at times.

Despite his new interest, he made sure to spend as much time with his wife and kids as possible while he kept in touch with his friends every other day. His correspondence with Jack thinned a bit however, but he trusted that Jack would know what to do when the time came. Besides, he didn't want to overthink this thing anyway. It had to be spontaneous for the most part. Brad just wanted to set the stage. The Play itself would unfold as it was supposed to. Or so he believed. God, he hoped! He really hoped that it wouldn't turn out to be a total let down. No, it won't, he thought. All of this is happening for a reason. He had to believe that. Something glorious and inspiring and maybe even cosmic was going to happen to them all and he just couldn't wait to get started!

So his days flew by in anticipation of the wondrous things to come. He thought often of the scene in the movie "The Doors", when Jim Morrison and his band mates went out to the desert sand dunes and tripped on Peyote. Brad felt that we all needed that amazement and awe that we are normally denied as human beings and that deep down we yearn for more than this mundane reality, whether we realized it consciously or not. There was another scene he loved where

Chapter 8

Jim was talking with a friend of his while flying to his next gig. Jim told his friend that he'd underestimated the audience and that what people really wanted wasn't two cars and a house; but something sacred. That really struck a chord in Brad and he thought about it every day now. He even watched the movie again for inspiration and felt that tingle of energy and anxious apprehension that came with the hope of something great on the threshold.

He stopped in at the local sporting goods store and got everything that he thought he'd need for the trip plus a couple of extra things in case Jason or Nick forgot to bring them.

Almost every chance he had while alone at night he locked the door to his room and took out the bag of Peyote. He stared at it with a mix of fear and wonder, feeling the weight of it in his hand. Such an amazing thing, he thought. That a plant, or cactus rather, could have such a profound effect on a person's mind and body. How much should they even eat? he wondered. Dipping his hand gently into the bag he pulled out a good sized button. One button each? Two...three? Hopefully Jack with all of his experience would know for sure. In fact, Brad thought that he should call him tomorrow just to double check.

Still so many things to work out. So many things to remember. As he held the Peyote button in his hand, he swore that he could sense its power. He must never forget to give this drug its due respect at all times.

His eyes glazed slightly as he remembered back to a time several years ago when he and Jason had taken L.S.D. together. They had gone hiking and wandering all over their little desert town, exploring new places and seeing things they had already been familiar with in a brand new light. At one time during the peak, they were walking down a well known street when the ground began lifting and pulsating beneath them. As they continued their walk, everything took a turn for the surreal and shadows started flowing beneath their feet like streams of water. It was at this point they realized that perhaps they had taken too much. They ran all the way back to Brad's little studio apartment and spent a hellish time trying to cope with what seemed to be the exact opposite of reality. Relentless and repetitive hallucinations threatened to completely consume their sanity and at one point Brad was convinced that they were never coming back. They ended up taking sleeping pills just to escape the unending madness that they had brought upon themselves. Yes, it was extremely important that they did not take too much!

A knock at the door brought him out of his reverie. It was the kids and they expected a story before bed time. He loved to make up stories for them and they loved hearing them. Well, tonight he'd make up a grand tale for them. One involving friends, the desert, and a sorcerer with mystical powers.

Chapter 9

Five a.m. Friday; the day of. Brad had spoken his farewells to his kids the night before which was tough to do, and now it was time to say goodbye to his wife. It'd be the first time that he'd be gone for more than a day without them in years. Luckily, his wife's younger sister decided to come over and stay with them for the weekend while he was gone. He hoped that she would be enough of a distraction until he returned. Her visit also allowed his wife to drive him to the rental agency so that they could have a few moments alone together.

Her concern and apprehension were crystal clear as she held him tight, acting as if it would be for the last time. Brad chuckled and assured her that everything would be fine and that he'd call her from a landline every chance he'd get if he had no cell phone coverage. He knew that it was very unlikely that he actually could but he had to tell her that in order to keep her from worrying. At least for now.

He watched her drive off with a hint of sadness after she dropped him off to pick up the rental. He didn't want to chance driving his own vehicle to New Mexico not knowing exactly where he'd even park or what state of mind he might be in. He'd get the insurance on the rental and not have to worry about any of that. He had arranged to pick Nick and Jason up at Nick's place which was about an hour from his house, and agreed that he would do all the driving. He had to agree to do practically everything just to get them to go along with his little scheme. But it would be worth it, he knew. Or hoped, once again. It had better, or they may never forgive him for this little deception. He had chosen a Jeep Wrangler, which had Four Wheel Drive, from the rental agency just in case and quickly loaded all the gear into the Jeep which included; camping equipment, water, food and snacks.

As he drove the freeway towards Nick's house he ran a mental checklist through his head to make sure that he hadn't forgotten anything. Feeling jazzed about the adventure he was soon to embark upon, he put some music on the stereo and relaxed himself for the cruise to pick up the fellas. "Not to Touch the Earth" drifted eerily through the stereo speakers off of his homemade "Doors Favorite Hits" CD, and he found himself singing along with Jim almost as if he were chanting a religious psalm. He had brought along plenty of the best psychedelic music he could find for the trip. He had made a mixed CD with songs from; Bob Marley, The Doors, Jimi Hendrix, The Grateful Dead, Led Zeppelin, Pink Floyd and even some Beatles. He loved the old Classic Rockers and knew that his friends would appreciate them too. It's what they'd grown up on and were familiar with.

During his last conversation with Jack, they had agreed to meet around dusk at a place about a mile away from their campsite. From there, Jack would lead them to a spot that he had scouted out for them that was far away from any intrusions or unforeseen campers who might be out near that area. Jack had also given him instructions on eating the Peyote.

"Each of you should eat one button at first with a piece of beef jerky. Wait half an hour and eat another, again with another piece of jerky. Continue this procedure until you've each consumed four buttons, and then stop. You should start to feel the effects by then and we will meet each other shortly after that. Timing is everything so keep your eyes on the clock. Remember to start eating the buttons two hours before we meet and no sooner. If you guys get all whacked out you may forget where to go and get lost."

Brad remembered the first time he had ever tried Peyote. It was a very small amount; like half a button, and it was still fresh because it hadn't been dried yet. He had liked the effect it had had on him though and he'd always hoped that one day he would be able to go the distance with a larger amount and really explore more of the levels and effects of that psychoactive Cactaceae. Well, that day was today! In fact, in just so many hours he would finally embark upon a journey that's been years in the waiting. He just hoped that he hadn't built this thing up so much that if he got let down, he might reconsider his faith in his spiritual beliefs. Brad had Cherokee blood somewhere in his lineage, so his father had told him, and ever since he'd turned twenty he had finally found the spirituality that he'd been searching for all his life. His mother had been Catholic and tried to raise him accordingly but it had just never felt right for him personally. After doing lots of research on Native American Culture and Mythology, he decided to dedicate his life to becoming a Warrior. At least in a certain sense. He prayed to the Great Spirit, the Mother Earth and the all powerful Universe and did his best to respect all forms of life. Then, when he started reading Carlos Castaneda, among others, everything else just fell into place. So he'd been off track for a while, but all that would change starting today. He was beginning to view this thing as a real test now and hoped that he would at least squeak by in passing it.

With all of the introspection and profound thought he was experiencing, he almost missed the exit for Nick's street. He couldn't believe that he'd gotten there so quickly and hurriedly ran through his mind the story that he'd propose to his two friends in order to keep them interested and their suspicions at bay. Hopefully Nick hadn't tried to prod Jason too much, and hopefully Jason hadn't volunteered too much information to Nick. He'd know right away as soon as he saw the first looks on their faces but whatever the case, he knew that it was too late for any of them to back out now. Or so again; he hoped.

He pulled up into Nick's driveway, shut the Jeep off and jumped out striding confidently up the walkway trying to appear cooler than he really felt at the moment.

His mind raced as he knocked loudly on the door and heard Nick's voice state loudly, "Come in."

As he walked through the door he saw Nick sitting on the couch, beer in hand, smiling at him.

"Hey, brother! Long time no see! Where's-" but before he could finish, Jason jumped out from behind the front door with an exaggerated Karate punch and yelled, "Whatowwww!"

Brad barely got his guard up in time and sidestepped the little maneuver, but it threw him off balance and he almost tripped.

"Whoa guy!" Brad yelled.

They both laughed and then Jason hugged him warmly.

"What's up man, how've you been?" Jason asked.

Jason and Brad had both been into martial arts since they were kids and both loved and idolized Bruce Lee. It was customary for one to attack the other, especially when they hadn't seen each other in a long time.

"I've been pretty good," Brad answered. "And how about this guy?" Brad asked as he approached Nick, who was already on his feet and walking towards him.

"Hey guy, what's up?" Nick asked, giving Brad a handshake and a hug.

"Same ol', same ol'. Still got your little apartment here, huh? That's cool. So, you guys ready for the incredible journey?"

"Yeah, let's do it," Nick said confidently. That was one thing Brad had always loved and admired about Nick. The guy was down to do damn near anything!

Chapter 9

"And you sir?" Brad asked, turning towards Jason.

"Oh I'm ready man. Start the expedition path finder! Let's go trail blazer!"

Man, it's good to be back with these guys again! Brad couldn't help but think. It was exciting to be sharing their energy again after so long, and it put Brad in an adventurous mood. They did a quick equipment check, then loaded up the Jeep and were soon on their way.

"So how long will it take us to get there?" Nick asked.

"It's over eight hundred miles so it will take us at least ten hours depending on traffic," Brad replied.

"Time for a long nap. I was up kinda late last night."

"What were you doin' old buddy? Talking to chicks online as usual? Hmmm?" Brad teased.

"Yeah...maybe," Nick retorted a little defensively.

"Well then you better get your beauty sleep while you can. Jay and I will try to keep it down to a dull roar."

"Yeah you do that," Nick quipped patronizingly.

"Go to bed you sonofa-" Brad said, letting it go at that.

He turned on some music and chatted with Jason for a while, then as Jason peeked in the back to make sure Nick was sleeping, Jason quietly asked, "All right man. What's really goin' on Brad? You in trouble with the wife, or the job or what?"

"No man. It's nothing like that. I just had an awakening recently that's all. It took long enough, but it got its hooks into me."

"Care to elaborate, old friend?"

"Well...I went out to New Mexico on business recently and something sorta...happened...to me while I was there. It actually started as I was driving on my way out and then an idea became cemented in my mind. It was to take this trip. With you guys. It's like the Universe was guiding me into everything. One thing led to another and here we are on our way to possibly experience one of the most profound and insightful adventures of our lives!"

Jason just sat there in silence and stared at Brad with an extremely unsure look on his face.

Without taking his eyes off of Brad he said, "Every time you talk this way it usually means that you have some kind of psychedelic surprise that you're going to spring on us at the last minute."

A hint of fear coming through in Jason's tone and rightfully so as he's going to soon see, Brad thought to himself.

"Come on you bastard! Let's have it! If I'm going to take part in something then you better come clean now so that I can start warming up to the idea!"

"Okay, okay!" Brad conceded. "I might have brought along a substantial amount of Peyote."

"Oh, Jesus!" Jason exclaimed. "Fucking Peyote? You do realize that I've never taken it before and I'm pretty sure that Nick hasn't either. And what about you?"

"I've tried it before!" Brad said defensively.

"Oh what, the time you ate that tiny little bit with your dad and went hiking up in the mountains? Dude! What have you gotten us into?"

"Relax! Hear me out before you panic okay?"

"This better be good," Jason replied, and Brad could see that he meant it.

"Okay. I met a man out in New Mexico right as I was starting to plan this trip. I accidentally left my laptop at the diner I was eating at and he found it for me. Turns out that this guy is a Native American Shaman. A Sorcerer! He's the real deal and he's agreed to guide us on a spiritual quest out there in the desert. We'll be meeting him in about nine hours from now."

Jason had a look of almost horror on his face and seemed truly aghast at this newest bit of information.

"I'm not even sure how to respond to that! How do you know that this guy is even legit?"

Chapter 9

"I did some checking up on him and I questioned him extensively." Both palpable lies. "He grew up out there on a Reservation and his Grandfather taught him everything he knows. He's a Yaqui Indian, just like-"

"Oh my God, don't say it! Just like don Juan from your Castaneda books right? Are you still reading those?"

"Well yeah, I picked one up again recently. What's wrong with that?"

"There's a very familiar feeling washing over me right now Brad! How many times did you get Nick and me to go hiking or camping out in the middle of the desert with you, looking for that 'something' that you always hoped that we would find but never did? We had some fun times, granted, but we never received any divine revelations did we? And we all got into trouble in some form or another over it didn't we?"

"Hey, that's not entirely true!" Brad shot back irritably.

"Oh, no?" Jason remarked casually. "How about the time we got lost on those trails up in the mountains when we were hiking at night? We ended up at that seriously spooky place that you liked to call Mordor and we all felt as though something really bad was going to happen to us at any moment. Thank God nothing ever did!"

Reflecting back, Brad remembered when there had been a couple of instances years ago, when he and Jason had found some man-made trails up in the northwestern mountains of Joshua Tree that led near the peak of one mountain top in particular. They had reached a certain area in which a jumbled cluster of large boulders sat right in their path and Brad refused to continue on. A strange ominous feeling had gripped him tightly and he felt certain that his death was waiting for him on the other side of those rocks. He became so frightened that he had to turn away and start back in the direction that they had just come from. Later, on another occasion, they went back to see if anything had changed and yet Brad still felt that unexplained anxiety and apprehension that he had come to recognize so well from that place. Again he flat out refused to go any further. It remained unexplained to this day and would likely stay that way forever.

"And...how about the time we got chased by those firefighters and later by the cops up through that canyon and we barely got away by hiding in that cave we found for hours? And what about-"

"Alright! Alright!" Brad interrupted irritably. "Look, that was a long time ago and we were young and maybe didn't go about it quite the right way. But this time is different. Can't you just reach way down into your reserves and trust me one more time?"

"You're right about us not being young anymore that's for sure. So you had better keep that in mind. As for the other, do you really even have to ask that? I'm here aren't I? And so is Nick."

"Thank you. So, are you ready to hear the plan now?"

"Lay it on me brother," Jason replied after a sigh of resignation.

"Good!"

So taking his time, Brad went over in detail and to the best of his ability; the plan, in all its wonder and mystery. Jason seemed amazingly calm through all of it and even offered some ideas on what to do first and what to take with them in case of an emergency. It made Brad extremely happy to see that his longtime friend was finally warming up to the trip.

"I'm still not sure about this medicine man friend of yours though."

"Just wait until you meet him and then you'll see. There really is something about him. I can't even describe it but you'll see it for yourself."

Once out of the city, the landscape changed to one of rugged mountainous terrain then eventually to desert, right before they got to Arizona. After that, the scenery was mostly just more desert until they drove again through the mountains and then noticed lots of

Chapter 9

Pine trees intermingled with Oak. Jason and Brad both enjoyed the beautiful views they witnessed and discussed them cheerfully. Nick woke up hours later and Brad went over the plan again, this time having Jason's supportive comments interjected here and there.

"So we need to start eating the Peyote about two hours before we rendezvous with Jack." At the mention of Peyote, Nick became extremely apprehensive. "I know, I know Nick. I'm a little nervous too and of course so is Jay, but it'll be okay, I'm telling you," Brad added, trying to calm him.

"Yeah dude, but you hear about hikers and people getting lost on trails in the mountains all the time on the news. Plus, what about mountain lions?" Nick asked fearfully. "And those hikers were sober even!"

"Ah, but don't forget we have a professional guide to lead us," Brad responded reassuringly.

Oh, so now he's a professional? Jason thought to himself. Brad had always been impulsive when it came to certain things, but this could be ridiculous. He was just going to have to have supreme faith in his friend yet one more time. He did take comfort in knowing that Brad now had a family and a good career and wouldn't take too many reckless chances in jeopardizing that. At least he believed he wouldn't.

"So...what do you guys want to listen to?" Brad asked, trying to direct their attention away from anxiety and concern.

"Put on some Hendrix," Nick said.

"You got it brother."

As "All Along the Watchtower," echoed out of the speakers, each of their thoughts drifted between the distant past to the almost immediate future. About an hour later they found themselves cruising down a long stretch of desert highway. The sun was approaching the western horizon behind them signifying a closeness towards the end of the day.

"Alright, men," Brad said in the tone of a general about to lead his troops into battle. "Now's the time, the time is now." He reached down into the middle console and drew forth the bag of Peyote ever so slowly as if it were a pouch full of precious jewels. "Jay, could you please distribute these so that we get one each for now?"

Jason now holding the bag for the very first time stared at it with a mixture of apprehension and wonderment, as he weighed it in his palm. Gently dipping his hand in, he pulled out a button and handed it to Brad.

"Here you go fearless leader."

Brad held it respectfully between his thumb and forefinger. Again Jason grabbed a button and handed it to Nick, who reached for it hesitantly. Lastly, he took one for himself clutching it tightly as he zip locked the bag.

As Jason stowed the bag back in the console, Brad gave one more little inspirational speech; "A toast! To friends, the guiding powers of the Cosmic Universe, and enlightenment!"

"Hear! Hear!" Jason and Nick echoed in unison.

"Nick? Please note the time."

"Four o'clock on the nose!"

"Perfect!" Brad said. "That'll make it easy to time these things. Everyone got a piece of jerky?" They all three held up their buttons and jerky as if they were the Three Musketeers crossing blades. "Here we go fellas. There's no turning back now!"

They all popped their buttons and chewed them as quickly as they could. With bitter reactions, they chased them down with the teriyaki jerky Brad had provided.

"Man!" Jason exclaimed. "These taste even worse than mushrooms!"

"Yech!" Nick agreed, taking a large gulp off of his bottled water. "Pretty bad! And we have to eat three more of those things? Maybe we should just wait a few hours and see what one does to us."

Chapter 9

"No! No, no, no! Can't deviate from the directions! No time to back out now fellas. We bought the ticket, now we take the ride! Don't worry, we'll be fine. Just have some faith."

A little while went by with more talk and music then Brad called for another time check.

"Four twenty," Nick stated.

"Whoa ho hooo! Four twenty bro!" Jason said in his best stoner voice. Where's the Ganja mon?"

"Yeah, right!" Brad scoffed. "Just how incoherent were you lookin' to get, guy? I'm seeking spirituality and peace, not tryin' to reenact the adventures of the late, great Hunter S. Thompson!"

"We were somewhere near New Mexico on the edge of the desert, when the drugs began to take hold..." Jason quoted in his best Hunter Thompson voice.

They all had a laugh at his perfectly timed witty comment and then proceeded to tell stories of their past psychedelic adventures. Soon enough it was four thirty and they repeated the process of button eating once again. They noticed that the air got cooler as it settled over the desert while they drove and they commented on it each in turn. They began chatting less and started taking more note of the scenery all around them.

"My God," Jason breathed. "It has been years since I've been out in the desert. There really is something awe inspiring about it, isn't there?"

"That's the Peyote talking guy!" Nick snickered.

"Fuck you, asshole!" Jason shot back angrily, his French temper surfacing. "Can't a guy get philosophical at a time like this?"

At that, Brad and Nick erupted into laughter. At first Jason appeared to get even angrier but then realized what he had said, and started to giggle as well.

"Oh shit! What time is it?" Brad asked, having lost track.

"Five o' two," said Nick, the official timekeeper at this point.

"We're late! Jay, could you please do the honors once again?"

"I'm on it," Jason replied in a serious tone. This time around they all remarked about how the taste wasn't so bad once you started to get used to it.

"Alright guys. After this, only one more button to go."

They all nodded their heads at that and once again began listening to music. At one point Nick very quietly commented that he thought he'd heard a noise coming from underneath the Jeep.

"What did it sound like?" Brad asked, showing only mild concern.

"Kinda like a scraping, vibrating sound. Like a low grinding noise. How's it been shifting?"

"A tiny bit rough now that you mention it," Brad said, lost in thought. "Good thing it's a rental huh?"

"Rental or not, it needs to get us where we're going. How would you like to be stranded out on the side of the road in the middle of the desert, tripping on Peyote with no cellular service?" Jason asked, pessimistically.

"Man, you paint a real pretty picture don't you?" Brad returned.

"Hey man, don't even talk like that or you'll jinx us," Nick said piping up from the back seat.

"Come on guys, relax! We'll be in town in less than half an hour, and besides…it seems to be shifting smoother now."

At Brad's proclamation they both seemed to relax visibly and Brad called for the time again.

"It's time for the last button, boys," Nick stated with authority.

They all cheered their last buttons together then downed them with the rest of the jerky. No more than then thirty seconds had passed when a horribly loud grinding sound came from underneath the Jeep. It started shifting back and forth between gears and Brad had to slow it way down and pull off onto the side of the road.

"Goddamnit! I don't believe this! This is your fault!" Brad screamed at Jason.

Chapter 9

"How the hell is this, my fault?"

"You cursed us with all that talk of breaking down, you asshole!"

"What? You wanna pin this on me? All I said was-"

"Alright, knock it off you two!" Nick said in a voice more commanding than they'd heard from him in a long time. "Look. You can see the town from here. Let's see if we can make it that far and call AAA or the rental agency. Then we can just wait for a new ride."

Jason and Brad both looked at each other sheepishly.

"Hey, I'm sorry man. I shouldn't have yelled at you," Brad said, somewhat embarrassed.

"Don't even worry," Jason replied. "I shouldn't have run my mouth like that anyway. It's just bad luck that's all. Let's keep it positive from here on out."

"Agreed," Brad stated, getting the Jeep back into gear then driving towards town at about twenty miles an hour. They arrived three minutes later and sought out the first hint of civilization which turned out to be a Circle K, or at least looked to have been owned by Circle K at one point.

As they pulled up and parked off to the side where a tow truck could access the Jeep easily, Brad turned to the boys, "Alright guys. How is everyone feeling? Are we cool? I know that this is gonna set us back a little on time but we'll be okay, right?"

"I feel okay," Jason replied. "How 'bout you Nick? You okay?"

"Yeah, I'm cool. But we better hurry up and get on with this before the Peyote fully kicks in and things get too intense."

"Let's go," Brad agreed.

They all went inside for cold drinks except for Brad who called the rental agency and apprised them of the situation. As he stood out front testing the strength of his cell phone signal, he suddenly noticed a guy who he hadn't seen when he'd first walked up, about twenty feet away. Sitting on the curb just hanging out, he caught Brad's eye and then quickly looked away. The rental agency apologized profusely and told him that they would send a tow truck and a brand new model Jeep out to him in no more than forty minutes.

Satisfied with that, Brad went inside to rejoin his slightly altered friends. They were restocking their jerky supply and buying trail mix and such, when Brad noticed something out of the corner of his eye. The guy who had been standing right outside of the store, came in and started perusing through the candy aisle. He was a classic version of the nineties grunge hippy; Camouflage shorts, tie dyed Nirvana T-shirt, scraggly unkempt dark brown hair and the attempt of a beard, albeit not a very good one.

As Brad caught up to Nick and Jason he asked, "So fellas, how are we doing?"

"Good," Jason answered. "Just replenishing our supply of munchies and getting some cold drinks."

"Hey, did you happen to notice the guy that just came in? He must have been standing outside the store when we first pulled up but I hadn't noticed him right away. The scruffy looking dude in the Nirvana shirt," Brad clarified.

"Yeah I saw him," Nick said.

"Well, what about him?" Jason asked, watching Brad as he kept stealing glances past him.

"He keeps looking over here. I think he's checking us out."

"What, like you think he knows us something?" Jason asked, apparently unperturbed.

"No, no. I mean like I bet he tries to ask us for money or a ride or something."

"No big deal, dude. We've got more important things to worry about right now. What did the rental agency say?"

"Oh, yeah. They'll be here in about forty minutes but maybe even less. And they're bringing us a brand new model Jeep too."

"Good," Jason said flippantly. "It's the least they can do."

Chapter 9

So knowing that they had some time, they took a few extra minutes to check out all that the store had to offer then made their purchases and walked back out to the Jeep.

"Well at least this stuff is already all packed up so it should be easy to transfer it once they get here," Brad offered.

As they sat in the Jeep listening to music, the hippy came out of the store and settled down against the wall leaning on his weathered backpack. He caught Brad's eye and jutted his chin up as if to say "What's up?" and Brad curtly responded back in the same manner, looking away immediately after. The last thing he wanted to do was give this freeloader some signal of an invite. The Grateful Dead drifted from the Wrangler's stereo and the hippy took notice, nodding his head and grooving to the music.

"I predict he'll make his move soon," Brad observed, staring off into the distance.

"Sooner than you think dude, here he comes," Jason replied.

"Yeeeaaah! Grateful Dead! Love those guys! Seen 'em eleven times man! Hey, what's up guys? How are you doing?"

"Were good bro," Jason jumped in, trying to be polite as he noticed the annoyed look on Brad's face.

"So what are you guys like…going camping or something?"

"Something like that," Brad answered a little irritably.

"Cool, cool," the hippy replied, unfazed. "So what happened to your ride? I heard it making an awful sound when you first pulled up. You guys gonna be okay? I could take a look at it for you if you want? My dad was a mechanic most of his life and he taught me quite a bit."

Slightly touched by the offer, Brad informed him of their plight and assured him that they'd be okay. Then Jason started a conversation with him and told him of their plans to go into the mountains.

Great! Brad thought to himself. Now he'll probably ask us for that ride.

"Oh cool man! Are you guys heading over to Center Circle? It's like a big, round, flat open space with gigantic boulders lining the entire outer edges of it. I know that whole area for miles. Love that place!"

"Yeah, actually we are," Brad responded, quite amazed. "What are you doing way out here in the boonies yourself?"

"Ah, well…I'm just kinda passing through really. Hitchhiking to Cali, then gonna meet up with some friends in Oregon and maybe hit Washington. No hurries, no worries."

"That's cool," Brad said.

"Hey…" the hippy said in a hushed tone as he advanced a few steps. "You guys interested in some mushrooms? They're really good! I've also got some killer bud if you're interested?"

"Nah man, we're cool," Brad assured him.

"You sure?" the hippy asked. "Very inexpensive. Trying to make some cash so's I can get a bite to eat."

"I think we're good but I'll tell you what…here's ten bucks if that'll help you out?"

"Oh dude, right on! Are you sure bro?"

"Yeah it's cool, don't worry about it."

"Thank you man, seriously! Hey, if you change your mind, you know…about those items, let me know. I will seriously hook you up!"

So they all chatted together for a while and as it turned out the hippy's name was Terry and he ended up being a pretty cool, down to earth guy and they all found themselves liking him. He told them some amazing stories and had a particularly funny type of humor and personality.

Time flew by and when the tow truck and rental arrived he wished them luck and made a hasty retreat back inside the store. As Brad signed the paperwork, Jason and Nick transferred all of their

Chapter 9

belongings over with amazing speed and efficiency. Soon the rental agent and tow truck driver were retreating down the highway and they noticed that evening was turning fast into night.

Brad started the Jeep and got ready to pull away when Terry walked out eating a freshly microwaved burrito while holding a huge soda. He caught sight of them and gave a wave of thanks and farewell. Brad waved back and looked over to Nick and Jason. They both had the same expression on their faces.

"I know that look," Brad said. "Alright, what do you guys think?"

"Well, he says he knows the area and that could come in handy if we get lost or separated from our guide. I mean, we're already late to meet him. He could end up being useful," Jason admitted.

"Nick?" Brad asked, turning towards him. After a moment's hesitation Nick answered, "Yeah. Why not? He seems like a pretty cool dude."

"Who knows?" Brad pondered aloud. "We might want to end up trying a little of those Shrooms after all. You never can tell. Alright then, let's ask him. Hey, Terry!" he yelled over to him.

As Terry came running up like a happy and faithful hound, Brad was sure that he already knew his answer.

Chapter 10

Driving east down the lonely highway, they all silently watched the sun go down into the mountains and enjoyed the cool desert breeze all the while.

"Amazing," Jason commented, almost in a whisper.

"Wait until you see the sun rise in this desert. It's even more spectacular if you can imagine that," Brad commented.

"I believe it," Jason agreed.

"So Terry...you ever read any Carlos Castaneda?" Brad asked, seeming only mildly curious.

After a moment's pause in thought, Terry said, "Oh yeah! Castaneda! Don Juan, the Indian Sorcerer right?"

"Yeah!" Brad said smiling. He had always felt a slight connection with people who were familiar with Castaneda's writing. "Have you read 'em all or just a few?"

"I've read all of them man! At least I'm pretty sure. Great stories!"

"So do you believe in any of those ideas or agree with his philosophies?"

Now normally around this time, Jason would intervene and sarcastically chastise Brad for giving someone the third degree about his beloved novelist and the enchanting don Juan character, having had to listen to Brad go on and on about him every hour. However, this time the circumstances were different. Brad was testing their

Chapter 10

newest crew member, and if he was to be a part of this mystical voyage then he would have to prove his state of mind to be similar if not akin to their own. This time Jason would not disapprove of his subtle tactics, redundant though they may seem to him.

"Oh, fully man! I've seen and heard things in this desert that you would not believe!" Terry replied dramatically.

The perfect answer, Brad thought to himself.

"I feel it only fair to warn you that we are on our way to have a journey of real self-discovery. We are currently feeling the effects of a serious substance and are on route to meet up with a Native American Shaman who has agreed to guide us in our endeavor. How do you feel about all that?" Brad asked seriously.

Nick and Jason both tightened visibly and waited to see Terry's reaction. There it was. Brad had laid all the cards out on the table in the blink of an eye and now they were about to find out if Terry was a real gambling man. If he was, then one more Musketeer would be welcomed into the fold, at least in a support capacity. If not, then they would be physically removing him forthwith, without any sympathies or explanations. After all, they didn't owe this guy anything and they barely even knew him. It was the mission at hand that was of the utmost importance now and they were too far into it to let some stranger spoil the journey and the fun. Boy how quickly their mindsets had changed!

They all tensed as Terry took a few seconds; which felt like an uncertain eternity, to respond. Their postures remained alert and ready for immediate action. Brad had the sudden mental image of Jason and Nick holding him by both hands and feet, whilst swinging his body like a swaying hammock and heave-hoing his ass out of the Wrangler at forty miles per hour.

"What are you guys on?" Terry asked back in an equally serious tone.

This only heightened the tension and escalated their suspense as they waited for Brad to give a reply. Even the mild mannered Nick who was always so calm and laid back seemed about to jump out of his own skin.

"Peyote," Brad stated with authority.

"Oh, right on man!" At that they all relaxed visibly. "I thought for a second that maybe you guys were on like heroin or cocaine or something, and I'm just not down with that. Hell, I even ate a few mushrooms myself right before I ran into you guys!"

"So we're all on the same page?" Brad asked, relief flooding through his body.

"For sure bro!" Terry replied enthusiastically.

As everyone took a few calming breaths, it got silent once again and they continued cruising down the long stretch of road towards their intended destination. As they pulled off onto the dirt road that would lead them to their parking spot, Brad called for a time check.

"Six twenty three," Nick called out from the back seat.

"Damn!" Brad exclaimed. "Were probably gonna be forty five minutes late to meet our guide."

"You don't think he'll ditch us do you?" Jason asked with intense concern in his expression. "You know, like think we're flaking out and not gonna show?"

"I don't believe that," Brad answered. "He'll wait for us. Trust me."

God I hope! Brad thought to himself. Whatever happened, Brad must at least keep the illusion of being positive and determined. As the road ended, Brad shot straight off through the desert trying to get as close to the giant group of boulders as he could. He wanted to get them as near to their campground as possible. Thirty seconds into the off-road excursion, he felt his stomach tighten with cramps. Then he noticed a flash of heat flood throughout his body.

"Hey man. Are you alright? You don't look so good," Terry inquired from the back seat.

Before Brad could reply, Nick piped up next to Terry, "Uh, hey man. Think you'd better pull over."

"I think I'll be alright," Brad said, trying to keep his composure.

"No man, stop! Let me out!" Nick shrieked.

Brad hit the brakes and Nick barely made it out of the Jeep before he started to vomit. Jason was hot on his heels, puking over the side of the Wrangler before he could even make it out the door. Like a chain reaction it happened. Brad actually made it a short ways out into the desert before a wave of nausea engulfed him completely, causing him to throw up as well.

Moments later they collected themselves and were back in the Jeep, slowly heading towards the campsite, with Terry in the back snickering at all of them.

"Shit guys, I'm sorry. I completely forgot about the puking part of taking Peyote. I think we're good now though," Brad tried to assure them.

With some groaning from his companions and more apologies from him, they continued on. After parking they loaded up their backpacks and went over to quickly set up camp, not sure if they'd even be back for it this night or the next morning. Once finished, they grabbed a good supply of water and snacks, then took off to go find their guide.

"Are you sure you'll know if we're heading in the right direction?" Jason asked with some urgency in the question.

"Yes. I remember seeing the spot he told me to meet him at, from here during the day, when I came out here to look at the area the first time."

Without further questioning they plowed ahead, a beautiful bright moon above them lighting the way. After a short time Terry made his way up near Brad and in a hushed tone asked, "So hey man, if you don't mind me asking; what spot are we meeting this guy at? Is it like near anywhere with a name?"

"Yeah, he said it's called the Little Mesa Verde."

"Little Mesa Verde?" Terry echoed in a slightly panicked tone. "Hey bro, I think we're going in the wrong direction. We need to turn southwest. See that big dark shape of a mountain over there about a mile? Pretty sure that's it."

"Are you sure man? I think we're supposed to keep heading west then go northwest. Isn't that it over there?" Brad asked, pointing to a spot out in the distance.

"I don't think so bro. I've hiked this area quite a bit and I'm pretty sure that's it," he said, looking off into the desert. "Just saying," Terry reiterated.

"Okay, man. You know this area better than me so I'll trust you."

Brad subtly began to make his way more south and soon declared that the dark shape of the mountain ahead was their designated meeting spot. As they marched along, Brad asked for a time check.

He got Nick's response, "Seven o' clock, bro."

"Wow! I don't know how we did it but were almost on time. Another few minutes and we'll be there. Let's run for it boys!"

Taking off like a Bighorn sheep being chased by a Puma, Brad ran towards the direction of the enormous grouping of rocks. The fellas took up pursuit and soon Brad was yipping like a coyote, adrenaline flowing through his body along with the Peyote at this point. He hurtled over bushes and leaped across small sandy ravines, the light of the moon glowing brightly all around them. They were all shouting excitedly now and the immense dark shape of the mountain loomed closer and closer ahead. Brad stopped about a hundred yards away from it and waited for the lads to reach him and catch their breaths.

"How are you guys feeling?" Brad's voice drifted, as if carried by the night air itself.

"I think that run just kicked the high into overdrive!" Jason responded. "I am really starting to feel the effects now. Feels good!"

"Same here!" Brad said with an enormous grin on his face. "How about you Nick?"

Chapter 10

"I feel...just capital!" he replied, quoting Curly Bill from the movie Tombstone, perfectly.

"Well...there she is, boys. Let's close the gap so that we can meet up with our guide."

Brad was just hoping that at the crucial moment of meeting Jack, he wouldn't completely blow it. Brad tried hard not to think about how horrible the situation could end up given that the facade was revealed right from the start. As they marched up to the north side of the mountain, Brad started to get a sinking feeling in the pit of his stomach and then he stopped hiking and stared upwards.

"Oh, no. No, no, no!"

"What's up dude?" Jason asked, recognizing a bad situation rapidly taking shape in front of them.

"This isn't Mesa Verde! This is just a giant mound of rocks! Dammit! I knew it!"

As Brad walked off cursing to himself, Jason trailed after him asking, "What? This isn't it? If you knew that then why did you lead us all the way over here?"

"Because Terr-" he started to say but then looked over to see Terry standing nearby hanging his head down sheepishly. Terry looked up to see Brad's face and gave a real "Dude I'm so sorry, I guess I was mistaken" look. Brad after a pause, completed his sentence saying, "Because terrible mistakes are made when you become too sure of yourself."

"Oookaaayyy..." Jason responded, patronizingly. "So what now? Are we lost? Where do we go?"

"Let me consult the map." After digging through his backpack for a flashlight and the map, Brad said, "Okay. We needed to go more north so let's just swing back this way and head over towards that direction. I'm sorry guys, I got a little mixed up for a second but I'm sure it's over there," he stated, pointing off into the distance.

"Okay. Let's just go," Jason said warily.

As they began to take off, Terry made his way up to Brad and said, "Hey bro, I'm really sorry."

"It's okay man. This whole area looks a lot alike. I've miscalculated a time or two and have gotten lost more than once myself."

"Well, thanks for not throwing me under the bus back there."

"Don't sweat it bro," Brad said looking at Terry, appreciating the sales terminology.

"Hey, check out that line of boulders over there," Terry commented, distracting Brad away from his mistake. "Kinda looks like Stonehenge, huh? Hey man, can we check it out?"

"Yeah, I don't know man. We're already late now and we still haven't even found this place yet."

"But we're walking right by it. Can't we just take a second to scope it out?"

With enthusiasm so similar to his own, Brad couldn't resist. Actually, he had wanted to check it out when he first saw it anyway.

Jason coming up from behind asked, "So, what's up? What are you two school girls gossiping about?"

"Uh…we thought we might stop and check this place out real quick."

"Which place? The one that looks like Stonehenge?"

"That's exactly what Terry just said a minute ago!"

"Cool. Well, let's do it but remember we've got a tight schedule to meet."

"Fair enough," Brad agreed, and received a nod from Nick as well.

As they explored the outer edge of the collection of strangely formed rocks they became mesmerized with the shadows that were cast by the giant stones in the moonlight. The slim, tall, pillar looking rocks seemed to be made out of some form of extrusive igneous granite, and looked as though they had sprouted straight out of the ground. They were smooth, grayish white slabs with streaks of quartz running coarsely throughout the stone in veins. There were several pieces collapsed across the tops of each other in certain places giving it a look very similar to that of the famous Stonehenge structure in Wiltshire, England.

"Hey guys, this is amazing!" Jason exclaimed, his voice barely above a whisper but resounding with perfect clarity.

"Whoa! Did you hear how Jason's voice sounded?" Nick asked, breaking his long silence. His voice reverberating through the columns of rocks much in the same manner that Jason's just had.

"Wow! Is it this place or are we really starting to trip on that Peyote?" Brad asked, his tone crisp and clear, trailing slight echoes at the ends of each emphasized syllable.

"Hey, Terry! How do we sound to you right now?"

"Pretty trippy, bro! But then again, I did eat a handful of mushrooms earlier so I'm feeling pretty 'in the zone' myself, if you know what I mean?"

"I think we do. Don't we guys?"

"Yeah...yeah we do," Nick and Jason both murmured at the same time, smiling.

As they continuously inspected the boulders, it was Terry that mentioned that they really ought to be going and once again they were out traversing the desert plains.

"Hey man, what's the name of your guide bro? I never even thought to ask," Terry inquired while hiking alongside Jason.

"You know what? I never even thought to ask either. Hey Nick! Do you know the name of our guide?"

"Uh...no man. Forgot to ask."

"Hey Brad!" Jason called out ahead. "What's the name of-" but was suddenly cut short when Brad started hissing, "Sssshhhh!" and crouched down behind a bush.

"What's up?" Jason whispered, sensing Brad's fear and apprehension.

He had been on many adventures with Brad in the past and knew when to take his friend seriously.

"I think there's something up ahead," Brad breathed cautiously, slightly peeking his head up from the brush to get a better view. "I could've sworn I saw something big move over there. There! See it? It just moved again! Shit! Am I seeing things? What is that?"

"I don't really see anything. Are you sure you're not just trippin' bro?" Jason asked, trying more to comfort himself then put up a valid argument.

By this time, all four of them were crouched down whispering and they all began breathing a little heavier.

"Let's go check it out," Nick said from the side, a streak of bravery desperately needed in their situation. As they slowly and ever so carefully approached the dark shape ahead, they saw that it was about eight feet tall and not moving.

They reached a distance of about ten feet away when Jason piped up and said, "Look man, it's just a boulder-"

Then at precisely that moment, a flash of light as if from a large fire flared up in front of them revealing a quick glimpse of a man. He was clad in Native American style clothes, including; an array of beaded necklaces, dark brown robe with feathers, and headband. He held a long wooden staff which he lifted high into the air before all went dark again. The sound of a rattle echoing in the night air was all that remained to be heard.

Terrified, they almost turned and ran when Brad shouted, "Wait! It's him!"

Cautiously walking back over with the boys in tow, Brad started to speak to the mystical apparition asking if it was indeed their guide. What he ended up talking to was a boulder about eight feet tall. Confused, they took a step closer when they heard someone speak from behind.

Chapter 10

"The answers you seek will not come from the stone," came a voice that could only be described as ethereal and otherworldly. Turning fast they saw their cryptic host standing in the moonlight, revealing himself in all his splendor.

"You're our...guide?" Jason asked, half questioning half stating, in a voice that sounded shell shocked.

"And you are late," he stated flatly. "Come. There is no time for talk now. We must arrive at the place of power very soon and there you may ask what you wish."

Turning away and starting off through the desert, he was twenty feet ahead before any of them even began to respond.

"Come on!" Brad said in a hushed whisper. "This is what we came here for!"

The boys began marching single file through the illuminated desert terrain, Jack leading and Terry following at the rear.

Hiking in silence and taking a seemingly southern direction, their shadows seemed to cast out ahead of them like visual echoes of their movements. The still, night air shrouded them in cool comfort while their footsteps were as silent as the clouds that slowly drifted through the sky overhead.

On they hiked, time appearing almost to stand still as they easily maneuvered around brush and over sand and stone. It seemed as though their energy was inexhaustible and they experienced neither fatigue nor shortness of breath.

How far have we gone? Brad thought to himself. Feels like we've been hiking for miles now. Boy, Jack is really playing his part. He almost had me convinced and I'm the only one who knows who he truly is!

Almost on cue, Jack called for a halt. He turned to Brad and stated, "I must speak to you alone. The rest of you will wait here. You will come with me now," he said to Brad as he turned and walked around a large boulder about thirty feet away.

Brad gave his friends a gesture of assurance and told them that he would be right back. Jogging lightly to catch up with Jack, he left the boys alone to talk with one another. He chuckled as he thought of what they were probably saying about their mysterious host right now!

As he rounded the boulder he saw Jack standing stoically next to an unlit fire pit. Jack just stared at Brad unflinchingly for a couple of seconds then broke down into whispering laughter.

"So what did you think? How was I? I know I laid it on a little thick but it's been awhile."

Brad breathed a sigh of relief and replied, "No, no. You did just fine! Hell, you almost had me fooled for a second there! How did you do that thing with the flash of light and being behind us so quick?"

"Ah, just smoke and mirrors my friend. Old Theatre tricks. I've got a bunch of 'em up my sleeve. So how are the boys? Do they suspect anything?"

"Not from what I can tell."

Jack took a step closer and said, "Let me take a good look at you." His eyes seemed to scan Brad from head to toe and after a few moments he looked right into Brad's eyes. "I'll bet you're really feeling the effects of that Mescaline now, eh? It looks as though you've timed it perfectly. I can tell that you're altered."

"Yeah, well we've had a few speed bumps coming out here. First our Jeep broke down then we picked up an extra body along the way and he led us in the wrong direction. That's why we're late. Then we stopped to check out these rocks-"

Jack listened to all of it with mild amusement, then interrupted Brad during his tirade and said, "Okay, Okay! Your friends are going to think that I ended up sacrificing you to my heathen gods if you don't get back there soon! In another hour or two you will be fully enjoying the effects of that Peyote so we had best keep this gig going. Just remember what I said about drinking. You really shouldn't have any alcohol while you're on this stuff. It could get you really sick."

"Don't worry Jack, we know the drill on that one. We got sick enough earlier. None of us are drinking tonight."

"Okay then. Now, about your friends…bring them back here. I've built a fire pit and I'll properly introduce myself to them. Go on, get going!"

Brad turned tail and quickly ran back to round up his friends.

"What the hell's going on?" Jason asked fearfully. "Felt like you were gone so long that we thought something might've happened to you."

"It's cool, I'm fine. We're all safe now. Follow me so that I can introduce you to our guide."

"What's his name Brad? You never did tell us," Jason asked, as all three trailed after Brad through the desert.

"He can introduce himself," Brad explained, as they rounded the corner of the large boulder.

Once again on cue, a fire blazed up and Jack standing in front of it crossed his arms and said, "I am Redfeather. The Spirit has guided me to you and before the sun rises, the night will have taught you more about yourselves than you could possibly have ever imagined."

A little overly dramatic and cryptic Brad thought, but off to a good start.

"I am familiar already with you," Jack said, looking squarely at Brad. "But the rest of you must now make introductions."

As they all walked over to stand around the fire, Jason leaned over and whispered in Nick's ear, "Is this guy for real?"

He received an elbow to the ribs as Brad whispered harshly, "Hey man, be cool! We don't know exactly what this guy is capable of!"

"Would you care to find out?" Jack asked.

At that, they both looked up amazed that he had heard their little exchange of words.

"Oh, I'm sorry Mr. Redfeather. I didn't mean any disrespect. It's just that this is a lot to take in all at once. I'm Jason, nice to meet you," he stammered awkwardly.

Jack nodded curtly and looked over to Nick, waiting expectantly.

"Aww, hey man. Yeah, I'm Nick, good to meet ya," Nick said, looking more than a little uncomfortable.

Jack then glanced off to the side in Terry's direction. Terry remained standing off in the background seeming extremely nervous and fidgety.

"Oh, yeah," Brad said, speaking up. "This is our new friend Terry. We picked him up on the way out here. We just met a little while ago."

As Jack eyed him with a disapproving glare, Terry remained quiet, looking away and to the ground. Jason finally spoke up, breaking the unpleasant moment.

"So Mr. Redfeather...umm...what's next? I mean, what do we do now?"

"Just Redfeather, Jason. Now, we wait by the fire for a sign from the Spirit. You have all ingested the buttons?" he asked, already knowing the answer.

"Yes," Brad confirmed. "We ate them on the way out here and we're really starting to feel it now. Right, guys?"

Nick and Jason both murmured their agreements, when Brad added, "Oh, except for Terry. But I think he ate some mushrooms earlier, didn't you Terry?"

Again a look of disdain as Jack's eyes shifted over to Terry's direction. Terry nodded and looked away again, obviously uncomfortable with Jack's scrutiny. Jack then broke his gaze and looked up towards the heavens and taking a deep breath, closed his eyes.

"I would like you all to feel comfortable around me. Close your eyes and take some deep breaths as I do. This is very important, so please trust me."

They all closed their eyes and tilted their heads up and back and began to breathe deeply. In a matter of seconds, all became perfectly calm and quiet. Only the sounds of their breathing and the crackling of the fire remained. Soon a perfectly serene atmosphere developed and they were all at peace within themselves and their surroundings. They felt each breath of air as it was sucked in and then circulated through their lungs and passageways. They noticed the warmth of their skin as the blood flowed through their veins and felt a sense of muscle relaxation better than that of a tranquilizer. Not even having realized it, they were all sitting down in front of the fire now.

"What you feel at this moment is the harmonious balance of energy that comes from the proper utilization of this particular power place," Jack explained, gently breaking the silence in a perfectly relaxed tone of voice. "All of our energies combined and working in a calm fluctuating sequence is the result of a focused concentration and meditation." Feeling very much as though enveloped in a cocoon of perfect bliss they all enjoyed being locked into the moment. "Now open your eyes," Jack said softly.

Just then, Jack gently nudged a small container of something flammable that he had strategically placed on a rock earlier, into the fire. The result was a small explosion of flames that lifted high up and burned brightly but only for an instant. Tiny cinders flew off and burned out into the night. They all gasped as they stared up into the sky, appreciating the exquisitely glowing tracers that followed each tiny spark as they slowly burned out high overhead.

All except for Brad. He had opened his eyes just a few moments before everyone else and was marveling at Jack's tactics. He found himself drawn in once again, and had watched as Jack kicked the small dish into the fire. A wake-up call to the fact that Jack was after all; just a vacuum cleaner salesman. A moment of sadness washed over him just then with that realization. It was amazing how he could allow himself to be pulled in knowing the truth about Jack, and yet it seemed to be happening almost every time! But then again, the Peyote probably had a lot to do with that.

Jack looked over at Brad with a crooked smile and gave him a wink. Brad had to stifle a giggle when he thought about the absurdity of it all. Well, it was his idea. He had better just go with it, relying on the belief that the Universe was a mysterious force that made everything transpire as it should.

"Everyone, stand up now," Jack said soothingly. "Feel free to talk about how you feel."

"That was unbelievable," Jason breathed. "I haven't felt that relaxed and at peace in years. I believe this really is a place of power!"

"My ancient ancestors discovered this area hundreds of years ago. It is sacred and is protected by forces of energy that deflect any and all that do not have permission to access it. We are welcome here tonight and should all give thanks that we have had a chance to bask in its power and energy."

"Thank you," Jason said to no one in particular, his eyes closed and head angled downward.

Again Brad almost lost it, thinking about how much Jason looked like he had just said "Amen" after a heartfelt prayer had just been said by a priest in church. The idea that this was starting to work, slowly manifested itself into his thoughts and the situation seemed as if it was one gigantic placebo. One that was actually working due to the amazing power of human belief. He felt the Peyote shifting through him in stages, so much more intense than the small dosage that he had taken the first time.

Looking to his companions, he clearly saw that its effect for them was nearly identical. Except for Terry of course, but he had eaten mushrooms and looked almost as relaxed as the rest of them.

Chapter 10

"It is time to douse the fire and continue on with the next step in our journey," Jack stated solemnly.

After extinguishing the fire, Jack took the lead once again in guiding them to their next location for self discovery. Catching up to Jack, Brad tried to nonchalantly strike up a quiet conversation with him.

"I have to admit, that was amazing. Did you make up all that stuff about that place and your ancestors?"

"You know, strangely enough, most of that is true. My grandfather took me out to that spot a few times trying to make me understand the significance of the area and what not. But most of the time I was too concerned with playing baseball or watching MTV to pay much attention to what he was telling me. What can I say? I was young and more into going to the Video Arcade than learning about my people's culture. Anyway, there really is supposed to be something about that little spot."

"Well, so far you've been worth every penny my friend and it seems to be working. Did you see everyone's reaction back there? Priceless!"

"You should have seen your own face. You looked as peaceful as a Buddhist Monk! Did you realize that you guys were perfectly stationary for twenty minutes back there? I timed you!" Jack exclaimed, pulling the sleeve of his robe back a bit to reveal a wristwatch.

"What?" Brad blurted loudly in disbelief.

"Ssshhh!" Jack whispered. "Better get back there with your friends, before they start suspecting something."

"But where are we going next?"

"Don't worry, you'll see. Have some faith in your guide huh?" Jack said with another knowing grin on his face.

Brad slowly lagged behind until the boys caught up to him and assaulted him with a barrage of questions.

"What's up? What were you guys talking about? Is everything cool?" They asked, everyone talking over the top of each other.

"Yes, yes, everything's fine! He's taking us to the next place now. I was just asking him questions about the area that's all. How are you guys doing? Everyone feeling good?"

A chorus of, "Yeah, we're feeling great," assured Brad that all was well for the moment. Having settled them down, it went quiet again as they continued their march single file through the desert.

After a short time Nick said, "Hey man, this looks kinda familiar. I think we were here earlier."

"Yeah, he's right," Jason confirmed. "Look...that Stonehenge spot is about fifty yards up ahead."

"I understand that you have all been here already, however, we must circle this area yet again," Jack announced, calling back to them, never slowing his stride even minutely. "Please continue to follow me."

As they approached the area of pillared stone, Jack turned left and started to circle the strange formation in a clockwise direction. With the boys in tow, they all methodically made their way around the rock formation several times never slowing. With each new completion of a circle they started to feel slightly more invigorated. Time went by and after what seemed like an enormous amount of completed circles, Jack broke off and started heading southeast back towards the direction of their campsite.

"What do you suppose that was all about?" Jason asked in exasperation. "That took forever!"

"Yeah but don't you feel better now? Like your energy has been renewed?" Brad responded.

"Actually I do, I-"

"Hey guys!" Nick said, interrupting as he caught up to them. "How many times do you think we went around in circles at that place?"

Chapter 10

"At least fifty," Brad answered, still walking.

"Felt more like a hundred!" Jason said piping up. "Took forever!"

"No, actually it didn't. I checked my watch right as we rolled up to that place and checked it again just now. It only took us eight minutes to walk all those laps around those rocks!" Nick excitedly informed them.

"Wow! Amazing! I guess that we didn't do as many circles as I thought," Brad replied.

"No man. We did exactly fifty, I counted them. You were right on the money!"

"Dude! Your Shaman friend is really starting to trip me out!" Jason expressed with panic in his voice.

"Just relax man," Brad said, trying to console his friend. "It's all part of the trip. We'll be okay. Trust me."

Jason seemed to calm a bit as he dropped back to his place in line. How the hell did he do that? Brad thought to himself, looking up ahead towards Jack. He started to wonder if it was the Peyote or if this mysterious desert was working its own wonder and magic upon them all.

Just then, Brad remembered their newest addition to the party and looked back to see if Terry was doing okay. Terry and Nick seemed to be chatting idly as they hiked and looked as if they were getting along well together.

Jason marched along right behind him looking all around as he went, admiring the desert landscape and beautiful moon up above. Jack trudged on up ahead with what seemed to be a singular purpose in mind. And Brad? He was just enjoying the hike and the feeling of a mind altering substance strengthening his awareness and reminding him of how amazing and fulfilling the simplest things in life could be.

As they hiked in what seemed to be the direction back to their camp, Brad took the opportunity to catch up with Jack and once again inquired as to their newest destination.

"We are going to the place where we were originally supposed to meet," Jack answered him.

"You mean Little Mesa Verde?"

"You got it, Hoss. So how are we doing so far? Are your friends holding up okay?"

"They're alright but you threw them for quite a loop with all those passes around the rocks earlier. We accomplished that in record time. How did you do that?"

Never missing a step, Jack turned to Brad whilst walking and said in all seriousness; "This particular desert has an immense power of its own, believe it or not, and you just witnessed some of it. I have no other explanation."

Waiting for Jack to erupt into laughter, Brad continued to stare at him. Instead, Jack just quickened his pace and moved back up to the front. That unsettled Brad substantially. He had suspected that might have been the reason but for Jack to confirm it for him really drove the point home.

He tried not to dwell on it too hard and his attention shifted when the dark shape of the Mesa Verde suddenly loomed ahead. In no time at all they were clambering right up the face of the behemoth, moving side to side while avoiding large bushes, boulders, and the occasional cactus with Jack leading unerringly.

As they neared the rise they had some trouble with the steep terrain and Terry lost his footing on the crumbly volcanic rock. Nick reached out and grabbed his hand only to be taken down along with him and they both slid about five feet down the mountainside. Jason and Brad were quick to respond, making their way back down as fast as they could to help out. Amazingly, Jack was already behind Nick and Terry, gently pushing them both upward and onward. Startled, Brad snapped his head back up towards the top where he had last seen Jack climb over and glimpsed something like a quick moving shadow which was gone in a heartbeat.

Chapter 10

As they finally climbed over the top and stopped to rest, Brad asked if they had sustained any injuries. Nick assured him however, that Jack stopped them before they could fall any further. After confirming that they were okay, Brad walked over to the edge of the mesa where Jack was gazing out over the valley.

"What just happened? Is there someone else up here with us right now?"

"What do you mean?" Jack asked, apparently confused.

"I saw you top the rise back there in front of us and then before I knew it…you were behind Nick and Terry! What's going on man?"

"You're mixed up. I circled back and came up behind you guys to make sure you all made it up to the top okay. It is really steep you know, and you guys have fallen prey to your clumsy, city slicker ways if I'm not mistaken."

"I saw you go over first!" Brad stated with conviction.

"No offense man, but didn't you eat four Peyote buttons earlier? Take it easy! I'm here to watch out for you guys. I've got your back!"

Feeling flustered but not wanting to start an argument in front of his friends, Brad let the matter drop. For now.

"Hey relax," Jack said soothingly. "I want to show you something. Check this out…" Gesturing with a sweep of his arm, he motioned out across the whole southeastern part of the valley. "I had almost forgotten how beautiful this was," he said quietly.

When Brad looked out, he was caught by surprise. The entire valley was bathed in the luminescent light of the moon and its effect was startling. There was a perfect stillness that had settled over everything and Brad stood there staring entranced by it all. He hadn't even noticed that the other three had come to stand right up beside him and they all gawked at the scene, taken in by the same inspiring spectacle.

"It's beautiful!" Jason gasped.

"You can see everything," Nick breathed.

They all continued to stare for long moments, transfixed by the beauty and majesty of the rugged terrain. Everything was accented by the moon's glow and the sky itself was nearly cloudless then, revealing an unending amount of stars twinkling dimly above. It was like a living picture. Amazingly still, yet alive. The cliffs off to the left shone with a beautiful brilliance while the right side of the canyon remained darkened in shadow. A testament to that everlasting environment, millions of years old. The small desert brush and native cacti left strange shadows which peppered the landscape below. Sandy washes widened and narrowed, crisscrossing all throughout the valley like lines on a map; beautifully peaceful and inviting.

"What's that shining way over there? Something's reflecting in the moonlight," Brad asked, turning towards Jack.

"That would be your vehicle," Jack stated calmly.

"Cool!" Jason almost shouted. "So that means our campsite is less than a mile away!"

"That is correct," Jack responded reassuringly.

"So what's next?" Brad inquired, never taking his eyes off the extraordinary view in front of him.

"We hike back down and you can get your campsite in order before we embark upon our next journey."

"Mr. Redfeather?" Jason asked meekly.

"Please, just call me Jack from here on out."

"Jack?" Jason asked again, feeling more comfortable now. "I just wanted to say thanks. I really had my doubts about this trip, but so far it has surpassed any and all of my expectations. I'm really glad we came."

"Yeah, same here," Brad and Nick both said in a chorus of gentle thanks.

Jack's reply was a warm smile as he looked over to them each in turn until he reached Terry. Then his look turned sour yet again and

Chapter 10

without taking his eyes off of Terry he said, "Don't thank me yet. We still have a long journey ahead."

Terry looked away nervously and began to shuffle his feet as Jack turned and headed straight down the side of the mesa.

"What the heck do you think that was all about?" Jason asked Brad when Jack seemed to be a good distance away. "Every time I start to feel comfortable around him he does something that brings us right back to square one!"

"I don't know. That was strange. Why don't you switch places with Nick and try to talk with Terry for a little bit and see what you can find out. Maybe they know each other from somewhere."

"Okay, good idea."

The hike back was uneventful. Just a steady march towards the Jeep with Brad turning occasionally to catch a glimpse of Jason talking to Terry, and Terry shrugging his shoulders quite a bit. As they neared the Wrangler, Brad noticed that Jack was nowhere in sight.

"Jack?" he called out quietly, then again a little louder.

They all joined up together a few yards from the Jeep and Jason asked, "Where's Jack?"

"Looks like he took off somewhere," Brad answered, seeming unsure.

Hearing that, Terry relaxed visibly. Nick took notice of that and asked him about it.

"Sorry man. That guy just kinda gives me the creeps."

"Do you know him from somewhere?" Brad asked, trying to keep the suspicion out of his voice.

"No man. Never seen him before tonight."

"Well, just give him a chance. It's probably in his nature to be mysterious."

"Sure bro, whatever you say," was Terry's only response.

"Well, let's set up camp," Jason said, trying to alleviate the tension.

After arranging camp and having some snacks and drinks, they all settled back and chatted about what they'd all been feeling and experiencing throughout the night. The common consensus was that they were amazingly stable for as much Mescaline as they'd ingested so far, Terry excluded. Everything had taken on a different perspective to be sure but they'd had no real hallucinations and very little intense introspection as of yet.

"Well, we can be sure that it's coming though," Brad stated with conviction, when suddenly he heard a small hissing sound behind him.

"Pssst!"

Turning around he saw nothing but then heard another whisper.

"Pssst! Hey!"

Recognizing it as Jack's voice, he got up, telling his friends that he was going to go water some bushes. Walking off towards a boulder some distance away, Brad almost ran right smack into Jack who was standing off in the shadows.

"Hey, watch it!" Jack chastised with a whisper.

"Sorry man. Sometimes it's hard to see out here even with all this moonlight."

"It's okay. So listen. What do you want to do next? Where do you want me to take you?"

"I don't know. You've been spot on so far. I guess just keep doing what you're doing. I don't think the Peyote has fully kicked in yet because we're not hallucinating or anything. At least not for the most part. Just some small tracers here and there."

"No it hasn't," Jack agreed eagerly. "Well, I had an idea. We could still meet up with those old Theatre pals of mine and..."

"Jack, no! I already told you that I don't want to do that. It's too risky."

Chapter 10

"But they'll look perfectly authentic! Well...mostly. They're only half Native American but their costumes are great! We did this play once called "Custer's Last Stand" and you should've seen 'em! They..."

"No Jack! For the last time, please!" Brad said looking back, trying to keep his voice down.

"Alright," Jack conceded in a sulking tone.

"So hey man, I wanted to ask you. What do you think of this guy that we picked up and brought along, Terry?"

Jack's countenance grew serious again and he said, "If you were smart you would immediately leave him behind once and for all."

"What? We can't just ditch him out here."

"That is exactly what you can and should do," Jack replied in all seriousness.

"We brought him with us and we can't just abandon him! Besides, he seems like a decent enough guy."

"Suit yourself," Jack replied indifferently. "Okay so what's next then? This is your show boss, I'm just the pretend guide, remember?"

"Okay. When I looked at the map earlier I thought I saw a pretty cool spot that had a canyon with tall cliffs and it was on the way to the power place that my friends had marked on the map."

"I think I might know where to find it," Jack said hopefully. "There are actually some cool Petroglyphs somewhere out near that area. Maybe we can look for them once we get there."

"Now you're talking!" Brad said enthusiastically. "So why don't you give us a little while longer before you dazzle us with another one of your grand entrances before you take us out?"

"You got it," Jack said, stepping back with a salute. "Kirk out."

Brad flinched, and then chuckled to himself as he walked back over to meet up with the fellas.

He found them all sitting in the Wrangler with the radio playing low, their heads back and eyes closed, they seemed totally relaxed.

As he got in the driver's seat and shut the door, he looked around to his buddies and his heart sank like the Titanic. A very familiar smell rose up into the air.

"What the hell?" he practically shouted. "Are you guys stoned? You're smoking weed?"

"Hey man, chill," Jason said calmly. "Nick found some killer Chronic someone accidentally left in between the back seats, and we couldn't resist."

Turning to Terry he asked, "So this isn't yours?"

"No bro. Not my stuff."

"This could ruin the experience!" Brad whined.

"Come on guy," Nick piped up from the back seat. "It'll be alright. Just a little to help mellow us out."

"Yeah, bro," Terry echoed. "Just a little. Come on, try some. It'll take the edge off. Look…they even left a pipe."

"No way man!" Brad replied angrily.

"We all did it. You have to do it now too and you know it," Jason argued, the deadpan look on his face leaving no room for debate.

"Sonofa bi-" Brad began to say looking down then back up at Jason who still just stared with conviction, his hand outstretched with the pipe in it. Nick and Terry started giggling as he took it from Jason but quickly quieted as Brad gave them a look as if to say, "Shut the hell up!" Terry gave a look back that said, "Sorry, man" and they all erupted into laughter once again as Brad lit up and took a deep breath, holding it in for a few moments before exhaling slowly.

"There," Jason said, taking the pipe away from him. "Don't you feel better now?"

And as a matter of fact, he did. He could feel a tingling sensation that started from his fingertips, and worked its way up to his head then down the rest of his entire body. It had been years since he had blazed but it was all coming back to him now. He was feeling more

Chapter 10

and more relaxed with each passing second and he could sense his racing mind trying to slow down to keep pace with the rest of him.

A wide grin took the place of the scowl that he had adorned only moments ago. It was then that he became extremely aware of the Peyote working its way through his system. A slight feeling of panic arose as he felt an intense rush of energy wash over him like an enormous wave of water. Water from an ocean of power; reminding him again of its presence just out there within reach. His brain tried in vain to process the immense complexities of a thousand different thoughts all running rampant through his mind at the same time. It was at that moment he was saved by a voice that seemed a thousand miles away.

"Wow man! This is good stuff. I'm really trippin' right now! Can't tell if it's the Mescaline or the Weed!"

He recognized it as Jason's voice and felt a calm envelop him knowing that his trusted friend was by his side.

"Hey Brad…" Jason continued. "Don't you have some cool tunes you could put on for us right now?"

Brad tried to answer but it appeared as if he'd melted halfway into his seat and his ability to speak had been somewhat disabled. He remained there relaxing until he heard Jason's voice once again.

"Brad?"

Brad glanced over towards the clock on the stereo, looked at it, and stated with certainty; "Seven thirty three."

After a few seconds he looked up to find Jason staring at him as if he had just fallen out of a Christmas Tree, and then they all started laughing.

"Some music, not the time you joker!" Jason said teasingly.

Brad realized then just how stoned he was. He made a supreme effort to sit up, then reached into the console and pulled out a CD. Miraculously, it was the one he'd had in mind and he smiled as he fed it into the stereo.

"What you got man?" Terry inquired from the backseat, his voice slow and slightly slurring.

"You'll see," Brad said, the smile ever widening on his face. Brad had put in the CD he'd recorded days earlier which contained the songs by all of his favorite psychedelic artists. The first song came through softly at the beginning and then got louder as Brad turned up the volume.

They all settled in and relaxed completely, enjoying the peaceful experience. None of them ever could have guessed what would happen next though. "Sun Is Shining" by Bob Marley, escaped the stereo in the form of tiny little waves of energy, gently enveloping them all. The experience got more intense as the bass came thumping through like the rhythmic sound of a pulsating heart.

They turned to their own individual thoughts then, each going to his own special place deep inside his mind.

Chapter 11

Jason was the first to find that the world around him had disappeared and he was now walking on soft earth, placing one foot in front of the other. He felt the brush of various types of foliage and palm fronds against his body as he moved past them on his way to...where was he even going? He didn't know. All he knew was that he was moving with a purpose and couldn't stop even if he had wanted to. His only companion was the reverberating sound of Marley in the distant background.

He began looking all around as he made his way to his unknown destination and clearly saw that he was in a tropical jungle of some sort. Beautifully colored parrots and other birds swooped down and landed on all sides of him and the sounds of the jungle began to become more apparent and enhanced. Dragonflies darted here and there and all manner of jungle life began to make itself known. He heard the chattering of monkeys close by and the roar of a large cat; possibly a tiger, off in the distance. But none of that startled him. He knew somehow that he was safe and more importantly, that he was about to discover something so wonderful and amazing, he may never be able to describe it in words.

The trail opened suddenly and he found himself in a small clearing, smooth and flat with a little stream at its edge. A beautiful waterfall cascaded down into a small pool creating an almost musical sound of its own. Tiny palm trees mixed with other vegetation encircled the entire area protectively.

As he advanced cautiously, he saw a figure sitting on a log next to a small fire. He could see that it was a man, though his back was to him, and he was softly playing a guitar. The man beckoned to him to take a seat directly across from him. Somehow he knew who he was about to meet despite the fact that it abandoned all reason and yet as he sat down and looked up, he was still shocked nonetheless.

"You look as doh you seen a ghost mon," the man said, his voice gentle yet exuding positive energy with every spoken syllable.

His Jamaican accent was thick, yet rich with wisdom and kindness.

"Are you a…ghost?" was all that Jason could muster as a reply.

"Well…if you want to call it dat! Whatever makes you feel comfortable. Let us just say dat I and I, am a spirit. I want you to be at ease mon, not on de edge."

"Are you…Bob Marley? I mean-" Jason stammered, "Are you really him? Is this a dream?"

"I am, was, and always will be him in your own mind. Right now for you I'm alive troo ma music, if dat elps to answer your question. But I know dat can't be what you really wanna be knowin' right now is it?" Bob asked in that heavy Rastafarian accent, smirking all the while.

Jason just watched him mesmerized as he strummed his guitar in perfect timing to accompany the music that he heard echoing in the background.

"There was so much that I always wanted to ask you but I never dreamed that I'd actually get the chance," Jason replied, his own voice like soft notes of music drifting up and out into the cool, tropical night.

"Ah! And rightfully so! But no one ever asks da right questions until it is too late and by den, dere be no one to answer dem!" he said with a warm chuckle. "Well den instead, I'll be talkin' and you just be listenin'. Would dot be okay for you mon?" Bob ended with a wide smile. Jason nodded his head eagerly hoping that whatever this experience was, it wouldn't end suddenly. "You must know den, dat dere is a reason dat you be ere wit me now," Bob said, pausing to look at Jason. "Is dat fair to say?"

Again Jason just nodded his head stupidly, trying hard to process the conversation, yet never taking his eyes off of his mystical host. Another soft chuckle escaped from Bob's grinning visage. "I know what you be tinkin. You be tinkin dat dis kind of ting is ridiculous and only appens in da movies. I and I, know how you feel and I and I, can understand your confusion. You don be knowin' where you be at and you can't even remember ow you got ere. Right? In fact, right now you be startin' ta believe dat I am just a manifestation of some deep psychological fantasy dat you ave always ad. Like a need to explain dat missin' part of your logical rationale. Don't you sometimes look ta me for answers and compare your lifestyle and choices to ma own set of beliefs and morals? What would Bob do, yes?" he asked, erupting into heartfelt laughter.

His mirth was infectious and Jason found himself lost in it as well and joined Bob in that laughter. "I know dat you take so many of ma words to heart and are always searchin' dem for some profound hidden meanin' but all in all, dey were meant to be taken more at face value. So many searchin' for de truth always be doin' just dat; searchin'. Instead of doin', dey be searchin'. Dey look to me for enlightenment when I and I myself was always more da student and not de teacher. Often Bob be askin' what Bob should do!"

He snickered quietly and for a second, Jason could see that he was reflecting on his former life.

His smile faded quickly then, and his manner became more businesslike in an instant. "Let me get serious for a moment now doh, okay mon? Every ting has led you up to dis point. You are ere, wit me now, because dere is some ting you need to know and remembar.

Listen carefully now for at one point in your life you will be needin' ta know it. You may not recall it anytime soon but it will be dere at da time when you need it most."

There was a dramatic pause and then Bob froze, remaining absolutely motionless, aside from his strumming, for what seemed like several seconds. Looking down at the ground in front of him yet not focusing on anything in particular he held the perfect likeness of a living statue except for the guitar which almost seemed to be strumming him and not the other way around.

Suddenly he looked up and straight into Jason's eyes and he began to speak. "Your thoughts and your energy…" he began but then his voice trailed off into silence like the last faint sounds of an echo reverberating through a long, deep canyon. It felt as though a mist was starting to settle over Jason's brain, clouding out any kind of focus or concentration. Then he experienced the sensation of moving forward at an incredible rate, much like falling; except not a free fall, but more like being on a roller coaster and plummeting straight down a track. He sensed that he was receiving information yet couldn't begin to decipher the message or where it was even coming from.

Suddenly he snapped to attention, feeling very much like he had just experienced a quick stop at the end of an amusement park ride. All had gone perfectly still and quiet. He leaned forward in his seat and slowly looked around to each of his comatose comrades. Still relaxed and comfortable in their seats with eyes closed, their labored breathing seemed to be almost in perfect unison.

"Comfortably Numb" by Pink Floyd began to emanate from the stereo now and Jason relaxed once again. Breathing deeply at first, then softly along with the rest, his eyes closed gently as he let himself slowly drift away once more. Soon his breathing coincided perfectly with the others and he drifted into the realm in between sleep and consciousness.

Chapter 12

During the Bob Marley song, Brad was very relaxed yet awake and philosophically immersed in thought. He began to have amazing recollections and started to analyze the different impacts that some of his former experiences had had on his life. The music seemed so far away now; like a pleasant background noise in a familiar workplace. It seemed as though he was suddenly hard at the task of remembering details of instances and recalling emotions that he'd felt before and after certain things had transpired.

He was pummeled with memories; most of which seemed to have had the most symbolic or spiritual significance in regards to truly affecting his life. He could recall turning corners and at times being completely off balance, metaphorically speaking, during certain stages of his life. He started to remember random things; places he'd been and trips he'd taken. Then suddenly he recalled a psychedelic trip that he had embarked upon in his youth.

It had started out with his friend Tim, who he had just picked up in town one afternoon. They were both around nineteen years old at the time, it was back in the early nineties, and Tim, as it turned out, was in possession of two sheets of White Blotter Acid. He had been making his rounds and hooking up various friends before meeting up with Brad.

Upon discovering this new information, Brad promptly inquired as to whether or not he might try a sample of Tim's goods and Tim cheerfully agreed. In fact, Tim insisted on trying some with him as well! However, Brad was a little leery as to the potency of the drug and was reluctant to take an entire hit therefore requested only half at first. This for some reason did not go over well with Tim, who demanded that he should take the whole thing or nothing at all.

The conclusion to the exchange ended with Brad deciding not to take any at all, having had a "recent experience" with not testing the waters properly so to speak, however, after hearing his bluff called, Tim backpedaled and soon acquiesced into agreeing to provide him with only half at first.

As they drove through town, heading nowhere in particular, Tim reached over to hand Brad his share and accidentally dropped it on the floorboard next to Brad's feet. Immediate panic ensued as Tim began to scream at Brad.

"Find it quick! Grab it! Grab it!"

Brad quickly pulled off to the side of the road and yelled back, "Where is it? I don't see it!"

Tim spotted it on the floorboard first and said, "There it is! Quick! Put it in your mouth!" Brad hastily did what he was told but as the tab settled in on his tongue, Brad had a suspicious feeling that something wasn't right. Looking over at Tim, he realized that his initial response had been correct judging by the "Cat who ate the Canary" look on Tim's face.

"That didn't feel like half a hit Tim," he said, the color draining from his face.

With a wide grin, Tim replied, "It wasn't. It was a whole hit!"

Brad, now realizing that he had been tricked, began to panic.

"How potent is this stuff?" he asked, his concern reflecting across his features.

Chapter 12

"I don't know," Tim admitted. "I haven't tried this kind yet. The last batch was amazing though! I guess we're the Guinea Pigs," he surmised, shrugging his shoulders with an exaggerated movement. Brad felt like leaping across and choking Tim at that precise moment, and had to make a supreme effort to resist that urge.

"I have somewhere I have to be today!" he practically shouted.

"Not me," Tim replied with an air of nonchalance.

"What if I get all jacked up, man? Then what am I supposed to do, huh?"

"Relax bro! I'll hang out with you for a couple of hours and it'll be fun. Come on, let's go to the carnival!"

Brad had no choice at this point but to go along with this new development and truthfully, the carnival sounded like fun to him.

So off they went, Brad still slightly fuming and Tim trying to console him. However, once they arrived, it was as though they were kids again.

Brad recalled the exhilarating rush of going on the Zipper, and the exquisite feeling of centrifugal force as they rode the Gravitron. The blurred shapes of people whizzed by and he caught brief glimpses of the spectacular lights of town, being so high up in the air. The whirring sounds of the machinery kept rising and falling in a perfect rhythm that almost seemed soothing.

At the time, he believed that he would never forget the experience, being so intense yet carefree, but somehow time not only heals all wounds but washes over precious memories as well. Leaving them disintegrated and barely recognizable upon the shores of our minds. Like Hendrix said; "Castles made of sand..."

After trying every ride in the park they left and ended up at the residence of their friend, Amber; a girl they had gone to high school with. Hanging out at Amber's house and watching some T.V. was a welcome shift to the adrenaline pumping action that they had just experienced.

The L.S.D. had been good so far and Brad was enjoying himself, however Amber soon discovered the secret of their altered state and had some fun at their expense. With distracting little head games she giggled away at their distress.

Soon they found themselves all laughing and television seemed to be more entertaining than it had been in a long time. Especially the episodes of "Married with Children".

It wasn't long though before Brad felt an apprehension upon the realization that soon he would have to leave, having made a previous commitment to a friend. And leave soon if he was going to make it on time. So he unglued himself from the couch and mustered up the courage to depart, bidding his farewells to Tim and Amber. After his assurance to several inquiries as to his ability to drive, he said his goodbyes and made his way out to his car.

He had a 1970 Pontiac Catalina at the time, and remembered sitting in it for a good fifteen minutes before he decided that he was, in fact, coherent enough to drive. It would only take about ten minutes to get to where he was going, but that day it felt like an eternity.

Using extra caution he drove slow, taking every back road that he could think of. No reason to take chances, he told himself. Jason was playing drums for a band at the time and happened to be performing at a gig over at the Playhouse in Joshua Tree that evening. He had invited Brad weeks ago and Brad had given his word that he would show.

Pulling into the parking lot, Brad paid special attention to gauging the depth and distance as he parked so as not to cause any damage to his vehicle or anyone else's. L.S.D can be funny that way. It can make you conscious of the tiniest of details and enhance your awareness of even the littlest things.

As Brad put on the black leather jacket that a friend of his had left in the car, he walked purposefully towards the back of the Play

House, scanning the area for his friend. Jason actually spotted him first and marched right up to him as Brad continued his approach. Jason was dressed like a complete redneck; with cowboy hat, western shirt, jeans and boots to match.

He was even chewing on a piece of hay which just added to the effect all the more and once he reached him said, "Howdy!" with his best southern drawl. The look on Brad's face must have been priceless just then for Jason gave a grin a country mile wide.

"Hey man, what's going on?" Brad stammered.

Jason looked at Brad as though he had just revealed himself completely.

While staring him square in the eye and smiling, he leaned in close and asked, "Are you on Acid?"

"Oh shit!" Brad responded with complete panic. "How could you tell? Do I look like it?" Jason erupted into laughter and Brad quickly broke down and told him what had transpired.

"Don't worry ol' buddy, you'll be fine," Jason responded reassuringly. "You can't even tell!" he smirked, snickering all the while.

As he led Brad in through the back door so that he wouldn't have to pay, he pointed out a good spot for him to sit and then made his way to his drum set down near the side of the stage. As it turned out, that night's band's leader was the High School Band teacher and it was his daughter who made her way down the aisle to end up sitting right next to Brad. She immediately introduced herself to Brad and the awkwardness began to ensue.

As mentioned earlier, Acid had a way of revealing even the smallest details, but it could also exaggerate things far beyond the way they might normally appear. Things such as physical features and mannerisms, for example. In this case the subject in question, who's name he's long since forgotten, looked to him just like the spitting image of Geddy Lee; the lead singer and bassist for the band Rush. Needless to say he was at a total loss as to how to handle the situation, especially when he could sense that the climax of the trip was soon to unfold. Anybody that's experienced in taking L.S.D. can tell you that even if you lose track of time, there is an internal mechanism so to speak, that helps to let you know when you are about to peak. And right around that point for Brad; alarm bells were ringing.

Thankfully the Play started just then, distracting Brad from wanting to run out of the theatre from lack of being able to cope with the situation. The Play was: "The Best Little Whorehouse in Texas," and scantily clad women began to filter onto the stage as the curtain was lifted. Brad was immediately drawn in and marveled at the costumes and stage acting, not to mention the provocative way in which the women walked and danced.

He was constantly distracted by Jason however, who was literally ten feet away from him and making ridiculous faces and gestures while he played his drums. It didn't help also that Geddy Lee was trying to make conversation almost the entire time and kept complimenting Brad on his leather jacket. At one point she asked to borrow it because she said she was cold and her advances took the uncomfortable feelings Brad had to a whole new level.

He finally received a welcome reprieve when she excused herself to use the restroom. Once again he found himself immediately immersed in the Play and while peaking on the L.S.D. learned something of which at the time, he was just beginning to comprehend and was of extreme importance. Life itself was like a Play, in most respects.

Perhaps it was the influence of his new found annoyance and seated neighbor, but the lyrics of a Rush song went swirling through his head. "All the world's indeed a stage, and we are merely players... performers and portrayers." The acting in certain scenes had felt so real and emotional to him that they tugged mercilessly on his heart strings. Could it have been the lighting or props that added to such

Chapter 12

an effect, or was it just the psychological state of mind that he was in? Either way, he was enormously affected by it and always kept a part of that knowledge hidden deep within his rationale.

He was coming down soon after the Play ended and was bidding Jason farewell and hastily retrieving his friend's jacket. He made his way home with the kind of melancholy that one often feels around sundown on a Sunday evening knowing that the weekend was over and the daily grind was soon to ensnare us all once again.

Brad felt as though he was drifting now, back to the present, leaving that whole scenario behind just as he did years ago. However this time, he made a specific mental note not to forget the vital message that he had been reintroduced to in regards to the human condition. His last thoughts were of the Greeks and what psychological genius's so many of them were for understanding this concept, and helping to share it with the world for generations to come.

He snapped back to attention to find his amigos relaxing peacefully to the sounds of Pink Floyd. He too, soon reclined back to his original position and began to stare at the moon with a new found peace and tranquility that he had not known or felt in several years.

Chapter 13

While Jason and Brad had been enjoying their little trips, Nick was about to experience one of his very own. He had been relaxing with his eyes closed, listening to the music, when the silence at the end of the Marley song actually alerted him as to a shift in his mind and body. In reality it was but four or five seconds, but in Nick's mind it was an eternity, and he became immediately conscious of a change in his level of awareness.

As "Comfortably Numb" slowly filtered out through the stereo in waves, Nick began to feel what some people would define as the beginning of an out of body experience. The regular human sensations of blood flow and heat in his limbs were replaced by a light ethereal feeling similar to floating or even gliding. Somehow he knew what was happening and embraced it with the understanding that something important or necessary was about to occur. He felt as if he were no longer breathing but rather existing as energy, and tried with an immense effort to focus all his concentration on what was unfolding within. Much like getting ready for the beginning of a movie right after the coming attractions and paying extra attention to the beginning so as not to miss anything crucial to the plot or outcome of the film.

Opening his eyes, he noticed a thick layer of fog all around him. Past the haze, he could dimly see the glow of various colored lights

Chapter 13

and then as the heavy mist slowly began to dissipate, he saw that he stood alone before an enormous stage.

Looking all around, Nick observed that he was in a gigantic auditorium that might have held twenty thousand people, and yet he stood alone. As he brought his gaze back full circle he stared at the stage in wonder as he saw the original members of Pink Floyd lined up near the front, instruments in hand. Appearing stoically and keeping in perfect rhythm with the song; they seemed somehow immortal. The clothes they wore looked to be of the late sixties, with their hair and sunglasses really accenting that style.

The music seemed to be emanating directly from them and he could literally see the waves of energy that they dispensed with every note that was being played. He'd never had a chance to see Pink Floyd perform live in concert but had heard about their light shows. In his wildest imaginations he never dreamed that there could be such masterful illuminations in reality as opposed to the ones that he was experiencing at this moment. Blues, reds, and greens all faded in and out of different hues with a holographic and laser-like quality which left him completely spellbound for several moments. His attention was drawn back over to the players and he watched intensely as Roger Waters plucked his Bass while David Gilmore picked intricate notes and strummed various chords out on his guitar. They both stepped closer and then stood right next to each other, directly in front of Nick's immediate line of sight. He locked eyes with them and then found he was unable to divert his gaze. Their eyes seemed like orbs of perfect energy and transmitted an aura of knowledge and experience unlike anything he'd ever witnessed before.

It was then that he realized that their eyes were the source of where the music was coming from! There was no equipment or anything electrical aside from their instruments. They projected the sounds straight from their very being, and the emanations from their eyes were the avenues upon which the music traveled!

Nick stood transfixed, sensing a real anticipation of an importance that was yet to come. Suddenly, the music and lights became as one, and they simultaneously throbbed like an intense heartbeat. Locked in that stare like a man in hypnosis, he felt himself being drawn in yet at the same time he recognized the release of information that was being dispensed from him. Thoughts, ideas, and feelings came streaming out in rays, willingly given at this point. Childhood memories and lost emotions emerged from deep within him at their slightest beckoning. And acceptance and understanding radiated forth from them like a warm, safe blanket to protect him as he dealt once again with so many of the things that he had blocked out and buried as a child. In turn, they exchanged and related memories and experiences of their own, helping to confirm that he had not been the only one suffering throughout the trials of life. Things that he had expected to be terrible and traumatic upon resurfacing were actually now interesting and explanatory. He understood at a rapid rate how human beings, one and all, shared similar thoughts and experiences no matter how bizarre or upsetting they might have seemed. In his mind he could see and feel the memory that one of them had had as a child engulfed in delirium with a high fever. The lyrics; "My hands felt just like two balloons," came through the air like the perfect punctuation to a point being made. Nick lost all sense of time and even of reality's existence at this stage of his trip, and left himself wide open to give and receive any and all knowledge that he might convey or interpret. He was allowing himself to become completely human on a massive scale, and it was embodying him with a peace he never dreamed he could have possibly attained. It was like an uncontrollable confession in which he was being psychologically absolved of all his doubts, angers and fears! Tears streamed down his face in rivulets and his entire body glowed with inner energy and tranquility.

 He actually chuckled when he realized that Pink Floyd had become his own personal Jesus Christ! Then there was that soft

Chapter 13

feeling of drifting, and he noticed the mist forming once again as the stage and players seemed to be fading off into the distance. The sound of the music dwindled down to a whisper and suddenly his eyes were open.

He was in the back seat of the Wrangler and had to wipe the moisture off his face from all the tears he'd just shed. He looked over to see the dark shape of Terry curled up against the door to his left. Taking a few deep breaths, he leaned forward with the intention of waking up his comrades to share what he'd just experienced but decided against it. It had been beyond amazing yet it was private and meant only for him. Besides, judging by the placid looks on the faces of his friends, who knows what they themselves might be experiencing? He wouldn't want to disturb them especially if they were going through even a tiny bit of what he himself had just felt. Nothing he had ever been through before had ever been so worth it!

Chapter 14

One by one, they slowly emerged from their peaceful states and became aware of each other through all the stretching and yawning that followed.

"Wow. Did we all pass out?" Jason asked, being the first to speak.

"Sure seems like it," Brad answered with a long exaggerated yawn. "Man. I had some seriously trippy dream...or whatever you wanna call it. How about you guys?"

A chorus of "Uh huhs" followed by nodding heads, seemed to be the general response.

"Well, I've gotta hit the old restroom," Brad announced, sluggishly pulling himself out of the Jeep. He carefully made his way out to the edge of the desert, slightly staggering and in somewhat of a daze. Trying to stand still but swaying a bit, he attempted to relieve his bladder when he heard a rustling sound in the bushes ahead of him. Suddenly remembering where he was and what he was doing, he whispered out harshly.

"Jack? Is that you? Jack..?"

Again the sound of something large in the brush directly ahead of him and he almost jumped out of his skin when he heard Jack's voice two feet away and directly behind him.

"Looking for me?" Jack asked in a mockingly dramatic tone. Brad had practically urinated all over himself, being so startled,

Chapter 14

and quickly zipped up while trying to catch his breath at the same time.

"Ha!" Jack exclaimed with whispered laughter. "Looks like I scared the piss out of you!" Jack had to cover his mouth to muffle his own laughter, he was giggling so hard.

"Very funny!" Brad chastised in a hissing whisper. "Where the hell have you been?"

"Just scouting the area, mon," Jack countered with a knowing smile.

"What's that supposed to mean?" Brad asked, trying his best to sound nonchalant.

"Come on! Are you kidding me? I could smell the Ganja from a hundred yards away! I didn't know you were planning on getting stoned on top of the Mescaline. That could get very tricky," he stated with a disapproving glare.

"Alright, alright!" Brad confessed. "We did get high, but I wasn't planning that. It just happened."

"Ya know, I gave up peer pressure way back in high school," Jack chided sarcastically.

"Okay! So anyway...what's next? Where are you taking us from here?"

"Well...there is a wash that leads up through a canyon that will eventually take us to that spring I was telling you about. How do you feel about that? It's a beautiful hike, especially in the moonlight. I think it might be near that spot on the map."

"Okay! Sounds good! So...I'm gonna head back to the Jeep to join the fellas. Wait a few minutes, then come get us okay?"

"Sounds like a real plan chief," Jack said, as he began walking back in the direction he came from. The way Jack; who was Native American, kept calling Brad; who was a white man; chief, got Brad every time and the irony was not lost on him.

"Oh, hey Jack," Brad whispered after him.

Jack half-turned back towards Brad, and lifting an eyebrow asked, "Yeah?"

"What was that sound I heard earlier coming from the bushes? I thought it was you but you were behind me."

"It was me," Jack stated with authority.

"What?" Brad exclaimed in a loud whisper. "How could it have been you? You were right behind me the whole time. Weren't you?"

"Smoke another, mon!" Jack said, chuckling as he turned and disappeared back out into the night.

"So..." Brad asked, as he slid back into the driver's seat of the Jeep. "how's everyone hangin'? Okay?"

"We're fine, but we were just wondering what we were going to do next?" Jason asked with an air of curiosity mixed with concern.

"I guess that would depend on our guide, he's-"

"Here," came a voice from the front of the Jeep. They turned to look and where just a moment before there had only been desert, they now found Jack standing there directly in front of them. "If you are all ready...we can go now."

Without waiting for any kind of a response, Jack turned and walked away. The four of them just stared at one another dumbfounded then scrambled to jump out of the Jeep, grab their packs, and catch up to Jack. Once again, they found themselves walking single file through the desert in a southwesterly direction.

"So where are we going now?" Jason asked Brad in a hushed tone.

"He's leading us through a canyon and to a natural spring that he knows about."

"How the hell do you know that?" Jason asked in disbelief.

"Because we talked about it when we first met and I can tell by the trail we're on, okay? Don't stress out! It'll be fine."

"I'm sorry man," Jason said apologetically. "I'm still high, and I think that the Mescaline is really starting to kick in now."

Chapter 14

"It's cool brotha," Brad said soothingly. "I'm feeling it too."

"Hey Brad," Jason retorted, catching his attention again. "Remember that time we bought that Acid from Wesley and walked all around town? We thought that it was bunk because we didn't feel anything for a long time and then we ended up at that chick's house, drank all that wine, and zang!"

"How could I forget that?" Brad asked, chuckling nostalgically. "That was one of the worst experiences I've ever had with wine. God, did I ever get sick!"

"Yeah, I remember!" Jason agreed, laughing. "But I took pretty good care of you that night, didn't I?"

"Yes, you sure did buddy."

Brad took a second to reflect back on that crazy night and how his friend had come through for him yet again. Jason had always been there for Brad no matter what, and Brad would always be eternally grateful for that.

"Hey Brad. Not to change the subject, but don't you find it eerie the way Jack keeps popping up all around us unexpectedly? I mean; one minute I think he's in front of us and the next, he's behind us. Or not there at all! Can you even attempt to explain any of that?"

"Well..." Brad pondered, "It reminds me a lot of how don Juan was always disappearing in those Castaneda books. It's like he almost has the ability to be in two places at once. Don't you think?"

Jason rolled his eyes and blew out an exasperated sigh.

"Boy, I sure walked into that one," he said sourly.

"What's that supposed to mean?" Brad fired back, getting offended.

"Every time we would go on a hike or little spiritual trip, you always had to throw that don Juan character into the mix. It was like you compared almost everything we did to those books!" Jason shot back without hesitation"

"I did not!" Brad argued defensively. "And even if I did, what is so wrong with that? Those books make a lot of sense and Carlos Castaneda was a brilliant and articulate author."

When he saw how rapidly upset his friend had become, Jason began to backpedal.

"Look man, I'm sorry. I didn't mean anything by it. It's just that sometimes you used to talk about it so much that I got tired of hearing it," he added, making matters worse.

"That's fine. Say no more. I won't ever mention any of it around you again…ever," Brad replied, spitting venom with every word as he picked up his pace.

Jason suddenly realized that he had just belittled something that was obviously very important to his friend and he suddenly felt ashamed. Sometimes he forgot how sensitive his old buddy really was and he hustled to catch back up to him.

"Brad, please. I'm sorry man. You're right. Castaneda did have some amazing insights and his writing was very intriguing. You go ahead and say whatever you feel whenever you feel it. I mean, that's what we're here for right? Sorry for pissing on your parade, really."

After hearing such a heartfelt spiel, Brad had no choice but to accept his apology.

"Alright," Brad conceded with a small sigh. "So anyway…" he went on, changing the subject, "I think we've got a good four or five mile hike ahead of us before we reach that spring. And I don't know if it's just me and I'm trippin'…but I keep noticing something out of the corners of my eyes. I keep thinking I see little things fly or run by but when I turn to catch a good look; nothing's there. You noticing anything like that?"

"Now that you mention it," Jason said with a spooked edge to his voice, "I just noticed as you were telling me."

Looking back, Brad could see that it was pretty much the same for Nick and Terry. They were glancing all around in various directions with a mixture of wonder and panic on their faces. As Brad turned back to face the front he was halted in mid step by the dark image of Jack who was suddenly standing right before him.

"This is called the Canyon of Shadows. It was often used by my people long ago as part of the journey that involved the Test of Manhood. It is a sacred place in which only the bravest and most worthy are allowed to travel."

Without another word, Jack was off leading the hike once more with a quick and purposeful pace. Jason turned to Brad with a look of horror in his eyes and then suddenly took off sprinting after Jack.

As he caught up to him he started stammering, "Uh, Jack? Excuse me. I'm sorry but...is this dangerous?"

"There is danger everywhere in life. Right now, you are the biggest threat to yourself. Be brave and vigilant and I'm sure that you will pass through just fine."

"Pass through?" Jason echoed fearfully. "Pass through what?"

Wow! Brad thought. Where does Jack come up with this stuff? He knew now without a doubt that he had picked the right man for the job. Jason just stood there dumbstruck and Brad gave him a reassuring pat on the shoulder as he passed him by. Brad chuckled to himself as he continued hiking, trying to constantly keep Jack within his sights.

It wasn't long before all three of the boys came running up and stopped him in mid-stride. They were all talking over the top of each other, asking Brad if they were safe and telling him of all the flitting shadows that kept invading their lines of sight. They seemed spooked to the point of irrational panic and Brad decided to call for a break.

"Okay. Let's all just stop and chill here for a minute. I admit that there is definitely something about this place, but it doesn't feel dangerous to me. Hey, Jack-" Brad said, calling out ahead to him.

"You may stop and rest here," Jack agreed, standing atop a rock directly up and to their left. They all gasped at the suddenness of his voice and appearance.

"Okay, who's got the backpack with the water? I need some," Brad asked, addressing everyone. Nick stepped forward with the pack and Brad immediately helped himself to a bottle. "Alright guys. Hang here for a minute while I go talk to Jack. I'll be right back, I promise."

He left his friends and started to scale up the rocky canyon in search of Jack. As he climbed, he noticed the color and texture of the smooth granite with its interesting detail and natural formation. He took care not to get too distracted however, as he carefully made his way up and over the slanted rock cliff. The moonlight accentuated shapes and shadows making it look and feel as though this genuinely was a spiritual place.

"It is a spiritual place," Jack said coming over the rise and offering Brad a hand, pulling him the last few feet up the ledge. "Very spiritual," he reiterated.

"How did you know-?" Brad started to stutter.

"It was written all over your face!" Jack replied laughing. "And plus, it was exactly what I was just thinking."

"Oh," Brad said, a little embarrassed.

"Hey Brad. Come check this out. I found this when I was a teenager and I just remembered that it was here." Jack led him over to a sandy little section in a tiny ravine that looked like it might have been a running waterfall years ago. "Look at these," Jack said, pointing out to a smooth, flat area. As Brad scanned the scene, he noticed dozens of grinding holes in all shapes and sizes worn smooth from work, weather and time. Kneeling down he inspected several of them, mesmerized by their perfect smoothness and circular shapes.

"Hey, buddy," Jack said, interrupting Brad's newest endeavor. "Can I get a drink of that water? I'm dying of thirst and I forgot to bring any," he begged, pointing to the water bottle Brad still held in his hand.

Chapter 14

"Sure thing," Brad answered, throwing the bottle the ten feet over to Jack.

He then watched as Jack fumbled and dropped it into a crevice in the rock behind him.

"Awww, son of a bitch!" Jack cursed, scrambling to get the water out of the wedge, way down in the rock.

"Sorry!" Brad snickered, as once again he reminded himself that this guy was just an actor. A damn good actor, but an actor nonetheless.

Jack chugged down most of the water and gave a satisfied, "Ahhhhh."

He then asked Brad, "So. What do you think?"

"I think the other fellas need to see this as well."

"Well, go call them up here. I'll keep my war paint on and ready. That is to say; I'll stay in character."

"You are outdoing yourself where that is concerned my friend. I'm so high on weed and Peyote right now that most of the time I keep convincing myself that you really are a Shaman!" Brad admitted with a nervous laugh.

"Thank you, thank you," Jack acknowledged, bowing twice. "Two years of College Theatre."

"But Jack. One thing is troubling me."

"Only one?" Jack asked with a laugh.

"Well, right now yes. What are all these fleeting little shadows that we keep seeing? Is this real or is it the Peyote doing a number on us?"

"Oh man! I forgot about the Shadows! I mean, this is called the Canyon of Shadows, but most people misinterpret that as to the moonlight playing off the rocks at night. I remember seeing them on my quest. Can you see them right now?"

"They're all around me," Brad replied, with a look of fear and confusion written all over his face.

"Alright man, well don't freak out. This is a very real part of the trip. What I said earlier was mostly true. I mean, I was using it for dramatic effect but this place was used in Spirit Quests many years ago. Those "Shadows" have no substance. They can't harm you. Just be careful where they might lead you. Some people get compelled to follow the wrong ones, or so the legends say, and they end up in trouble."

"Wrong ones? What kind of trouble?" Brad asked, approaching Jack with a startled look on his face.

"It's hard to say. Just be careful and pass the info on to the other boys. I've gotta go now, nature's calling. I'll meet up with you in about half an hour back over this way, okay?"

"Uhh...okay," was all that Brad could manage to say. His mind raced to try and understand what possible significance any of this could have on their trip.

He heard Jack in the distance talking to himself, "Now where the hell could I find something that resembles leaves? Hey Brad...do you have any toi...wup, nevermind!"

As if in a trance, Brad made his way over to the edge of the ravine and looking down, shouted out to his compatriots.

"Guys! Come up here and see what I've discovered!"

"Hey, I'm the one that showed you!" he heard Jack say out in the distance.

"Ssshhh!" Brad hissed at him.

Soon his friends were climbing over the top of the rock and once there, all three stared in amazement at the scene before them. Even Brad was once again taken in as they all gazed upon the rows of scattered grinding holes lining the entire wash for as far as the eye could see in the moonlight.

"What are all these holes?" Nick asked in an interested tone.

"Grinding holes," Jason clarified. "Man. We've never seen more than one or two of them in an area, huh Brad?"

Chapter 14

"I know, right?" Brad agreed. "Imagine the community of people that used to live here."

"Hey guys, look what I found!" Nick shouted with excitement.

"Wow! Nice arrowhead!" Jason said, inspecting the artifact and holding it up for all to see. It looked to be chipped from Obsidian and it had been beautifully crafted with extreme care and artistry.

"That's a big one," Brad commented. "Probably used to take down a deer, Bighorn sheep or maybe even a mountain lion."

Terry looked up with total alarm written all over his face.

"Mountain lion? There are mountain lions out here?"

"Well, yeah...sure man. I thought you knew that. Haven't you been hiking out here before? I thought you were familiar with this area."

"Oh, yeah man," Terry stammered. "I mean, I've been all through here, it's just...I've never seen one myself before. At least up here, man."

Jason and Brad both looked over to each other with doubtful and concerned stares.

"See guys, I told you!" Nick said chiming in. "What are we gonna do if we run into one of those?"

As his voice rose, the look on Terry's face bordered on panic.

"Just stop right there guys! You're starting to freak out. We'll be fine. I brought a large hunting knife and don't forget that we have Jack here to guide and help us. Not to mention that we're talking about hundreds of years ago when all kinds of wild animals used to roam these hills. I'm sure that by now they are extremely rare even in these parts."

Brad's assurance immediately calmed them and they pretty much forgot all about it and continued inspecting the holes and searching for more relics. But now it was Brad's turn to worry.

He looked off into the direction that Jack had gone and wondered what they would do if approached by something dangerous. He'd never even considered bringing a firearm along and he was the only one who knew Jack's real identity. At this point it would be utter chaos if they found out the truth.

He disregarded those thoughts and said a silent prayer to the Great Spirit and the Universe, asking for protection over them all. In no time he was back with his friends, scouring the ground for further signs of the lost civilization that once inhabited that area. Minutes later they all heard a voice and looked up to see Jack perched upon a rock, beckoning them to continue their journey.

After scaling down the cliff, they were once again on their way heading southwest and through the mysterious Canyon of Shadows. The march took on a somber tone and soon they were again surrounded with fast, flittering shadows which seemed to be caught more by their peripheral vision than with straight on eyesight. They darted here and there, and the sidelong glances that they got were all that they could really use to ascertain the shapes and sizes of the disturbing anomalies.

Finally Jack called for a halt and a meditation, upon seeing the discontent and fearful reactions that the Shadows were causing.

"We will sit down right here in the middle of this wash. Once again as I speak, I want you all to relax. This area is filled with energy, but most of all it is filled with whatever energy is projected into it. Do not succumb to fear or frustration. Let your minds be filled with the wonder of this place, and realize that you have the power to create a positive environment for yourselves. The Shadows may seem frightful but that is not their nature. Listen to their movements. Concentrate on their patterns. There is much that you can learn from them if you'll open your minds and be attentive. Many Braves have followed Shadows and reached unsurpassed levels in the attainment of knowledge. Keep your thoughts separate from your instincts and let your energy guide you."

Jack's voice was a soothing mixture of confidence and compassion and soon the boys found themselves falling into

Chapter 14

a trance. Jack began to sound farther and farther away until all sound faded from hearing. The last thing Brad could make out Jack saying was; "Trust in the strength of your spirit, but beware..." Brad thought; what an amazing and insightful speech that was that Jack just concocted for them. I hope the very last part was designed purely for dramatic effect!

Then suddenly Brad realized that he was standing. His eyes were still closed but he could tell by the feeling of gravity washing down his body that he was upright. Slowly, he opened his eyes and looked around.

He was alone in a section of the canyon that was unknown to him. As he scanned his surroundings he stopped short, noticing a very dark shape contrasted against the cliffs directly in front of him. As he moved his head to the side, he noticed that the shape was frozen in place and not just a shadow that was cast from the rock by the moonlight. Moving his head back and forth he felt as though he was witnessing an almost 3-D optical illusion. Slowly extending his arm out he reached straight ahead to gauge the distance between himself and the shape. Suddenly the dark shape darted backwards and then slowly moved upward, ever higher, until it was almost directly above him and then he lost sight of it against the night sky. Scanning the sky above and seeing no trace of it, he turned completely around and immediately saw the shape not more than three feet from his face. Staring directly into the massless void, he realized that there were no longer little Shadows constantly flying all around him. The black shape appeared to be somewhat rectangular and as near as he could tell; maybe two feet in height and about a foot wide. Then the patch of darkness started slowly bobbing up and down in a manner which seemed to be beckoning him.

"What do you wish of me?" Brad asked, his voice an eerie, hollow echo which startled even himself upon realizing that he had just spoken when he hadn't intended to.

The dark shape stopped its bobbing movements and slowly backed away from him, halting after only a short distance. It repeated its movements until Brad understood that it wished for him to follow. Without hesitation, he began striding purposefully after the elusive shape beseeching him.

It led him down a white, sandy wash augmented by large smooth boulders which had been worn and shaped by time and weather. Never once looking down yet at the same time completely sure of his footing, he marched on mechanically after the inviting entity that floated always just out of reach in front of him.

Driven by purpose to an unknown destination he continued on, never even questioning the outcome let alone the possibility of danger. After what seemed about two minutes of walking, the Shadow slowly began its ascent upward amidst some boulders on the right side of the wash. Approaching his mysterious new guide he noticed another smaller wash coming down from the canyon; a little tributary of sorts, and he immediately commenced to follow it upwards.

It switchbacked to and fro and gradually increased in incline until it ended right at the top of the canyon. Turning his head, he spotted a ledge to his immediate left and caught just a glimpse of his Shadow guide disappearing into the dark side of the mountain there.

Carefully climbing up the ledge, he soon found himself standing before the entrance of a moderately sized cave. He stepped forth cautiously, no longer seeing any trace of the dark shape that had led him there. Walking into the cave, he could clearly see by the moonlight that it was about the size of a large bedroom and very circular in shape. After a brief inspection, he sat down in the very center of the cave on the floor, and began relaxing his body to get comfortable. From where he sat, he had a beautiful view of the wash and most of the valley below as the light of the moon continued to cast a soft glow over the desert landscape. Closing his eyes he

Chapter 14

felt calm and relaxed yet noticed a radiant energy surging through him. All at once he was hit with a substantial jolt which appeared to come straight from the ground and rose up throughout his entire body and he was suddenly shocked into an immediate elevation in awareness. His hearing became keener and his eyesight suddenly as sharp as a hawk's. He could sense life's energies all around him, even though he couldn't physically see them all. It was as if his Hunter's instinct had fully kicked in within the blink of an eye. He sensed the tiny life force of a silent cricket and heard the breathing of a desert Chuckwalla lizard sleeping no more than ten feet away from him. Something inside was telling him how to harness the ability to sustain and change to this level of awareness. It was compelling him to understand how it was possible and to remember how it could be done when needed. His body was now the perfect receptor for his brain's ultrafast signals without even the slightest bit of interference and all at once he understood that this was how human beings were meant to function. It was the most basic process and yet it was something that mankind had all but completely lost over the centuries.

Out of all the different types of drugs and enhancers he had tried in his lifetime, this was by far the most pure and aware that he'd ever felt. Nothing else had even come close and he didn't want the feeling to ever end. This was what a true human being should feel like. No outside interference or corruption of thought from society's dogmatic teachings of conformity or negativity. Just a human being; perfectly honest with oneself. An important realization occurred to him just then; he was sitting directly upon another power spot! Don Juan had taught Carlos how to find and utilize certain places in the desert which emanated power and energy directly from the earth. Brad had found a few of these spots before in the past, usually while out hiking alone, and he had let his instincts take over and guide him. But never anything like this! Still, a specific memory made its way into his mind just then.

He began to remember the first time he had ever stumbled upon a power spot. He had been hiking along the ridge of a large canyon and after a time, stopped for a rest. His attention soon became drawn towards various rocks; mostly of the same size and near the area where he was sitting. After a time, he got up and started very nonchalantly placing them all around until he had formed a perfect circle. Then, he proceeded to construct straight lines throughout the circle until all edges met one another and indicated the four directions. He noticed his pace quickening and his movements getting faster as he neared to completion. He had felt a thriving energy building from within and instead of being exhausted from all his effort, he instead actually seemed rejuvenated. When he felt that he had finished, he stepped back and looked upon his work with amazement and appreciation. He had built a complete Native American style Medicine Wheel!

At that point in time he had not known exactly what it was that he had built, yet he admired its beauty and design all the same. He hadn't even read any of Castaneda's books yet, but later on he looked back on it with an enormous appreciation for the power of the Universe and its energy in guiding him. It was indeed an amazing rush that he'd felt and yet it paled in comparison to what he was feeling right now. He sensed that this particular spot had been utilized by very powerful Sorcerers for hundreds if not thousands of years, and the implications of his finding it tonight were staggering. That Shadow had led him there and he voiced a silent prayer of thanks to it and to the Universe, for being able to experience something so intense and insightful.

Suddenly, he found himself up and on his feet. He walked to the lip of the ledge and stared out at the mystical beauty of the desert that stretched out before him. There was something magical about that open expanse of rugged terrain that held a mysterious energy and power which tugged at one's very soul. It was almost as if it held a thousand lost memories that time had kept secret but not forgotten.

Chapter 14

Only the moon could ever know with its heavenly brilliance, what passions, tragedies and accomplishments, had transpired across this amazing landscape. And only the sun could have kept witness to the dreams and sorrows of all the different forms of life which had traveled in some way or another, across it. The amount of contemplation he was experiencing just then would have staggered a sober person, but thanks to his heightened awareness, he received it all as a blessing to his mind and his spirit.

Feeling supercharged, he hopped the six feet off of the cliff into the wash and made his way down towards the valley to see where this new energy might lead him next.

As he walked, his thought process shifted gears. He began to analyze himself and why he loved certain things yet feared or disliked others. He had always been attracted to specific things in his life and now he realized that it was mostly the energy that attracted him and not always the physical or mental aspects involved. He thought about the different kinds of music that he'd listened to during certain phases and stages of his life.

For instance, he had always been a fan of The Doors music. More for its psychedelic and Bluesy quality than anything else, but it wasn't until he'd had a certain dream that he became really taken with the Doors, and more precisely; Jim Morrison.

He'd had a dream one night in which he'd stumbled upon a house in the countryside, somewhere not far from a city, and tried to find out if it was for rent. It was small; more like a cottage really, and upon arriving he was let in the front door by someone who looked as though he was from the era of either the mid or late sixties. He had on the kind of colorful and stylish attire that would have been worn by the hippies at Woodstock. Walking through the kitchen he found himself in a small room that was somewhat attached, containing multiple people just hanging about. He remembered that the walls were a plain white color with random pictures and decorations hanging here and there, but nothing special that really stood out. There were some people sitting on a couch and upon seeing the one at the end, he was startled with astonishment. The man stood up and pleasantly introduced himself.

"Hi, I'm Jim," he said in a calm and friendly voice.

"Jim Morrison?" Brad asked in disbelief. "Of The Doors?"

"Oh, you've heard of us?" Jim asked with warmness and satisfaction in his tone.

"Oh man, I can't believe this!" Brad had exclaimed. "I'm a huge fan of your music!"

Jim promptly introduced him to all the other members of the band. Ray Manzarek, who was sitting at the other end of the couch, waved curtly at Brad. Robby Krieger, who was standing over by the corner leaning on the kitchen counter. And John Densmore, who was in the kitchen by the refrigerator talking with another guy.

Brad remembered chatting with Jim as if they had been old friends and how honest and open Jim was when speaking about things. He had the heart and soul of a poet, and Brad remembered thinking of how badly depicted Jim had been by Hollywood's misinterpreted version of him. He was very intelligent and down to earth and Brad felt an immediate kinship with him. It was hard to recall much more than that, but he felt upon awakening that he had truly met Jim Morrison.

He couldn't explain it, but in his heart he knew that he had talked with the man that everyone recognized as an unstable and out of control rock star. He had gotten to know the real Jim, albeit just for a brief amount of time, and he knew that no one could ever convince him otherwise. After that, he learned all that he could about the man who seemed so much of a kindred spirit, if not a darker reflection of himself.

In researching Jim, everything he read and watched just bolstered the fact that he really was the same man that he'd had the great

Chapter 14

fortune to meet and exchange ideas and life's philosophies with. To this day, Jim had been a steady influence and reminder in almost everything that he did in life.

Continuing with his trek, he thought of other bands and music that had influenced and inspired him. He had always loved watching local and underground musicians play and had had the pleasure of meeting some amazing and wonderful people.

Having moved out to the desert from L.A. as a child, he grew up mostly in Joshua Tree, California, and had been lucky enough to witness the birth of some great new sounds and talent.

One such band he could easily recall was Gram Rabbit. He remembered hearing their edgy, powerfully played sounds, accompanied by Jesika von Rabbit's sultry psychedelic voice. They had derived the first part of their name from Gram Parsons, who was an amazing Country Rock singer from the late sixties and early seventies. He was legendary for his ability to croon sad Country ballads that genuinely told the tale of true heartbreak, depression, loss, and celebration. He had died at the young age of twenty seven, just like so many of the other greats of that eclectic era. He was Brad's favorite Country Western singer and songwriter.

He remembered the first time he had met Jesika up at Pappy and Harriet's in Pioneertown, California. He'd felt as if they'd had an immediate connection in energy and talked for a long time about the music they loved, people they knew, and just life in general. They were almost the exact same age, with the exception of Jesika having him beat by two days. She was stunningly beautiful and had a genuine and sweet humbleness about her that captivated Brad to no end. When on stage, she mesmerized her audience with a sensual and seductive charm and had an amazing talent for creating a new type of sound which was almost indescribable and beyond categorizing.

That same afternoon, Brad had also met Todd; the guitarist and crucial counterpart that defined the other half of the band. Todd had a warmth and shyness that made him endearing to everyone around and yet he carried a quiet intensity that could not be overlooked. Always courteous and quick to give a hug, Todd had a big heart and Brad was always happy to see him. He felt truly privileged to be able to call them both friends.

The local scene where he had once lived was all tied in together with a conglomeration of musicians, writers and artists, among other types.

One amazing local artist in particular, who was a mutual friend of the Rabbits as well, was Bret Philpot. As far as human beings went, Bret was about as genuine as you could get. Many of his paintings were very dark and intense and conducted an energy to the onlooker that drew you in at once with fascination and respect. Bret's emotions, fears and passions swept through you in waves as you gazed upon his textured and beautifully enhanced canvases. The energy within the artistry virtually projected back out at the viewer, and tended to spark an immediate reaction. Not only was his art fantastic, but as a person, Bret was by far one of the most compassionate and non-judgmental souls that Brad had ever known. He radiated positive energy and could make you glow from just being in the same room with him. Bret was one of the few people that Brad trusted implicitly and rightfully so, for throughout all of their years of friendship, he had most certainly earned it.

In his youth, Brad had also lived in a town called Yucca Valley which was located about thirty miles above Palm Springs and ten miles away from The Joshua Tree National Monument. That whole high desert area, and even some of the low desert, was the mecca for new and amazing talent to rise from. So many great musicians and bands had originated from or near there, and many of them were some of Brad's favorites. Kyuss, Queens of the Stone Age, The Eagles of Death Metal, and Unsound were just a few among many others.

Chapter 14

Yet another which really stood out for him that he admired and appreciated, was a band called Death on Wednesday. Hailing from the Huntington Beach area, he had first seen them headline in Anaheim with another favorite band of his called Three Bad Jacks. Three Bad Jacks was fronted by his friend Elvis and represented a vintage Rockabilly sound that was like no other. This band did something that he'd never seen before; they set their instruments on fire and played them as the flames licked away at their arms and faces. It never got old to see and it was exciting every time they did it. Unfortunately, they had to stop for a while after the Great White incident in Rhode Island. Elvis was amazingly talented and Brad had appreciated how he'd always taken the time to talk with him and thank him for coming out to their shows.

He had actually been talking to Elvis the night that he had first seen Death on Wednesday perform on stage. He was quickly distracted from his conversation though, by the haunting and melodic singing of front man and guitarist; Nate Lawler. Nate's voice was entrancing and had a rhythmic style and sound comparable to Morrissey. He could only begin to describe their music as the Smiths meets Social Distortion and that description still fell drastically short of capturing what they really were. He couldn't even count how many times their music had gotten him through some of the hardest chapters of his life. Somehow their melancholy sound had inspired him to push through intolerable levels of depression and come out all the stronger for his efforts. He would always owe Lawler and the band a debt of gratitude and hoped to show his thanks by remaining a true fan to the music. He would continue to watch and support them in the hopes that one day they would be as renowned and respected as he knew they deserved.

When thinking of it, he felt exactly the same way about Todd and Jesika. And Elvis for that matter! So many talented musicians deserved a chance at worldwide awareness but were overlooked by a mainstream music industry that's more concerned about sales, radio publicity, and trend popularity than it is about the real need for a genuine message. A way to strengthen the human condition and experience the emotional and psychological aspects which make us all human beings. Musicians like Ryan Bingham and Jesse Dayton, were masterful at conveying those messages, and their music was crucial in helping people to understand life and even themselves. At least in Brad's opinion. He felt as though great artists like these had been overlooked for far too long. How strange he mused, that he'd never really contemplated just how important to his life music really was.

By this time, he found himself out in a wide open field with randomly scattered brush and rocks here and there. All of a sudden he stopped for a reason that he couldn't explain and then looked up to see something directly in front of him. It was a patch of darkness; partially blocking his view of the mountain range. Confused at first, he took a step back then realized that it was just his mysterious Shadow guide.

"Oh, it's you! So where are you going to lead me to this time? Back to my friends I hope?" Brad asked aloud and in an amused tone.

Suddenly the shape began to move towards him and he knew immediately that something was wrong. A feeling of panic overwhelmed him as the shape grew larger and larger in size as it approached him. He then realized that the shape was not growing in size, it had just been far away and was now practically on top of him. This was not the Shadow guide from earlier but something else entirely. Something terrifying!

Trying to back away quickly, he ended up falling down but hurriedly picked himself up and ran as fast as he could, away from the nightmarish figure looming above him. Like a giant Manta ray, the horrible shape hovered over him threatening to envelop him at any second. Out of stark fear he kept looking back only to find that the terrible mass was only a few feet away from him; a pitch black void radiating a vacuum of pure darkness. He sensed that he was in mortal danger and if this monstrosity caught him it would possess his entire being in a most terrible manner. His only thoughts now were of escape, and he desperately searched the landscape dead ahead for an area in which he might hide in order to elude his surreal attacker.

Sprinting with everything he had, he made straight for the edge of the valley hoping to find a cave or hole big enough for him to hide out in until the sinister apparition hopefully passed him by. He considered for a moment just lying down and curling up in a fetal position in hopes that it would continue by overhead, when an alarm went off in his mind telling him that it would be a dangerous mistake. So he just kept on running. Yet, as fast as he ran, the entity slowly and inexorably began closing the distance between them. At one point he shrieked as he felt its touch on his back like a wave of icy electricity streaming down his spine. That terrifying sensation caused him to excel his speed to a new level and he looked back once more to see if he had finally gained the lead. With a tiny sense of relief, he saw that he had started to outdistance it but when he turned back around he practically screamed in horror. He had run right off of a huge cliff and into a free fall, kicking and flailing frantically to no avail. A two hundred foot drop to the valley far below was all that was in store for him now. After a second he just closed his eyes and said a quick prayer in which he hoped that the Great Spirit would take him into his lodge. He felt a rush of wind and a jolt, but no impact!

He opened his eyes and found himself sitting back in the wash with his friends. Glancing around he saw that they were all resting just like him; with their arms hung loosely down at their sides, legs criss-crossed beneath them. They seemed as if they were all in a meditative state of being, probably experiencing their own reflections or adventures much in the same way he just had. He then looked over to Jack, half expecting to find him gone and instead saw Jack staring at him knowingly.

"Where were you just now?" he asked.

Taking a deep breath and exhaling it, Brad answered, "Man! I just had the most terrifying yet amazing experience ever! It was like a dream only more vivid and I can still remember every detail. Have I been sitting here the entire time?"

"Entire time?" Jack asked rhetorically as he chuckled. "You only closed your eyes about two minutes ago. I could tell something was happening though because you went from an extremely peaceful state to one in which your body started twitching uncontrollably. I was going to try and snap you out of it if you hadn't come out on your own real soon, but here you are!"

"Two minutes? You must be mistaken! I was out hiking for at least an hour! I found a cave! I was chased by…" Brad's thoughts trailed off with his sentence.

"By what?" Jack asked, seemingly intrigued.

"Never mind," Brad digressed. "So how are the boys doing?"

"They are in a deeply altered state of consciousness. Not asleep, but in a meditative state of non-ordinary reality. Just like you were."

Non-ordinary reality. That was a term Carlos Castaneda used when talking about Sorcery. But earlier Jack acted like he had never heard of Castaneda. He would have to touch on that later, but for now he had other questions.

"I need to talk with you about some things. Should we go somewhere so that the boys won't be able to hear us?"

"We can talk all you want right here. Trust me. They are totally disconnected from our reality right now. I've seen it before," Jack assured him.

"Okay then. First of all, what time is it? I lost all concept of it ever since we started hiking out here. Will the sun be coming up soon?"

Chapter 14

"In about a few hours I'd say."

"Wow. I was beginning to think that time had ceased altogether, but it's finally caught up with us. So what's next? Are you still taking us to that spring? And when are we going back to our campsite?"

"I am still taking you to that natural spring I told you about and you can sleep there if you need to. After that, we can decide what else you want to do. It depends on how far you want to go with this, podner. This is your journey of self-discovery so you tell me when you've had enough."

With a wild gleam in his eye, Brad shot Jack a wicked grin.

"This keeps getting better and better as far as I'm concerned. I want to keep going. I think something's happening inside me, like an awakening. I don't think I've ever felt this alive!"

"In that case, I think you had better take some more Peyote, and soon I'd say. I can see its effect on you is about moderate and if you want to go deeper then you'll need to increase the dosage. But that decision is up to you fellers."

"I'll talk with these guys and see how they feel about it. One more thing. I wanted to know more about what you think of Terry. I know you mentioned that you disapprove but we picked him up at a liquor store and let him come along in case we couldn't find you because he said that he knew this area real well. He hasn't taken anything other than mushrooms...or so he says," he added looking over at Terry who was sitting slightly slumped and swaying back and forth almost imperceptibly. Brad turned his gaze back towards Jack and found him staring at Terry intensely with disapproving contempt.

"Again I say; you should leave him behind and do it real soon. He can only cause you grief."

Brad looked back over to Jack, shocked. "What? Just leave him out here? I told you we can't do that! We're responsible for him in a sense. We can't just abandon him out here!"

"That is exactly what you can and will do if you are smart, and you will do it now. We'll all get up and leave him right where he is sitting to awaken alone and without all of you to depend on."

Again Brad looked at Jack with an expression of pure appall on his face. "You're kidding right? I mean, I could tell from the start that you weren't crazy about the guy but you wouldn't seriously leave him out here all alone to fend for himself? I know we just met him and all so we don't actually know him, but he can't be all that bad."

Jack, never taking his eyes off of Terry replied, "I am dead serious. Do what you think is best but very soon you may regret that decision."

Brad watched Jack for a few moments, marveling at his intensity and his ability to go back and forth from comical to serious.

"So, anyway!" Jack said suddenly, bringing his attention back to Brad and lightening his tone by several shades. "Are you ready for the next leg of the journey? What do you think of my acting skills so far? Not bad, eh?"

"You are phenomenal indeed, Jack! You've got me coming and going most of the time and I guess that just adds to the trip. I can tell that the boys still don't know what to think of you! I'm ready, but what about these fellas? Should we wake them?"

"No need. Time to get my game face on."

With that, Brad noticed them all regaining their regular clarity at the same time and looked back at Jack with puzzled curiosity only to find Jack stone-faced and serious once again, playing his part to perfection.

"Hey, fellas! Glad to have you back," Brad greeted in a sincere and sober tone.

"Take a moment to stabilize yourselves and we will continue on with your journey," Jack said soothingly.

After some stretching and brief chit-chat, they were again on the march up through the sandy wash. Soon though, they were out of the canyon and into a large expanse of flat desert that stretched off for miles out into the distance. It looked to Brad as if they were centered in a large valley with gigantic rock boulder mountains lining its edges.

With all of them feeling very peaceful and serene, they enjoyed the steady calming monotony of just putting one foot in front of the other, and it became very pleasant as they hiked across the dry desert landscape. The moon appeared to have barely made its celestial arch over the sky for all the time that it seemed they'd traveled so far. Soon they approached another canyon, only the cliffs of this one appeared to be lined with tall, smooth, red rock.

They then followed a small, dry wash up to the entrance of a moderately sized rock river basin and hiked the gradual incline up its angular surface. Upon reaching the center they noticed a warm change in the temperature, and used caution as they felt the slick surface of the rock underneath their feet.

"Watch your step. The bedrock here has seen years of water and wind erosion making it very slippery," Jack called out to them as he moved forward, carefully picking his way across the smoothed surfaces of the many boulders.

Over, down, and around various types of soft sand, gravel and rock, they hiked until they finally rounded a bend which opened into another circular clearing. It was surrounded by vertical cliffs, rust colored with lighter shades of red and orange, which were easily visible in the bright moonlight. There was a very warm air mass that filled the entire enclosed area and each of them noticed it right away.

Comments of; "Wow! You feel that?" and "Man, it's warm in here" softly echoed up and out of the canyon.

Jack led them straight ahead to an enormous gray boulder which seemed attached to a length of flat, smooth and solid bedrock; also gray in color. As they circled around to the front side of the immense boulder, they were amazed to see that it was actually a naturally carved cave. Almost as if it had been hand chiseled from the outside in, the edges were smooth and formed a high and wide half-circle like the entrance to a hut. They all filed in after Jack and found the interior spacious yet cozy, and emanating a feeling of peace, comfort and security.

"What an amazing cave...structure...whatever this is!" Jason commented in an exasperated tone.

"Was this man-made, Jack?" Brad asked in wonderment.

"It was originally formed naturally; mostly by wind and water. However the legends say that the Ancients had a hand in chipping and shaping it in certain ways and when they did, they left strong traces of their energy within. You can feel completely at ease in this place for it is and has been protected for hundreds of years."

"It's amazing!" Nick proclaimed, carefully scanning the interior's edges and studying the small details crafted into the rock. While the guys were all exploring the inside of the cave, Jack motioned with his chin for Brad to join him outside.

"I'll be right back fellas," Brad said, as he made his exit, ducking out quickly. He found Jack over by the backside of the cave waiting for him.

"Hey Brad, listen. I'm going to head back to town real quick and go to Carl's Jr. for a hamburger. I'm starving! I parked my car about a mile away from your vehicle. Do you want me to stop by and check on your campsite and Jeep for you?"

"Yes, thank you Jack! That would be awesome! What time will you be back?"

"Aww, not long. About an hour or two I think. The water in this spring is pure and even okay to drink if need be so you guys will be fine till I get back."

"What spring?"

"Oh man! I completely forgot to tell you. Come check this out... but wait! First, what are you gonna do while I'm gone? Pretty soon you should start eating more buttons because the sun will be coming up in about an hour or two, I'm guessing. Do you have any left I hope?"

"Yes. We actually have only eaten about half so far, but will we be okay with you gone?"

"Oh, I'm sure you'll be fine as long as you keep yourselves occupied. I won't be gone that long. What will you do? Any ideas?"

"As a matter of fact, I've been considering that and I think that you should assign all of us certain things to do. In Castaneda's books, he said that don Juan would give him tasks to complete during some of his psychedelic journeys."

"Like what?" Jack asked inquisitively.

"Well...random things, really. Don't worry, I'll think of something."

"Okay, you're the boss, boss. Now follow me!"

Walking back over near the front-side of the cave, they continued heading down towards the edge of the bedrock and looked over it. There was a small, clear stream quietly trickling down to form a pool of water about five feet away. Brad stared at the natural wonder with mouth agape like an astonished man who had just learned a valuable secret.

"Oh, man! I can't wait to show the guys. They're gonna flip!"

"Okay then. You're all set so let me just go announce my departure and I'll be on my way."

As they entered the ancient dwelling they found the boys exactly as they had left them; still admiring the details of the cave's formations with intensity.

"Ahem," Jack cleared his throat, trying to get their attention. "I am leaving for a short time and have assigned you all tasks to perform until I get back. Brad will tell you all what to do and you should follow the instructions to the letter. It's very important. This area holds many powerful secrets and my hopes are that you begin to discover some of them. This cave is a safe zone and nothing can harm you here so take comfort in that until I return," he finished stoically. Without even a backward glance, he left the cave and was on his way.

Brad's friends hardly even noted his exit, so intent on feeling the various textures as well as studying the intricate designs forged into the walls of the cave. After watching Jack depart, Brad turned his attention back towards his friends and made an announcement.

"Alright guys. Gather around and listen up. Jack has gone on some kind of mysterious errand, and has given each of us a certain task to perform for our own spiritual growth and enlightenment. But first we will need another dose of buttons and with the sun coming up soon we might just be able to time this thing perfectly."

"What about Terry though?" Nick asked from the far end of the enclosure. "Do we have enough for all of us? Terry hasn't even taken any yet. Have you?" he inquired, looking over at Terry.

Terry just looked down sheepishly. "Nah, man. That's okay, I don't need any."

Brad and Jason exchanged concerned looks. "Well, if he's with us then he needs to be part of this trip right?" Jason asked seriously.

"I agree," Brad confirmed.

"Hey man! I've got some mushrooms I can eat! That will help me keep up with you guys!"

Jason looked to Nick and Nick turned to Brad. Terry in turn, looked questioningly at all three.

"Alright," Brad consented. "That should be okay. In the meantime, let's get our buttons ready."

Walking over to pick up his pack, he noticed the back zipper undone. In a flash of panic, he delved his hand inside searching for the Peyote. Not finding it there, he began frantically checking all the pockets but to no avail.

"It's gone," he stated dismally.

Chapter 14

"What?" Jason cried in an alarmed pitch.

"Someone left the zipper open to the pocket that I had the Peyote stashed in. It's gone. Probably out there in the middle of the desert. Who could say where?"

Jason let out an exasperated groan.

"Should we try and go look for it?" Nick asked, already suspecting the answer.

"I think we're screwed guys," is all that Brad could offer at that point.

"Who the hell left the zipper open anyway?" Jason yelled.

"Don't look at me," Brad said.

"Or me," Nick echoed.

"Well I sure as hell didn't!" Jason exclaimed.

As one, they all turned to look at Terry, who stood slouching with his hands in his pockets, a guilty look spreading across his countenance.

"I...uh...might have accidentally...uh...left it open when I was looking for the water earlier. Man, I'm really sorry guys. I'll help you look for it."

Brad could see Jason's blood pressure rising and just as he was about to start a cursing extravaganza, Brad interjected.

"Okay, what's done is done and there's no changing that now."

"So what do we do then?" Jason asked in a dry, cutting tone.

"Well, we'll just have to wait for Jack to get back and hope that he can acquire some more for us. It's not the end of the world."

They all slumped down to the floor and sat with their backs to the wall in a gesture of defeat except for Terry who remained standing, shuffling his feet nervously as usual.

After a few silent moments in which you could hear a pin drop, Nick spoke up saying, "Hey! Why don't we just eat some of those mushrooms Terry brought with him? That should keep us going until we figure something else out."

Jason looked over at Brad hopefully. "What do you think?" he asked.

"I don't know man. It might be a bad idea to mix the two."

"Come on man! I can already feel this high starting to wear off and it wasn't even as intense as I thought it would be to begin with. It's been great, don't get me wrong, but don't you feel like you need more? I know I do."

Brad looked to Nick who nodded his assent.

With a sigh, Brad conceded, "Okay. Where are these magical mushrooms of yours Terry? Bring 'em out. Let's have' em!"

Terry, who'd been shifting uneasily, looked up seemingly caught unaware.

"Oh right man. Sure. They're in my backpack."

The guys all waited calmly, resigned to their newfound option. After a few moments of circling the inside of the cave searching for his pack, they heard Terry mumble, "Ummm..."

Jason looked up and asked, "What is it?"

"Well...uhhh...my pack's not here."

"You've gotta be kidding me." Jason spat through gritted teeth.

They all fell silent again, then after a few painstaking minutes Terry shouted, "Hey!" startling Nick who was closest to him. "I remember where I left it! I set it down next to a boulder right before we started hiking into this canyon! I can find it, I know I can," he offered confidently, waiting for a response from the others.

"Well, let's go then," Jason grumbled, storming out of the cave and leaving the others behind.

"I'm sorry man," Terry apologized solemnly.

"It's okay man," Brad replied, putting his hand on Terry's shoulder. "We all make mistakes, nobody's perfect. Jason just has a bit of a quick temper sometimes, that's all."

"Are we going or what?" Jason shouted from outside the cave right on cue. They all made their way out and were soon retracing

Chapter 14

their steps, hiking carefully back across the smooth boulders of the canyon.

"We've got to be careful," Brad stated loudly. "We don't have Jack to guide us now and we don't want to get lost."

They got to a certain point in which they could no longer see any footprints or trace of their passing and Brad called for a halt.

"Alright guys. I don't recognize this area. Does anyone remember which way we came in?"

They all glanced around with evident looks of uncertainty.

"Didn't we pass by that pointy, spire looking rock, on our way in? I think it was on our left," Nick offered hopefully.

"Shit man. I can't remember," Jason cursed.

"You could be right," Brad agreed optimistically.

"Yeah, what the hell," Jason stated more than asked. "Let's go."

As they started off again, they noticed that Terry had lagged behind. They all stopped, looking at him expectantly.

"You know...I think we came in this way," Terry said pointing off to the right. "Yeah, that little wash looks really familiar to me. I think we should try it."

Without question, the boys all headed back and over the way Terry had indicated, and soon found themselves in a maze of twists and turns. Maneuvering their way down tiny, dried up waterfalls, and up and over slick water worn boulders, they ended up looking down the edge of a vertical cliff which had a sheer drop off of at least twenty five feet straight down.

"Well this isn't it," Brad stated angrily, as he turned the boys around to go back the way they came. It became increasingly evident however, that they were lost and Jason's frustration levels were approaching a critical mass.

"Look. I have an idea. I'll hike up to that tall cliff and get a better view of our surroundings. It'll just take me a few minutes so you boys relax while I go scout it out," Brad said, then abruptly turned and left.

Having grown up for the better part of his life out in the desert, Brad's climbing skills were excellent to say the very least. True, he had been out of practice but the ability was always there when he needed it. In no time he was at the top scanning the entire area, and spotted the entrance to where they came in, about a half mile away. Making a note of the best course to follow, he climbed back down with a grin on his face like a hero awaiting his homecoming.

"Follow me gents! I'll show you the way!"

Very soon they arrived at the entrance and then sat down waiting for Terry to reclaim his lost backpack. He began wandering all around a bit nervously from area to area trying to pinpoint the location with apparently no luck whatsoever.

"I know I left it leaning against a boulder right around here," he said, as he paced back and forth.

"Well, let's help him," Brad said, prodding his other two friends into action. They all took to the task, going off in various directions, meandering to and fro, in search of what was soon starting to seem like a mythical creature.

"You don't think someone could have found it do you?" Nick asked, as he passed by Brad on his search.

"Extremely doubtful," Brad replied. "I didn't see any other tracks aside from ours when we first showed back up here, and I looked."

After another ten minutes or so, Jason pulled Brad aside.

"Hey look man, this is a wild goose chase. I didn't say anything earlier, but I think that Terry has been hittin' his pipe this whole time since he's been on board with us. It's not that I have anything against weed, obviously, I just don't trust his memory. I think he's way too high…and not in a good way. Who knows where he left that damn pack of his? Let's head back. The sun will be coming up soon and we might just make it back to the cave in time to catch Jack in case he goes out looking for us."

Chapter 14

Brad hadn't even considered the idea that upon Jack arriving back at the cave and not finding them there, he, himself, might go out searching for them.

"You're right. Let's abandon this mission and head back."

Brad announced their departure and they all fell back in line and began the march to the cave, Terry looking like a whipped dog with his tail between his legs. They made it back quickly this time though, mostly following their own tracks, and while circling the outer edge of the cave, Nick spotted something.

"What's that?" he asked curiously, as they walked back around and over to the object in question.

"It's Terry's backpack!" Jason shouted with glee.

They all cheered except for Terry who approached the object somewhat tentatively, and then quickly picking it up, headed directly for the cave. The other three exchanged curious looks and followed after him. They all sat down and waited expectantly as Terry perused through the pockets in his pack, one by one, coming up short.

Jason's smile turned to a frown as Terry looked up and announced, "I can't find them."

With a look of defeat, he hung his head down and slumped his shoulders. Nick and Jason both looked to Brad angrily, while Brad continued to stare deadpan at Terry who refused to look up.

"Terry? Can I talk to you outside for a minute?" Brad asked calmly.

Terry got up quietly and followed Brad out of the cave, leaving Jason and Nick looking after them as they went. Once around the backside, Brad stopped and turned toward Terry who seemed almost on the verge of tears.

"Hey man, relax. It's okay." Brad reassured him. After a moment, Terry calmed down and looked up at Brad. "You wanna tell me what's really going on here?" he asked Terry gently. "Talk to me. I'm not gonna get angry with you. You never did have any mushrooms did you?" Terry looked away, and then shook his head no, confirming Brad's suspicions. "So why the deceit?"

"I just really wanted you guys to like me," Terry answered, starting to choke up. "I don't know anyone out here and I really wanted to hang out with someone again. I did have some mushrooms earlier, but I sold them to the guy behind the register at the liquor store and I ate the rest when you guys weren't looking. I'm sorry."

Brad looked down and gave a heavy sigh. He had the brief mental image of the store clerk transfixed by the hallucinatory tracers coming off of his fingers as he wiggled them before his eyes. Must be nice, he thought.

"Okay man. I'll cover for you one more time, but from here on out, no more dishonesty! Deal?"

"Deal!" Terry agreed, nodding his head emphatically.

"Alright. Let's go back inside and face the music."

As they entered the cave, Brad found Nick and Jason whispering back and forth to each other in conspiratorial tones but quickly ceased as they both made their way inside. Brad cleared his throat then announced; "As it turns out, Terry might have lost his mushrooms back at the liquor store in town, as that was the last time he checked to make sure he still had them. Isn't that right?"

"Uhh...yeah," Terry stammered. "I'm sorry guys. I should have double checked before we left."

Jason groaned again and Nick just rolled his eyes.

"So anyway, let's relax a bit until Jack gets back."

"But what about those little tasks Jack said we should do?" Nick asked, concerned.

"Well, when Jack gets back, hopefully he'll have more buttons and we can take some and start on them," Brad replied.

"Yeah. If he even has any. Seems to be a real shortage of psychedelics around here," Jason countered sarcastically.

Chapter 14

"Hey man, I said I was sorry!" Terry shot back angrily.

Jason snapped his head up and looked at Terry, obviously infuriated and apparently about to start yelling back, when Brad interrupted from the side.

"Jason!" Brad said sharply. Jason looked up at Brad a bit fearfully, obviously caught off guard. "Do you still have any jerky in your backpack? I could really use some."

Jason reached over for his pack responding, "Yeah, I had some saved for the next time we ate more buttons." Reaching in, he pulled out a large, zip lock bag with a perplexed look on his face. "What's this?" he asked, looking at it in confusion.

Upon spying the bag, Brad rushed over and quickly snatched it from his hands. Holding it up above his head like an offering to the gods, he shouted; "It's our Peyote!" They all looked to one another in disbelief as if they might be dreaming, when Brad explained; "Nick! You must have accidentally put it in Jason's bag with the jerky, instead of mine, after we ate some the first time!"

They all cheered like Vikings after a hard fought and won battle and Jason quickly assembled them all into a tight knit circle as he began dividing up the once lost treasure. Terry however, stayed over against the far wall as they started setting up.

"Come on Terry, get over here!" Brad called out to him.

"Yeah, man," Nick agreed.

Jason piped up next saying, "Yeah come on bro. It's all good. Come partake with us!"

For the first time, Terry got very serious with them.

"No guys. You go ahead. I've put you through enough. I'll hang back on this round. It's more important that you guys make sure you all have enough. It's about you. I'm just a tag along. Really, I mean it."

"You're sure?" Brad asked quietly.

"Positive. I can hang back just in case you guys get a little too far out there."

"Okay," Brad replied indifferently.

"Hey Brad," Nick asked anxiously. "Do you think that maybe this time we should eat them all at once instead of at half hour intervals? I mean…the sun will be coming up soon and maybe it will have a stronger effect on us this time."

Looking from Nick to Brad expectantly, Jason chimed in asking, "Yeah man, why not? It's already in our systems and we have Terry here to watch over us in case we go around the bend."

Glancing over at Terry who nodded curtly, Brad looked down to the sand of the cave floor. Yeah, that's just what we need, he thought; a guy like this, looking after us if we get blasted out of our minds. Throwing caution and good sense into the wind, he agreed, hopefully not regrettably. Nick cleared a space right in the middle of them and very ritualistically set the buttons out and started counting them.

"So, there are twelve left which means four apiece," he stated as fact.

"We should still eat some jerky with them though," Jason added seriously.

"Hey guys, I hope you don't think I'm being melodramatic, but I would really like for all of us to do something before we embark upon yet another journey," Brad said. "I think we should all give silent thanks to the Universe and to whatever powers that be, and ask that they guide and guard us on our next adventure."

"I think that's a great idea," Jason concurred, and Nick nodded his agreement.

They closed their eyes and fell into a deep silence, and in their own ways, expressed their appreciation and gratitude for what they'd already experienced and for what was next to come. Upon opening their eyes, they all reached for a button at the same time and initiated the consumption.

In no time at all, the buttons were devoured and most of the jerky was gone. Still sitting, they all relaxed their limbs and started rolling

Chapter 14

their heads around to stretch out their neck muscles. Terry was like an unnoticed ghost in the corner, quiet and serious, watching their reactions with an almost sober intensity.

After a few more moments, they stood up and began looking around trying to gauge the effects of the dosage that they'd just ingested. They began wandering all about the cave and each became captivated by the tiny details of its interior. Terry remained quietly passive in a corner and watched with amusement as they pored over the inner walls, scrutinizing each minute marking and carefully carved shape.

Suddenly, Nick looked up in panic and rushed out of the cave with Brad and Jason soon running quickly behind him. Very curious but still calm, Terry casually strolled outside to find them all side by side, over by a boulder with hands on their knees, lurched over puking.

"Are you guys alright?" he asked.

"Yeah man. We'll be alright," Brad answered, speaking for the rest of them. "I think it was just worse this time around because we ate them all at once instead of little by little."

"For sure man," Jason added, spitting out the last little bit.

"When you guys feel better, maybe you should head back to the cave and relax for a few."

Terry walked back inside the cave and sat down next to the battery powered lantern they had set up earlier, and got comfortable.

Very soon after, the boys all shuffled in and taking their places in the middle, began relaxing by doing some deep breathing.

After a bit, Nick looked up at Brad and asked, "What do we do now?"

Jason then stared at Brad expectantly as Brad contemplated the question.

Looking down at the sandy cave floor and almost getting lost in the small circular shapes he saw there, Brad suddenly snapped to attention and said, "Oh yeah! We all have tasks that we're supposed to do before Jack gets back!"

"Oh, yeah," Jason and Nick both quietly echoed, their voices sounding calm and hollow.

"So then...who does what? Did Jack tell you what we're all supposed to do?"

"Ummm yeah... he said that we should-"

"Hey you know what?" Terry blurted out from the side interrupting him. "The weather outside is perfect right now. We should all go out and consider this some more under the night sky."

The boys both looked from Terry back over to Brad who just sat there with a blank expression on his face, staring up at Terry.

Terry winked at Brad who then seemed to understand and said loudly, "Yes! Let's do that!"

Terry then swiftly exited the cave as the other three slowly got up and made their way out, one at a time, trailing after him. The first thing they all noticed was the clarity of the early morning sky. With the dawn still a good hour or two away, billions of stars sparkled brilliantly creating an enchanting tapestry of wonder directly overhead. Admiring the glittering lights from above, a loud "Ahem" from the side, alerted them yet again to Terry's presence.

"Hey Brad, can I speak to you for a moment?"

Brad stared at Terry stupidly until Terry gave him a quick gesture, jerking his head to the side.

"Yeah man, sure. I'll be right back guys."

The boys were so enamored with their view of the stars that they hardly even noticed him leaving.

"Hey man, I'm going to stay here at the cave and hold down the fort but if you guys need me at any time, just holler. And try not to go too far, okay?"

"Uhh...yeah, sure Terry. I'm gonna go round up the guys right now so that we can get right to work on our tasks."

Chapter 14

Terry gave Brad a smile and a nod, and then headed straight back to the cave. Watching Terry go, Brad felt as though he reminded him of someone. It's interesting how irritated they all were with him earlier and now as he watched him leave, he had only respect and appreciation for him.

He was quickly distracted from his reverie by the sound of his friends calling him back over to admire the stars.

"Brad, you've just got to witness this! Do you see what we're seeing?"

Brad couldn't help but give a chuckle when he caught sight of his fellow adventurers. They were both staring straight up at the sky with about as dumbfounded a look as ever existed. Jaws agape with eyes wide open; almost to the point of popping out of their skulls! It was as if they didn't dare look away even for a second, for fear of missing something fantastic.

"Brad," he heard Nick ask softly, "Do you see?"

Brad was completely intrigued now because he'd known Nick for over a decade and had never seen such an expression on his face before. Walking up to stand right in between the two, he slowly lifted his head up towards the heavens, and what happened next was something that would stay with him for the rest of his life. He didn't see it right away because it took just a moment for his eyes to adjust, but then he began to notice an awareness drifting through his mind. It was almost as if his head was slowly being submerged into a very thick form of liquid. He saw the shine of countless stars and had trouble at first discerning anything else, and then it hit him. As if a veil had been pulled from his eyes, everything came into indescribable focus. He could see millions of brightly burning stars all in front, behind, and side by side, with a depth perception that he never would have believed possible. From their position, the tall cliffs behind them blocked the moon and therefore left their view of the sky darkened to the perfect pitch to enable them to enjoy the amazing light show overhead.

He saw them all simultaneously, but he could identify each shining light as if it were the only one presently existing in that beautiful night sky! He tried to fathom how he could see them collectively, yet individually, at the same time and began to understand. It was as if he had learned a language that couldn't be spoken or read yet perfectly described their existence! Soft rays of shimmering light emanated from each star, and engulfed his entire body leaving him calm and tranquil. He could actually see in detail the amazing luminescent rays pulsating like ethereal jellyfish, floating down in perfect precision to wash over and through his very being! It was by far the most fantastic thing he had ever witnessed, and to realize that it happened on a nightly basis, only he'd never been in the proper state of awareness to truly appreciate it, staggered him. A subtle, ancient light and energy which came from a source that had actually sent it millions of years ago.

He realized then that he must look just as silly as his friends, and that his jaw was probably hitting the ground as well! They must be in another power spot, he reasoned. This simplest and most ordinary of experiences held him breathless for several moments and he absorbed as much of the relaxing, yet rich energy as he could.

After some time, his hypnotic trance was broken somehow and he thought about the tasks that he and his altered friends needed to perform. According to Jack that is; which was really just according to him. What should he tell the boys that they must do? Their state of mind was becoming more heightened by the minute and he needed to come up with something spiritual, something symbolic. But what? He began searching his brain for ideas and like a spark of inspiration; he remembered some of the unique stories from the Castaneda books that he knew so well. He recalled some of the strange and almost comical tasks that don Juan used to insist that Carlos complete. Maybe with a little improvisation he could incorporate some of those, as well as come up with a few of his own. He decided then that it was time to break the fellas free from their astronomical spell.

"Alright guys," he began to proclaim loudly, shaking their attention loose so that they looked to him somewhat startled. "Here's what you must do. Nick; you must first find a bush. But not just any desert scrub. Find one that is thriving out here in this dry region. Communicate with it. Talk to it. Seek answers and energy from it," Brad stated with authority.

Without waiting for any kind of a response, he turned to Jason, "Jay; you must locate and discover your Spirit Animal. You may not know what it is right away, but chances are that it will reveal itself to you."

Jason and Nick both looked to each other, doubt written all over their faces.

"A bush?" Nick asked skeptically.

"How long do I look for?" Jason asked slightly panicked. "And where do I even start looking? Are you sure this is right?"

For a brief moment, Brad hesitated. *Am I doing the right thing?* he thought to himself.

"Yes. These were Jack's instructions, and we must follow them to the letter like he said," Brad answered, gaining confidence from his own words.

"Okay," Jason conceded meekly. "What about you though? What are you gonna do?"

"I have my own task set before me," he answered, leaving no room for debate. "And Terry will remain here as he is not part of this expedition. We are not far from the cave and we should all meet up in time to get back here shortly before sunrise. So that gives us all at least an hour, maybe longer." Scanning all around in a full circle, Brad ordered Nick first, pointing out a direction for him to start in. "Nick; you head northwest, over that way. And Jason...you should head east, back that way. Let the energies of this desert and the Universe guide you. I will head south now and afterwards meet you right back here on the trail. Don't get lost!" he said rather sternly. Putting his left and right hand on each of their shoulders, he gave them a firm squeeze then lightened his countenance and with an almost sympathetic look he asked, "Okay?"

Again, Nick and Jason just looked to one another then quietly agreed. Without hesitation, Brad was on his way heading back towards the direction of the cave. He almost felt a little guilty for putting the guys through all this but he believed that whatever was meant to happen would come to pass, and that included him as well. Considering that, he thought about everything that had already transpired so far this night that may just forever change them. And the journey wasn't even halfway through yet!

Chapter 15

Looking back only once to make sure that the boys were heading off towards their separate ways, Brad then concentrated on the self chosen path in front of him. After a short distance, before he reached the cave, he took a left and went back up through another sandy wash which led him through yet another canyon. He continued his march for at least a half a mile before he stopped to get a better look at his surroundings.

Tall vertical cliffs of dark, red sandstone lined the edges of the canyon, and he suddenly noticed strange markings and carvings that spanned them from top to bottom sporadically. He decided to inspect them closer and approached a group of them that were about eye level. Once again the light of the moon helped him in discerning what it was he was looking at and then suddenly it became evident.

"Petroglyphs!" he whispered to himself excitedly.

He scanned the wash all around the immediate area to make sure that he was safe and then began to focus all of his attention on the primitive artwork directly in front of him. At first, the designs didn't seem like anything other than basic etchings and grooves in the rock until he got so close that his nose was almost touching the cliff. Then in the moonlight he could see the way the stone had been chiseled, each marking having tiny punctuations to accent each individual symbol and picture.

On a whim, he ran his hands over the carvings to determine their depth and texture and received a light tingle on his fingertips that ran slightly up his arms. Backing away abruptly, he looked the cliff up, and down, questioningly. Had he really just felt that? Taking a step forward, he cautiously placed his fingertips onto the stone, once more ready to jump backwards at any time, and he felt it again. He retracted his digits quickly then inexplicably and almost against his own will, he placed both hands on the cliff wall, pressing hard against the myriad of symbols, and closed his eyes. His mind became immediately flooded with thoughts and brief images that seemed to stem from the crafted carvings. That amazing sensation of tingling energy assaulted him on a grand scale, riveting throughout his entire body. Not painful, but intense.

He sensed feelings and emotions streaming forth from the rock, but most of all; he felt memories. Memories of people, nature, and power. Those symbols were not just historical documentations of a certain race of people. Nor were they directions or instructions for finding or locating areas and tribes. They were tiny conduits for power and energy that existed and were imbued within the stone. A way for Shamans and Sorcerers to pass down knowledge and information that would always be pertinent and important throughout all of time! And he was lucky enough to find them and experience their residual energy and possibly gain insight and wisdom into that eternal question of existence!

On some level he felt like an appliance that had been plugged into a power source and was now processing the electricity that created the utilization of function.

He felt his mind begin to wander when suddenly his internal, spiritual instincts took over completely. From head to toe, the power washed all through him but not necessarily on just a physical level. It felt as though he had transcended mind and body, yet expanded both to become one singular form. His brain did not send messages to his nerves nor did his body tell his brain that it was functioning. He was now of one consciousness, and he was absorbing and processing on so many different levels that an ordinary person in a normal lucid state of mind would most likely have gone insane. If one had gazed upon him in that instant, they would have seen one big, oblong mass of luminous energy.

He tried in vain to retain some semblance of a reference point in order to maintain at least a small form of self-recognition. Though he had no control over what was happening, he slipped in and out of a vague awareness of what he normally was as a human being. Flashes of coherency that warned of danger, danced through his thoughts. Like a faraway voice; reminding him of a certain plane of ordinary reality. It was as though he were in an elevator that was constantly rushing him up and down through certain floors of awareness. He was only able to glimpse inside of each one, and only for an instant. He began to understand then, the construct of this particular power and how it was bound within the cliff. Limited yet limitless. He was paralyzed in the grips of that power, very much like a person who had encountered a stream of electricity and was caught helpless in its clutches. Then it was fading and his stare on the symbols rose higher and higher until it became stars and sky, and his eyes closed. He awoke seconds later to find that he was lying on his back in the soft sand, and blinked his eyes as he struggled to stand.

"Thank God I'm free of that!" he exclaimed aloud in an exhausted and frazzled voice.

Leaning up against a small rock on shaky legs, he stared at the glyphs in awe. If he dared to touch the cliff once more, would it happen again? Did it happen to him because of the level of awareness he was in or because of the cliff itself? Or could anyone touch those carvings and experience what he had, just then? Well, he knew he was not going to touch them again just to find out!

Gaining his composure, he turned away from the cliff and started to follow the wash up to see if it led to any more interesting locations. He hadn't gone far before he reached a very unusual area in which the wash narrowed then opened into a wide expanse of soft sand which had probably been a pool of water at one time. What grabbed his attention foremost, were the strange rock formations surrounding its edges. There were several rock ledges on the outer rim that formed tiers and looked very much like giant mushrooms, jutting out from the rest of the boulders and rock piles.

Approaching them carefully, he cautiously climbed onto one of the lower ledges. He immediately started walking and jumping from stone to stone going up and down the entire section, picking up his pace as he went along. It was very similar to running across bleachers at a stadium he thought, except that he was going in a steady circle. It seemed like a good way to burn off some of his pent up energy and kill some time as well.

After a while, he began to slow down and suddenly noticed many smooth, flat stones scattered along the edges as well, and some that had fallen in between. He stopped abruptly and picked one up for a closer look. They were miniature versions of the strange, flat boulders he'd just been traversing and he set one down right in the middle of the rock ledge that he currently stood upon. Out of the corner of his eye he spotted a couple more and proceeded to stack them one on top of the other, until he'd created a small rock sculpture about a foot and a half high.

After admiring his handy work, he began to grab more rocks and proceeded to the next ledge to build another. He realized that it was not very practical but it sure was fun! Just the act of creating something, silly though it may be, filled him with a renewed vigor and he fully immersed himself into his newest project.

Thirty minutes later, he stepped back to evaluate his artistry and beamed in awe at the numerous stone sentinels, which although

Chapter 15

were scattered, lined the entire area. They stood shining in the moonlight like tiny testaments to his altered and enlightened state of consciousness. Nodding his head in satisfaction he felt as though his task was complete.

"I wonder how the other fellas are getting along?" he muttered aloud to himself.

Chapter 16

After hiking for about half a mile, Nick surveyed his new surroundings with no small amount of bewilderment and anticipation.

"What am I doing out here?" he mumbled softly to himself.

Looking out into the distance as far as he could see, he slowly turned in a three hundred and sixty degree circle searching for some clue as to what direction to continue in. In its vast beauty the night desert all looked the same to him.

He began walking north but stopped and looked back after only about ten steps, completely unsure if he was headed in the right direction or not. Again he started walking, but back towards the way from whence he just came. Stopping after another ten paces he realized that he was right back where he had started. Frustrated, he sat down in the sand and entertained the notion of just waiting there before heading back to find the other guys to tell them that his efforts had ended in failure. As he tucked in his feet, he set his arms across his knees and put his head down, figuring that he might as well get comfortable; he could be there for a while. After a few deep relaxing breaths he started talking to himself.

"Why am I looking for a bush? What am I going to learn from a shrub? Sounds like something out of a Monty Python movie. You must find a shrubbery!" he announced in an exaggerated English accent to himself, cackling at the idea. "Feel ridiculous," he breathed, exhaling an exasperated sigh.

Glancing down, he saw a tiny little desert scrub and decided that he had nothing to lose.

"Hey there, little...bush. How are you?"

Waiting for a response, he gave another sigh.

"So how about this weather?"

After staring intently at the wild shrub for another twenty seconds and still receiving no response, he gave up. He closed his eyes and started taking deep breaths to calm himself, expecting that he may have to wait awhile, and soon began to feel more relaxed. While he found his breathing had become more calculated, he realized that his mind had also become more alert. An image of the desert landscape that he had just previously viewed suddenly appeared inside his head, only it was as if he had a more aerial viewpoint to it all. It was much like the feeling he had experienced earlier in the Jeep but much more intense and directed. Then he felt himself floating higher and higher and then suddenly he was moving forward.

Soaring over the desert terrain, his new found sight took him north through the desert plains which were riddled with tiny washes, rock clusters and vegetation. He soon reached a field cropped with various types of indigenous desert plants and abruptly ceased hovering. Among these, there was one in particular that stood out from all the rest. It was greener, larger, and located almost exactly in the middle of all the other plant life in that particular field. His focus faded back and he snapped to, suddenly realizing that he was up and walking through a small wash heading north through the canyon. Looking left to right, he wondered how long he had actually been walking but didn't stop or slow his pace to consider.

It wasn't long before he started to recognize the area that was in his vision, even at a ground level perspective, and veered over towards the spot that he believed would mark his destination. Hiking over a small hill and exiting the wash, he stopped dead in his tracks. He couldn't see it yet but he most certainly sensed it. Very slowly he advanced step by cautious step towards what he knew he would soon find, and a subtle tightness gripped his throat causing him to swallow hard. Five more paces and he stood before it, understanding beyond the shadow of a doubt that this was exactly what he was meant to find. There directly in front of him was a giant lush and thriving Datura inoxia plant. There was no mistaking what it was even though Nick knew almost nothing about indigenous desert plant life. Brad had pointed this particular plant out to him on several occasions while hiking. Even with only the moon's glow for light, he could see that it was extremely healthy and had a darker, richer, green color than the surrounding plants that were near it. Its branches had spread out in all directions, taking over the immediate area. Its large white flowers had strangely blossomed in the moonlight, and the plant adorned round spiked pods underneath its thin, viney stems. He found that he was transfixed by its beauty, and admired the healthy state of the plant as it seemed to have been rooted in a patch of soft, almost beach-like white sand.

Kneeling down, he found himself mentally paying tribute to this magnificent specimen and sensed that this plant was more than just alive. It was defying the climate and the elements. He found himself thinking that Brad was right after all, and must have received incredible insight from Jack to have known that he would end up here in this encounter. Such strange thoughts for Nick to have, analyzing a situation like this! But then again, he was under the influence of a serious psychedelic drug.

Suddenly his internal dialogue became distracted by something and he found his thoughts drifting back towards that marvelous plant. It seemed to be pulling his attention toward it like a magnet! Abandoning all of his pointless thoughts, he found his attention utterly devoted to the amazing life form that lay before him. He felt a strange beckoning as though the plant was trying to establish communication with him and suddenly he remembered Brad's directions.

"Hello," Nick said confidently. "I'm glad that I finally found you," he stated as if talking to an old friend that he hadn't seen in years.

This time he didn't feel silly in the least but instead relieved and excited as he addressed his newly discovered acquaintance. He in turn, received a message of greeting and contentment which enveloped him like the welcoming feeling of being invited into the house of a close relative. He felt safe and happy and sensed that the Datura plant was feeding off of his positive responses as well. As he stood there marveling at the plant, he found himself conversing with it; telling it of his adventures so far and of how he came to be precisely where he was now. It was almost as if he was talking to an animal; one of intelligence and understanding. Knowing that it couldn't respond verbally, it still somehow expressed wisdom and energy.

A slight wave of euphoria engulfed Nick all of a sudden and he noticed that his vision grew sharper and his senses became more alert. He knew then without a doubt that the Mescaline had ascended him even higher in his awareness.

Leaning in closer, he asked the plant out loud if he might have permission to respectively touch it and feel the texture of its leaves. He wanted as well, to admire the sweet smell of its beautifully long trumpet shaped flowers. Inviting waves of energy flowed forth from the plant, and once again he felt magnetically drawn in to its power. For that was exactly what Brad had called it; a power plant. How many times had they seen these plants growing wild and he had only briefly stopped to glimpse them without much interest? Only Brad had ever really given this plant its due and had always acknowledged it with respect. Well from now on; Nick would do the same!

Reaching in, he carefully ran his fingers over the wide, thick green leaves noticing how smooth the texture was and stared intently at the lightly colored detailed veins which ran throughout. Gently cradling a large white blossom in his hand, he bent closer to smell it and caught an amazing fragrance like the smell of honey and newly fallen rain. He found it hard to release the silky smooth petals that came to rest so delicately in his fingers and sensed that this was the most vulnerable part of the plant. Catching sight of a large round pod beneath a slender stem, he respectfully lowered the flower down as he reached in with his other hand to grasp the spiky, dark green orb, which brushed abrasively across his palm. He sensed great power there and looked on in awe at the beauty and perfection nature had instilled when creating every aspect of this plant.

His attention stirred and became redirected to the opposite end of the plant, so he stood up and walked around to the backside and knelt down to consider the source of this new calling. He stood again suddenly, and his breath caught in his chest as he fully viewed the immense foliage. In its entirety; its diameter ranged somewhere around ten feet in an almost perfect circle. It reminded him somewhat of an octopus with its thick, dense center and long reaching vine-like branches that were similar to tentacles. In a way he almost felt as though the entire plant was capable of enveloping him at any given moment, and dragging him down to the depths of the mysterious infinite.

Kneeling again, he returned his attention down toward a particular stem which just happened to be the one nearest him, and he noticed an imperfection. Impulsively reaching down he began to grab for a brownish object underneath the slim branch but stopped, abruptly realizing that he had not asked for permission. Again, so strange! How many times had he brushed plants aside, stepping on them and even cutting them down without giving it a second thought? Yet are plants not a form of life on this planet just like everything else that should be given consideration in the cycle of life and death?

Chapter 16

His contemplation was respected and the plant conveyed its approval as well as its permission in inspecting it further. In fact, the plant was even inviting him in with more subtle thoughts of intrigue and the possibility of learning some new secret. He curbed any further hesitation and in reaching down to lift the branch, he found another pod there. This particular pod was not green however but brown and withered, and it detached at the first touch of his fingers as they encompassed it. A sense of shock hit him hard then as if he'd just broken a piece of fine Chinaware but received a soothing message from the plant letting him know that he had done nothing wrong. The Datura plant wished him to have it as a gift. A gift of power; the plant's energy communicated.

Standing up straight, he sent a message of thanks and appreciation to the plant for the gift as well as the amazing experience. Holding the pod in his hand as if it were an egg, Nick began his hike back to the cave, beaming with energy and the satisfying feeling that he had more than fulfilled his task.

Chapter 17

Casually striding beneath the light of the moon, Jason picked his way easily through the desolate yet beautiful terrain. He was in no hurry as he marched confidently across the desert wilderness, and enjoyed the cool breeze that glided through his hair and filtered over his body. He knew that he had a specific purpose but didn't worry at all, having a new found faith in that, what was meant to happen; would happen. Just when it was supposed to. And why? Because he was starting to believe. He had experienced too much in such a short amount of time not to. He also suspected that he was far from done, as he considered this trip.

With the Peyote running strong in his blood stream he was rapidly gaining an admiration, if not an understanding, for things in this life working beyond his control. Sensing a deep introspection beginning to dominate his thoughts, he sat down on a flat comfortable boulder and allowed himself to be immersed.

Twenty four hours ago he was a different person; at least in the conventional ways of thinking and philosophy. The one thing that he knew about himself which he felt to be one of his greatest attributes; was his ability to recall his former self and adapt to intense situations such as these. He had only ever just needed a good jolt to remind him of everything which he had so easily forgotten or pushed aside throughout the years. Everyday life had an amazing way of

Chapter 17

shrouding the truth and all that was real. Or rather, the mundane human existence with its constant reasoning and logic did. Almost everyone connected to one another on a certain wavelength, and we all expected and believed in only certain things; mostly because we were programmed. It seemed as if this in itself was the core eliminator to almost any real spiritual enlightenment. However, if we were all in better tune with one another then wouldn't there be a likelier chance for one beautiful, singular consciousness? One real, true belief system that was tailor made for the individual, yet without limits, and for the sole honest purpose of each person on the planet? All of us connected and able to contribute our individual energy for the benefit of everyone collectively; worldwide. Probably not likely to happen as he was again realizing if not just remembering; that every single individual must discover their own destiny as well as true spiritual beliefs. Like in death; we may live our entire lives around others but we must all face death and the infinite alone. These were the thoughts that drifted through his mind, assaulting his logical human side and though they frightened him at times, they also bolstered and strengthened his beliefs.

He could almost recall a time when these revelations were an everyday part of his former life and he used them daily to the benefit of carrying on with his earthly existence. How the hell had he forgotten them? They used to help him understand so much as he acted out his life's routines, trying so hard at times just to make sense of it all. He had always been a deep thinker and he probably over analyzed much in his life, and to his own torment he might add, but it was what always kept him different from the rest. Different from all of those condemned souls who were content with everything convenient and materialistic in life. All those followers that just wanted to be like everyone else and be accepted. Of course there was no avoiding a fair amount of these things, especially in this age of technology and society, but it was perfectly clear to him at that moment just how dangerously mankind was pushing its own limits. Human beings had forsaken that which was most precious to their existence for the shallow and cheap distraction of something temporary and material.

No one could possibly know the price we all would pay but Jason decided then and there that he would extricate himself from the herd. His specific deviation and rebellion would be in a sense; his own tiny form of revolution. One in which he planned to nurture and feed with his spiritual side hoping that one day, even his last day; it would yield the fruits and rewards in which most could only dream of.

Man this is good Peyote! he thought to himself, grinning foolishly. Slowly drifting out of his contemplations, he looked up from the sandy desert floor and froze. No more than thirty feet away was a large coyote watching him intently. He lost all track of time as he just stared back at his inquisitive visitor for what could have been seconds or minutes. If it hadn't been so close then he surely would have believed that his eyes were playing tricks on him. It was looking at him head on and so motionless, that he almost believed it could have been a statue.

Rising ever so slowly, he stood straight up and saw the coyote shift its stance to the left, revealing the entire length of its body from nose to tail. Very slowly he sat back down, afraid of spooking this most interesting creature, and yet the animal remained perfectly still.

Fearing that more movement might scare it away, he tried to communicate with it telepathically. Projecting very non-threatening thoughts, he tried greeting his furry spectator but received no noticeable response.

After a few moments and more unsuccessful attempts he sighed, hanging his head down limply. Only then did he look back up to notice the animal had taken a few cautious steps backwards. Freezing in place, he continued to stare at the skittish creature and then noticed its eyes. Turning its head slightly, they caught the full moon's light causing them to glow eerily, yet curiously at him. The coyote had fur that seemed somewhat thicker than normal and retained a silhouette like that of a small wolf in Jason's eyes.

On a sudden whim, he decided to abruptly stand to see what reaction he might illicit, but the wild desert dweller still made no move whatsoever. He took a step forward; neither slowly nor cautiously, and still got no response from the animal. Ten more steps brought him so close that he was about fifteen feet away from the coyote and then it finally responded by skittering away a couple of feet. Jason stopped dead in his tracks fearing that he might have scared it away for good and held his breath, hoping to find otherwise. He didn't want to ruin his encounter, for he was intrigued with this animal way too much! The coyote continued to eye him curiously instead of suspiciously and so Jason stepped forth yet again. However, once he got too close the coyote turned and trotted away, stopping after a few steps to look back at him; beckoning.

What an unusual critter! he thought to himself. Then it dawned on him like an epiphany. His task! The reason that he was out there alone in that rugged expanse of desert! Brad's vague instructions echoed through his mind. He was to search for, then engage with his spirit animal. How had he not seen it sooner? Those distracting introspections brought on by the Mescaline had diverted him from his true course, but only momentarily. The coyote then began a slow purposeful trot away so Jason began to follow it.

Striding with purpose now he followed the animal, wondering where it would lead him and what he would soon discover.

Over windswept hills and gravelly washes he hiked, always the coyote just ahead and always glancing back at him to ensure that he was still following. The trail twisted and turned narrowly between boulders at times and across brush filled plains at others.

For the most part he was intrigued with the prospect of gaining some spiritual enlightenment, especially the knowledge which might be attained from a primitive source like a Spirit Animal. However in the corner of his mind he feared to be going too far, spiritually and physically, and tried to keep his bearings so that he wouldn't get too lost in either. The point itself was to get lost so that he might discover something that he had been missing, but that nagging voice…that rational side, was admonishing him to stay alert and be ready for a catastrophe. He wanted to abandon that side of himself altogether and immerse his being into the magic of what was happening, but his instincts would not fully allow that so he was caught somewhere in the middle; and it kept him more than a little on edge. The further he went, the harder he had to try to dismiss the warning bells which were sounding in his head and tightening his stomach.

After a while he just focused on the mysterious guide that led him, trusting that he had a purpose and believing that something amazing lay in store for him. He would receive a revelation from some higher calling. Yes! That had to be it! His fear must have stemmed from his rational mind trying to build up some sort of logical defense against the mystical wisdom that he was soon to discover. Just over the next hill, or maybe around the next bend! Something magical and spiritual, he kept telling himself.

All of a sudden, his mystic guide broke into a run up a steep hill and he lost sight of it as it went over the other side.

"This is it!" he whispered to himself excitedly, and he raced up the hill, losing his balance as he ran down the other side, falling to his knees in the dirt.

It didn't matter though, because he knew he had reached his destination! He could sense it!

Standing back up, he staggered a few feet ahead grinning from ear to ear. However, once he took in the full view of his surroundings, he gasped in shock as he saw that he had landed right in the middle of a large pack of vicious, snarling coyotes.

Remaining motionless, the smile completely disappeared from his lips. Slowly turning his head left to right, he could see that he

Chapter 17

was in the midst of at least fifteen to twenty very ravenous coyotes, all growling at him with hunger.

"Ohhh shit," he whispered almost breathless.

Jason wondered how it all could have gone so terribly wrong, when he noticed out of the corner of his eye his original guide. He saw now that it was a female and although large for her gender, she was dwarfed in comparison to the angry males of this very malicious looking pack. She stood behind two of them with what he swore to be a smirk on her face, and it suddenly became clear to him. This wild canine had not been guiding him and hadn't led him here for enlightenment. She had set him up to become their dinner.

Somehow his mind instantaneously flashed back to stories that he had heard about female coyotes leading domesticated male dogs that were hoping to mate, out into the wild, only to be set upon and eaten by other coyotes. Never had he heard of a case involving humans though, for coyotes usually avoided all contact with people as that seemed part of their nature and instinct. These Hell Hounds however, obviously didn't follow that program and had no fear of man; especially one who was stupid enough to allow himself to be caught helpless out in the middle of nowhere!

Snapping back to reality, he could actually feel the menacing vibrations all around him and the atmosphere was so thick with malevolence that you could cut it with a knife. That feeling of awakening to find that you are actually in a nightmare situation assaulted his senses and terror gripped him like the very specter of death itself.

His panic was his only saving grace however, for as the first crazed, slavering beast leaped from atop a flat boulder with jaws agape for his throat, he reacted and ducked beneath the airborne demon. Rushing forward he actually caught the two directly ahead by surprise and they parted for him like the Red Sea. He was all motion now, leaving any thoughts of fear behind, as he raced away as fast as his legs and feet could transport him. He had no idea how he could possibly outrun a pack of vicious, wild canines and knew that he didn't even have time to contemplate that right now. So he ran for his life; the devil dogs yipping at his very heels.

Barreling through large desert sage and scrambling over rocks he raced, using every ounce of strength he had, and pushed his lungs until they felt like they were about to collapse. Finally gaining a bit of a lead, he spotted a large group of boulders and sprinted towards them with everything he had left, for he could feel the fierce, hysterical beasts closing in on him.

Covering the last stretch of ground, he ran up the side of a slanted rock which connected to a large cluster of other granite boulders. Praying that the murderous animals couldn't climb as well as he could, he hoped to catch at least a brief respite so that he might find his breath and reassess the situation.

Gaining the high ground and climbing up a jutting outcrop on one of the taller boulders, he looked down anxiously to ensure that he was indeed safe for now. Unfortunately, he wasn't. Doubled over with his hands on his knees and gulping large amounts of air, he sucked in a huge gasping breath as he saw two coyotes with ridiculously good climbing skills, clambering up the angled ledge with hunger and murderous intent written all over their furry faces.

Not waiting to find out whether they could jump the distance to his rock or not, he quickly scanned his surroundings, frantically searching for some escape. Then he thought he found it. Pushing aside the branches of a large, scraggly bush growing straight out of the rock, he saw what looked like an entrance to a tiny cave or cubbyhole. A quick look back told him that the coyotes couldn't see him, and he practically dove through the bush and into the dark hole. As he stumbled in he saw that it widened out into a spacious little area and crouching down against a rock, he held his breath. He listened anxiously to the scuffling sounds of the determined little monsters

Chapter 17

searching just outside for him. He could hear them sniffing around and brushing by the shrub that guarded the secret entrance way. He prayed that they wouldn't catch his scent and rush in on him because he knew that there would be no place left to run. Outside the sounds of yipping and growling reached an almost unbearable pitch. Feeling around, he grabbed a sizable rock to throw, seeing as how in his brilliance he had not brought along a weapon of any kind for this trip.

Glancing all about and frantically looking for any other means of escape; he found nothing. Tiny beams of moonlight streamed down from above, filtering throughout the cave, showing no reprieves. He knew that it wouldn't be much longer before those terrible hunters stormed in and surrounded him and all he could hear now was the sound of his own heart beating loudly, fearfully. The incessant growling was so close now that he almost thought it was coming from inside the small cave.

His heart then literally stopped beating for a second and caught in his throat as he spotted two glowing, yellow eyes staring hatefully at him from the far end of the enclosure. He remained frozen as they slowly began to float over towards him and he whispered, "God, they've gotten in," when he suddenly realized the horrible truth of the situation. Emitting a low growl and stalking straight up to him was a large, angry mountain lion. Too paralyzed to react, he crouched motionless as the beast hissed at him and swiped a huge paw right towards his face.

Jumping back at the last possible fraction of a second was all that saved him from razor sharp claws tearing into the side of his head. He could feel the whoosh of air from the powerful swing as he fell over backwards. Luckily, he somehow flipped around halfway before hitting the ground and scrambled back out of the den with speed that he had not thought possible for a human being.

Crashing back out through the bush and breaking into a fast climb, he saw a coyote standing directly ahead, blocking his way.

When the canine caught sight of him it remembered his last little ploy and instead of moving aside, it stood its ground and crouched down bracing itself for a leap again at his throat. Jason was willing to take his chances and didn't slow even for a second. He rushed forward and to his horror tripped, his foot catching in a crevice taking him down fast with his already quickened momentum.

While falling forward, he looked up briefly expecting to see a triumphant snarl on the feral animal's face as it went in for the kill but instead saw a look of terror. Then he felt it. Something brushing over the top of him, knocking him even harder, flat against the rock and he saw the coyote overtaken by a flash of tan fur and muscle. Another coyote close by, failed to react in time and suffered terrible consequences. The cougar, never even slowing down, twisted its body sideways and brought a powerful arm up to rake the by-standing coyote in the face. The dog tumbled backward and off the rock and he saw the puma divert its attention back to the first canine; shredding its neck with its strong jaws in a killing move. But it wasn't done yet. Bounding down from the boulders, it leaped amidst the pack on the ground and proceeded to inflict devastation upon the remaining members of the group; leaving a trail of blood and fur in its deadly wake. While a few did stand their ground, and even a few attacked, most scurried off into the desert as fast and as far as their little legs could take them.

Jason watched it all as if in a trance and might have even become the last victim if not for a large moth. It fluttered in his face just then, distracting him from the horrendous scene and bringing him back to a more alert state of awareness. Swatting at the moth reflexively, he slowly stood and then began to carefully climb up and over the other side of the small mountain. He could only pray that the cougar would still be too busy with the coyotes to notice him sneaking away. Escaping to the sounds of growling and yelping, he found his feet again on the desert floor and took off running like a man in an Olympic foot race.

Steering into a large wash, he ran for what seemed like an eternity. Just as his lungs felt likely to burst, he stopped to listen for any signs of pursuit. Hearing none, he slumped down into the sand with his back against the edge of the wash, and tried to relax. He found that he was thoroughly disoriented and exhausted from everything that he had experienced in just the last few minutes.

"I can't believe that just happened!" he breathed aloud to himself.

It was definitely the closest he'd ever come to death and the psychological toll from it all, was finally starting to manifest itself into his altered state of mind. On the one hand; he was happy just to be alive. But on the other hand; he wondered why something so horrifying had to happen to him. Especially at that particular point in time! He had expected an enchanting version of Heaven and instead received a frightening reality of a brief Hell.

His brain began producing thoughts of paranoia, along with feelings of fear and negativity. He imagined the effects that this way of thinking would have on him psychologically, being that his traumatic experience was so recent, and he became far too disheveled. He could sense that he was going down a dark road but couldn't restore himself back to his prior state. The adrenaline was still pumping through his veins and his lungs were burning from too much physical exertion and lack of oxygen.

With his eyes darting left to right, he failed to see the flittering object hovering right in front of his face and only noticed it when it bopped him on the nose. Waving his hand annoyingly, he strained his eyes to see what newest assailant had found him and saw another moth flying back and forth about a foot away. Man, the moths are really out for me tonight! he thought to himself, momentarily distracted. Then upon closer inspection he discovered something amazing.

He had noticed earlier, albeit very briefly, that the first moth he'd seen had an interesting wing coloration. Though it was but a quick glimpse, he saw two large dark brown dots in the middle of its pale, white wings as well as the same brown coloration lining its wing's edges. Twice this type of moth had distracted him and both times its distractions had really saved him. Instinctively reaching out his hand, the moth immediately landed on his index finger, tickling him with its fuzzy little body. Same type of moth, or same moth? he wondered. It was rather large; probably about the size of a Monarch butterfly, but how could it have found him here? He was certain that he must have run at least a mile away from that violent, dangerous scene and as fast as he could, to boot. Could this little moth somehow have followed him? He wanted to shrug that thought away but as he looked into the large black orbs of his tiny little friend he couldn't help but feel something stir inside of him. Like a cross between a long lost recollection and a new found revelation.

He remained transfixed by the moth's steady gaze and the continual movement of its small, fuzzy antennae, waving up and down hypnotically. A wave of severe drowsiness overtook him then, most likely due to his recent ordeal, and his shoulders slumped along with his head down against his chest. And then...nothingness. Surrounded in darkness, he was only vaguely aware that he even existed. Then an image flashed by. That feeling of being somewhere in between asleep and awake, as well as the sensation of floating, encompassed his being.

Again that fleeting image like a stream of random light, crossed through his limited field of vision. Trying his hardest to focus on the source of the fluctuating light, it suddenly froze; creating an arcing beam of luminescence directly in front of his face. He found it indescribably beautiful and felt his thoughts and energy drawn toward it as though a huge part of him was being absorbed into the anomaly. He had a keen sense of understanding growing from within and found that his attention was honed to the sharpness of a razors edge. Suddenly, inside his mind he asked a question; What do I need to know? Immediately he was encapsulated inside a framework in which millions of thoughts along with limitless knowledge assaulted him on every possible level. Each new epiphany and idea that penetrated his protective cocoon seemed to be ingraining itself into his brain, and even every fiber of his being, almost instantaneously. Every conceivable answer to his question was formulated into pertinent knowledge which he then soaked up like a limitless sponge in an ocean of information.

But it was too much. The intensity was overwhelming him and his reaction became one of panic. Mentally, he tried retracting his initial inquiry because he realized that it was far too broad in terms of a question and with far too many possibilities for a response.

Everything came to an immediate halt and he knew peace within his mind once again. Sensing that he was dealing with a powerful entity of some sort, he decided to be more careful and specific with his next question. Why is this amazing phenomenon happening to me right now? The question emanated from his thoughts and floated out into the unknown.

It was not a voice that answered him, rather a wave of information and understanding; one which his mind easily processed and comprehended on more levels than he could ever rationally decipher.

The source that the knowledge was radiating from conveyed to him many thoughts at once and yet he was able to follow an appropriate pattern that guided him through the general message. This powerful beacon of energy and information introduced to him an understanding of what was happening, as well as what had already happened in order to help lead him up to this most crucial event. First; arriving in the desert, followed by the consumption of the Peyote. Then, his experiences involving the various power places he had encountered. Lastly; the most recent situation involving the trickery of the devious coyote and the confrontation with the puma.

He had shifted levels of awareness several times and for a specific purpose; to arrive at this particular state of attention and gain this precious insight. The last scenario involving the coyotes and the mountain lion were specifically meant to be traumatic in order to jolt his core being and heighten his state of awareness to a level in which he would become an open vessel. A vessel in which knowledge could be freely passed and appreciated, as well as kept safe and intact from the destruction of his rational mind.

A person in a sober state of ordinary reality would have refused or dismissed such thoughts and messages as madness. Jason however, saw now how he could distinguish the two but that was due only to his current heightened awareness.

His satisfaction with such an explanation was in itself a monumental achievement, as he knew now that the logical side of his brain had surrendered its defenses. He was now ready for enlightenment. After his unexpected brush with Hell, his expected version of Heaven had finally arrived! He knew that he was fully able to let go now, so he did.

He suddenly felt as if he was being swallowed into the vacuum of an endless void; everything compressing within and without him. Then he was released, and became freer than he'd ever felt in his life! It was as if he'd eaten all the fruit from the Tree of Knowledge, and had become the tree itself! There was really no describable way to righteously interpret just what he had evolved into in that instant, so he didn't bother to try. To even attempt to, would demean the entire experience and he knew that he had no time to waste in doing that. So he just opened himself completely and received willingly. Trusting in the forces that be, to instill him with the wisdom that he had been meant to attain.

Chapter 17

Still hypnotized by the luminous arc, he followed every fluctuating movement as it slowly swayed from side to side; shimmering all the while. Time had lost all meaning and appropriately so. Then the luminescent light and the weightless sensation began to deplete and he felt a heavy darkness creep in along with the fading of the arc, which grew smaller and less bright.

The realization of being grounded had settled in, and with heavy lids he opened his eyes. The moth was still perched upon his thumb and forefinger and he immediately noticed the striking and naturally artistic patterns that were evident along the edges of its wings. For only a moment was he able to stare dumbfounded before the insect took flight, lifting its chubby, furry little body, until it traveled higher and higher into the night sky, finally disappearing from view. Very mechanically, Jason stood up and began the hike back to his friends in a state of peaceful bliss and contentment.

All three of them arrived at the exact area that they had left from at virtually the same time. The relief was evident on their faces when they spotted each other, and as they closed the distance, they greeted one another earnestly. Silently hiking back down to their sacred dwelling they found Jack waiting for them.

"Jack! It's good to see you!" Brad said genuinely. "How long have you been here waiting for us?"

"Exactly long enough," Jack answered confidently. "Terry has gone out exploring and will be back around dawn I expect."

"Terry!" They all said in stereo.

"I had forgotten all about him!" Brad remarked, with echoes of "So did I" coming from the other two.

Jack looked at all three of them curiously, then nodded his head. "Did you all fulfill your tasks?" he asked, already figuring he knew the answer.

"And then some," Jason mumbled under his breath.

"Then you three should gather to discuss it. You can relax down by the water while the sun rises."

"Water?" Nick and Jason both asked as one.

"Oh yeah! You guys have gotta see this!" Brad said excitedly. "Jack...how much longer before sun up?"

"About half an hour," he replied. "Head down to the stream now and I will meet you there shortly."

Without another word, Brad led them down to the pool where he heard a chorus of "oohs" and "ahs" as the boys caught the sparkle of the water glistening from the last of the early morning moonlight. Taking off their hiking boots and rolling up their pants, they sat down and dipped their toes in, letting out sighs and groans of relief. The cool, clear water rippled against their legs and soothed their aching feet, bringing a relaxed feeling of pleasure.

"Man, have I got a story for you guys!" Jason said, leaning his head back and enjoying every bit of the well earned respite.

"So do I!" Nick added, and Brad nodded his head in agreement before commenting.

"And I, as well, but let's wait for Jack so that he can hear it all as we tell it."

"Jack is already here," came a voice from a ledge about ten feet away and up above them.

Slightly startled, they all flinched then relaxed again as Jack said, "Brad...you will speak first."

Upon Jack's declaration, Nick and Jason both turned to Brad expectantly. Taking a deep breath then exhaling it slowly, Brad began to recount his experience; all the while, the boys listened intently with undivided attention.

They reacted with awe and recognition as Brad described the many thoughts and emotions he had encountered. When he was done, a nod from Jack to Jason began a whole new tale of adventure and intrigue. More of the same reactions were seen and heard as he finished, albeit a bit more horrified in places, and finally Nick gave his testimony as to what he'd witnessed. Through it all, Jack just watched and listened stone-faced. Then, at the end of Nick's recounting, a spectacular thing happened.

They had noticed the sky beginning to grow lighter with the approach of dawn but had kept their focus solely on one another's storytelling. They all looked up then suddenly and gasped at the gorgeous event transpiring all around them. The sun crept up over the eastern horizon and set the water to glitter like newly polished diamonds. In turn they followed the light to its ascent over the entire valley, like a curtain being lifted to reveal the desert dawn in all of its splendid glory. It was a once in a lifetime experience, especially to be observed under their altered conditions.

Gazing all about, they basked in the beauty of the marvelous desert awakening. Jack finally broke the tranquility by quietly recommending that they retire to the cave for some much needed sleep. At the mention of sleep, they all immediately began yawning as if merely the suggestion could send them off into slumber. As they gathered their things and went inside, Jack pulled Brad aside at the last minute and ushered him over to the back of the cave. Once alone, Jack began talking.

"Man! I can't believe all of that actually happened to you guys! Are you sure you're not just trippin' really hard?"

"No way Jack. It happened. At least to me. I can't speak for the other guys, but I know what I saw and felt."

Studying him for a moment, Jack just shook his head then nodded.

"Wow. Well, I guess it's all working out the way you planned then, yes?"

Upon mentioning his former scheme, Brad began to get a little nervous. He had gotten so swept up in his trip that he had forgotten all about his little deception. And what about Terry? He still wasn't back yet and Brad had momentarily forgotten all about their strange new friend.

"Don't worry about Terry," Jack said, seeming to read his mind. "I found him napping when I came in and he awoke and said he was going to go hike around and that he'd be back soon."

Brad looked at Jack then nodded his head.

"I think I'll go get a little bit of shuteye, if that's okay?"

"Go right ahead sir. I'll keep watch," Jack replied briskly. "And when you wake up, I've got a surprise to show you!"

Jack gave him a wink then walked down toward the direction of the pool. By the time Brad had reached the inside of the cave he saw Nick and Jason both curled up against the rock wall, sleeping in the soft sand contentedly. He picked up his backpack, and using it as a pillow, joined his friends in slumber.

Chapter 18

As he opened his eyes, filtered light trickled in causing him to squint slightly, and his eyelids fluttered rapidly as he tried to adjust. The first thing he noticed was that he was in the cave alone but he knew that the boys couldn't be far, as they'd left their backpacks behind. Taking a moment to drink some bottled water and splash some on his face, he tried to gather his wits, still heavily feeling the effects of the Mescaline.

The first waking thoughts that entered his mind were negative. What am I doing here? he contemplated. I've deceived my friends into joining me out in the middle of this desert, and for what? What do I really hope to get out of all this? He sighed, his heart feeling heavy at the moment. Just then, Terry strolled into the cave like he owned it and caught sight of Brad.

"Hey, how's it goin' man?" he asked, trying to make conversation.

For some strange reason, Terry's mere presence had an annoying effect on Brad.

"Good, just waking up. How have you been? We didn't see you after we left last night."

"Ah, pretty good. I went out looking around, after you guys went on your mission, and when I got back this morning you all were crashed out. How was the hike for you guys?"

At the mention of his adventure just hours earlier, Brad began to smile helplessly.

"It was amazing! I discovered something so..." his voice trailed off as he tried in vain to recollect.

"Sooo...what?" Terry prompted him.

"I'm having a hard time remembering all of a sudden. I found something really important but I can't recall what it was."

"If it was important, you'll remember it."

In just a few moments time, Brad went from feeling annoyed with Terry; to being comforted by his company. Thinking about that, he stared at Terry for a long moment while Terry just looked down at the ground shifting his feet. It was interesting how this stranger could seem so familiar at times and unknown at others. Not wanting to make him feel uncomfortable, he kept the conversation going.

"So where are the other fellas at?" Brad asked.

"Oh...they're down there at the stream, taking a little dip. They told me to come check on you to see if you were awake, and to tell you to go down there."

"Okay," Brad said, standing up and grabbing some granola bars out of his pack. "Let's go."

Once down at the pool, another smile immediately crept across his lips as he spotted his two friends, splashing and playing like two happy porpoises.

"Hey! Look who's awake!" Jason shouted, ducking his head under the water and popping back up again.

"Come on in for a swim!" Nick said, chiming in.

"You don't have to tell me twice!" Brad exclaimed cheerfully, as he stripped down to his boxers and cannonballed in.

Nick and Jason immediately started splashing him and they all created a loud watery raucous, allowing themselves to feel like kids again.

"Hey, Terry! You comin' in?" Brad asked playfully.

Chapter 18

"Aw, we already asked him a bunch of times but he's too scared!" Jason interjected loudly over the sound of splashing water.

"Nah, I'm cool man. You guys have fun." Terry said, confirming Jason's comment.

"Where's Jack? Gone again?" Brad inquired.

"Yeah, he left as soon as Terry came back this morning. Said he'd meet us at the Jeep in a little while. He told us what trail to follow that will lead us right back to it," Jason informed him.

"Okay..." Brad replied, leaving an unanswered thought hanging in the air.

He looked to Terry for some sort of explanation but Terry just shrugged in response. Brad swam over to where he had set his breakfast down and quickly ate both granola bars. He felt a real sense of hunger due to the small amount of food he'd had in the last twenty four hours. He turned around to ask Terry another question only to find him heading back to the cave again.

"What time do you think it is?" Brad asked the boys, his question directed towards either one of them.

"It's probably about ten thirty by now," Jason answered while dunking Nick's head under the water.

"You mean we've only slept about four hours?"

"I guess," he replied, receiving a mouth full of water as Nick got him back.

"What do you suppose Terry is up to right now?" Brad asked curiously.

Nick put his thumb and forefinger together and then to his lips making the universal sign for a person smoking a Joint. Then he and Jason both started giggling as they continued on with their water wrestling match. For an instant Brad felt that irritable feeling again but shook it off as two sets of arms reached in to grab him, dragging him into the deeper part of the pool to continue the shenanigans.

About half an hour later, the boys were all feeling refreshed, although still quite altered, and they packed up and hit the trail that Jack had marked out for them. Being daylight now, they were all able to take in the full view of the fantastic scenery that surrounded them in every direction.

There were more red rock cliffs; standing time worn yet majestic, along with amazing cloud formations drifting overhead. The desert foliage was sparse and the landscape turned to one of mostly rusty orange and red colored rock, which came up from the earth seemingly everywhere.

Then after a short time they spotted more tall, red cliffs out in the distance. Just a few at first, then more and more stretching out to the horizon. Terry seemed to be having a hard time through a lot of it though, and tripped or slid more than once, bringing doubtful and suspicious glances from all the boys. He also started complaining which in a roundabout way caused them to start complaining. What initially began as a pleasant hike turned into them listening to Terry's whining and bracing for his next act of clumsiness.

"Are you okay man?" Jason asked him skeptically at one point.

"Yeah, why?" Terry questioned him back.

"It's just that I thought you said you were good at hiking and knew this area?"

"Oh…well, uh…maybe not this exact area, but I have hiked around these mountains before. You know, I think it might be my shoes too, man."

Nick just rolled his eyes and Jason gave Brad a "Yeah, I'm sure that must be it" look of sarcasm, and then let the subject drop. Terry's poor balance and hiking skills shouldn't have been much of a concern for the other three except that one of the biggest problems was; that whenever they tried to help him up after a fall or keep him from stumbling, he almost always ended up taking that person down to the ground with him. Strange, Brad thought. He hadn't remembered him being that clumsy before. Maybe he was just really high. Who knows?

Continuing on, they eventually spotted the Jeep and soon all of them raced the last quarter mile to see who could get there first. Amazingly enough, Terry took the lead and beat them all! As they stood around huffing and puffing, Terry just sat down calmly and waited for them to regain their composure.

"I can't believe it! How in the hell did you pull that off?" Jason asked, between breaths.

"I don't know man," Terry said smiling slyly. "I guess I just found my inner-coordination!"

Looking over to Nick, Brad could see him smirking as well, and they all broke into heartfelt laughter.

"Yeah. That...or we just got hustled!" Jason shouted back jokingly.

The laughter died immediately though as Jack came walking up with a look of displeasure on his face.

"I see you've all made it back," he observed.

He looked each of them over in turn and when he got to Terry he barely gave him a glance, and a distasteful one at that.

"Take a few minutes to rest and pack some food and water. We head out to our next destination soon."

With that, he stalked off leaving them all looking to one another bewildered.

"Mr. Personality, huh?" Jason remarked quietly, once Jack was some distance away.

"Well, I didn't hire him for his personality. I hired him to guide us where we need to go and so far I'd say that he's done alright."

"Yeah, that's true," Nick murmured.

"I know," Jason admitted. "He's just so stern all the time. I wish he'd lighten up."

At that, Brad almost broke out into laughter. If they only knew! The real Jack had one of the most easy going and ridiculous personalities that Brad had ever known!

"Yeah, I hear ya," Brad conceded, trying his hardest to keep a straight face. "Why don't you guys get some water and snacks ready? I think I'll go talk to Jack real quick."

Striding off after Jack, he looked back once more to make sure that the boys were indeed packing some things and then he took off in the same direction that he had just seen Jack heading. After rounding a boulder out of sight of the boys, he stopped in his tracks.

"Where you goin' city boy?" came a voice behind him and as he turned he saw Jack standing there with what looked almost like a piece of wheat hanging out of his mouth. Brad snickered in spite of himself and stared at Jack as he shook his head.

"Man, you are too much!"

"Is that a good thing or a bad thing?" Jack asked, the grin never leaving his face.

"I'll tell you when I figure that out! Hey Jack, you've got to ease up just a bit. You're starting to make the fellas too nervous. You're coming across a little..." Jack cocked his head slightly to the side and raised his eyebrows waiting for Brad's inevitable comment, "strict, to put it politely."

"I thought that's what you wanted!" Jack whined. "You know, Shaman...Medicine Man? By all accounts they were meant to be taken seriously, ya know?"

"Yeah, I know. I'm just sayin'...maybe show a little more charisma. More charm."

"By Jove old chap, I can be as charming as a prince if need be," Jack countered with a perfect English accent. "And don't forget...I still have friends that could make an appearance tonight around the campfire if you want. Just give me the word," he added, reminding Brad for about the third time.

Chapter 18

"Okay...not that charming, and God no! I don't want anyone to ruin my game plan! I don't know how the guys would react. To tell you the truth, I myself keep going in and out of an intense Mescaline high and sometimes almost can't tell night from day."

At the mention of his own condition, he happened to look up at the sky and witnessed a fantastic spectacle involving the puffy gray and white Cumulonimbus clouds overhead. One in particular looked just like the face of a Greek God; Zeus himself perhaps, and it seemed to be staring right down at him in silent judgment.

His jaw must have been hanging wide open for he heard Jack whisper, "What do you see up there? Hee! Hee!"

"Do you see that...?" Brad asked, his voice trailing off.

"See what?" Jack replied, answering his question with a question, trying to contain his laughter.

"Never mind."

"Hey man, you're not trippin' out on me are you?" Jack said with a playful, yet doubtful look on his face.

Brad looked over at him and seriously replied, "Maybe."

Then they both erupted into laughter.

"It's just that those clouds..." And again, Brad spaced off into the distance.

"How about those clouds over there?" Jack asked, pointing south with a gesture of his chin, indicating a mass of dark clouds which looked to be about ten miles away. "Those look like rain clouds to me, don't ya think?"

Gazing off in the direction Jack had just pointed to, Brad concluded that he was probably correct and started to worry.

"Aw, Dammit! I checked the forecast for this weekend and it didn't call for rain in this area!"

"Since when can the Weatherman predict the weather, let alone the future?"

Brad looked at Jack as if he had just fallen off a turnip truck.

"What?"

"Back to the Future! You've never seen that movie? Remember when Marty's about to go back to his own time in the future in the Delorean and he has to use the lightning that strikes the clock tower? Remember? Marty? Doc? Oh...never mind. I'm a huge movie guy."

"I see," Brad said somewhat snidely. "So are we gonna get rained on or what?"

"Yes! But it will be awesome, trust me! This next place is hidden and I almost forgot about it because I've only been there once, and that was years ago, but I'm sure that I can find it again."

"How far is it and what's there?"

"It's about three miles from here and I wouldn't want to ruin the surprise by telling you!" Jack said with a wink. "So...you wanna check to see if the boys are ready, and then we'll go?"

"Okay. I'll be right back, Jack." Brad turned and started away, then looked back to ask Jack something else and found him already gone. "He's getting too good at this," Brad said with a chuckle and went back to see the boys.

Very soon after, the men were marching south; Nick carrying a backpack with water and snacks as well as a knife through the insistence of Jason.

Jack spearheaded the hike from the front while a shy and nervous Terry brought up the rear. Having watched Terry for a while now, Brad clearly saw the anxious sidelong glances that Terry gave Jack every so often. Brad figured that there was a missing piece to the puzzle somewhere and wondered if it would ever come to light.

Was bringing Terry along a mistake? After all, he hadn't cleared that with Jack. In a way, Jack really was responsible for all of them and Brad had assured Jack that his influence on the other two was secure as far as getting them to go along with this trip. But Terry was a bit of a wild card. No one really knew anything about him and Brad had already caught him in more than one lie. Yet, there was definitely

Chapter 18

something about him. At times he was unbelievably frustrating and unstable but at other times he was well grounded and thoughtful, and had surprised them all. They had all found themselves relating to him in some form or another and could be quite comfortable around him as if they'd always known him. Did they know him from their past somehow? He was a mystery, no doubt about it.

Looking back at Nick and Jason, he saw that they seemed to be in really good spirits; chatting with each other and throwing the occasional comment back to Terry as well. Content with that, Brad gazed out at the horizon and towards their soon to be next destination.

All the while though, Brad kept looking up to the clouds. He saw a multitude of different unique shapes and formations and always there were the faces in the clouds. Almost like statues in their clarity; the visages of Greek Gods with their masked features, casting down judgment and overseeing their journey.

About thirty minutes later, they arrived at a rocky escarpment with more red cliffs and as they approached it they began to feel a definite energy radiating all around it. A very old and strong form of energy. They all slowed their pace a little and looked to Jack with questioning expressions on their faces.

Never even slowing, Jack drove forward purposefully as they twisted their way through the valley and into a narrow rocky ravine. They arrived in a sandy little wash enclosed on both sides by more of the red rock formations that they'd seen earlier, and ended smack dab into a cliff wall. Once stopped, they all looked around and at each other searching for a hint of some sign of what was to come next. Jack stood there patiently watching them, gauging their reactions.

"Now, what?" Jason asked through gritted teeth, looking to Brad for some sort of an explanation.

The sky had begun to grow dark and a slight feeling of tension had crept its way into their midst.

"This place is an extremely well kept and guarded secret, and it's been that way for hundreds of years. It's with enormous privilege that you are allowed to be here today to witness this event." Jack's tone was almost like that of a Carnival Barker as he addressed them all.

"What are we supposed to see here Jack?" Brad asked skeptically.

"Not right here!" Jack answered enthusiastically. "Observe..."

As Jack stepped aside, the boys noticed a tiny cleft that nature had cut directly into the cliff; no wider than a person.

"This is a secret entrance. The only entrance actually, to where we're going. It will be a tight squeeze most of the way there but the rewards will be great." Brad looked on at Jack with admiration, for he had definitely lightened his tone and had even added a level of mystery and intrigue to their newest adventure. "Follow me!" Jack said cheerfully, and twisting sideways he slid into the crevice slightly scraping his body as he went.

Brad went next, then Jason with Nick and Terry at the end. Once past the entrance it widened out a bit and all of them were able to walk forth without any difficulty.

While marching along, Brad couldn't help but admire nature's profound construction in designing the area. Swirls of tan and red, decorated the walls of the tight spaced cliffs in fantastic patterns much like the cliffs of the Grand Canyon or mesas in Red Rock Arizona; only much more intricate. The floor of the narrow defile was mostly soft white sand but occasionally turned into smooth, dark grayish, blue colored bedrock at times.

Every so often, Brad looked up to catch a glimpse of the darkening sky overhead and there were the clouds again. He saw one that resembled the perfect image of a flying dragon and stumbled, almost falling, while admiring its unusually clear caricature. He looked back once to see the rest of the guys all marching along with purpose, their faces the picture of determination. The only sounds being that of their footsteps echoing off the canyon walls.

Chapter 18

More than a few times they were forced to physically squeeze their bodies through tight spaces and had to slow down and wait on one another. Then the canyon suddenly widened and the wash ended at a large boulder that was wedged into the sides of the narrow cliff walls. It completely blocked their way except for a small three foot space in the damp sand beneath it. Without hesitation, Jack got down in the dirt and wriggled his way under the boulder while the boys just stared at one another with uncertainty.

All was silent until they heard Jack's voice call out from the other side, "Well, what are you waiting for?"

After a moment's pause, Brad took the initiative and got down on his belly, slowly worming his way through. He could hear the others right behind him crunching and sliding atop the gravelly sand, so he kept on slithering the fifteen feet or so to get to the other side of their cumbersome obstacle.

Reaching the end, Brad pulled himself slowly to his feet and discovered that he now stood at the threshold of what looked like a large, naturally formed rock amphitheater. His gaze stopped right in the center however, for there ahead of him was a cluster of huge green saguaro cacti. He spotted Jack at the far end of the circular structure leaning against the cliff with a grin that stretched from ear to ear. The others came out one by one, and then stood awestruck by this newest wonder and absolute miracle of nature.

As they walked around the edges and passed by the enormous cacti, they got an even better understanding of just how gigantic they were; for they dwarfed even the largest saguaros that they'd ever seen. Jack motioned for them to quickly join him underneath a large ledge at the opposite end of the entrance and they complied quickly as his gestures seemed quite urgent.

"Everyone come over here," he said, ushering them all to be seated on what looked like a natural rock bench. "You are all going to witness an event that has rarely been seen by anyone other than

Sorcerers or men of power. This place is the most sacred area in this region of the desert and has been kept from prying eyes ever since its creation. Certain ancient Toltec sorcerers that once made their pilgrimage from central Mexico discovered this amazing enclosure and it's said that the spirits not only guided them here, but also in what to create."

Again Brad marveled at Jack's new disposition, sounding more now like an optimistic tour guide than a serious, hardened Medicine Man.

"You've obviously noticed the gigantic saguaro cacti protruding from the ground here in the center of this rocky arena, but look more closely at the ground. It is formed entirely out of the cliffs and bedrock except for the naturally cut holes in which the cacti grow from, that contain sand and rich clay desert earth. Also note the slanted formation of this amphitheater, as the rock angles upward from the ground at a precise degree and in a perfect circle. There is a reason for all of this as you will soon see, and hopefully appreciate, what many others will never have the chance to witness."

Brad noticed everyone's eyes were glued to Jack now as he delivered his amazing and insightful speech. All of them watched him intently, hanging on his every word.

"No one can say exactly when the Ancients planted these saguaros, but we know that it was hundreds of years ago. Come and look closer at the one in the very center."

Jack motioned for them to follow him down near the edge of the cluster and they all audibly gasped, for where they had all thought there to be at least three saguaros growing closely together in the middle; it was actually only one.

To say that the cactus was gigantic, fell drastically short of a description. The thickest part of its trunk probably measured around eight to ten feet in diameter, and it was at least thirty five feet tall. By Brad's account, it had to be the largest in the world. It

Chapter 18

had several thick branches shooting out in different directions with clusters of tiny unopened flower buds at the tips of each. The other saguaros were very healthy, without so much as a spot of brown in any of them, but this unprecedented mammoth exuded amazing vitality and seemed bursting with life. Brad had been to Redwood forests before while vacationing up north, and had seen the amazing spectacle of the hundreds of gigantic trees; with some even big enough to drive a car through, but that experience was nothing like this. He had seen pictures before his trip, therefore knew that trees could get that large. He had no idea that anything like this could have ever existed. Back when he lived in the high desert, there were a few huge saguaros growing in front of his old barber shop, but even their size seemed only moderate in comparison to these living megaliths.

A crack of thunder in the distance snapped them to, and Jack ushered them all back over to the bench where he seated himself in the middle, continuing his spiel. The boys listened but never took their eyes off of the giant saguaro.

"Once a year, usually in the summer, this area gets hit by a good thunderstorm and the showers always help these amazing cacti sustain their life in this harsh environment. So with all that said... enjoy the show. Because it's about to begin!"

Looking around the enclosure, Brad understood how it could have been kept a secret. The entire place was completely confined within the cliff and even from an aerial point of view, would probably blend in with and be overshadowed by the protruding rock formations above. Even aircraft flying directly overhead would have missed it.

"Brad...look!" Jason whispered, drawing his attention out into the distance opposite them.

Dark clouds came drifting in fast and they saw bolts of lightning flashing intermittently all throughout them. The booming sound of thunder startled them as the first drops of rain began to fall

all around and increase as the seconds ticked by. Staying dry and protected thanks to the ledge they were under, they had a perfect unhindered view of the unfolding spectacle taking place before them.

"Watch the water!" Jack said loudly as the sound of the rain began to increase. The water formed rivulets which traveled down the angled rock and pooled below into the cactus garden.

It was then very cleverly irrigated into the holes of the bedrock from which the cacti sprouted from, and it seemed as though none of it was wasted; all to the benefit of those wondrous forms of nature. The rain came down in sheets so hard that they completely lost sight of the cacti and had to shout to be heard over the deafening roar of the cascading water.

"Jack, what is that?" Brad heard Nick shout, and as he turned to look over at Nick, he saw a knowing smile spread across Jack's face.

"Just keep watching," Jack replied calmly, his voice somehow clear through all of the tumult.

Brad looked back to the saguaros and squinted, trying to see what Nick was referring to and physically flinched. Strange shapes soared and swooped among the cacti leaving brief watery trails as they crisscrossed each other amidst the storm. They almost seemed like the shapes of large winged, majestic birds, and Brad pictured in his mind the legendary Phoenix; only one of water instead of fire. It was an amazing pageant that took place before them all with those strange elemental creatures diving and gliding over and between the large towering cacti. He found himself short of breath just watching it all and suddenly heard a voice close by, startling him.

"I told you this would be cool," Jack commented, speaking right into Brad's ear; somehow having moved undetected and now sitting right next to him.

"What are those things, Jack?"

"Well...what I was told was that they are the powerful spirits of nature and maybe even those of the sorcerers that planted them

Chapter 18

here. Their spirits forever bound and enduring through the lives of these cacti."

"That's the most beautiful thing I've ever heard," Brad commented, barely above a whisper.

Jack looked at Brad appreciatively and nodded his head. Sneaking a glimpse at his friends, Brad saw that they were all enjoying the show just as much; their faces filled with awe and wonder. Then as quickly as it had begun, it ceased. The shapes disappeared with the rain, and the sun shined brightly as the last crack of thunder was heard in the distance.

"That was unbelievable!" Nick exclaimed off to the side.

"Wait!" Jack said sharply, holding out his hand in a halting gesture. "It's not over yet!"

They all followed Jack's gaze back down to the giant, green behemoths and waited to see what would happen next. At first it seemed as though they were viewing a mirage as the glistening cacti shimmered in the sunlight, radiating a visible glowing energy. Then the saguaros all seemed to be vibrating and shaking with that energy, while giving off an aura of pure power and suddenly an amazing phenomenon occurred. The small budded clusters of flowers that tipped the ends of each branch began to subtly shake, then open, revealing bright beautifully colored petals of pink, purple, orange and red. Drenched in water, they seemed to sparkle like jewels in the warm light of the sun and Brad could see that the boys were shedding tears of admiration and joy for the wonderful display of life they were witnessing. There was a tangible feeling of energy in the air, almost like a change in season, and it filled their hearts with satisfaction and yearning, leaving them all completely enamored with the experience.

Brad understood now why he had associated those watery phantoms with that of a Phoenix. The legendary Phoenix was said to be new life rising from ashes, and they had definitely seen a display of rejuvenation at its finest!

"Well, we'd better get going before the bees get here. Aside from the indigenous desert birds in this area, insects are the only other associates of these silent giants," Jack informed them as he began walking.

On cue, a number of bees began to infiltrate the scene all buzzing loudly in search of new pollen and nectar; which they knew they'd now find at this most sacred place. As they quickly scurried under the boulder, Brad took one final look back, thinking that he may never see the likes of anything this fantastic ever again. Although, he thought; they weren't done yet!

Chapter 19

After squeezing their way back through the narrow cleft, the troop headed out of the canyon and back up the wash that had led them there. Hiking leisurely and with everyone in a peaceful contented state, Jack continued to march the boys through the wide, sandy wash until he suddenly called for a halt. As they all rested in a shady area of overhanging rock, Jack subtly motioned to Brad and then disappeared soon after. Meeting up with Jack around the corner and down the wash a ways, he inquired as to the secret meeting.

"Hey buddy, I need to take off again for a little while and run into town but I'll meet you back at the campfire later tonight. Maybe even sooner if I can."

"What's going on this time, Jack?" he asked, slightly annoyed. "Hungry again?"

"Well, yeah!" Jack responded sarcastically. "I need to eat too ya know! But also, I need to talk to some people. Don't worry! I'll be back later. You boys will be fine."

"Okay Jack," Brad said, conceding.

After all, they could probably use some more time to themselves anyway.

"See ya!" Jack chirped happily, as he took off down the wash and then scurried up the trail.

Brad walked back once again shaking his head and chuckling to himself. Upon reaching the others, Jason immediately asked where Jack was, acting as if he probably already knew the answer.

"Jack had to leave again you guys, but he will meet us back at camp tonight."

"What?" Jason whined in a high pitched tone. "Is this guy Gandalf or what? Why is it that every time we turn around he's gone again?"

Brad just shrugged his shoulders and walked over to sit down next to Nick.

"Well, we can find our way back to the campsite easily enough so what do you say we do a little exploring while we're out here?"

None of them seemed to be paying too much attention to him at that moment, so after waiting a few seconds, with a sigh he took off thinking that they would eventually figure it out anyway.

Brad ventured off towards the west, while Nick, Jason and Terry all meandered around the wash, climbing rocks and scanning their surroundings. Brad was grateful to have another moment alone and switched onto autopilot as he hiked off towards the horizon, letting his thoughts drift with the desert breeze.

Memories from his past crept in, and a melancholy feeling much like that of a Sunday Neurosis, settled in all throughout him. As he looked to the ground he slowed a bit, noticing a definite change in the geography of the land.

A slight shine caught his eye and he reached down to find a beautiful specimen of a quartz crystal shard about the size of his pinky. Holding it up to the light he smiled, admiring the clarity along with the smooth cut and shape of the stone.

Suddenly, a memory of a time years ago began to enter his mind, making him smile even wider. He had gone hiking with his friend Bret one afternoon, in the rugged desert mountains above their friend Reggie's house, and they had made an amazing discovery.

Chapter 19

After traversing steep hills with brush and Cholla strewn landscape, they had ended up on what looked like an old utility road, long out of use. Brad had noticed a crystal, much like the one he had just found lying on the ground, and told Bret to start scouring the area on the off chance that there may be more.

They soon found a scarce trail of the clear crystals and their search eventually led them to a large mound of quartz jutting straight out of the mountainside. There were pieces so clear and beautifully cut, that one could have purchased them in a New Age shop. Digging excitedly and comparing their finds with one another, they could have stayed out there indefinitely, so unique was their discovery.

After a time though, Brad got the idea that they should involve Reggie in their adventurous little endeavor and called him on his cell phone, goading him into joining the fun. Reggie was another one of Brad's friends that he hadn't been in touch with for years and in thinking back, he realized that he had always considered Reggie as more than just a friend; but as a brother. Even more so than his real brother who had never been there for him growing up. However, a very reluctant Reggie coming off of a long and hard day at work needed some serious convincing, so Brad played up their find to monumental proportions.

As the boys kept digging, Bret, having discovered the biggest one yet; a large, green, rough cut crystal almost the size of his fist, decided to take a break. Bret soon spotted Reggie going down the steep mountainside opposite them and then coming back up the sandy wash towards them, and notified Brad. Brad, having a very mischievous side to him, especially in those days, came up with a great idea to have a little fun at their old buddy's expense.

Calling Bret over he said, "Hey I've got an idea! Let's mess with him by showing him the ugliest rocks we can find, and pretend that they were our great discovery to see how he'll react!"

Of course Bret was all for the deception as he could never pass up the chance to pull on his dear friend's leg at every opportunity. Coming up the mountainside even at fifty feet away, they could clearly see the sour look on Reggie's face as he panted his way up to the both of them and demanded at once to see their "precious" finds. Brad immediately produced some of the ugliest and dirtiest rocks he could find; most of which even a three year old child wouldn't bother with. The look of doubt was beyond evident on Reggie's face and only got worse as Bret rushed over with childlike abandon and proudly showed him his collection which, if one could believe, was even worse than Brad's.

"Look at these!" Bret squealed, beaming with pride, eager to reveal his findings.

It was clear to them both that Reggie was appalled, but their act had been so convincing that he just couldn't offer any insults. Sitting down on the ground with a look of utter disappointment, he seemed as though he may get physically ill. He had just hiked three miles through rugged terrain after already working a twelve hour day, only to deal with this; two idiot friends who he didn't have the heart to be honest with, as he believed, that they believed; they had just discovered the find of the century!

Trying their hardest to stifle their giggling, Bret nudged Brad and motioned towards Reggie indicating that it was time to reveal the facade, and they both approached him with the real crystals in hand. Reggie, hardly wanting to look up at that point glanced at them, and then quickly did a double take, looking as though his eyes would pop right out of his head!

Brad and Bret both erupted into laughter as Reggie, with a look of astonishment on his face, asked, "Wow, where did you find those?"

They led him directly to the large mound and then the three of them proceeded to search the hill for more crystals, all finding some amazing pieces and going back home that day with plenty of

Chapter 19

great quartz as well as fond memories. Brad snickered helplessly at that old memory, realizing just how much he missed those two dear friends of his.

Pocketing his new found item, he continued heading west towards some large boulders that he saw scattered in the distance. Casually strolling along, he caught sight of a bright flash out of the corner of his eye and looked up to see another thunderstorm heading directly towards him. Looking back he realized that he was a half mile or more away from his friends and couldn't outrun this one, so he sought out whatever shelter he could close by.

Jogging over to an outcropping of boulders bordering a small wash, he found a little space that was tucked under an overhanging ledge and felt confident that it would keep him dry. As the sky again turned gray, his mind wandered back to more memories of his past and the soft sound of falling rain actually helped him regress back to another time. He began to recall again certain times he had shared with good friends and talented people back when he had lived in the high desert.

As the rain pelted the rocks and dirt he was reminded of his favorite song by his good friend Scott Wexton; also known as The Voodoo Organist. "It's raining again. It's raining again. Where's the sun? Where's my gun? Where's everyone?" While the slow melodic harmonies replayed inside his head, they brought back nostalgic memories of time spent with Scott. He had really cherished those in-depth and philosophical conversations that they had shared together on many an occasion. Scott was a very intelligent guy and had a brilliant mind which only aided in the creativity of his music. He was an amazing organist and all around accomplished musician, performing almost all of his live shows solo. He consistently entranced his audiences as he manipulated sounds like an artist molded clay. Scott owned a local shop in town called Hoodoo, and Brad missed the times in which they would hang out there discussing everything from politics and religion, to music and art. He had always considered himself lucky to call Scott and his wife Lisa; friends, and always enjoyed surrounding himself with people as accepting and talented as them.

His mind wandered further and he began to think of another friend of his named Wade Crawford. Wade was a musician that played an old edgy style of Country music that Brad had loved and had grown up listening to.

Brad was a Seventies kid and had pretty much grown up in the bars that his dad loved to frequent. He recalled shooting pool and playing Pac-Man, amidst fetching beers for bikers and old Country Western desert rats. He remembered hearing Merle Haggard, Waylon Jennings and Willie Nelson on the jukebox as well as many others like Patsy Cline, Dolly Parton and Loretta Lynn. Back then, Country music had a real raw, gritty, yet beautiful down home sound to him and spoke of the troubles, hardships, and suffering that people dealt with in matters of love and life. They just didn't play it that way anymore and most of the Pop Country ballads that droned out through the radio stations of today were simply no comparison to the real thing back in those days, he felt.

Wade was one of the few exceptions and kept that traditional Country style in his music. He had an amazing gift for bringing back that type of old school sound with his steady, rhythmic guitar strumming, and straight from the heart voice. As the water collected and started to slowly trickle down the wash, Brad recalled his favorite song that Wade always performed incredibly on stage. It was called "New Orleans" and as tiny streams began to formulate their way down the small ravine, he remembered the key lyrics in the song; "Flow me down the river to Tennessee, and tell my baby that I'm finally free. And they buried me in New Orleans." Brad and Wade had gotten along right from the first time they'd met and Brad could see the potential Wade had for success. They both shared a love of

Chapter 19

David Allen Coe and Hank Williams One, Two and Three, and talked at length about The Doors; who they both loved above all else. Brad remembered watching Wade play and telling himself; One day, that man is going to make it big.

Fond memories of those great people seemed to be all he had left of them now. He vowed that when he got back, he'd begin to maintain a stronger level of correspondence and would definitely keep in touch on a more regular basis. As the storm let up once again, and just as quickly as the first time, he decided that it was time to go back and rejoin his friends.

Upon arriving, it looked to him as though none of them had moved more than twenty feet in all the time he'd been gone.

"What's up fellas? What have you been doing?"

"Not much man," Nick answered lazily.

"We've just been waiting on you. Where have you been?" Jason demanded irritably. "We thought you got lost or something. Where did you go for so long?"

"I went out exploring! I told you guys that right before I left, didn't you hear me?"

"No!" Jason exclaimed. "We asked Terry where you went and he said that you went to go take a leak or something. We thought you were coming right back!"

They all looked over to Terry who seemed oblivious, or at least acted like it.

"What's up?" he asked, snapping out of his haze.

"Never mind," Brad said, shaking his head.

This was definitely one of those times when he did not appreciate Terry's presence.

"Well damn, man!" Jason shouted. "I would've gone looking around too but I thought we were waiting on you!"

"We've still got time," Brad said, trying to utilize a calming tone to settle Jason down, recognizing that his patience was wearing thin. "Come on, let's go!" Brad shouted cheerfully, and they took off back up the trail with Brad meandering in and out of it, looking all around at the scenery and occasionally down at the ground for interesting rocks.

Jason's manner didn't seem to improve one bit and Brad thought that maybe they should separate to give Jason and Nick a break from Terry for a while. Stopping in the middle of the trail he spoke up.

"Hey guys, why don't we split up for a little while? I'll take Terry with me and we'll go check out that mesa over there. You guys can explore for a bit and we'll meet back on the trail in thirty minutes. Sound good?"

"Sounds great," a very sarcastic Jason replied, and he and Nick immediately moved out north, trying to put some distance between them as quickly as possible.

Nick looked back once and shook his head saying, "Good luck."

Brad breathed a small sigh as they moved out of sight, then he turned his attention back towards Terry.

"Well, what do you say Terry? Ready to go check out that mesa over there?" he asked, pointing it out to him.

"Huh?" Terry shot back, obviously paying no attention.

"That mesa over there. Let's go check it out."

"Oh yeah, sure man. Okay," he responded absently.

At only about five minutes in, Brad already felt like he was babysitting and he was not happy about it. Terry moved too slow and went the wrong way more than a few times and Brad soon became frustrated. As they neared the mesa, however, Brad forgot about Terry momentarily and began to scan the rugged mountain, finding its natural structure very interesting.

Once at the base of the low, flat topped mountain, Brad exclaimed, "Woooaahh! I was wondering what those strange brown lines running down the edges were. They're lava flows! Look at that!"

Chapter 19

Terry just gazed at them stupidly, as if he had not been entirely awakened from a nap, and Brad ran forth eager to get a closer look at this intriguing natural phenomenon.

Reaching the bottom of the nearest flow, he marveled at the enormous amount of pure volcanic rock which was rich, dark brown in color and riddled with porous holes. Brad began carefully picking his way up through the ancient solidified river and the sharpened, jagged rocks shifted uneasily beneath his feet causing him to lose his balance repeatedly. He could hear Terry slipping and sliding across the volcanic rocks back behind him but chose to pay him no mind, so captivated was he by such a geological occurrence. He had seen mesas like this from a distance, with their dark brown stripes stretching down all sides, but had never gotten this up close and personal with one before.

As he stood in the center of the volcanic dry, rock river and looked up, he got a real understanding of what it must have been like thousands if not millions of years ago. These mountains had erupted fire and molten rock, spewing it down the mountainside in all directions, and the devastation and heat had probably been indescribable.

After a few moments he had seen enough and felt satisfied with what he'd viewed, so then headed back down the rugged lava flow to the bottom where Terry sat on a boulder awaiting his return. He was ready to leave, but decided that he would really love to take a souvenir to remind him of this place and the experience that he'd had there. He started looking around as Terry just sat there complacently, and in overturning a few rocks, found a couple of pieces that he thought were unique and beautiful.

"Hey, Terry. I want to bring two of these rocks back, so can you carry one for me while I grab the other?"

"Uh...yeah. Sure man, I guess," he answered dismally, not seeming too thrilled at all about having to do any extra work.

Inspecting the two rocks and more talking to himself than to Terry, he mumbled, "I think I'm going to send one to my friend Bret. Which one do you think I should give to him; this one, or this one?"

As Terry began to respond, they both suddenly heard a loud crashing sound like something in between an avalanche and a bunch of wild stampeding animals coming right down the mountainside directly towards them. Looking up, they both staggered backwards, terrified by the sheer sound and ferocity of whatever danger now assaulted them. Fully expecting to see a herd of huge beasts bearing down on them, they instead saw nothing. A second later, their attentions turned to a large desert bush that was directly in front of them and to their left which shook violently as if there were a dozen angry apes within, trying to aggressively threaten any trespassers. Two seconds later a similar bush about fifteen feet away and again to their left, shook almost as violently as the first.

Then all was quiet except for the sound of Brad's volcanic rocks hitting the ground along with their own heavy breathing.

Frozen in place, Brad asked, "What the hell was that?"

"I don't know man," Terry gasped. "At first I thought we were being attacked by a huge mountain lion or bear, the way that sound came crashing down the mountain!"

"So did I!" Brad exclaimed and continued, "Did you see the way that bush was shaking? Like something was rattling it from the inside!"

"Maybe it was just the wind," Terry said unconvincingly.

"No way man," Brad said calmly, trying to rationalize it in his mind. "Did you see the way it jumped from one bush to the other? There wasn't even a breeze blowing when it happened. I think I know what it was now…Wowww! I've read about these things but had never encountered one till now."

"Let's go man, I'm scared!" Terry whined.

"It's okay man. It won't hurt us but we'd better leave these rocks here, just in case."

Chapter 19

"Fine man, come on let's go!"

"Wow," Brad repeated, as they both took cautious steps backwards, never taking their eyes off the area that harbored the strange entity.

Quickly picking up the pace, they put some distance between themselves and the mesa and Terry asked Brad, "What was that thing?"

"It was an Ally," Brad replied confidently. "I read about them in a few of Castaneda's books but never dreamed that one day I'd actually experience the energy of one myself. They are powerful forces that exist out in the desert. I guess you could call them spirits, but not in a ghostlike sense. Don Juan told Carlos that attaining the knowledge and energy of an Ally was about the greatest gift you could ever hope to receive as far as power."

"That was terrifying!" Terry exclaimed.

"Yes it was!" Brad agreed. "I think it was defending that area and must have felt threatened because it sure let us know it was there, didn't it? It's a good thing we left those rocks behind! Who knows what might have happened if we hadn't. Maybe nothing at all. Maybe something terrible! You know, come to think of it...I've heard stories about people taking lava rocks from certain sacred places in the Hawaiian Islands and being suddenly cursed with bad luck. They even try mailing them back to the locals sometimes!"

Brad saw that Terry was visibly shaken and he gave him a friendly pat on the shoulder to try and console him as they made their way back down the trail to meet the other boys.

"Man, you guys won't believe what just happened to us!" Brad said to Jason and Nick, as he came walking up with Terry.

They both stood up as Brad approached them and waited with arms crossed to hear the story.

"Well?" Jason prompted. "Don't keep us in suspenders!"

Brad excitedly rehashed the experience using hand gestures for emphasis and a lot of emotion, really driving the point home.

Nick and Jason both stared at him with a fair amount of uncertainty, if not disbelief, and when he finished they both looked at each other, then at Terry.

"Is that really how it happened?" Jason asked with more than a little skepticism.

"Uh, well yeah…I guess," was all Terry could manage to say.

"Come on Terry!" Brad practically screamed. "Tell them! You were there too! You saw it!"

"Yeah, I don't know man. Could have just been the wind," he said lamely.

"Just the wi-" Brad started to say, but then threw his hands up in defeat and stalked off leaving them all standing there looking after him.

Brad had practically relived the event just through the telling of it and now felt shook up all over again. He was hoping for some backup from Terry concerning the terrifying situation and it looked now as if he wasn't going to get it. The boys probably thought that he was just exaggerating his description. His constant references to Carlos Castaneda and don Juan probably made him look all the more desperate in convincing them that the situation was something other than what it really was. Now thanks to Terry, they would probably just believe it was a freak occurrence.

"Stupid Terry!" Brad hissed under his breath, as he stalked off into the desert to be alone so that he could gather his thoughts and assure himself that he really had felt and experienced the whole thing.

"Hey Brad! Come back man," Jason yelled.

"Yeah man, come back. We believe you," Nick said, trying to appeal to Brad's hurt feelings.

Brad paused, taking a deep breath, and then started shuffling back over to the guys.

"Alright," he said. "Let's just get going."

With that, they all commenced with hiking again, knowing better than to argue with Brad when he was in that kind of mood. They began to head back to the campsite and the Jeep, with Brad still fuming and Terry lagging behind indifferently. They soon reached a fork in the trail however, and found themselves at a loss as to whether they should go left or right, and unfortunately Jack was not there to guide them and they couldn't remember.

"Well, boys," Brad said. "I can't remember which way we came in, can you? Was it the left trail or the right?"

Both Nick and Jason shrugged their shoulders, when all of a sudden in a rare act of participation, Terry stepped up confidently and said, "It's the left one."

Raising his eyebrows at Terry with a look of total skepticism, Brad asked, "The left one?"

"Yes, it's definitely that one," he said, pointing down at the trail in question.

Brad, still feeling irked from Terry's lack of support in recounting the last little adventure they were on, was obviously doubtful.

"You're sure?" he asked, never taking his eyes off Terry.

"Yes."

"Positive?"

"I'm telling you, I remember," Terry insisted stubbornly, standing firm and folding his arms across his chest for emphasis.

"Okay. Then we're going this way," Brad stated, taking the trail to the right in a bold move of defiance against Terry.

Jason and Nick both followed right behind him, feeling the same as Brad about Terry's directional skills.

"Okaaaay..." Terry replied as he fell in line at the end, shaking his head but going along with it.

About ten minutes into their hike, it became painfully apparent that Terry had indeed been correct and they were going way out of their way and in the wrong direction.

They ended up in a large wash that became a cul-de-sac and had to stop to figure out whether to go on or double back. Brad again volunteered to climb to a higher point to reassess the situation, seeing as how his disregard got them there in the first place.

He climbed out of the wash and toward a small group of boulders to see if he could spot a shortcut to connect back up to the correct trail.

Moments after Brad had left, Nick and Jason began wandering around the wash, looking at various rock formations. Nick looked down and found a beautiful smooth, round river rock then called out to Jason as he bent down to pick it up.

"Hey, Jay! Check this out!"

Jason walked over and inspected the stone, agreeing that it was beautiful and very interesting. "Nice! Look, there are more. Lots more!"

As they both perused through the sand, inspecting several different rocks like they were collecting Easter eggs, Terry just looked on without interest, waiting for Brad to return.

"I think I'll take a few of these back with us," Jason announced. "Memoirs of our adventures out in this God forsaken wash to nowhere!"

He and Nick both laughed as they started grabbing as many as their greedy little hands could hold. A moment later they heard a noise; distant at first, then closer and high pitched. It seemed to come from far away but then was practically on top of them in a matter of just a few seconds. As it got louder, Terry stood up, looking all around while Jason and Nick remained rooted in place.

"Well guys, it looks like we'll have to double back because I don't see any way to get through to the trail-" Brad started to say, coming off the ridge and sliding down into the wash.

He saw the looks of panic imprinted on all of their faces though and cut his sentence short, sensing their alarm.

"What is it?" he asked fearfully and with an anxious tone to his voice.

He'd been through too much out in this unpredictable desert to not take everything seriously at this point.

"Listen!" Jason commanded curtly, and Brad cocked his head a little trying to see if he could distinguish any certain noises.

Another high pitched whine and something seemed to zoom right over their heads. It happened again and again and Brad tried real hard to discern what the noise might be and where it was coming from. There seemed to be an invisible trajectory which started from outside the wash and to the south of them and it whistled right past them to the left and directly overhead.

"Is someone shooting at us?" Terry asked, his tone clearly bordering on panic.

"No," Brad answered immediately.

There would have been a report and mostly an impact if a shot had been fired, unless there was a sniper using a silencer, Brad concluded. He seriously doubted that though. It almost sounded to him like an insect, but the path that it traveled was one-way and not something going back and forth. As it whistled overhead he tried following the sound with his ears, then with his eyes, and while whipping his head to the left, he noticed Nick holding a stack of rocks in his hand.

Looking from Nick to Jason, he realized that they both probably intended on taking the river rocks and shouted, "What are you doing with those?"

"We were gonna take a few back with us..." Nick stammered.

"Drop em!" Brad yelled.

Even as they threw down their rocks, the sound became higher pitched and more frequent.

"Run!" Brad screamed, and they all took off after him back down through the wash, sprinting as if their lives depended on it.

When they got a good distance away, Jason asked Brad between breaths, "What was that?"

"I don't know," he gasped. "It almost sounded like some sort of invisible alien death ray, if that's any way to describe it!"

"But what would cause that?" Nick asked, just as startled as the others. Brad looked from Nick over to Terry.

"Why didn't you warn them about the rocks? You know what happened to us earlier! You should have reminded them!"

Terry just stared at Brad uncomprehendingly and Brad turned back to Nick and Jason asking, "You believe me now?"

Jason and Nick stared at each other shocked, the belief now evident on both of their faces.

"Come on. I think we're safe, but no more souvenirs! Don't try taking anything else from this desert! Too many forces lurking about," he said, craning his neck around in all directions as he led the boys back up the wash and to the proper trail.

Chapter 20

As they approached their camp, they saw Jack walking past the Jeep with a stack of firewood in his arms. Dropping the wood into a newly built fire pit, he dusted off his hands and with a grin, walked up to meet them.

Jack's smile disappeared completely when he noticed how distraught the boys were, and in a serious tone immediately asked them, "What happened?"

Nick and Jason both seemed like they wanted to say something but appeared to be at a loss for words. Jack looked at Brad questioningly and Brad just scrunched up his face and shook his head as he continued to walk past him.

Recognizing their apprehension, Jack tried to change the subject and announced, "Well anyway, despite the fact that there is an almost full moon tonight, I thought we should have a fire as it might be slightly chillier than normal on account of the rainy weather. Brad, I'll need to talk to you alone for a minute."

Brad just nodded his head as the boys made their way towards the Jeep to sit down and relax for a moment. Once out of sight, Jack asked Brad about what happened.

"There's a lot of strange activity out here in this desert Jack, and we've been running right smack into it!" Brad said irritably, raising his voice and looking at Jack accusingly.

"Heyyyy!" Jack responded, holding up his hands defensively. "You're the one that wanted to come out here, remember? I'm just the guide!"

Calming down a bit, Brad said, "Sorry Jack. I didn't mean to snap at you. It's just that we've been through a lot and most of it, not so good lately."

"It's okay!" Jack said, flashing that disarming smile of his.

"Jack?" Brad began seriously.

"Yes Brad?" Jack responded with mock seriousness.

"I know I've asked you your opinion on Terry already, but...do you know him from somewhere?"

Jack's smile was gone in a heartbeat.

"Yeah, I know him," he answered seriously. Brad, taken back by that statement, looked at Jack with a ghastly expression. "I know his type anyway," Jack clarified.

"Well what does that mean, exactly? I have been really on the fence about this guy and now he's got us all on edge. It's not like he goes out of his way to trip us up but it seems to be what he does nonetheless. He's like a bad luck charm, and we're beginning to feel like we're cursed for just having him around."

Jack nodded his head through it all, agreeing with Brad silently, and almost seemed to have a look of slight pity in his eyes.

"I can tell you that he is only going to cause you more problems. I can see that you've all formed some sort of bond with him but you should send him packing. It's really for the best. Please take my word for it before you end up regretting it." Scrutinizing every word Jack said, Brad went silent for a moment then lowered his head.

"I'll talk to the boys about it," he replied.

Jack nodded his head curtly and then proceeded with other business.

"Sit down for a minute Brad," he said gently.

Chapter 20

As Brad and Jack both sat down, Brad looked up at him curiously. Jack had definitely shifted personalities once again and became much more earnest and concerned.

"How is your trip so far Brad? Is it everything you hoped it would be? How's the Mescaline treating you?"

"It's good, but not quite what I expected," Brad honestly answered, to all three questions.

"It never is," Jack admitted, in a tone reflecting melancholy.

He stared out into the distance towards the afternoon sun as it made its slow arc across the sky and at that moment, he seemed far, far away. Brad watched Jack with a puzzled look on his face and Jack snapped his attention back to Brad once more.

"This is the last night isn't it? You're leaving tomorrow, yes?"

"Yes. Tomorrow, probably late morning. Why Jack? What's up? Are you worried about getting paid? I've got your money in the-"

"No, no. Nothing like that," Jack interrupted, and then hesitated for a brief moment before proceeding, "I acquired some more Peyote for you earlier today. I got it from a good friend and it's fresh from the mountains way down in southern New Mexico. And...it was blessed by a Shaman from a tribe of Mescalero Indians. So what I want to know is...how far are you willing to take this trip? The amount of Peyote you've all had so far should have put you in a pretty good twist but are you ready to go around the bend? If you desire profound answers, then you've got to be willing to go all the way. So are you?"

Brad stared at Jack now as if he was looking through him, or even seeing him for the first time. In a way it frightened, yet comforted him simultaneously.

"Yes," he said, before he realized that he was even answering. "And I speak for all of us."

Apparently hoping to receive that answer, Jack smiled and nodded his head as he gave Brad a leather pouch which he had already been holding in his hand.

"I'm sorry Brad. I have to leave again but I'll be back tonight, hopefully to join you around the campfire."

Without any further explanation, Jack stood and walked off just as Jason and Nick came over. Jason said hello to Jack, who gave him only a slight nod as he continued to move past him. Jason threw both his hands up and looked to Brad with an offended expression on his face and Brad just waved it away as if telling him not to worry about it.

"So what did Jack have to say then?" Jason asked, his tone thick with impatience, apparently knowing Jack well enough by now to figure out that something was going on. "And what's with all the secret conversations anyway? Why can't we ever be involved?"

Brad looked to Nick who also seemed to be waiting for an answer to that question.

"Well, Jack had to leave again. Apparently he has something to take care of, but he'll be back tonight."

"Awww!" Jason began in an exasperated tone. "Why bother? He's barely been with us the entire time!" he complained, as he continued raising his voice. "He's always-"

"He's done what I've asked him to do," Brad said, cutting Jason off sharply from starting his tirade. "For all of us. Just because he's not here every second doesn't mean otherwise." Brad's tone left no room for debate and Jason was shocked into silence by it. "He's done a lot more for us then some people I might add," Brad continued, turning his head slightly and shifting his gaze over towards Terry who still sat in the Jeep, oblivious to their conversation. Jason followed his stare then looked back to Nick who shrugged his shoulders and nodded his head in agreement.

"Okay. Point taken. So, what happens next?"

"Have a seat," Brad offered, gesturing to them both. Once they were seated, Brad revealed the news.

"Jack was able to procure some more Peyote for us," he announced, then waited for a reaction from them before carrying on. They both just continued to stare at him, waiting for the rest of the story.

"Only this Peyote is rare and special. He says it's fresh and was blessed by a Native American Medicine Man from the Mescalero tribe south of here," he continued, trying to add a tone of intrigue to his sales pitch. "He knows we're going back tomorrow and thought we might need it for our last night out. So what do you guys say?"

"You want to take more?" Jason asked in a tone of astonishment.

"Yes I do," Brad replied with certainty. "I can only speak for myself when I say that I've come to understand a lot more about life, than I can ever remember learning, but I don't quite feel 'there' yet. Do you guys?"

Jason turned to Nick who seemed to be staring at the ground. Then he looked away and paused to really consider Brad's assessment.

"Okay. Let's do it. One last hurrah, shall we say?"

This is what Brad loved about Jason. He would always back your play no matter what the odds, as long as he was appreciated for it, and right now Brad felt like hugging him! Jason looked back to Nick, who kept his gaze locked on the ground yet nodded his head affirmatively.

"Alright, then!" Brad said excitedly. "Let's see what we've got!"

He pulled out the leather pouch and dipped his hand inside.

"What, right now?" Jason asked, his voice rising.

"Yes, when else?" Brad responded.

Jason looking again to Nick saw him mechanically nodding his head, never taking his vacant stare away from the ground.

"What about Terry?" Jason asked quietly, glancing back over towards Terry who was taking a nap as he sat in the Jeep, his head resting against the door, snoring loudly.

"What about him?" Brad asked in an angry tone. "That was actually another thing that Jack wanted me to talk to you guys about.

He says that we should ditch him. I can't say for sure but I suspect that Jack may know Terry from somewhere and he sure as hell doesn't like him. I told him I would speak to you guys about it but I think that he's right."

Looking shocked, Jason stared at Brad in disbelief.

"Hey man, I'm not crazy about the guy either but you think we should bail on him? What if something happens to him? That would make us somewhat responsible. Besides, how would we do it anyway? No one here is in any condition to drive him back except for Jack and he's disappeared again!"

"Okay look," Brad said, trying to keep his voice calm. "The guy hasn't really contributed even one thing and he causes nothing but trouble. And don't forget...he hasn't taken any Peyote, it's only been us. I've got nothing against Weed but he's probably just been stoned this whole time and he can take care of himself if need be. We are in no way bound to this guy. Remember that it was us helping him out. We brought him along out of pity or some sense of strange obligation...whatever you want to call it, but it's just not working out." Brad's voice rose to a high pitch at the very end, then all went quiet.

There was a long moment of silence and then Nick spoke up startling them both.

"Brad's right. I'm tired of this guy. The things he says and does. I don't know what it is about him but I almost love and hate him at the same time. Like a brother or a family member; only one who just fucks up all the time. But I'm with Brad. He's gotta go. We need to lose him once and for all. He's just been bringing down my trip for a while now."

Brad gaped at Nick with his hand still frozen inside the pouch and almost had to pick his jaw up off the ground. Nick had just perfectly articulated everything that he had come to realize about Terry, but couldn't confirm within himself. Nick had obviously been

Chapter 20

thinking about this for some time now. He looked to Jason and saw an expression which must have mirrored his own. They all remained silent for some moments before Brad spoke again.

"I have an idea. Since Jack is gone and we can't drive him back into town, let's just walk him out. We can hike almost all the way back to town, then lose him. He doesn't really know this area, he was full of it! Once we get close, we'll show him where town is then ditch him. He'll never find his way back here before we leave tomorrow I'm sure of it," he ended confidently.

Nick and Jason both reluctantly agreed, and then turned back to look at Terry who was now awake and seemed to be staring at all three as if he had been aware that he was being talked about.

Sitting in the Jeep he asked, "Hey, what are you guys doing over there?"

"Nothing man, just hanging out!" Jason yelled back trying to sound inconspicuous. "We're going for another hike soon so get your rest while you can!" he added, looking back to Nick and Brad with an expression like he'd just been caught doing something he wasn't supposed to.

Terry slumped his head back against the door and was snoring again within seconds.

"Alright then, it's agreed. Let's eat this Peyote and then we'll head on out."

Brad withdrew his hand, and they all leaned in to view what they were up against, and saw fresh, dark green buttons piled in his palm.

"We'll need some jerky," Jason suggested, as he stared at the potent looking succulents. Nick suddenly thrust forth a bag of jerky he'd been holding that no one had even noticed.

"All at once?" Jason asked, fearing that he already knew the answer. A nod from both the other two confirmed his suspicions.

"Here we go again..." Brad said, exhaling a deep breath.

Quietly taking supplies from the Jeep afterwards, they began setting up around the campfire and rolled a few large boulders over to its edges so that they could have something to sit on later.

All the while as they worked, Terry, having finally awoke, lounged in the Wrangler watching them; apparently too lazy to provide any help. As far as they could remember in fact, Terry hadn't lifted one finger or really done any type of physical work to help them out; except for carrying a backpack maybe. Soon after they were all set up, Jason turned to Brad, and Brad then looked to Nick for confirmation. Nick in turn looked over at Terry, then back at the boys and nodded his head quickly, affirming their intentions. Taking the initiative, Nick turned and casually walked over to Terry and had a quiet conversation with him while Jason and Brad looked on apprehensively.

"He may not go for it man," Jason whispered at Brad. "He kinda acts like he's onto us. Do you think he heard us talking earlier?"

"No. He was too far away. Don't worry Jay. He doesn't suspect anything."

Nick came walking back and once he was close enough, Jason asked, "What did you tell him?"

"I told him that we were about to lead him out to the middle of the desert so that we could ditch him because we're tired of all his shit," Nick reported seriously.

Brad and Jason stared at him dumbfounded, actually believing what he had just said, Nick's face looking so deadpan.

"Well, that's what I wanted to say to him anyway," he continued sheepishly.

Jason and Brad both let out deep sighs of relief and started chuckling at Nick's humorous deception.

"I told him we wanted to take one more hike around the desert before we come back and have a campfire later tonight, and he bought it."

Chapter 20

"You done good buddy boy," Brad said, clapping Nick on the shoulder. "Let's go be done with this business then."

Turning around to go fetch Terry, they all gasped to find him standing a few feet behind them.

"What's going on guys? You seem a little on edge."

His tone was crisper and more sober than usual, throwing the boys off a bit and making them wonder whether or not he had indeed suspected what was about to happen.

"You just startled us, is all," Jason replied, trying to act casual.

"So we're going for another hike, huh?"

Everything quieted down all of a sudden and went deathly still. Even the slight breeze that was blowing abruptly ceased.

"Okay, but this time can we make it a short one?"

Exhaling their held breaths, Jason immediately grabbed a backpack and checked its contents for water and emergency snacks.

"Alright then. Let's go," Terry said, grabbing his backpack and stalking off in the exact direction that they had planned to go, leaving them all standing behind gawking after him as he left.

"Oh man, he knows. He has to!" Jason said in a low voice. "Nick, you didn't really tell him did you?"

"No man!" Nick whispered back harshly. "I told him we were going hiking. That's all!"

"Alright, well there's nothing to do now, but to do it," Brad said determinedly. They all took up the trail after Terry who had already gotten a sizable lead on them and wasn't slowing. About three quarters of a mile out Jason called up to Terry, "Hey man, wait up!"

Terry stopped dead in his tracks, remaining face forward and without turning to look at them, he waited. Once they caught up, without a word he hiked on; never looking back and continuing like a man marching to his death.

The tension only increased as time went by and the boys all exchanged worried glances with one another, each of them wondering if they should just abandon the mission.

The sun started getting close to the western horizon on their left, and they found Terry again a good twenty yards up ahead and hiking steadily. The three boys stopped and huddled together discussing what to do next and they noticed that Terry stopped a distance away also, waiting for them with his back turned.

"Look guys," Brad said after some quiet debating. "It's too late to turn back now, even if he knows. It's for the best. I know you guys aren't crazy about Jack but I trust him, and he says we need to do this."

Terry, who couldn't possibly have heard them from such a distance, seemed to cock his head slightly almost as if he was listening to every word.

"Then let's get it over with," Jason said angrily, pushing past Brad and Nick as he moved forward to catch up to Terry.

"He's upset," Nick commented with obvious recognition. "He hates this kind of deceit and it's starting to eat away at him."

"As with us all I'd say," Brad agreed sadly, thinking that if Jason had this kind of reaction to deceit, what would he do if he found out about Brad's little ploy? Would he ditch him just like they intended to ditch Terry? He shivered at the thought of it.

Jason, having caught up with Terry, hiked alongside him chatting idly as Brad and Nick trailed a distance behind. Eventually Nick trotted up and joined them, constantly looking back and forth between the two as he added to the dialogue here and there. Finally Brad sprinted up to join all three and they hiked along side by side, commenting on the weather and the desert's beauty around this time of year.

All of a sudden Terry stopped short and stood perfectly still. The boys ceased their hiking and turned as one to look back at Terry questioningly. Without looking up he began to speak.

"Look, you guys. I know that I haven't been the best company on this journey of yours, and I'm really sorry about that. I just wanted to thank you for bringing me along in the first place and tell you that I've come to really connect with you all in such a short amount of time. I hope you're not too mad about anything that I've done and don't hold it against me."

Nick and Jason both walked back over to Terry and put a reassuring hand on his shoulder then turned back towards Brad with looks of compassion which begged for an appeal on Terry's behalf. Brad walked over to Terry and standing directly before him, calmly called his name. Terry looked up with tears welling in his eyes, and Brad felt a pang of sudden sadness deep within his heart.

At that moment they all felt terribly guilty and Brad was on the verge of changing his mind. From somewhere however, the memory of a voice called out to him and he heard Jack echoing inside his head. He knew then that despite how hard this would be, they must see it through to its end.

"It's alright Terry," Brad said soothingly. "Don't frown on it too hard."

Brad turned and stalked off then, leaving Terry to wipe his tears and Jason and Nick soon followed after him.

"Well?" Jason asked, he and Nick both waiting expectantly for the response that they hoped to get from him.

"Terry!" Brad called out. As Terry came jogging over, looking more like a whipped dog than they'd ever seen, Brad continued, "What are you waiting for? Let's go!"

Terry's smile spread widely across his lips and he bounded off into the direction they were originally heading while Nick and Jason just gave Brad looks of disgust and disappointment.

"Come on," Brad said in a tone leaving no room for argument.

Once again they were on their way and the sun continued its descent down towards the mountains in its inevitable quest for sleep.

With Terry's spirits soaring, he continually bantered with the fellas, to their dismay, and soon they approached a large canyon wall with tall granite cliffs that spired out at the top.

All but Terry recognized that wall as the one they'd seen when they left town the night before, and knew that town was only a few miles in on the other side. The night before! Brad thought. Had it really only been that long? It felt as though they'd been at this for a week and yet it had been less than forty eight hours! Brad noticed then that they were much farther to the west now than when they'd originally driven in. He hoped that they could lose Terry on the other side of those mountains and backtrack their way to the campsite without him following their trail.

Occasionally glancing towards Nick and Jason, he could see that they were so upset that they didn't even want to look at him. Taking it with a grain of salt, Brad kept going, knowing that this was a task that must be completed. So far, the Peyote had not fully kicked in yet and he hoped to be rid of Terry before it did.

Upon reaching the base of the mountain, Brad saw a narrow wash which looked as though it might lead them straight through the canyon and steered them towards it. Terry seemingly oblivious, followed right along chatting incessantly, while Jason and Nick with sour faces, steadily kept pace. About halfway through, Brad stopped and looked up to the top of the canyon.

"What's that up there?" he asked loudly.

Nick and Jason both shot curious stares up in the direction that Brad had just indicated.

"What do you see man?" Terry asked, coming over to stand right beside Brad, trying hard to focus his sights near the canyon's top.

"I don't know. It's strange. I think I'm gonna go check it out. Wanna go with me?" he asked Terry.

Catching on, Nick and Jason both turned to Brad with incredulous stares then angrily looked away.

Chapter 20

"Come on guys!" Terry said cheerfully. "Let's all go!"

Jason and Nick turned away and went to sit down on a flat boulder that lined the edge of the wash.

"Nah man, you go," Nick said with his back turned to him.

"Yeah, come on Terry. You and me," Brad offered optimistically, and patted Terry on the back as he went by him, climbing up the wash and towards the large boulders set into the mountainside.

Shrugging his shoulders and giving it no further thought, Terry sprinted to keep up with Brad as they picked their way carefully up the rock strewn canyon. Looking back only once, Brad could see Jason and Nick staring up at them, the guilt and disappointment evident on both of their faces even at that distance. Once at the top, Brad continued making his way, climbing carefully along the high ridge as the wind whistled all across the mountain top.

"So where is this thing that you thought you saw?" Terry yelled over at Brad, trying to elevate his voice above the soaring wind.

"I think it was over here," Brad answered with mock earnestness. "It could have been a bobcat or something but it was moving."

"Oh, man! We're chasing an animal?" Terry asked dishearteningly.

"Look Terry!" Brad responded, trying to distract his attention. "There's town," he announced, pointing off to the northeast, directing Terry's gaze.

"Oh, yeah. Wow. I didn't realize that we'd hiked so far already."

"Yeah, how about that," Brad commented distantly. "Look! There it is!" he exclaimed excitedly, pointing down near the bottom of the mountain. "Let's go get a closer look."

"Where man? I don't see anything."

"Come on, follow me!" Brad said bounding down the mountainside, pretending to be intrigued. Terry hesitated, looking back toward the way they came in; obviously uncertain as to whether or not he should follow. Not having much choice in the matter at that point he raced to catch up with Brad and soon they were at the very bottom, walking through a field of green desert scrub.

"Well, I think we lost it man. Are you ready to head back?" Terry asked with an edge of fear and apprehension in his tone.

"I know it came this way," Brad replied, continuing the facade.

"At this rate we're gonna end up in town man. Don't you think we should head back?"

"Yeah...okay," Brad sighed resignedly, knowing that the jig was up. It was now or never, so Brad made his play. "Hey, Terry. Before we head back I think I should tell you something."

Terry looked to Brad with concern, noting his tone. "What's up man?"

"Well, the reason the fellas didn't want to go with us back there is because they're pretty upset."

"They are? But, why?" Terry watched the steady look on Brad's face and started to slowly comprehend. "Oh. I see," he said in a tone of defeat.

"Try not to take it too hard man," Brad said encouragingly. "I'm just not sure if they want you around anymore. These things just happen." Terry, looking at the ground dejectedly, nodded his head. "Well, hey man, I've gotta take a leak. I'll be back in a minute," Brad's voice choked as he was unable to keep up the charade any longer and just wanted this to be over.

Again Terry just nodded as Brad stalked away. Looking back only once, he saw the sorrowful look on Terry's face and what he thought might be teardrops hitting the ground. Once at the mountains edge, Brad climbed straight up without hesitation, noticing a sick feeling rising within his stomach.

He reached the top in no time and stood looking back down to Terry who was already walking off into the distance, heading straight towards town. He cringed at the sight, feeling as though he had just betrayed his best friend, and vomited all down the side of the cliff, losing his balance and almost falling off the precipice.

"I probably deserve to fall," he muttered aloud with self-deprecation.

He began to stagger back along the ridge shakily, not at all wanting to confront his friends when he got down and yet he felt spiritually lifted in a way.

Stopping suddenly, he took a wide stance, planting his feet firmly onto the rock and held both arms out wide in a gesture of submission to the powers that be. Feeling the wind buffet all around and against him, he sensed a cleansing that only nature itself could provide. Taking deep breaths, he closed his eyes and rooted himself to the rock, enjoying the high elevation and the healing warmth of the late afternoon sun on his face. Opening his eyes, he gazed up towards the Heavens and saw a spectacular sight causing his heart to leap for joy. There, circling about forty feet directly overhead was a magnificent looking Red Tailed hawk gliding with the air currents, its beautiful feathers shimmering in the sun.

Brad had always believed in omens of a certain nature, and this glorious creature soaring with the breeze had always marked good luck soon to come. It was very comforting for him to see such a sign, especially at a time like this. There were two very significant omens that he had learned to acknowledge, once he had strengthened himself in his beliefs, and both were birds.

The Red Tailed hawk; which was always a welcomed sign, indicating fortune and happiness in times to come.

The other was the owl; which was ominous and foreboding. Always forecasting trouble, tragedy, and sometimes even death. Some cultures believed that owls represented wisdom and knowledge. Definitely not so for him.

He recalled the time specifically in which he'd had the worst encounter with the owl that he'd ever known. He was driving home from a friend's house late one night when he was around the age of twenty five, and an owl flew down out of the night sky and directly at his windshield. He stared in terror and fascination as it plummeted straight towards him. He thought for sure that it would burst right through his windshield and deliver him to Death itself but at the last possible second, it glanced off the glass and flew back out into the night. He had seen its face clearly and remembered the horrible intensity that had shown in its eyes. At that moment he'd felt as if someone had hit him in the chest with a sledgehammer, and he struggled just to breathe.

Later that night while he was asleep, his Appendix burst. He was sick for three days before finally being sent to the hospital for emergency surgery and he almost died. He'd never forget the excruciating week that he'd spent in the hospital, battling infections, as well as the six weeks of painstaking recovery at home thereafter. If he never saw another owl again, it would be too soon.

The most obscure part about those omens though, was that he never knew exactly how to interpret them. He usually tried to base his experience off of whatever emotion he was instinctually feeling at the time. When he saw a hawk, his heart was light and happy. When he saw an owl, he would always try to take every possible precaution to keep himself and his loved ones safe.

Today he was thankful for this omen.

Coming out of his reflective reverie, he continued back along the ridge and down the canyon to meet up with his awaiting comrades.

Approaching the two men, he saw them leaning up against the same rock nauseously, with two piles of puke not far from where they stood.

"So that's why I threw up!" he whispered to himself, again forgetting about how the consumption of Peyote almost always induced vomiting.

Chapter 20

Noting his approach, Jason wiped his mouth and asked, "Is it done?"

"It is," Brad replied solemnly.

"Fine then, let's get out of here," he said, and they all began the hike out of the canyon, and soon found themselves walking back across the immense desert plains that they had previously traveled on their way in.

They began meandering aimlessly, wandering off in different directions, only to meet right back up again to continue on the trail. They soon reached a group of rocks that stood out all alone in the open expanse and without words, sat down on the ground in a tight circle all facing one another.

The Mescaline was running strong now, and they found themselves preoccupied with looking all around, surveying their surroundings until Brad spoke up.

"Are you guys feeling this?"

Directing their attention towards him they nodded in unison, having facial expressions in between those of fear and expectation. "Gather near, boys," he said, draping his arms around each of them and pulling them in closer and more protectively. "I think we've just been through a slightly traumatic experience and we need to really support one another right now."

Leaning in and resting their heads together, Nick asked in a voice slow and thick with pain, "Brad, why did that have to happen?"

"I don't know Nick," Brad replied, his own voice sounding as if it were being played back off of a tape recorder in slow motion. "But honestly, don't you feel better?"

"I do," Nick answered with slurred speech that sounded as if it had been pulled from quicksand.

"Soundsss soooo sssssstrange!" Jason observed, startling himself with the grating hiss of his own vocal chords.

"Remember when we raced Terry back to our campsite?" Nick asked, chuckling at the recent but distant seeming memory.

They all laughed at that and then began to tell comical stories of Terry's antics, almost as if they were talking about a man who was no longer alive. They reminisced about his clumsiness and awkward demeanor, especially when he had been around Jack.

Soon Jason stood up swaying uncontrollably, like a man who'd had too much to drink, and staggered away laughing to himself. Nick then joined him and they both stumbled off into the desert, stopping here and there to admire the wildflowers or interesting landmarks in the distance.

Brad stayed behind and sat down, leaning back against a rock he'd found to be the perfect shape to generate the comfort he required to relax, and began to stare up into the sky. He saw a row of clouds coming in from the south and watched as they slowly drifted downward towards him. Simultaneously and from the north came a second mass of clouds which also caught his attention, and soon he found he was mesmerized. His eyes locked onto the spectacle that unfolded before him. Clouds usually only came in from one direction, mostly due to the wind currents, and he noted the beginning of a strange occurrence. As both masses of clouds approached each other they began to create a whirlpool effect, and joined together to form a virtual corkscrew of ethereal mist. Thin wispy trails, like fingers, began to drift straight down towards him in a spiraling pattern. Brad's smile stretched from ear to ear and his breath came in short gasps.

"Do you guys see this?" he asked, just barely above a whisper, laughing quietly and uncontrollably to himself. "It's like a show, just for me!" he giggled, as he just repeated the word "Wow" over and over again to himself. He could hardly fathom the natural effect that was occurring at that moment and believed that the Gods must have been smiling down their approval at him. His gratefulness was unbounded with appreciation to be allowed to have such an enlightening and beautiful experience such as this.

Chapter 20

He wanted to look over and call to the boys to come witness the event but he dared not take his eyes away even for a second, afraid that he may lose the wonderful view that he was treasuring every moment of.

A few moments later, Nick and Jason strolled right up to where Brad was lounging. They crept up on him from behind, grabbing his arm in an attempt to scare him. Brad would have been startled indeed, if he could have stopped himself from laughing so hard.

Acknowledging their presence he asked, "Can you guys see what I'm seeing?"

In between snickers, they both asked what it was that he thought he was experiencing.

"This!" he said, extending his arms out to the sky.

"We're seeing a lot of things right now!" Jason chortled, and he and Nick both broke into laughter.

"You guys have got to see this! Come sit here!" Standing unsteadily, he walked out of the natural circle of rocks in order to enable them both to lay back and witness the marvel.

A chorus of "Wows" quickly ensued as Brad said, "See! I told you!" However, in looking back up, Brad didn't see nearly the same miraculous event that had just taken a hold of him.

Then getting an idea, he told the boys to make room for him and he took a place right next to Nick and in looking up again, he saw more of the marvel that he had just witnessed.

"I get it! I get it now!" Brad shouted with glee. "We're in a power spot! Watch...if you get up and stand over there you won't see it like this. You have to be right in here!"

Jason got up and walked a foot or so, testing Brad's theory, and sure enough found out that he was right.

Lying back down, they all watched in pure fascination, until Jason quickly turned to Brad and said, "Look at my eyes!" Brad did so and gasped audibly, being shaken by what he saw. Jason's pupils were enormous and sparkling like glistening onyx and the intensity of the sight scared Brad enough to cause him to quickly tear his gaze away.

Slowly turning back to Jason he said, "Your eyes look like those of a scared rabbit!"

They all laughed then and Jason leaned over showing Nick as well, who just said, "Whoooooaaa!"

"Hazel Ra!" Brad stated, quoting their all-time favorite animated movie; Watership Down, his voice shimmering off into the distance.

Brad could remember the first time he'd watched that movie and he had fallen in love with it right away. He had never looked at rabbits the same again after that. The author of the book; Richard Adams, had a fascinating way of giving them personalities and even their own sort of lingo. The adventures and dangers that they'd experienced all seemed so relatable to Brad in some way. He immediately shared it with Jason who loved it as well; the disturbing yet uplifting story having stuck with them both.

"There's a dog loose in the woods!" Jason replied, his voice trailing off into echoes perfectly mocking a specific scene in the film.

"How do my eyes look?" Brad and Nick both asked almost simultaneously. Inspecting each of them Jason shouted out; "We're all scared rabbits!"

After more joking, laughter and movie quotes, the clouds began to dissipate and the boys realized that the show was over. They rose and stretched, and began staring all about, looking for the next interesting thing.

Jason announced his need to relieve his bladder and took off stumbling towards some large bushes.

In a mischievous tone, Nick turned to Brad and said, "Come on!" and they started sprinting off towards a large deep ravine not far away.

"Hey, wait for me!" they heard Jason shout out, off in the distance.

Chapter 20

"Don't worry!" Brad yelled back. "We're only going right over here!"

As they continued running, they could hear Jason yelling after them.

"Over where?" he asked, his voice sounding tiny and far away.

"Maybe we should wait for him," Brad noted with concern looking back.

"Aw, don't worry, we won't go too far," Nick assured him.

Easily convinced, Brad followed him down into the wash where they strolled casually, constantly surveying their surroundings, when all of a sudden Nick cried out in alarm and pointed towards the ground.

"Brad, look!"

Directing his gaze to the sand, Brad saw several large and small patches of bright red, spattering the floor of the wash.

"What is that?" Brad asked, grabbing Nick by the arm, obviously frightened.

Nick leaned in a little closer and shrieked, "It's blood!"

"Blood?" Brad echoed frantically.

Looking up and all around Nick said, "Maybe there was a mountain lion and it just killed something!"

They both turned to run in panic but only got a few feet away when Brad said, "Wait!"

Taking a few tentative steps back towards the crimson blotches, he slowly looked down and said, "Hey! It's not blood! They're plants!"

Cautiously returning to stand next to Brad, Nick saw for himself and they both looked at each other and started laughing. Up close, the tiny, red plants had a tangle of intricate vines all interwoven with one another, but from afar, the brightly colored stems gave off the deceptive appearance of blood stains.

Hearing Jason's voice trailing from up over the rise, Brad yelled excitedly, "Come on!" and they raced back over to meet up with him, immediately telling him about their ridiculous mistake.

"Hey, you guys! Look at this patch of wildflowers I found over here!" he said excitedly, leading the boys out further away from the original place of power.

The first thing Brad noticed was how much greener the entire area looked. Wild crabgrass seemed to sprout from several areas along with dark green tufts of wheat-looking bushes. Then, within a short distance they were in the midst of an enormous field of blossoming, desert wildflowers.

Walking carefully in between them so as not to crush even a single one, they gaped at the beautiful sight of multicolored flowers which looked to have just freshly bloomed from the rain.

Looking down on them they seemed to have a three dimensional appearance and the contrast of the shadows they gave off due to the setting sun only amplified the psychedelic experience.

"Beautiful, huh?" Jason asked rhetorically. "But check this out!" he said slyly. "Stop and kneel down and just stare at one for a minute."

Brad and Nick both complied without question, and soon Brad understood exactly what Jason was talking about. The clarity in the color of the petals, which stood out above all else, was spectacular to say the least. So rich and vibrant that Brad couldn't ever have recalled seeing such a pleasing and more gorgeous sight within nature. The tiny details of not only the petal's colors, but also their designs and formations, were mesmerizing.

"Keep watching!" Jason said expectantly, and Brad noticed a very subtle and surreal effect starting to take place. Concentrating on one blossom in particular, he could see the energy radiating from the flower as it rose up the stem and encompassed the petals, before slowly fluctuating up and out towards him. It was just like it had been with the stars the night before, only so much closer, and he could actually feel small amounts of real living energy emanating from it!

Then he stood up and broadened his gaze out towards the entire field and saw a sea of fluctuating energy. It was like an ocean of blossoms gently swaying with an intricate rhythm, all their own. He couldn't help but feel pure elation in what he saw. Nature is in itself a language, and at that moment he understood it perfectly. Smiling ridiculously, he couldn't remember being that happy in his entire life.

"This is what I've been waiting for!" he said joyously to himself. "This is why I came out here!"

With his spirits soaring, he basked in the wonderment of it all. Feeling an immense connection to everything pure and beautiful.

Everywhere he looked he saw energy; in the scrubs on the hillside, the grass on the ground and even in inanimate objects such as rocks and sand. It all radiated a definite power and it contributed to the existence that we all shared on this planet.

It was a true revelation and yet somehow deep down, it was something that he had already known. The Native American tribes on this planet had always understood that and had been one of the few races of humans to have ever learned to live in perfect harmony with the earth. Brad felt that he now understood how they had, experiencing such an intense oneness with nature at that moment.

Looking over at his best friends, he felt an enormous sense of camaraderie with them and knew that he had done the right thing by convincing them to come along on this journey. Walking away in no certain direction, he just let his mood take him wherever it may and looked back only once to see Jason and Nick doing the same as well.

Wandering aimlessly, Brad found himself walking alongside some giant boulders which lined the edge of a mountain not far from the area that the boys were still exploring.

Walking directly up to a high, steep cliff, he began to inspect the various crisscrossing lines and markings which mapped the face of the jutting rock. He found it so strange and interesting to see how the rock was naturally formed; probably deep within the earth before a cataclysmic event forced it above the surface.

A song by another one of his favorite bands called The Shins, drifted into his thoughts just then. His favorite song by them in fact; "Past and Pending" replayed in his mind. As he stared at the primitively etched markings, he experienced another wave of melancholy. The lyrics repeating "Lose yourself, in lines dissecting," sent long lost emotions of a time in his youth when the world was so different and everything meant something else.

Back then, his thoughts and feelings were almost the antithesis of what they are now; with of course the innocence of youth and lack of responsibility being a huge factor in that. He began to remember again the carefree days; when the only person he really had to worry about was himself. How different life had been! He would go to work and put his eight hours in at his crappy little job, but when he was done he could go home to his little apartment, get stoned, then go hiking with his buddies and enjoy nature and the company of good friends. He worked, ate, slept, paid his rent and bills, and just repeated the process week after week, month after month and he had never been happier. Somewhere along the lines however, he fell in love, had kids, and had to truly stabilize his life's patterns for the sake of his loved ones.

Gone were the days of just quitting a job because you weren't happy with it. No longer was he able to just come home from a hard day of work and go get high with friends and then skip off into the desert. Thinking of that cold, hard fact really tugged at his heartstrings just then.

It was rare for him to reflect back on life in this manner as he was normally like a soldier who just pushed on because of necessity and obligation. Having children especially, changed everything in that you ceased doing what might be best for you, so that you could do what was best for them and really that's the way it should be. Most of the time, he had been more than happy to do so; getting a different type of satisfaction out of his lifestyle now.

Chapter 20

Coming to conclusions like this had always bolstered Brad's reserve and helped confirm that he was doing the right thing. He had taught himself to live with as little regret as possible, and that had always helped him in moving forward in his life. Not just for his own sake, mind you, but for the sake of the ones whom he loved and cared about. So in this way of thinking, he was able to sustain a form of peace within himself. But was it enough? If it was then why was he out here? The real question. He had finally gotten down to it. He had obviously felt the need for something more and in putting those thoughts out to the Universe; he had ended up here. What was all this, really? Just a fun psychedelic trip to take to escape, and rehash old memories, or was it something profoundly more? How had he gone from an ordinary state of being and contentment, to where he was now? The trip to the desert certainly triggered it, but he had also gotten to a point in his life where he had been seriously asking himself just what sort of legacy he would leave behind. His children were part of his legacy of course, but what would he end up contributing to this world in the brief time that he had been put on this planet? He had always been a strong believer in making a difference, no matter how small, and always for the better.

Those things were extremely important to him. So far, he couldn't honestly say that he'd done much more than that on the smallest of scales. He knew that he was a good, generous and decent person, and so far that had been enough. Nothing had felt better to him than when he helped out another life form, be it human, plant or animal. What was he doing right now though, in this place, with his friends? Was it really to their benefit? He'd actually had more selfish motives when first designing this trip and now he was self analyzing his every move, especially concerning those who really trusted him. What would they take away from all this? What would they do if they found out that it was all a scam? That Jack wasn't who he had told them he was and that he actually had no problems with work or at home? And what would Nick say when he found out that Jason had no real problems either? Would they hate him? Or would it even matter, considering all the amazing things that they had already witnessed and the amazing things that were probably yet to come?

That last batch of Mescaline he had ingested was taking him way past his usual boundaries for introspection and while he couldn't say that he was very comfortable with it, he could at least admit that it was necessary. He knew then what he had to do. He had to give up whatever illusion of power and control that he thought he might have possessed, and trust completely in the forces that be. At least he would do his humanly best to try. Despite any subliminal reservations he might harbor contrary to this self agreement, he couldn't help but feel like something magnificent was soon to transpire. Already so much had happened to really shake his foundations and create new awareness that it wasn't hard for him to believe that more was just around the corner.

Smiling at that, he realized that the entire time he had been reflecting on all of this, he had been staring deeply into the various lines and roughly etched grooves which surfaced the rock he faced. Stepping back and regaining his focus, he nodded his head in a show of respect and recognition before turning to leave. With the lyrics of the song fading within his mind he walked away triumphantly, not once looking back.

Upon his return, Brad found Nick and Jason both lying down flat on their backs in the middle of the field of wildflowers, staring up at the sky peacefully. Chuckling to himself, he stood there with his hands on his hips shaking his head as he looked down at them.

"You guys should see yourselves!" he snickered.

Nick looked up a bit startled, apparently shocked at Brad's sudden appearance, but then went right back to looking at the clouds.

"Okay fellas," Brad said, clapping his hands together. "You guys ready to hit the trail? Go back to camp?"

Chapter 20

"Awww. It's so beautiful here," Jason groaned, as he pulled himself up to lean on one elbow. "Let's just stay here forever!"

"Yeah!" Nick agreed, still staring at the sky.

"Hey! This ain't Woodstock, you hippies!" Brad shouted as if he was some kind of sports coach. "Up! Up! Let's go, let's go!"

After more groans of disappointment, soon the boys were up and on their feet, Nick trailing wildflowers from his hair. Brad pointed at him and began laughing hysterically and when Jason caught sight of him, he did as well.

Catching on, Nick began brushing the flowers off his head feeling somewhat embarrassed. He then turned sharply and pointed his finger at Jason saying, "Take a look at yourself guy!"

Brad looked back over to Jason, and on a closer inspection saw that he had numerous flowers all tucked into his shirt collar and sleeves as well as the belt buckle of his pants.

Roaring with laughter Brad practically shouted, "You guys do look like you just came back from Woodstock!"

They all laughed heartily then and Jason threw out a quick Jimi Hendrix air guitar rendition of "Purple Haze" just for good measure.

"Come along flower children!" Brad said lightheartedly, as he began the trail that led them back to camp.

By the time they reached the Jeep the sun had just settled behind the mountains on the westward horizon, and in moments it was gone, leaving them in a tranquil state of twilight. With the light gone they felt a noticeable change in temperature and even a slight chill in the air. Rooting through the Wrangler they all found flannels and long sleeve shirts to wear, then headed over towards the fire pit.

"Well, should we get this thing started?" Brad asked, searching his backpack for a lighter.

"When is Jack due to be back?" Jason asked, and as Brad looked up he jokingly said, "Hey, that rhymed!"

Jason, not very amused, just continued to stare at Brad.

"I honestly don't know," Brad admitted with a sigh.

"Well then, why wait?" he shot back harshly, walking over to the Jeep to stand next to Nick who seemed to be trying to sort through some camping gear.

Brad sympathized with Jason's frustration because he didn't know the truth of things. He probably figured that Jack was neglecting his duties as their guide and was angry about it. Jason thought that Jack was running the show when in reality it was just Brad. How frustrated would he be upon finding out that little fact? Brad wondered yet again.

Shrugging away such useless thoughts, he focused on the task at hand and soon the small fire he had ignited was growing larger by the second. He watched as the flames first attacked the kindling then expanded to start licking away against the underside of the thicker branches. His eyes were reeled into the scene as the fire began to take its hold, consuming the small brush as it tried desperately to maintain a hold on the larger pieces. "We're gonna need more wood," Brad mumbled to himself then tore his gaze away from the fire as he turned and walked toward the Jeep. As he got closer, he heard music and by the time he reached the boys, he could identify the song. It was "Castles Made of Sand" by Jimi Hendrix; the very song that he had been thinking about the night before. Jason and Nick were both lounging in the back seat, listening, while staring at the ever darkening sky.

"I'm gonna go collect some more firewood, guys," Brad notified them. "We don't have enough to last us the night. Feel free to join me if you want."

He stood there waiting for some kind of a response when Jason said, "Yeah, okay man. Make sure you get enough. Thanks!"

Looking over at Nick, Brad could see that he would definitely not be joining him either as both seemed much too comfortable in their present jobs of doing nothing.

Chapter 20

With an exasperated sigh, Brad trekked out into the desert hoping to use the last of the twilight to help him find some dry pieces of wood to burn. Luckily enough, he found an old dead Mesquite tree and after inspecting it thoroughly, he proceeded to heft the larger branches back to camp and over near the fire pit. After about five trips, Brad was quite certain that he'd stocked a sufficient amount of wood and respectively thanked the tree for its contribution. He then went back for a drink of water and checked on the boys. They had fallen asleep, so Brad turned off the car stereo and gently nudged Jason then Nick.

"Rise and shine boys," he said softly, trying to be as polite as he could so as not to raise any hostility or unwanted anger from either of them. "We're all stocked up on fire wood now and we've got quite a blaze going. Thought you boys might wanna come check it out."

After some yawning and stretching, the guys exited the Jeep and sluggishly made their way over to the fire. When they got there, Jack was sitting on one of the rocks in the outer circle waiting for them.

"Jack!" Brad almost shouted, walking over and sitting down across from him. Nick and Jason both took their places around the fire, looking at Jack expectantly.

"Hello Searchers," Jack said, smiling warmly all the while. "There is a noticeable difference about you all. You look much better! How do you feel?"

"Feeling great, Jack!" Brad answered, speaking up for all of them.

Jack smiled at Brad in approval until Jason spoke up from the side, "Yeah, we're all good but where have you been?"

As Jack turned his stare over towards Jason, his smile disappeared and the boys could literally feel the goosebumps tingling the flesh on their arms.

"I have been away but always near," Jack said coldly yet calmly. "I have watched from afar and close by when needed, yet I have allowed you to maintain the necessary freedom to truly discover yourselves. I have done no more and no less than what your spirits and energy needed me to."

Seeming to visibly shrink under Jack's powerful gaze, Jason looked to Brad and began to stutter incoherently. Jack in turn, stood and stalked off into the desert night. For a few seconds there was a tense feeling in their midst which bewildered even Brad.

"Aw, way to go man!" Nick whispered harshly. "Why do you always have to go questioning the guy?"

"I'm sorry guys," Jason whined. "I just-"

As Brad stood up and walked after Jack he could hear Jason continue to babble apologies in the fading distance. Expecting to find Jack at any moment or around any corner, Brad kept walking, constantly looking all around the camp's perimeter. He eventually found Jack sitting on a rock, looking up into the night sky, and so approached him.

"Hey Jack, you okay?"

"Oh, I'm fine!" he replied, taking his attention off the stars to focus on Brad. "I hope I didn't scare your friend too much back there! I just don't appreciate always being second-guessed."

"Nah, he'll be fine. He gets a little impatient sometimes but I guess you put him in his place!"

Chuckling at that notion, Brad suddenly stopped laughing when he heard Jack's soft yet crisp voice say, "Brad. Come closer." Almost as if under some spell, Brad walked straight over to Jack, whereas Jack then immediately shined a small flashlight right into his eyes.

"Oh, ho, ho! Man! You should see the size of your pupils right now! That last batch of Peyote is really doing a number on you guys isn't it?" Jack laughed almost uncontrollably. Brad joined in his laughter and Jack had to stifle his snickering just to get out his next question. "You sure you guys are doing okay?"

"Yes, we're good," Brad answered. "We got rid of Terry."

"I can see that. I can't imagine how hard that must have been for you. For all of you. It truly is for the best. I'm proud of you Brad."

The last time anyone had told Brad that they were proud of him in such a manner was his father, and to hear it again now after so many years warmed his heart.

"So Jack...what's next?"

"Umm...I don't know man. I'm kind of out of tricks at this point. What more did you want? I thought that you guys would probably just hang out at the fire circle all night telling stories, then get some sleep and head back in the morning."

"Well, yeah. I guess so..." Brad replied, the disappointment evident in his voice.

There was a silence between the two of them until Jack spoke up suddenly.

"Hey, I know! Why don't I get my friends that I mentioned to come out and pay you guys a little visit? They're a bit younger than us but they have great costumes and they're really good actors! They're always looking for a reason to practice. We took acting when we were all in Theatre together years ago when I was-"

"No Jack! Please!" Brad said loudly, cutting him off, and then quickly looked back towards camp to make sure that he hadn't been overheard. Lowering his voice he quietly said, "No thank you, Jack. I don't want to risk it."

Jack looked down sheepishly, and then turned his head away from Brad as though his feelings were hurt.

"I was just trying to help," he said meekly out into the desert night.

"I know, it's okay. You know what? We'll be fine. You've done so much already. You've more than earned that money Jack and I can't thank you enough for all your help."

Jack looked back to Brad and smiled shyly. "Well...it's actually been fun. I haven't had a chance to do an acting gig like this in years!"

"And you were marvelous Jack!"

"Thank you again!" Jack said, bowing like a man on stage after a riveting performance. "But you're sure-"

"Yes! Thanks, but no thanks!" Brad said adamantly, cutting Jack off from the question that he knew was coming.

"Alrighty then!" Jack exclaimed in his best Jim Carrey impression of Ace Ventura.

"Do you think you'll be back later tonight Jack?"

"No, I don't suspect so. It looks like you guys can take it from here."

"Okay. So, I'll plan on giving you the cash tomorrow morning before we leave then. That way we can say goodbye. Does that work for you?"

"Sounds real good to me, Hoss!" Jack agreed, smiling widely. "So I'll see you guys in the morning. Have fun and be safe!"

"Thanks Jack!" Brad said, then turned and walked straight back to the fire, where he found the boys still in their places and seemingly a bit calmer.

"You alright?" Brad asked Jason, as he sat down on a rock and picked up his bottle of water taking a long drink.

"Yeah man, I'm sorry-"

"Hey, don't even worry about it! Jack may act a little edgy sometimes but he's really one of the good ones. At least from what I know of him. Anyway, what were you guys talking about while I was gone?"

"Oh, well Nick and I were talking about when we were kids growing up, and where we used to live and such."

"Ah, then!" Brad said enthusiastically. "Let's keep it going!"

So Nick picked up the thread of a story that he had been telling about some childhood friends of his, while Brad and Jason both listened with genuine interest. It wasn't often that Nick opened up

Chapter 20

like this and they were going to take advantage of that and absorb any information that he was willing to share about himself.

Soon it was Jason's turn and he recounted some nostalgic times that he had spent with his family, mostly his parents. Nick commented to Jason about how lucky he was to have spent real quality time with his dad, especially as he himself had never been very close with his father.

Brad took it all in with interest and admiration and soon it was his turn to do the telling.

"Come on Brad!" Jason goaded him. "You must have at least a couple of stories for us! You had great parents! Your mom was the sweetest and we both remember your dad real well. Man he was something else! You've gotta have some stories about him!"

"Yeah, come on man!" Nick started in from the side, supporting Jason. "Let's hear one!"

Brad had lost both his parents years earlier to cancer and at times found it somewhat hard even discussing them.

Oddly enough though he felt very at ease just then and nodded his head saying, "Okay, okay. Well first of all, I loved my mom very much and she was the strongest woman I ever knew. But I can't recollect any real interesting tales concerning her. My Pop however..."

As his voice trailed off, Nick and Jason looked at each other and smiled knowingly.

"Did I ever tell you guys about the time I drove my dad home and got chased by the cops when I was a kid?" he asked sincerely.

"Noooo!!!" They both replied in unison.

"Okay. Well, here it goes..."

Brad first cleared his throat while reflecting back on that adventure, and then he began his narrative.

"Well, Dad and I used to love going to the Drive-in movies on the weekends when I'd go to visit, and I'll never forget what happened on one particular night. I was about ten and a half years old then and Pop sent me to the snack bar to get him a large coke and whatever snacks and drink I wanted. You guys remember how my old man loved to drink his whiskey right?"

"Oh, yeah!" they both agreed, smiling widely.

"So when I'd come back he would always take the lid off his soda and tell me to drink as much off the top as I could. Then he would commence to pour in a half pint of whiskey and stir it all up. That way he could sit back and have a drink while we watched the show. It probably would have bothered me a lot more, even as a kid, except that my dad could drive better drunk than most people could sober, not that I'm condoning it or anything.

"Anyway, on this night whilst driving home after the show, I made the mistake of asking him if driving was a hard thing to do.

"'No, not at all he said!' and he pulled off onto a dirt road. 'I'll show ya! It's easy!'

"I tried my best to get out of the situation which I unwittingly put myself into, but to no avail. Dad insisted.

"So I hesitantly got into the driver's seat, barely even being able to see over the steering wheel of his 1981 Ford Econoline Van.

"'Just go slow,' he told me, so I began to creep along a desolate dirt road which led towards the general direction of his place about four miles away. It was scary at first but then I was doing great; picking up speed and avoiding any and all obstacles in the road. I was even starting to feel like a real big shot, that is until we ran out of dirt road and had to get back onto the pavement. So Dad, more than slightly inebriated, tells me to keep going and be careful, refusing to take back the wheel even though I begged him to. So then we're traveling down this paved road at around ten thirty, eleven o'clock at night and I see a car heading towards us and it starts flashing its lights.

Chapter 20

"'Ah, you've got your high beams on,' Dad tells me. 'You gotta hit that button on the floorboard down there on the left.' Well, I, being barely able to even touch the gas pedal was at a loss.

"'Where, Dad?' I kept asking him over and over again, trying to feel for it with my left foot while maintaining pressure on the gas with my right, and also keep my attention on the road.

"'It's right down there! On the left!' he kept saying, and all the while the car approaching us kept flashing its lights at me. Finally, the guy passed by and Dad said, 'Never mind.' Feeling slightly relieved but still stressed, I pleaded with my dad again to take the wheel but he wouldn't. Said I was doing fine.

"It wasn't long before another car approached and this one started flashing us even more fanatically than the last guy, and again my dad kept barking at me to hit the high beam button! Despite my best efforts I just couldn't find it and as the car drew closer and closer I got more and more frantic. As soon as it passed us by, Dad said, 'Shit! That was a cop, and he's turning around! Floor it!' Reacting instantly, I put the pedal to the metal and in seconds was roaring down the road at around seventy miles an hour!"

Gasps and giggles flowed forth from Nick and Jason as they listened to the story with glee.

"So there I am, a ten year old kid, driving his drunk dad at seventy miles an hour, and getting chased by the police!

"Dad said, 'Quick, turn here!' and I spun around the corner of a dirt road at what felt like about forty miles an hour, sliding through the sand and desert then turning the wheel hard trying not to over correct, my dad looking out the back window constantly.

"'Turn off your lights!' he yelled, and I searched in a panic for the knob, finally finding it on the dashboard. Streaming along a dirt road at around fifty miles per hour at night with no headlights, while being chased by the cops will get your adrenaline going, let me tell ya!

"'Coast in here!' Dad said, as I turned into the long driveway that led to his place, scraping bushes and trees into his opened window most of the way while Dad cursed out obscenities. I pulled to a stop and he reached over, put it in Park and turned the key off and told me to be quiet. We both watched as the cop slowly drove down the road trying to find some evidence of our passing, then continued on his way out of sight. Once the threat was gone Dad said, 'Ah, you did great pal!' clapping me on the shoulder. 'Come on, let's go in.'

"I must have stayed there frozen behind that wheel for several seconds, bordering on hyperventilation, before I finally stumbled out of the van and went inside. And that was my dad for ya!"

"Unbelievable!" Nick breathed as he and Jason just stared at Brad shocked. Then they all erupted into snickering laughter.

Brad had come to realize later on in life that his father had taught him a valuable lesson that night; that we are all capable of surviving and overcoming some of the most outlandish situations in life, even as children. While the boys just kept chuckling, Brad looked up to the sky and silently mouthed the words, "Love you Pop."

So the story telling continued on into the night. The boys reminisced about long forgotten adventures, each helping the others out in remembering different details and characters. Eventually Brad noticed that Nick was holding something in his hand but couldn't tell at all what it was. Reaching the end of one of their stories, Brad looked over at Nick curiously and asked him, "Hey Nick. What are you holding in your hand?"

Catching Jason's attention as well, they both stared at Nick expectantly.

"Huh?" Nick asked, looking down almost as if he had been unaware that he'd been holding anything. "Oh, yeah! You guys remember when we went out last night to complete our little tasks?" Jason and Brad both nodded as one. "Well, this is the pod I got from the plant I found. It's special...well at least to me."

Chapter 20

"Let us see it!" Jason begged Nick.

Opening his hand and leaning in closer to the fire light, Nick exposed his precious gift.

"What is that?" Jason asked, unimpressed.

"It's a seed pod!" Brad said excitedly. "From a Datura plant! You know, Jimson Weed?"

"Uh, okay..." Jason said, obviously not really caring much about it at all.

"I'm not sure what I'm supposed to do with it, but I know that it means something. I just don't know what," he said in a sad and puzzled voice.

"Can I hold it Nick?" Brad asked politely.

"Sure!" Nick said, happily handing it over to Brad as if it were a Rubik's Cube that he hadn't been able to solve but maybe Brad could.

Turning it over in his hand, it split open a little, pouring out a few brown, dried up seeds.

"You know..." Brad began.

"What?" Nick asked hopefully.

"Uh oh," Jason said from the side, recognizing Brad's tone as one foretelling possible trouble.

Ignoring Jason completely he responded, "I know that people actually eat the seeds, although if not done in the right amount it can be extremely dangerous. But I also know that you can smoke them once they're this dried out."

Jason looked at Brad skeptically. He then looked to Nick then back at Brad again.

"Nooo! No! You guys can't be serious!"

However, judging by the looks on both of their faces, they most certainly were.

Jason just stared down at the ground shaking his head.

"If we do it, we all do it together," Brad said, looking over at Jason already knowing that Nick was all in on this one.

"Seriously?" Jason whined, while Nick continually nodded his head affirmatively.

"I found it for a reason," Nick said. "We were meant to do this."

Exhaling a huge breath, Jason looked back at Brad who had already poured some of the seeds into his palm before handing the pod back over to Nick. Outvoted and outgunned, Jason knew it would be futile to resist.

"What are we gonna use to smoke it out of?" Jason asked hopefully, thinking that he'd just found a loophole in getting himself off the hook with this one.

"We'll use the pipe we found in the back seat of the Wrangler yesterday," Nick retorted, checkmating Jason into the unorthodox maneuver.

"Damn," Jason muttered under his breath as Nick grinned at him slyly.

"I'll go grab it!" Nick said happily, and rushed off to the Jeep.

While he was gone Jason whispered, "You sure you wanna do this?"

"Yeah, why not? Nick really wants to and we need to support him. I've never seen him so 'gung ho' about wanting to do something. What's got you so worried anyway?"

Jason stared at Brad intensely for a few moments before replying, "Remember what happened last time when you tried that Spice stuff?"

Brad's face lost all color and he swallowed hard.

Remember? How could he ever forget that night? Years ago they had both been at a friends house for a visit, and not having seen him in a long time they chatted for a while trying to bridge the gap. At one point, their friend took out a marijuana pipe and started smoking it. Knowing that his job administered regular drug tests, they turned and looked at each other in astonishment.

"Oh it's not weed," he clarified. "I started smoking this other stuff that you can order through the mail or get from the local smoke shop and it won't show up on a drug test. It's called Spice, and it gets you pretty high."

"Hmmm..." Brad contemplated. "Interesting. You're positive that it won't show up on a drug test?"

"Yep. I've already been tested and it was all clear."

Looking at Jason, Brad asked, "What do you think?"

"Yeah, sure. Why not? Might be a good way for you to have fun and still beat the system."

Jason knew that at the time, Brad's employers also drug screened on occasion but Brad had always been too responsible to take a chance.

So they passed the pipe around and Brad took an enormous amount of smoke into his lungs, holding it in at length before exhaling. He didn't notice anything at first but then thirty seconds later it hit him like a shotgun blast. Tunnel vision completely took over his range of sight and a terrible sense of paranoia gripped him like a madman in the throes of insanity. He felt a wave of pure panic and judging by the looks on his friends faces, it emanated from him. Jason glanced at him then did an immediate double take.

"Hey man, are you okay?"

"I don't think so," Brad responded, rising from his seat, stumbling for the sliding glass door, trying to make his way outside as calmly as he could.

The smoking mixture assaulted him on every level and not in any way good. Once out front he paced the driveway, cursing and swearing with paranoia, convinced that his friend had mixed marijuana in with the strange herbs, and got horrifically worried that he would now fail a drug test and lose his job. But that wasn't the worst of it. He was rapidly losing all of his capacity for logical thinking and his sight was getting more and more out of focus. He had to try extremely hard just to maintain some semblance of rational thought, and he became dizzy and lightheaded. When his friends came looking for him, he feigned exhaustion from a long day and stressed his need to get home because he had to work early the next morning.

After some apologies to his friend, he threw his keys at Jason and demanded that he take him as far away from there and as fast as he could.

As they drove Brad began to suspect that he might have been having a possible allergic reaction to the drug, and that thought only heightened his fear and panic. He found it hard to breathe and lost all sense of direction and normal awareness, not even knowing what day it was. He tried to drink some water but found it nearly impossible to swallow. The scenario was pretty close at times to the epic scene from the movie "Up in Smoke" where Cheech had smoked too much of Chong's dynamite weed and had a total meltdown. Jason had to scream at Brad to mellow out and remind him just to breathe. More than once, Brad considered having Jason take him straight to the E.R.

By the time they reached Brad's place he was in even worse shape. He'd developed an intense headache and eventually ended up vomiting. Jason had to use Brad's truck to drive himself home because Brad was nowhere near in any kind of shape to do it himself. Jason stayed with Brad most of that night though, and took care of him. Brad would be forever grateful and indebted to Jason for that. Jason had looked after Brad more times than he could count in their long standing friendship, and Brad loved him for it.

That was one hell of a lesson Brad had learned about trying experimental drugs! Snapping out of his reverie, he looked up to find Jason studying him curiously.

"You know, you raise a damn good point Jay! But in defense, I can say that I have tried this before, and more than once, and was okay with it. I'll risk it for Nick's sake."

"Man! You are one hell of a friend!" Jason said shaking his head in disbelief.

Chapter 20

"So are you Jay," Brad pointed out to him.

"Okay. Let's do it," Jason replied, finally fully acquiescing to the endeavor.

"Yeah, let's!" Nick said giddily as he sat back down, pipe in hand.

"Is there still weed in that?" Brad asked with concern.

"Nah. It's all gone. I emptied it out just to be sure."

"Okay," Brad said, fully trusting Nick.

Taking the pipe from Nick, he set the seeds down on the boulder and started grinding them up a bit with a smaller rock. Scooping up as much as he could, he filled the bowl of the pipe then handed it back to Nick who already had a lighter. Taking a long draw off the pipe, Nick filled his lungs and then handed it off to Brad with a trail of dense smoke escaping from the bowl. Brad waited for a few seconds to see what kind of reaction Nick was going to have and when he saw Nick calmly exhaling the thick smoke, he decided to go in for his share. Sparking the bowl, Brad inhaled deeply, feeling the textured smoke flow down his throat and filter into his chest and lungs. He didn't hold it in too long though and it felt a little harsh as he blew it out. He could taste the flavor of the bitter, dry seeds and he could also slightly taste marijuana. Handing it over to Jason, he coughed a couple of times then reached down to grab his bottle of water and took a drink to soothe his throat. Jason took a good sized hit and then handed it back over to Nick.

"I can still taste the weed in that pipe," Brad declared to Nick, who was obviously already aware.

"Yeah, it's probably still got some resin in it but I doubt that it will do anything to counteract the effect," Nick replied without worry.

Brad looked at him and shrugged, conceding to his point. After all, it was too late now. Nick took another hit of the Jimson Weed and handed it back to Brad again.

"I don't know man," he hesitated, a little concerned. "Shouldn't we wait a while to see what effect this will have on us before we do much more?"

"You can wait if you want but hand it over here!" Jason commanded boldly, leaning over and taking the pipe from Brad.

Brad watched as Jason took a fairly good sized draw, exhaling smoke through his mouth and nose at the same time. He blew out so much that Brad almost expected it to come out of his ears as well! Jason then handed Nick the pipe again but this time Nick just waved it away. Offering it up to Brad once more, he set it down as he saw Brad shaking his head. Then all of a sudden, even though it was already night, everything got just a little bit darker. A slightly ominous feeling took hold and the three men just stared back and forth at one another.

"Did you guys feel that?" Brad asked with a hint of fear in his voice.

"I definitely felt that," Jason responded, confirming what Brad was sensing as Nick just nodded his head emphatically.

"Well...this is it fellas! Enlightenment or bust!" Brad said, giggling at his own self-made proclamation, while Nick and Jason continued to look around anxiously.

Brad noticed their frightened expressions and tried to put them both more at ease.

"So I don't know about you guys, but so far I have learned a lot on this trip. So many things in my life that I needed to address, and I was finally able to do some much needed analytical thinking."

"Oh yeah man," Jason returned, focusing all of his attention on Brad. "We never had a chance to talk about any of that. So what's going on with you anyway? Is everything gonna be alright with work and the wife and kids?"

Nick looked from Brad to Jason then back to Brad again confused.

Chapter 20

"What do you mean what's going on with him? What's going on with you? You're the reason I came out here in the first place. Are you okay?" Nick asked with concern.

"Me?" Jason answered dramatically. "I came out here to support this guy!" he said, pointing to Brad.

"Brad?" They both asked simultaneously.

"Uh, well...you see...I...uh..." Brad stammered, looking guilty as sin. "I kinda told Nick that you had a problem, so that I could get him out here," he admitted, addressing Jason.

"What?" Jason practically screamed. "I don't have a problem! Brad's the one who wanted...no scratch that; needed to come out here! I'm just here for him. He said you were too."

"Dude!" Nick exclaimed with disappointment evident in his tone. "You didn't have to make up a story just to get me to come out here man. You could have told me the truth."

"I would have!" Brad whined, "But I didn't think you would have come!"

"So the cat's out of the bag, huh Brad? What else aren't you telling us?" Jason asked angrily.

Brad looked at Jason and then seemed to look past him, his eyes going distant. If their reaction to his first little fib was this bad, then what would they do if they found out about Jack? He began to feel seriously panicked because he knew that at this point, he couldn't lie to them anymore, but being that they were all so intensely altered, he feared their ultimate reactions may prove extremely unpredictable and it truly scared him. He was so close to making it all the way through this trip without having to reveal his sordid little plans and mild deceits. God how he wished for a miracle at that point in time! Anything just to stall them or take their attention off this newly revealed facade!

And he got it. Just as Jason was about to really lay into him, Nick shushed them both as he listened intently, slowly scanning the area all around him in the dark.

"What-" Jason started to ask when Nick cut him off.

"I heard something."

After a few seconds of total silence, they all began to hear it.

Footsteps and the distant sound of people talking. As one, they all turned toward the direction of the noises and saw four young men walking forth from the desert and straight into their midst.

"Hey there guys!" the one in the very front called out as he approached. "We saw your campfire from way back there and thought we'd come say hello!" he announced cheerfully. As they all stood lined up together, he asked, "Is it okay if we join you?"

Jason shot Brad a questioning look and Brad, never taking his eyes off the four, responded, "Yeah sure guys! Pull up a seat wherever you can find one."

After they'd all sat down, the one who initially spoke to Brad made introductions.

"Hey, I'm Jake. This is Gabe, that's Eli, and that over there is Zeke," he finished, pointing out each member of his party.

Brad then addressing Jake said, "I'm Brad, that's Jason and that and over there is Nick."

A bunch of "Hellos" and "Nice to meet ya's" ensued thereafter and then a silence as they all quieted down and waited for the other side to start a conversation. Without being rude, Brad looked each of them over noticing that they were probably of Native American descent or possibly Mexican; or both. They had very tan skin with prominent stoic features and all had thick black hair; not necessarily long but a bit shaggy. After a moment of pondering, Brad got a notion and spoke up.

"Your names…"

"Yes?" Jake asked, looking curiously at Brad.

"They're biblical names aren't they?"

As the new visitors looked to one another they seemed a bit astonished, and then started chuckling to themselves.

"You know, you're the first person that's ever gotten that right away! My given name is Jacob, his is Gabriel, and that's Elijah and Isaac. How did you pick up on that so quickly?"

All heads turned to Brad awaiting a response and Brad just looked down at the dirt and replied, "You know, I'm not really sure. It just occurred to me."

After some more moments of silence, and not the comfortable kind, Nick spoke up capturing everyone's attention.

"So what are you guys doing way out here?"

"Oh, we just came from town and are headed back to the reservation," Jake answered.

So they are Native American, Brad thought to himself confirming his earlier suspicions.

"Normally we hike back more west of here but we spotted your fire and thought we'd see who was camping. So what are you guys doing way out here?" Gabe asked, speaking up from across the fire.

"Well..." Jason started to respond, "We actually came out here to support the whim of a friend."

The four young men exchanged confused glances and before anyone else could speak again, Brad interjected, not wanting the conversation to go down an awkward road.

"So anyway, I'm curious..." Brad began, drawing all eyes back to him. "You guys look Native American. Are you?" They all responded affirmatively, and so Brad continued. "How did you guys get your names then?"

Eli spoke up for the first time then and said, "I like this guy! He's very observant!"

More like very high, Brad thought to himself as he began to really feel the effects of the Datura creeping in and grow more intense by the minute. Looking at Jason and Nick, who kept blinking their eyes in order to refocus, he saw that they were probably feeling much the same way.

"Well..." Zeke chimed in, "why don't we let Jake tell that story? He's schooled the best out of all of us in the ways of Literature and Theatre and can probably tell it better than anyone."

"Sounds good!" Brad said, looking over to Nick and Jason who were both nodding their heads.

"Okay!" Jake said enthusiastically. "Well, we were all born on the Res and are pretty much as close as brothers. Our mothers were Missionaries who came here from the Midwest with a group of other Christians back in the late seventies. Apparently, they had some idea that the Natives out here were nothing but a bunch of hedonistic savages that were in dire need of saving! What's really funny is that from what we've been told, our mothers were actually the most fanatic in the group! All of the people on the Reservation hated them at first because they insisted on conversion, and wouldn't stop spreading the Word of God!"

"Wow!" Brad remarked, intrigued. Not only by the story, but by the storytelling as well. Zeke was right, Jake was marvelous! Using hand gestures and accentuating the tone and timbre of his voice to reel in the listener.

"So what happened?" Jason asked, equally as curious.

"Eventually the group left, giving up on our people as a lost cause, but our mothers decided to stay. They refused to admit defeat and probably stayed on out of pure stubbornness!"

They all had a good laugh then, picturing conservative white women staying in Teepees and living off the land even though they hated it, just to prove a point.

"So one night, the man who was the Shaman of our tribe back then said that he had received a sign of some sort and tricked them into drinking Peyote tea on the first night of the Sun and Moon Dance. It's lucky that they didn't lose it altogether because it was said that they drank a lot!"

Jason, Nick and Brad, all snuck quick glances at one another, trying not to be too conspicuous at the reference to Peyote. The other three guys were grinning widely now for they knew the story well and what was going to happen next.

"Normally they called such traditions sacrilegious and would have nothing to do with them, but when that Peyote kicked in... Pow! They had no choice! They danced all night and most of the next morning until they collapsed, and our elders took them in and cared for them as if they were one of our own. They must have had some serious revelations because they were never the same again after that. They started learning all of our customs and fell in love with our fathers. Then they had us! We were all born within a few months of each other, and we have an incredible bond."

"Are your moms' still living on the Reservation?" Nick asked from the side.

"Yep!" Jake replied cheerfully. "Still there! Right now they're all back in the Midwest visiting with friends and family though. The craziest thing is that now they go back there and try to convert Christians into joining our way of life! They call it: Way of the Truth.

"Wow!" Jason, Brad and Nick all responded as one.

All went silent again, and Brad pondered the story they were just told. There was so much symbolism and significance in it that just about anyone could probably take some sort of lesson away from it. Looking back up at Jake who just sat there staring at the fire, smiling, Brad couldn't help but think about how much he looked like a younger version of an ancient warrior from some long ago tribe that had been lost to the ages. He marveled at the irony in the story, never doubting for a second its authenticity.

"But your parents still gave you biblical names!" Brad blurted out, bringing them back to the original point of the story.

"Yes," Jake said nodding his head, pleased that Brad had picked up on that. "When we were born they insisted on it. I guess it's funny, well rather more strange than funny, but no matter how strong your belief system is; there is always that tiny bit of uncertainty. Whether it was out of fear, doubt or respect, we may never know, but they felt it was appropriate. Perhaps they wanted never to forget where they came from and how far they've come. Anyhow, we were all raised to believe in Native culture and we sure are glad for that, aren't we guys?"

"Amen!" the three shouted in unison, and Brad and the boys looked up with shocked expressions.

The four young men erupted into hysterical laughter which soon infected everyone and they all chuckled until their sides ached.

As the boys all chatted amongst themselves, Brad just stared into the dancing flames, thinking about how unpredictable life could be and how just when you thought you'd found stability, the Universe could turn you upside down and show you otherwise. He also sensed that the effects of the Jimson Weed were accelerating, and quite rapidly now. He felt a slight bit of a marijuana high as well, which he hoped wouldn't counteract any positive insights he'd been searching for and cause him to feel paranoid. Something had been nagging at him ever since the beginning of the story but he just couldn't put his finger on it. Something to do with these new found friends of theirs. What was it? he screamed at himself inside of his own mind. Soon he started to feel as though he couldn't even handle being around anyone anymore and he desperately sought to find a way to leave and be alone. He was thinking all these desperate thoughts when he was brought back from his contemplative paranoia by a word; Jack.

"Yeah, we know Jack!" Jake said to Jason, obviously just having been asked if he knew of him.

Pure panic raced through Brad's brain as it occurred to him; these were Jack's friends! The ones he had talked about! They were

Chapter 20

the acting buddies that he had tried so hard to involve in Brad's trip! He didn't have to send them over to put on a show, for they had found them all on their own and purely by accident! Brad had never even considered that as a possibility. They were about to blow his whole plan and reveal Jack for who he truly was and it would be completely unintentional. Talk about irony! Brad thought, and he felt sick to his stomach. How would Jason and Nick react? What would their new friends think? He had to get out of there. Standing quickly, he staggered off towards the direction of the rock mountain without a word to anyone.

"Hey, where you going?" Jason called out after him. "Are you okay?"

"Yeah, I just need to take a leak," Brad croaked, stumbling off towards the cliffs.

Once he reached the base, he leaned his hand up against a rock, feeling flushed and fevered, knowing that the jig was up. It didn't help that he was extremely stoned as well, and the high just got more and more intense. He started thinking about what he might say to his friends and then realized that he didn't want to think about any of that just now. He began to wander aimlessly through the canyon until he reached a dead end within the wash. Not to be deterred, he started climbing the slick, gray rock near the bottom until he reached a ledge in which he could get a better foothold. The texture of the rock became more abrasive and he drove himself on, climbing from tier to tier, trying to get as high up and as far away as possible. Leaning against a ledge and breathing heavily from the strenuous climb, he could still hear their voices. Seeing the glow from the fire, he slowly trudged towards the edge of the precipice and looked down trying to get a clear view of the boys below.

"I hope your friend is alright," Jake commented with concern, looking back in the direction that Brad had originally left in.

"He'll be fine," Brad heard Jason respond with perfect clarity. "So anyway, tell us about Jack."

"Oh, yeah! That guy! What a character!"

Brad couldn't stand to hear anymore, knowing that he'd been done in. It was his own fault too. Why couldn't he just have been honest with his friends right from the start? He wouldn't blame them if they just took the Jeep and left him stranded out in the middle of that desert. He'd probably earned that. Turning back toward the cliff, he started climbing higher. He knew that he could never climb high enough to get out of this situation but he may as well try.

Stepping onto boulders and scraping through the rugged mountain brush, he toiled on. Eventually he got very near to the top and found another large wash which wound its way up through another canyon. It looked as though it would probably come out on the very top so he headed off that way but then slowed and came to a stop. The terrain had changed dramatically and he noticed a lot of Desert Oak growing sporadically among the edges as well as some scraggly pines. The scenery immediately reminded him of a place he used to love to go hiking up in Pioneertown.

He and his dad, or sometimes friends, would hike all around the mountains there and would almost always end up at Pappy and Harriet's for a drink or some dinner afterward.

He could remember being a boy no more than seven or eight years old when Pappy used to roam the bar and restaurant, talking with customers and friends, telling stories. He could even vaguely remember a somewhat whiskey buzzed Pappy, sitting him down on his knee and asking him how he was doing and if he was being good or not. Pappy had always been a really kind man. Sometimes a little gruff, but then again that was common to most of those old timers back then. Harriet was always the sweetest woman ever, giving him cokes and handing him beers to take to his dad back when people allowed kids to handle alcohol and be inside bars.

Chapter 20

That was a lifetime ago to him now. He remembered some years later hearing about Pappy having passed away and it greatly saddened him. He wasn't sure what became of Harriet but he knew that two ladies from New York, Robyn and Linda, had ended up buying the place and kept it going. There were a few close calls, he had heard, with fires and financial hardships, which had almost forced the place to close down but they had endured. Those gals had ended up really putting that place on the map and had secured some of the biggest names in music to come play there. In doing so, it attracted people from hundreds and even thousands of miles around. Robyn always remembered him and embraced him with a warm hug while sweet Linda always had a drink for him readily on hand. The warmth and western décor of that place was memorable and he always felt comfortable and at home there. Yes, wherever Pappy was looking down from, he had to be proud of those girls indeed for carrying on the legacy!

Standing at the edge of the wash, the much needed distraction of that memory gave Brad a warm feeling all over just thinking about it, but then suddenly something snapped him out of his reverie. All went deathly still around him without so much as even a slight breeze in the night air and he found his attention drawn up towards the top of the sandy wash. Marveling at the shiny luminescence of the moon's light reflecting off the cliffs, he looked up to the moon itself. Then unexplainably, he sensed something near. Jerking his head back towards the wash he waited and listened.

"Brrraaaaaaad..." came a voice, calling out his name in a chilling, otherworldly tone.

His entire body grew ice cold and he froze in his tracks. The voice sounded as if it were almost carried by a breeze and yet it felt more as if it had been inside his head. He reasoned that it must have been the wind and relaxed a bit until he heard it again, only more faint.

"Brrraaaaddd..."

That repeated calling left no doubt this time, and he had not felt even a trace of a breeze just then. There was something beckoning him to continue up the wash, and again he stood rooted to the spot. Then very cautiously he began to creep his way up the white sandy wash, not knowing what to expect from one moment to the next.

When he finally reached a bend near the top of the wash, he stopped. He had not again heard the voice since the second time it had called out to him yet he definitely felt as if something were still drawing him up towards it. He couldn't describe it but somehow he knew that if he continued on with his journey; something was going to change him. He couldn't even begin to guess what would happen but he knew one thing for certain; he would never be the same again. He took a few steps back towards the cliff he had originally climbed, and saw the faint glow of the fire reminding him that his friends were down there waiting for him. He hesitated then, and that was all the incentive he needed, being as spooked as he was at that moment, and turning tail he ran back.

He climbed down the cliff tiers as fast as he could, scraping himself on the jagged rocks and bristly desert brush, and soon found himself back at the bottom approaching the fire pit where his friends awaited.

Chapter 21

"Hey man, where did you run off to?" Jason asked with concern, when he saw Brad come striding forth from the desert, looking bruised and shaken. "We were starting to get worried about you."

Staring down at the ground the entire time as he approached, Brad suddenly looked up to see that the newcomers had departed and it was only Nick and Jason who remained.

"Where'd they go?" Brad asked in a monotone voice.

"Aw, they had to get back they said, but wanted us to tell you goodbye and that they hope you're feeling okay," Nick answered from the side.

Sitting back down on his rock, Brad waited for the axe to fall. After a long silence in which Nick and Jason just stared at Brad curiously, Brad finally dared to ask.

"So what did they have to say about Jack?" he inquired, wincing in anticipation of their response.

"Oh, it was the wrong guy." Jason clarified. "Not the same Jack. They were talking about a friend that lives in the next town over." Brad was so shocked that he almost collapsed. He released a gigantic sigh of relief, and then nodded his head hopefully. "Hey man, are you sure you're okay?" Jason asked again.

"Yes, I'll be fine now!" Brad replied, gaining his composure. Jason and Nick stared at one another with concern evident on their faces.

"Brad," Jason called to him in a serious tone. "What happened to you man? You are obviously shook up. Tell us!"

Brad glanced at Nick then, who eyed him expectantly.

Two things raced through Brad's brain then; he wanted desperately to tell them about the voice that he'd heard call his name and the feelings that he had experienced along with it, but more importantly he wanted to tell them everything. The truth about Jack and the truth about him wanting to come out here. He wanted to try to explain to them everything that was going on inside of him. All of it; once and for all. He was so close to doing it that he started to open his mouth to speak but then closed it again and looked back down at the ground, shaking his head. He was so vulnerable at that point that he felt as though he just couldn't survive another onslaught of negative energy. Especially from his best friends. So his fear kept him in his shell.

"I can't right now guys…I just can't. I'm sorry."

His window of opportunity shattered, he retreated back within himself feeling like a traitor. Here were his two best friends reaching out to him, wanting to help him, and he still couldn't take the first step. As he stared guiltily at the ground he heard Jason blow out an exasperated sigh, clearly aimed at him.

"You know what Brad? I'm starting to get really tired of all this. You bring us all the way out here to the middle of nowhere, pump us full of drugs, then lead us on some never ending adventure, and for what? Why are we even doing this? You still haven't told us! We've been patient and supportive and what do we get back? Secrets and silence! Well I'm sick of it!" he ended, getting up and storming off in a huff out into the desert dramatically.

Brad watched him go and looked up in shock, for out of the corner of his eye he saw the white fleeting image of what could only have been an owl flying overhead. Brad sucked in his breath and looked to Nick, fearing the worst.

Chapter 21

"I hate to say it, guy, but he has a point. I'm high as a kite right now but I can still see that you're hiding something. I just hope that whatever it is, it's worth causing this rift in our friendship."

"B..b..b...b-" Brad stammered, but never got the sentence out, noticing a dark shape move out in the distance behind Nick, and all sounds ceased.

Nick, picking up on it by the look on Brad's face, turned and squinted out into the darkness behind him.

"I saw something move out there." Brad spoke barely above a whisper.

"I see it too," Nick said, sounding somewhat alarmed. "Jay, is that you?" he called out into the night, waiting for a response.

"What?" Jason asked in an aggravated tone, walking back in from the opposite direction to rejoin them at the fire.

"There's something moving out there," Brad stated, pointing out towards the darkness. "See...there!" Brad whispered harshly.

Jason, obviously seeing it too, suddenly looked a little spooked as well and all three tensed in trepid anticipation.

"Who's out there?" Jason yelled in about as brave a tone as he could muster.

The dark outline of a person approached slowly and they all held their breaths in anticipation. As the form almost reached the fire, a very familiar feeling began to wash over them all, and then a person stepped into the light.

It was Terry.

"Terry...is that you?" Jason managed to squeak out.

"Hey guys," he confirmed. "I didn't have anywhere else to go so I came back looking for you. I saw the fire and knew it'd be you guys."

The mood immediately took a turn for the surreal and all three of the boys just stared at him, jaws agape. As Terry stood there with his head hanging down, no one knew what to say and the awkward silence seemed to be endless.

"Ummmm...how are you doing Terry?" Brad finally managed to spit out, not having a clue as to what else to say.

"I'm okay, I guess," he answered in a forlorn manner.

More silence. Brad looked to Jason who seemed ashamed and then to Nick who looked beyond embarrassed. Knowing that this couldn't go anywhere good, Brad took the initiative and called over to Jason.

"Jay, can I talk to you for a second?"

"Uh...yeah sure man," Jason said, quickly getting up to join Brad as he began heading over to the Jeep.

"Hey Nick, we'll be right back."

Nick looked over at them both with an "Aww, come on guys, don't leave me here alone with him!" look, but Brad and Jason just kept walking.

Once at the Jeep and out of earshot, Jason turned to Brad.

"Oh my God! Is this really happening? What the hell are we supposed to do? I don't know about you but I am way too high to deal with this right now!"

"I am too. I can't believe he came back! What is wrong with this guy?"

"I don't know man but I am trippin' out right now! And we just left poor Nick with him. What should we do?"

"We've gotta ditch him somehow. This is all wrong. Can't you feel it?" Brad asked, as he reached over and grabbed a backpack, stuffing bottles of water inside.

"It's oppressive and I definitely feel it!" Jason answered.

Nodding his head, Brad said, "Let's call Nick over here."

"Hey Nick!" Jason yelled out to him immediately. "Can you come over here for a moment alone please?" They both waited as Nick excused himself away from Terry and hurriedly walked over to the Wrangler.

Chapter 21

"Hey," he said, once he got right next to them and they all huddled in close.

"How's he look to you?" Brad asked Nick.

"Man, he has a strange look about him and he's acting really nervous. Thank God you called me over! I was getting nervous!"

"Look guys," Brad said, "We are all really high on weed, Datura and Peyote, and personally I don't think we should have to deal with this right now. Let's ditch Terry and go find somewhere to chill out. He'll be fine here until we figure out what to do."

Brad got no arguments from his partners and so reached down and grabbed his pack, strapping it to his back.

"Okay, so how do we do this?" Jason asked, constantly looking back over his shoulder to see if Terry was listening.

"Jason, you go first. Head west then start going south behind him and hike for about a mile, then stop. Nick, you go next. Try to follow Jason's tracks. They shouldn't be too hard to see with the light of the moon to help. Once I know you guys are clear and Terry isn't following, I'll head out and track you both down."

Jason, not needing to be told twice, took straight off into the desert heading west. After a minute and a nod from Brad, Nick hurriedly followed. Then Brad was left there standing alone watching Terry, who had seated himself on one of the rocks and seemed to be looking all around for them.

"Who are you? What do you want from us?" he whispered to himself as he continued staring at him.

There was definitely more going on here than Brad could understand at the moment and he knew that he needed to put some distance between Terry and themselves. Slowly edging his way through the shadows, Brad headed west in hopes of picking up their trail, while also eluding any attempts made by Terry to follow. Once he got a considerable distance away, he used some dried out desert brush to erase any of the footprints that they might have left behind in their escape attempt. Brad discovered their tracks with ease and continued to sweep away all evidence of their passing. It wasn't long before he spotted the boys sitting down next to a cluster of boulders and hurried to join them.

"There's Brad," he heard Nick notify Jason.

"Did he see you?" Jason asked, the fear thick in his voice.

"No, and I covered up all our tracks so that he couldn't follow either. We should be okay," Brad stated, trying to comfort him.

"Why the hell did he come back anyway? What is his problem?" Jason asked, sounding almost hysterical.

"I don't know but I was getting some seriously weird vibes from him."

"Yeah man, I did not enjoy being left alone with him even for a minute when you guys went to talk," Nick added in a worried tone.

"You don't think he's some kind of stalker do you?" Jason asked, adding more fear to the already bizarre situation.

"What if he wants to kill us?" Nick asked, raising the level of panic.

"Look guys, we need to calm down. We're safe for now, but let's just stay away from him till we can figure this thing out," Brad responded, asserting his role as the leader.

"What do we do now? Where do we go?" Jason asked, sounding truly frightened.

"We'll keep heading south," Brad answered. There's a large mountain range down that way that I saw on the map before we came out here and it should be far enough away from camp. Jack had also mentioned it before, so I had marked it and committed it to memory. We can wait it out there for a while."

"Where is Jack anyway? We need him now more than ever and he's gone!" Jason practically yelled.

"Okay, this isn't doing us any good arguing about it. We should-"

Chapter 21

"This is your fault to begin with Brad!" Jason accused. "Why did you make us ditch Terry anyway? He wasn't that bad, and now for all we know, he may be seeking vengeance against us for leaving him in the first place!"

"Okay Jay, I know you're upset, but listen to what you're saying," Brad argued back, trying to keep his voice calm. "Nick, don't you think-"

"Hey man, don't drag me into this!" Nick fired back.

Brad, feeling unbelievably frustrated, started to get overwhelmed by the negativity that was being thrust upon him. As Jason and Nick both started ganging up on him, he lost his cool and began to yell back at them.

He practically got in a face to face shouting match with Jason when Nick shrieked from the side, "Guys! Look!"

As Brad and Jason followed Nick's pointing finger, they saw the shadowy image of Terry steadily approaching their position.

"Oh my God!" Jason breathed. "What do we do?"

"Run for it!" Brad yelled, and they took off like a shot, running south through the moonlit desert. Like a scene out of a horror movie, Brad looked back to see Terry stalking mechanically after them.

Brad increased his speed, passing the other two, and they struggled to keep up with him, trying not to trip or fall off any unforeseen cliffs up ahead. They ran on and on, Brad leading the way until they rounded the side of a large mountain and stopped to catch their breaths. Panting heavily, their lungs felt as though they were about to collapse from exhaustion.

In between breaths, Nick asked, "What is...wrong with that... guy? Is he on...Angel Dust or...something?"

"I don't know," Brad replied helplessly.

"Hey look!" Jason said excitedly, as he turned his head from scanning the desert behind him to the scene ahead.

In the moonlight the three could see a wide, dry lake bed that stretched on for about a half a mile, and at the far end were gigantic sand dunes. The large, pale mounds were lit by the moon and cast a multitude of shadows in various shapes against the dry flat terrain.

"Let's go," Brad said, glancing back for any trace of their persistent pursuer.

As they reached the first set of dunes, he looked back one last time searching for any sign of Terry. Seeing none, he concentrated on climbing the first sandy hill that loomed directly ahead of him, sinking in and sliding with each step. Up each dune and down the other side they went, never stopping, each of them occasionally craning their necks around expecting to see Terry at any moment. About a half a mile into the hike, they climbed up an enormous dune which seemed to level out at the top, and Brad called for a halt.

"Alright guys, let's stop and catch our breath," he said, sliding the pack off his shoulders. Neither of them resisted the suggestion, and they all took seats in the sand, trying to contain their labored breathing in between gulps of water.

"Well if he does try to follow, he won't have a hard time finding us now," Jason said, indicating the fresh tracks strewn across the otherwise untainted sand dunes.

"What do we do if he keeps following, Brad?" Nick asked in a frightened and serious tone.

"If worse comes to worse, we'll do what we have to," Brad answered, pulling out a large, wicked looking hunting knife from within the backpack.

"Are you serious?" Jason squeaked, gasping. "You're gonna kill the guy?" he asked, shrinking away from the blade.

"Look man, I don't want to hurt anybody. Least of all some guy who is probably defenseless and unskilled in fighting, but what does he want? Do you really think that he just wants to hang out with us at this point? He can see that we want nothing to do with him but he

Chapter 21

just keeps coming on like the goddamn Terminator! I'm just saying that if he is truly unstable and does try to attack us, we at least have some measure of protection."

"How did he even find his way back? And in the dark no less?" Jason asked.

"I bet he followed those Native guys on their way back from town," Nick guessed, confirming Brad's original suspicions.

"That's what I was thinking too," Brad agreed. Jason exhaled an enormous sigh and they all went quiet. "Okay guys, listen," Brad began, taking the initiative. "We're all really freaked out right now and we need to focus. That Jimson Weed we smoked really did a number on us and combined with the Peyote we've eaten, we're all flying high. Now that I think about it, this whole thing with Terry is really ridiculous. He's just a hippy stoner that doesn't have any friends and has no place to go. He's not going to hurt us and he probably already went back to town by now. For all we know he may have some harmless disorder that impairs his judgment when it comes to being social."

His words had a significant impact on the boys and he could see them relaxing their rigid postures as a result of his little proclamation. "Come on fellas, let's tighten it up," he said, calling for them to all gather close and sit together in a circle. As Nick reached over to grab the backpack, the leather pouch that Jack had given Brad earlier fell out and with it a button of Peyote.

"Hey Brad, look," Nick said, scooping them both up and handing them over to him.

"Well! There was still a button left! I must've missed that one!" Brad said happily.

Brushing the sand off it the best he could, he held it up in the moonlight.

"So, what do you say boys? Three ways?" Brad turned to Jason and noting the worry on his face tried to console him. "It'll be fine Jay. This will be good for us."

Jason never taking his eyes off the button nodded his consent and Brad turned to Nick and got a single nod from him. Taking the hunting knife back out of its sheath, Brad meticulously cut the last button into thirds and handed them each a piece. They all began to chew their pieces and Brad said a silent prayer to the Great Spirit as he consumed his.

"What now?" Jason asked, as they looked upon one another.

"Let's just relax for a bit," Brad said, sheathing the knife and setting it down close by his side. "This is our last night out here and we should make the most of it. We should just take some deep breaths and let the Mescaline show us the way."

As they all lowered their heads and began to inhale and exhale breaths of air, Brad began to really consider the amount of Peyote they'd consumed. How many buttons had they eaten again? He couldn't even remember! Way more than he had originally planned, that's for sure! The Mescaline was good though and it had taken them all to places within their own minds that even he hadn't counted on.

The Datura however, was a different story. It hadn't been a bad trip so far but it had certainly been more on the dark side. In truth, he still could not tell whether they had peaked on the high from it yet or if it was instead more of a steady buzz that just kept going and eventually leveled out. He wasn't sure but he didn't think so.

He remembered one of the times that he had done it back in his youth. It seemed like he'd reached a high point in the trip where he had done some serious reckoning with reality as well as the altered state that it put him in. When he drank the juice that he and his friends as teenagers had made from the seeds, he recalled how badly it had affected their vision. Everything got real blurry near the end and the loss of sight had caused them to panic. He remembered also, the vivid colorful dreams he'd had for well over a week each night even after the trip.

Chapter 21

They were like nothing he had ever experienced before. It had gotten to the point, to where he couldn't wait to go to sleep every night because each time was like going to some spectacularly surreal amusement park. He experienced exhilarant emotions and saw strange yet amazing things and places with abstract people, animals, and weird objects of a futuristic nature. Bright neon lights of all colors bordered the edges of almost every scene he found himself a part of. He encountered strange, magical contraptions whose components were technologically advanced beyond any human understanding. Just possessing those items seemed to be more the prime focus than anything, but utilizing them was yet another means to further the adventures within the dream. Very much like a video game he realized, and wondered what the point of it all might have really been.

Or was there even supposed to be a point? He had felt for most of his life that everything in some form or another was significant. It was the only way to retain any real sanity when one truly pondered it. The human mind could only take so much chaos before it cracked. Everyone craved stability whether they realized it or not. It was inherent within us. Believing that life was just one big joke would only get you so far. Brad, like don Juan, believed that we were all just luminous beings and that everything was energy. Even Einstein had believed as much; at least about the energy.

Re-emerging from his contemplations he looked over to check on his friends and saw that they were experiencing some sort of introspection as well. How long had they been sitting there reflecting, he had to wonder?

Suddenly, Brad sensed a familiar feeling rising from the pit of his stomach and looked to his friends in panic.

They all looked up simultaneously then and Brad managed to squeak out, "Uh oh."

He suddenly remembered again the vomiting side effect of Mescaline and opened his mouth, his eyes going wide. A loud hiccup was all that escaped his lips however, and he just stared at the boys shocked. Another hiccup sounded out through the night and echoed off the canyon walls which bordered the dunes on both sides. Brad had a look on his face like a baby who had just burped for the first time and Nick and Jason both started laughing. Their laughter turned to uncontrollable hiccups as well and then Brad started laughing in between his hiccups.

"Apparently...hiccup...we didn't take enough to...hiccup...puke. Only enough...hiccup to give us the...hiccup...hiccups!"

They all had a heartfelt laugh at that and immediately their mood changed to one of clowning.

"Hey, Jason!" Brad said, in between chuckles. "Try standing on your head while you take a drink of water!"

To their surprise, Jason did indeed stand on his head, and reaching for his water bottle took a drink. Something incredible started to happen then. As Jason gulped down the water from his unusual position, he slowly began to fall backwards.

Right as Brad and Nick reached out for him, he fell completely over and to their utter amazement, did a tuck and roll popping right back up like an acrobat and said, "Ta-da!" without spilling even one drop. "Look!" he exclaimed, "No more hiccups!"

"How did you-" Brad started to ask, when all of a sudden Jason shouted, "Nick! Let's see what you can do!"

Nick, being startled by Jason's yell, stopped in mid hiccup, and looked over to Brad and said, "Hey! They're gone!"

Brad realized that something was happening now and they all seemed to be in the grips of some fantastic force of energy.

"Well...?" Jason reiterated towards Nick.

"After smoking all that Jimson and taking that last piece of Peyote, I feel like I'm sidewinding!" he said, flipping over onto his side.

He began literally slithering through the sand just like a rattlesnake, even creating patterns almost identical to that of a

Chapter 21

Sidewinder! His body writhed and twisted down the side of the dune while Jason stood with his hands on his hips, beaming at the sight. Brad was completely astounded by Nick's bodily contortions, not thinking it even possible for a human being to move in such a manner. It was like witnessing a magic act, and once Nick got halfway down the dune, he began to make his way back up to the top and once there he popped up to a standing position as if the feat had been nothing at all!

"Bravo!" Jason commended, as he clapped his hands, looking over to Brad and motioning for him to do the same.

As the clapping died down, without a word, they both looked to Brad expectantly to see what sort of trickery he might perform. Brad, seeming to be at a loss, looked at the ground then up to the sky as if asking the stars for help.

A thought suddenly occurred to him then and as he turned from the night sky back over to his friends, he seemed as if he had received a sudden epiphany and announced, "I can make it snow stars…look up!"

With puzzled expressions, Jason and Nick went from looking at Brad to staring up at the sky and what they saw made them gasp loudly. All the stars of the night started to sparkle and grow brighter and their light began to emanate downward; slowly drifting towards them. Tiny, fluorescent flakes filtered down from the stars themselves, like floating dandelions that disappeared once they reached the ground. The star-flakes fell in tiny little circlets of energy, and as they all reached out to touch them, the miniature particles of light dissipated away into nothingness upon impact. Thousands of tiny flurries of starlight continued to fall steadily, and the boys just watched and giggled, mesmerized. Brad realized then that his hand had been in his front pocket grasping something, and when he pulled it out, he saw the crystal that he had found earlier. Another realization dawned on him just then. This was the spot that Dan and Troy had marked for him on the map! He had finally found it! He now felt as though their weekend hike was absolutely complete.

"Okay Brad. You've got us beat! How did you do that?" Jason asked, distracting him.

"I just realized..." Brad answered confidently, "that we can do anything! It's our ordinary state of being that's dominated by reality, which stops us. We're peaking right now. Don't you guys feel it?"

"I do!" Nick said, and once more he slid back down into the sand and slithered around with glee, laughing and smiling the entire time.

Jason yelled, "I think I'll go for a swim!" and immediately dove down into the sand, virtually swimming all around in it!

As he glided all throughout the dunes, he even backstroked his way past Brad, smiling as he went by! What does this remind me of? Brad thought to himself. Don Genaro! Don Juan's Sorcerer associate from the Castaneda books! Brad remembered how don Genaro would astound Carlos with his ability to swim around on the floor of whichever abode they happened to be in, trying to teach Carlos to change his state of awareness.

It was a spectacle which boggled the mind and apparently it was meant to. The actions themselves contradicted logic and therefore helped to eliminate logical rationale. It was an effort to transport the apprentice into a higher state of awareness helping him to enter the realm of the Sorcerer.

"Guys!" Brad shouted excitedly. "We're in the Sorcerers Realm right now! It's real! It exists!" Jason and Nick both stopped their antics and stood up, sand pouring off their bodies and clothes. "Hey! I just thought of something!" Brad said, quickly reaching down for the backpack. He pulled out a store bought bag of dehydrated fruit and holding it out cheerfully said, "Try this!"

They all grabbed a handful and began popping them into their mouths, one at a time.

"Mmmmmm!" Jason and Nick both expressed.

Chapter 21

"Oh my God! This is so good!" Brad said, in between bites.

Psychedelics could sometimes sharpen the taste buds and Brad had a feeling that this would be one of those times. Each bite was so tangy, sweet and flavorful, that they all commented on how it was the best thing that they'd ever eaten in their lives. It was as if they were truly tasting them for the first time!

The star-flakes continued drifting slowly down which only added to the experience. The texture of the dehydrated fruit was dry, yet crisp, and they savored each piece as they stuffed them into their mouths. It was a great experience and when they ran out, they started losing the distraction from eating and began to notice a feeling building up inside of them. The sky ceased its downfall of light play and the boys all stood together closely, as a very serious feeling settled in among the three. They all looked up to the heavens and spoke while watching the stars.

"I can feel the Datura speaking to me," Nick commented unexpectedly from the side.

"I feel it too Nick," Jason agreed, staring back at Nick with a look of recognition.

Funny that I don't so much, Brad thought to himself. As Brad surveyed the entire area around them he noticed that the dunes were just like those out of "The Doors" movie.

"I'm just realizing something," he said, and Nick and Jason turned their attention towards him and listened intently. "In the movie; The Doors, Jim Morrison talked about an ancient snake, seven miles long. He said that the world's history was imprinted on its scales and that it was a monster of energy, devouring consciousness, and digesting power. If it sensed fear then it would eat you instantly, but if you kissed it on the tongue without fear then it would take you to the gardens through the gate. To the other side; till the end of time. In Castaneda's books; the Sorcerer don Juan talked about The Eagle and a thousand points of light. He described The Eagle as being an unfathomable amount of energy in which all other energies eventually returned to. He also described filaments of light which emanated from all living creatures and formed a direct path to The Eagle. He said that when your light burns as bright as it ever will, The Eagle may pluck you away if it can, in order to maintain its unimaginable power. I think Jim was talking about the same thing, only he imagined a different version of it. We're all just energy and we exist in accordance with the balance of power that flows all throughout the planet, and even the Universe. I understand it now. It's so beautiful!"

Jason and Nick were both nodding in earnest agreement.

"It's like this planet," Jason began. "All life and death are tied into one another."

"Yeah!" Nick agreed. "The energy that flows through everything is like-"

"Yeah!" Jason said, interrupting. "It's like when humans were created and-"

"We were introduced to this planet," Nick said, finishing his sentence for him.

"And thousands of years ago we were-"

"Established here and taught to-"

"Yes!" Jason agreed before the sentence could even be finished.

They went back and forth like this and Brad realized that they were actually reading each other's minds! He stared astounded and listened to the best of his ability but he couldn't keep up.

They talked about advanced theories and unbelievable concepts, as if the secrets of the Universe were unfolding right before their very eyes, yet he was unable to comprehend it like they could!

Thinking back, he realized that they had smoked more of the Jimson Weed than he had and now the gift of knowledge was theirs for the taking. He still felt the Mescaline running strong within him yet he was getting left behind.

"Wait! Wait!" he pleaded with them. "Slow down! I can't follow you!"

But the boys just increased their velocity, unable to slow down, as the knowledge of the ages flowed forth from their lips. They weren't even speaking in whole sentences at all now and were finishing each other's thoughts after only a few words.

Brad looked on helplessly as their enlightenment reached new heights and he heard Nick say, "And there's a giant Amethyst crystal-"

"And it's at the center of the earth-" Jason continued.

"And it controls-" Nick added.

"Yeah!" Jason finished.

Brad cried out in frustration, "I can't keep up with you guys!"

Then Nick and Jason both stopped as if coming to one last enormous realization, and stared at one another. Brad wondered what possible conclusion they could have arrived at, when Jason and Nick both suddenly looked up to the stars silently, as if their ultimate thesis ended there. Brad looked up then too and suddenly; nothing that he saw seemed real.

The night sky looked like a dark canvas with lights set into it and he began to wonder if it all wasn't just an illusion.

"What were you guys talking about just now?" he asked in an insistent tone.

"I don't know," Jason admitted, snapping out of his contemplations. "I...can't really remember."

Turning to Nick questioningly, Brad stared at him waiting for a response.

"I lost it," Nick said sadly. "But for a moment...I had the answers. I knew it all. Everything."

They both turned to Brad confused, and stared at him with tears in their eyes. As the two of them began to softly weep, Brad walked over and wrapped them both in a comforting embrace. They all broke down in sobs at the love that they then felt for one another, as well as everything beautiful that existed. Then they started to calm down and Brad spoke to them.

"Let me tell you what I know; we are all just energy. Everything; living or inanimate. We need to burn as bright and as often as we can, without any fear of death. Now that we know the truth, we can live our lives accordingly. The most important things are; love and happiness. We need to accept everyone and everything, and help others. We don't ever need to fear death because death is nothing to fear. It is only a life of fear and hate, wasted and misspent, that one should fear. If we live a positive life of honesty, generosity and love, then the spirit that flows throughout the Universe will always watch over us. I could willingly die for that belief, because no matter how we go and wherever we go, we will be taken care of. We'll live like warriors! Let's start now!"

As he looked to his two dearest comrades he saw only agreement in their eyes. He ended by stepping back and thrusting forth his hand, waiting for the other two to take hold. Jason clasped it first, then Nick grabbed onto them both tightly.

"Thank you for this Brad," Jason said, tears streaming from his eyes.

He looked over to Nick, who nodded as tiny, salty rivulets ran down his cheeks as well. Then sensing something, they all looked back toward the entrance of the canyon and caught a glimpse of a shadow disappearing behind a sand dune.

"Was that Terry?" Nick asked, slightly alarmed.

"Aw I doubt it. Probably just some animal, or something," Brad replied, trying to maintain the positive vibrations that they had manifested amongst themselves. "Come on guys. Let's go back."

As they began their journey back across the dunes, Nick asked, "What if Terry is waiting for us at camp?"

"You know, I kinda hope he is," Brad responded lightheartedly. "Are you guys still afraid?"

Chapter 21

"Actually, no," Jason stated with confidence.

"No, I guess not," Nick said in sudden realization.

"It's kinda funny," Jason pointed out, "remember how scared Terry was of running into a mountain lion and then we became scared that we might run back into Terry?" he chuckled with ironic amusement.

"Yep! Well, we'll see if he's there when we get back," was all that Brad could offer in response.

Upon reaching camp they saw no sign or trace of Terry anywhere to be found. They all even scoured the immediate area calling out his name, but he was nowhere in sight. They settled back down by the fire and as Brad added more wood to the dying coals, they began to again tell stories of their past. The mood was somber, yet without sadness as they reminisced about times of old, and even spoke of times to come. So it went, until they ran out of wood and the fire eventually died down almost completely.

"Think I'm about ready for bed," Jason reported. "It's gotta be around two in the morning by now."

"It is almost two," Nick confirmed. "I just checked the clock in the Jeep," he said, walking back to the fire with his sleeping bag in his hand.

"Think I'll go get mine," Jason announced, when he spotted Nick unrolling his bag by the dying embers of the fire circle. "What about you Brad?" he asked. "Aren't you gonna hit the hay as well? Man, you've got to be as exhausted as we are!"

"I am tired," Brad admitted. "But I think I'll go hang out in the Jeep and listen to some music for a while first."

"Suit yourself," Jason said, looking over at Nick who was already snuggled up inside his sleeping bag and rapidly drifting off to slumberland by the looks of it.

"Good night Nick," Jason called out to him.

"Yeah, good night guys," he responded sleepily. "I'm beat."

In seconds, Nick was snoring softly and Brad and Jason just chuckled as they watched him.

"Awwww!" Jason said exaggeratedly. "Poor little guy's all tuckered out!"

"Indeed," Brad agreed.

"I really feel the come down now man, don't you?" Jason asked Brad.

"Yes, most certainly. Definitely not my favorite feeling in the world and there's no mistaking it, that's for sure."

"Yeah, I bet we'll feel just peachy in the morning too."

"It already is morning, you silly guy!" Brad laughed.

"You know what I mean!" Jason countered irritably. "Good night Brad. It's been one hell of a trip."

"It sure has! Good night my friend."

With a grunt, Jason rolled over onto his side and soon Brad could tell by his rhythmic breathing that he was fast asleep.

Looking at his two friends then, he realized just how much he really loved them. Their bond was even stronger than brothers and he would die for them if need be. He wouldn't have wanted to be anywhere else or with anybody else at that moment. His friends had come out to support him and endured all types of trials and unforeseen events, and all for his sake because he had asked them. How many people did he know or even still have in his life that he could say the same about? Throughout his friendships while growing up, he could pretty much count them on both hands, at least aside from family. There were of course Jason and Nick, who in just the last two days had been to Heaven and Hell and back again!

There were Bret and Reggie who had also proved their friendships true, time and time again.

There were also his friends Josh and Tony. Josh was of a breed that hardly existed anymore. He had an intelligence that Brad easily

Chapter 21

connected with and it was one of the things Brad had always liked and respected about him. No nonsense and hard as a coffin nail, he was literally the toughest guy Brad had ever known. Josh reminded Brad of a modern day Viking; not only with his looks but also because of his physical strength and brutal temper; which often led to the bodily harm of anyone who crossed him. Those two had been in and out of countless scrapes during their younger, wilder days, and had gotten each other's back through situations which would have had most people running for the hills. When Josh gave you his word you could take it to the bank, and if you needed his help; he was there.

Tony was another friend who was good to have there when the cards were down. The parties he threw back in the day were legendary and could go from good wholesome fun to somewhat violent, pretty quickly. Tony had the ability to happily take things to the next level when needed, without even a thought as to the consequences. Good people and good friends both, these were men of action and overall: very dangerous. He couldn't think of many others that he'd want backing him up at any given time and he would always be thankful for their friendship.

As the dying embers of the fire smoldered down, the light dissipated quite dramatically and Brad decided it was time to head over to the Jeep. He casually walked over to the nearest rocks to relieve his bladder and as he did he noticed their curious formation. They reminded him of some place.

"Cap Rock!" he stated in recognition, and as he zipped up, he moved closer to inspect it better and indeed it was very similar in shape and structure.

It caused him to again reflect on the memory of an amazing and talented spirit. When Brad had first started listening to Gram Parsons years ago, he fell in love with the music immediately and began to research the story of the man known as the Grievous Angel.

Gram had loved going out to the Joshua Tree National Park back in the early seventies and there was one place in particular which was said to have been his favorite: Cap Rock. Apparently he loved that area so much that he had made a pact with his best friend and manager Phil Kaufman. Gram insisted that when he passed away, Phil must take his body there to be burned so that his spirit could be forever free to roam that beautiful mysterious stretch of desert. The story and the music had so captivated Brad that he used to go up there every year on the anniversary of Gram's death and pay his respects to the Cowboy Angel.

He could still remember the eerie stillness of the crisp desert nights and the almost spooky feeling he experienced as he hiked to get to the memorial spot. He also remembered the feeling of comfort he got as he lit a candle for Gram and spoke to him, reminding him of how dearly he was missed by all his fans and loved ones. Gram had passed away at the Joshua Tree Inn and his body had been hijacked by Phil while it was on route to a flight back south. Brad was almost positive that Gram's spirit still roamed the desert from time to time, especially when called upon. He would always pay it tribute by bringing along a little stereo in which to play Gram's songs on, and would usually take shots of whiskey and cheers them all to him.

His most memorable time had been when he had gone up to Cap Rock with some friends and they had brought along some beer to drink and marker pens to write Gram a message on the memorial stone; where they usually lit his candle. Shortly after they arrived though, they had spotted a truck with bright headlights and soon feared that they would be caught by a Park Ranger. It was a day use area only, and people were restricted from being allowed to visit there at night. It was indeed a ranger, and in no time he pulled right up to the edge of the street and fixed a glaring spotlight right on their position.

"What should we do?" someone asked. "Should we run?"

Chapter 21

"Don't move," Brad had replied calmly, yet seriously. "Stay perfectly still. Gram will protect us."

The blindingly, bright light enveloped everybody, revealing them all against the rocky landscape, and there was no way that they could not have been seen. Yet they weren't, for after a few more passes with his floodlight, the ranger turned it off and drove back the other way towards the station.

"Did that really just happen?" someone asked. "They had to have seen us! There's no way they could've missed us!"

"Gram kept us safe," Brad stated, leaving no room for argument. "Thanks Gram," he said, as he knelt down next to his candle, offering a silent prayer to him as the others just gawked in disbelief.

Brad knew that Gram had been a special kind of spirit, one who had died much too young and could have been as big as Johnny Cash or Willie Nelson, if he'd but had his chance. In the years to follow he couldn't convince anyone else to go back up there at night except for one person; his amazing friend Samantha.

From the first moment they'd met, they had connected on a certain level which was extremely rare and had formed a bond of trust and friendship; the likes of which Brad had not known in years. Sam had a sparkling personality and a witty sense of humor which Brad had admired almost as much as her loving and generous nature. Her most notable physical trademark was her beautiful, golden curly hair for which she was renowned among her friends. Her mischievous smile only accented her beautiful features and always made you wonder what she might be up to next. Brad would always respect and appreciate the special love they'd had for one another.

So every year on September 19th they would head up to Cap Rock in the Joshua Tree National Monument and visit the spirit of the Grievous Angel. Brad had never taken her friendship for granted and the rewards in the form of the many adventures they had once shared together were great.

"So many memories," he whispered, taking a last look at the bouldered structure before he turned and started back for the Wrangler.

Stopping in to check on his companions, he found them sleeping soundly and so headed over to the vehicle. He turned on the stereo, putting his mixed psychedelic CD back on and then hopped over into the back seat and got in a comfortable position. He definitely felt the effects of the Mescaline winding down now in his bloodstream and was pretty sure that the Datura high was all but gone. "Riders on the Storm" by The Doors, softly trickled from the speakers and he sensed another introspection coming on. Listening closely to the lyrics, the line; "Into this world we're thrown" resonated in his mind.

He began to think about society and the everyday life in which people scurried from one moment to the next. Everyone constantly worked for that small amount of rest or fun that they tried so hard to earn for themselves. Brad included! It was almost like not seeing the forest for the trees. Was it purpose that drove us all or do we drive ourselves for our purpose? So few stopped to really take the time to recognize and appreciate life's beauties because we're all too busy striving for more. It didn't help either, that modern technology had us all distracted to a point in which we practically ignored what was right in front of our faces in order to concentrate on something a thousand miles away. Technology could be great, to be fair, but most of us got too swept up in it and failed to use it in moderation, mostly due to a lack of well earned self discipline. It's an age of communication and yet how many families can't truly express their love for one another because they're too distracted with what other people are doing? It seemed as if we're all just trying to deal with the cards we've been given the best we can, but can't we all try to do better? "Into this world we're thrown" is true, but we all have a choice and no one can make that decision for us.

Chapter 21

Brad could remember an instance several years ago in which he was so caught up in the task at hand, he might have inadvertently killed himself. He was nineteen years old and hiking around in the mountains near his old apartment with his friend Jeff Cooper. He and Jeff used to cause all kinds of mischief and mayhem growing up in the rougher parts of Joshua Tree when they were young. When bored, there was really no telling what one might get into, especially when one lived out in the desert with little parental guidance. On just such an occasion, they had taken some L.S.D. and had gone exploring in the rock strewn mountains near a place they called Coyote Hole.

Coyote Hole was a place where they all would often go hiking as teenagers, and on the weekends they would have fire pits and hold parties there as well. It was a well known and notorious spot for many people back then and thinking about it now, he found it easy to understand why. That place had a very strong energy about it that attracted the locals like a magnet.

There was an old utility road which led into a wash and about a mile up the wash, it ended into a canyon with a moderately large, dry waterfall. The rock was dark and smooth, and had a slippery texture, having been well worn from the ages. Certain Native Americans once inhabited that area and old relics and traces of their existence were not hard to find if one knew where to look. In the rare, desert rainy season, the waterfall often trickled with a tiny stream of water which the indigenous wildlife must have greatly appreciated. It was a beautiful and somewhat secluded little canyon, yet on a dark night it could seem ominous and mysterious as well.

So as he and Jeff were hiking, they made their way through Coyote Hole then headed northeast along the mountain ridge and ended up along the backside of a small rocky area. The Acid had taken its hold pretty strongly and their energy levels started to rise as they began to explore a previously unknown section of the mountainside.

The sky had grown dark gray and tiny droplets of rain started to fall lightly all around them enhancing their experience. As mist began to form on the edge of the mountain, there was a real ethereal and mystical feeling settling in, like something from a Led Zeppelin song.

One of them stepped on a loose boulder, accidentally dislodging it, and it went tumbling down the mountainside crashing against other boulders and bushes as it went. In watching its descent they noticed that it created huge sparks when colliding with other rocks, followed by a faint wisp of sulfur which rose into the air. Upon seeing this, it didn't take long before they began intentionally dislodging rocks, sending them down the mountainside and watching the effect with awe and pleasure. It seemed that the bigger the boulder; the better the effect, so they tried finding the largest ones they could; that weren't too deeply embedded into the hill.

They came across one gigantic, rectangular shaped boulder, which had some give, but needed a lot of work to be set free. As they both sweated feverishly at removing obstructing rocks at its base, as well as trying to dig it free, they lost all sight of safety and common sense. The rock in question was a good eight feet tall by five feet wide and probably weighed at least four tons. Jeff worked from the top behind the boulder while Brad was right in front, practically underneath it. At one point it shifted significantly and Brad jumped to the side as it settled back into place.

Looking from the boulder to Jeff, he asked, "What am I doing? I'm gonna smash myself!"

"Yeah, what are you doing?" Jeff asked with concern.

Just then, realizing the possible dangers which they had put themselves in, Brad decided that they should quit that little endeavor for the day and so headed back to his place. The next morning, Jeff came by with another friend and asked if he wanted to go finish rolling the boulder and Brad wisely declined. About an hour later he actually heard it crashing down the mountainside and looked out in that direction, shaking his head and wincing slightly. He could have been killed by that enormous rock! Crushed to bits! What a stupid way to die, he thought and wondered just what a person might have to say at a eulogy in which that were the case!

Physically speaking, he could have died or been horribly maimed, but psychologically speaking, many of us do stupid things in an attempt to attain what we think we desire, not realizing the possible ramifications. We get caught up in the moment or lose sight of the bigger picture and just create bad habits in which we no longer use conscious decision making. Mistaking what we want, for what we need.

He and Jeff had many such adventures and learned quite a few lessons growing up. The last he'd heard, Jeff had become an acclaimed tattoo artist and was very successful, owning a few of his own shops and doing great. That thought made him happy. He began to really miss the people who had been such an integral part of his young life growing up.

He suddenly remembered his friend Cain, who owned a place called Domeland which was right on the way to Pappy and Harriets off of Pioneertown road. Cain had a warm, easy personality and the two of them had hit it off right from the start. He was into art and music just like Brad and they'd talked for great lengths of time about it. Cain possessed a tremendous amount of positive energy along with his agreeable nature and had always inspired Brad. He loved Cain's get-togethers and always appreciated being invited.

Brad also began to consider how interesting it was to see the different things that people were into, and had a passion for. So many people were into sports or racing but Brad had always loved books, movies and writing. He was probably not that interested in sports because his dad had never been into them; except for boxing and martial arts. Brad had always respected all sports for their physical aspects and dedication to self and team discipline though.

What Brad had loved more than anything was music. To him, music was the ultimate form of self-expression. It was and always would be; timeless. Music could lift you up or bring you down, but usually in a good way. So many times in life, music had helped him through some torrid emotional states and gave him hope and inspiration to continue on.

Reading was probably his second biggest influence. His dad had possessed an insatiable appetite for books and had easily read over a thousand of them in his lifetime. Brad must have inherited some of that from him and often found solace and satisfaction in the many novels and stories that he'd read. So many characters inspired him and had a direct part in the formation of the person that he was today.

His all-time favorite author was R.A. Salvatore; who was a writer of fantasy novels, and had a brilliant ability for description and imagination. His most famed character was a Dark Elf named Drizzt Do'Urden. Drizzt was a pure spirit who had grown up in a society of treachery and evil and despite overwhelming odds, had discovered his true self and escaped. His introspections and adventures were legendary and Brad could recall on several occasions relating to his character in many ways and on many levels.

Another favorite of his was Robert E. Howard's character; Conan. Brad had read some of the books but found that the magazine comics were the best; having amazing artistry and exciting storylines. Conan was a warrior and adventurer who seemed to be charmed by the Gods in his existence, which was dangerous and battle-filled. He had a righteous nature and a good heart but had always found himself fighting against insurmountable odds just to stay alive. He thought the movies were okay, but never totally accurate with portraying who he really was. That is, until Conan the Barbarian with Jason Momoa came out. Jason was the first to fully emphasize Conan's brutal abilities on and off the battlefield, and Brad truly respected his acting and version of the character.

Chapter 21

He had also loved Louis L'amour's stories and had been touched deeply by the strong family bond Louis had created with his characters in the Sacketts series.

Brad's biggest male influence in life however, aside from his father, had been his uncle John Leslie, whom people referred to as "Les". His dad used to tell him stories of his physical strength and intellect that Brad never got tired of hearing. It was said that his uncle could lift four hundred pounds over his head and that he had a genius I.Q. When tired of an argument one would hear him say; "When a wise man argues with a fool, it makes two fools," before he just turned and walked away. He was taken while he was very young in life but the memories of his stories continued to inspire Brad to this very day.

Brad had also idolized Bruce Lee as a boy, constantly amazed at his strength and lightning fast reflexes and abilities. His philosophies and comparisons to the earthly elements always intrigued Brad as well, even as an adult.

Later he had discovered another true icon and gained enormous respect for Steve Irwin; The Crocodile Hunter. He had never seen a man so happily devote his life to the animals he loved, even though it constantly put him in extreme danger. He doubted if anyone in the last hundred years or so, had faced death on so many occasions in only one lifetime!

Everything Brad had loved and appreciated in all these characters pointed to love, strength, honesty and loyalty. So many of those precious values had become lost throughout the recent years. Nowadays, people liked the villains and talentless trash that had somehow found their way into the media or television. Brad didn't watch television. He either read books or watched movies. He felt that giving commercial advertisements even a second of your time corrupted your free thinking, and only opened a gateway for the media to get a foothold into the subliminal brainwashing process that they seemed so adept at. All television did, these days anyway, was glamorize the shallow and uneducated. At least for the most part, he felt.

"Where are the heroes?" he wondered aloud.

Why had everyone turned to glorifying ignorance and negativity? He may seem old fashioned in thinking that way, but he felt as though that was what was really bringing this country down. Some of the characters he idolized were immersed in adversity and even violence, but they always emerged victorious and they maintained their integrity. He didn't advocate violence but he was no stranger to it either. It seemed an unfortunate condition of human existence but perhaps if we could all fully evolve one day, we could leave it in our past.

With so many thoughts and reflections, Brad's mind began spinning and he decided to step away from it for a minute by listening to the next song which came through the stereo. It was "Lucy in the Sky with Diamonds" by the Beatles, and he remembered as a child his dad telling him a story about how he had taken some really good L.S.D. back in the sixties and listened to that song with some friends. He'd said that he had actually pictured himself floating down a stream and remembered feeling as though it was like he was on a ride at Disneyland. He literally saw rocking horse people eating marshmallow pies! Man, they must've had great Acid back in the sixties! That had been one of Brad's favorite stories and he always thought of it whenever he heard that song.

He thought about how much he missed his parents and about how happy he would be to see his wife and kids again when he got home. A wave of fatigue engulfed him at last, and he felt his eyelids grow heavy as his entire body relaxed. The last thing he heard was, "Look for the girl with the sun in her eyes, and she's gone..." before drifting off and he remembered thinking; I need to turn off the radio

Chapter 21

or we'll have a dead battery in the morning! It was too late though, for the comforting darkness had already enveloped him.

Brad awoke with a start to a clicking sound and looked up to see the dark shadow of a figure looming above him.

"Terry?" he croaked hoarsely with fear.

"No buddy, it's just me, Jack. I turned your stereo off so that it wouldn't kill the battery."

"Jack!" Brad exclaimed groggily. "I thought you were Terry come back," he sighed in relief.

"Nope, just me."

"We told Terry to leave but he came back and then we ran-" Brad started to babble incoherently before Jack cut him off.

"I wouldn't worry about him," Jack said soothingly. Brad relaxed considerably hearing Jack's calming tone. "Did you guys have a good adventure? Did you find what you came out here for?"

"That, and more," Brad squeaked, as he tried in vain to focus his eyes on Jack's vague outline.

"Good for you my friend. Get some rest now, you've definitely earned it."

"Will we see you in the morning?" Brad asked, trying his hardest just to stay awake.

"I'll see you…" Jack responded, and everything faded to black as Brad once again drifted off into unconsciousness.

Chapter 22

The first thing Brad noticed as he awoke was the sensation of heat on his face and then he heard the buzzing of a fly somewhere near him. As he opened his eyes against the glare of the sun, he suddenly realized where he was. Sitting up straight, he clicked on the power to the Jeep, checking the clock to find that it was ten thirty three in the morning. A movement ahead and to his left caught his attention as Nick rose up from the ground stretching. Jason soon awoke and in trying to sit up, gave out a groan of pain.

"Ahhhrrr! Been a while since I slept on ground that hard! What time is it?"

"It's ten thirty," Brad informed, approaching them both. "How do you guys feel?"

"A little burned out but okay I guess," Nick said, reaching for the bottle of water that Brad extended to him. Handing one to Jason, Brad then took a seat on a rock and blew out an exhausted sigh.

"That was one hell of a ride, eh boys?" Brad asked, chuckling to himself.

"That's putting it politely!" Jason quipped, and they all erupted into laughter.

"I had some weird dreams last night man," Nick said, looking over at Brad, then at Jason.

"Me too, brother," Jason confirmed.

"Jack came back after we went to sleep last night," Brad announced, bringing their attention back to him. "Unless that was

Chapter 22

just a dream too. He asked how we were, I think. He also said not to worry about Terry."

"Right now the only thing I'm worried about is getting some breakfast!" Jason said grouchily.

"Alright then, let's pack it up!" Brad countered, and began to fill the fire pit with dirt to ensure that it was out for good.

In no time, they were ready to go and while the other two were already seated inside the Jeep, Brad stood out by the hood, looking all around hoping to spot Jack.

"Is he supposed to meet us this morning?" Jason called out from the passenger's seat.

"I think I remember him saying that he would..." Brad answered, but after a few moments he jumped into the Wrangler and started the ignition. "Maybe we'll spot him in town. Let's go eat at the cafe I was telling you guys about and see if we can find him there."

Soon they were at the diner loading up on nutrients like; bacon, scrambled eggs and toast, and were all feeling much better. As Brad went to pay the check he asked the waitress, who he didn't recognize, if she knew Jack and if he'd been there earlier that morning.

"Who?" was all the response he got. He left it at that and they again piled into the Jeep and began to drive their way west and back to the places they called home.

Chapter 23

Once on the long desert stretch of highway they rode in silence for some time, each seeming to be peacefully reflecting on his experiences. After some time Brad began to feel a strangeness building inside of him. It didn't appear bad in nature and seemed to be more like a new found awareness. His blood felt warmer within his veins and there was a light feeling in his heart and head. Looking over to his comrades he was startled to find that they had a visible aura all about their bodies! Hues of amber waves seemed to surround them and Jason spoke up about it first.

"Brad! You should see yourself!"

"I can feel it!" Brad responded. "I know I must be glowing because you guys definitely are!"

Glancing into the rear view mirror, Brad confirmed that his first assessment was correct and began to smile widely, looking back and forth to both his friends.

"Is it the Peyote?" Nick asked from the back seat.

"No!" Brad answered confidently. "It's just us!"

"I feel great!" Jason announced, and they all grinned with the knowledge that they had something amazing welling up from deep inside of themselves.

"I think we're taking some of that energy from the hike back home with us!" Brad said, brimming with joy.

Chapter 23

"I believe you're right!" Jason agreed.

For a moment Brad considered telling the boys the truth about Jack but realized that it probably wouldn't matter at this point anyway, and might only serve to bring them down when right now they were feeling so high. Instead he decided to go in a different direction with his thoughts.

"Okay guys. What have we learned from all this?"

"What haven't we learned, would be a better question if you asked me!" Nick retorted, piping up from the back again.

"I think we learned that there is much, much more to achieve from life," Jason answered seriously. "We need to really step back and even outside of ourselves, to get a better view of things." Brad looked at Jason respectively, for that was precisely what he had just been thinking. "Soon we will go right back to being our anxious, thoughtless, programmed selves and will have forgotten most of the amazing things that we learned on this trip though," he continued.

"Therefore..." Brad prompted, and Jason and Nick both looked at him knowingly.

"We need to do this at least once a year so we don't forget!" Nick and Jason both answered loudly and simultaneously in stereo.

"Exactly!" Brad exclaimed.

As they cruised down the highway, Brad turned on the stereo and "Ramble On" by Led Zeppelin began to filter softly from the speakers. The serene sound of Jimmy Page's acoustic guitar filled the morning air and seemed as if it actually enhanced the amazing glow that they possessed.

It was nearing the end of September and summer was coming to its close, ushering in beautiful autumn weather now, and the breeze seemed a bit crisper, becoming even more vibrant and refreshing. The music was now their vehicle and they let it take them with the wind as they drove the open highway towards the distant mountains.

Far off ahead of them and on a mesa to the northwest, two figures stood casually looking down on them with satisfaction. Troy and Dan watched as they made their way homebound and could distinctly see their wondrous glowing outlines even at that distance. Turning to each other they smiled and began to laugh joyously before returning their attention back down towards the three searchers. They then looked from the boys over to two other figures standing down in a stretch of desert off the highway.

Jack stood stoically; like a marble statue, as Terry who seemed extremely nervous, stood only a few feet ahead and to the left of him. Jack looked out on the boys in admiration as Terry's physical form began to shimmer and vibrate; almost like a television station losing reception. His entire being dissipated completely then and Jack smiled as the last trace of him vanished from existence.

From the moment Brad had expressed his desires to take this trip, the Universe had begun working its complex yet simple constructs in making it so. The power and energy of the Universe is infinite and flows around us all, brilliant in the ways of directing its will.

Brad hadn't realized his subconscious need until he had first visited the desert, although in truth, the ball had begun rolling even before then. Spilling his coffee on his laptop was just the first act in a sequence of steps he would undertake in making his much needed experience a reality. The grand design unfolded accordingly, as first he acquired the Peyote from the apprentices Dan and Troy, and then hired Jack as his guide.

Many people were unwittingly factored into the larger scheme, but Troy and Dan had been knowing and willing participants from the start. The four young Native American apprentices had known as well, and had played their parts perfectly after all; never once giving away Jack's true identity. And all those power spots that he had encountered in the desert with the help of Jack and the mysterious forces that resided out there, only helped to align his

Chapter 23

energies properly. He had even inadvertently parked the Jeep on top of one over by the campsite! All those amazing experiences would stay ingrained in him forever.

What Brad never could have known for sure however; was the entire truth of it all. Terry had only ever been just a personification, collectively manifested, of mostly all of his and his friends worst traits; fear, anger, laziness, impatience and so forth. Once they overcame their inferior mental and psychological hindrances; Terry ceased to exist.

As Jack continued to watch them depart, his eyes slowly pooled into black orbs as dark as liquid night, shining out vast reflections of knowledge that resided deep within. Even after everything he had experienced, Brad had never come to guess the truth; that Jack truly had been a Sorcerer all along.

www.ingramcontent.com/pod-product-compliance
Lightning Source LLC
LaVergne TN
LVHW011803060526
838200LV00053B/3661